BLADE OF TRUTH

Also by Amanda Briar

The Dawnlin Trilogy
Dawn of Hope
Blade of Truth

BLADE OF TRUTH

AMANDA BRIAR

FUN
SIZE

PUBLISHING

Fun Size Publishing is an imprint of Fun Size Media LLC.

Fun Size Media LLC
Antioch, CA 94509
business@funsizemedia.com

Editing by K. Morton Editing Services

Formatting by Fun Size Publishing

Cover Art by Fun Size Publishing

Map Design by Fun Size Publishing
Original Illustrations from Map Effects Fantasy Map Builder

Library of Congress Control Number: 2025900970

Paperback
ISBN 978-1-964819-07-5

Hardcover
ISBN 978-1-964819-08-2

Special Edition Paperback
ISBN 978-1-964819-09-9

Special Edition Hardcover
ISBN 978-1-964819-10-5

Ebook
ISBN 978-1-964819-06-8

Audiobook
ISBN 978-1-964819-11-2

Published in March 2025

www.amandabriar.com

AUTHOR'S NOTE

Blade of Truth is a New Adult Fantasy Romance novel filled with adventure and high stakes. The story includes mention of loss of family and friends, death/illness/injury of loved ones, adult language, abduction, captivity, isolation, starvation, violence, drowning, abandonment, mental and emotional manipulation, on page gaslighting, life or death situations, alcohol use, consensual but undesired physical contact, deceptive behaviors, physical injury, and explicit sexual content. Readers who are sensitive to these themes please take note.

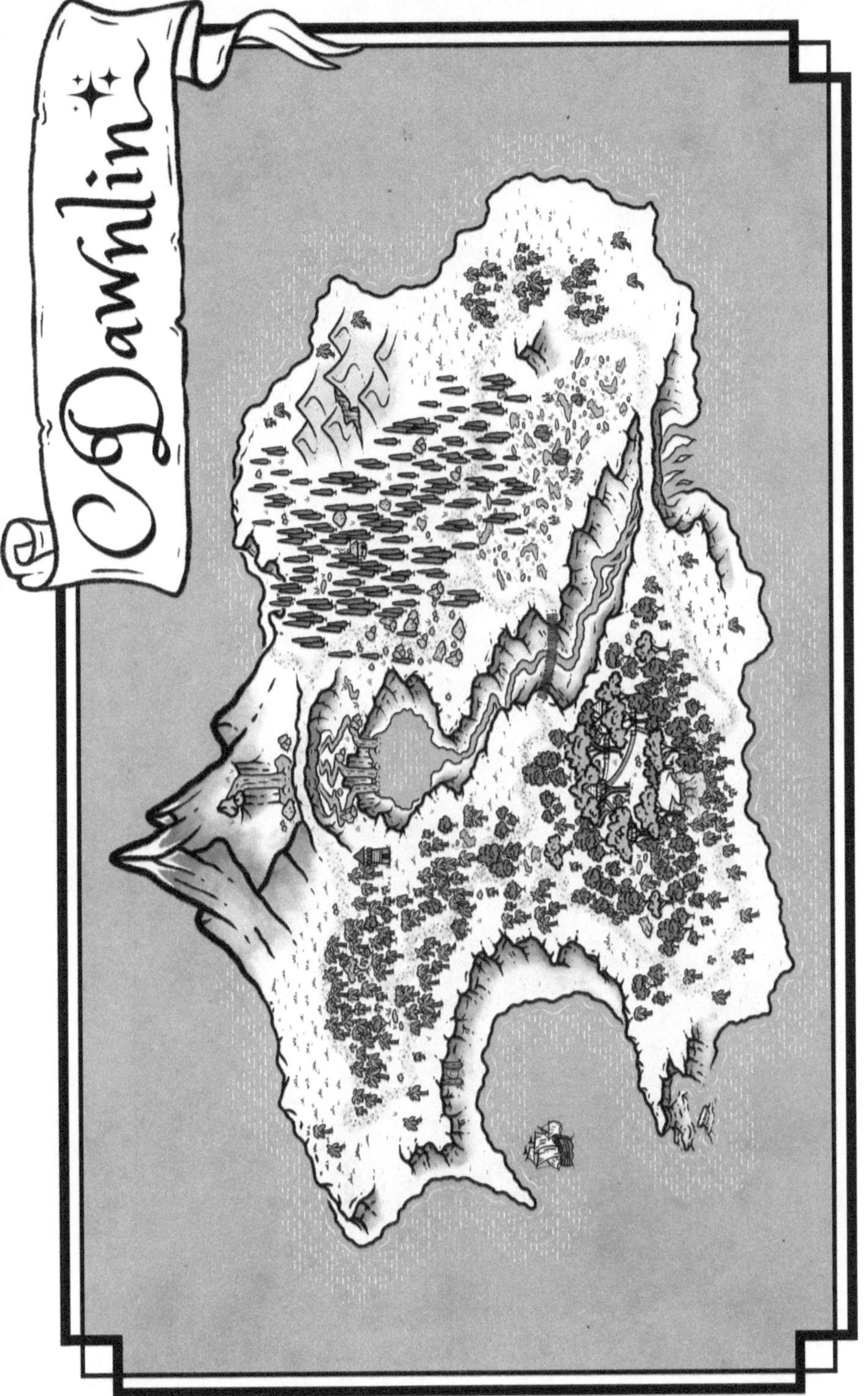
Dawnlin

BLADE OF TRUTH

PROLOGUE

here is she?

The man paced in the road, his worry escalating as time ticked away. She was never late. She always came when she promised. Today was the same as all their other days, the way they'd spent the last few years of their lives.

Except for him, today was different.

Today was the day he planned to tell her how she had enraptured him, how after years of being by her side as only a friend, he wished to be more. He wanted to shower her with the love that had been living in his heart since they were children together.

But she was not here.

His mind reeled with places she could be, replaying their conversations to see if there was something he did not recall, some plan that had changed. He didn't want to leave.

What if he missed her? What if he went out looking for her, and she arrived thinking he'd abandoned their plans?

But what if she needed help?

His chest tightened as he continued to pace, garnering looks from those passing by. Nothing could happen to her. He wouldn't allow it. Not until the last breath left his body, and he faced the gods to answer for his time in this world.

He did not know how long to wait, how long to continue to flounder in this state of torture before he succumbed to the worry and fear and went searching for her.

She was always steady and calculated. She kept him grounded when he'd been lost, and hopeful for the future.

He could not lose her.

He *would* not lose her.

He just needed to find her.

His hands clenched at his sides, opening and closing with every step as he scanned the surrounding roads. His gaze flickered to every face, searching for hers. He didn't even need to see her face to know it was her. He'd been so attuned to her presence, the shape of her body, the sound of her movements over the years, that he could pick her out of a crowd in an instant.

If anything good came from this worry, it was that his love for her was never in question. He knew his feelings were strong, but the moment her safety was uncertain, they intensified. He'd only hoped they wouldn't scare her away, for the fear of not having her in his life was too much for him to fathom. He hoped that instead of being afraid of their lives together changing, she would return everything he's felt for her, without a shred of doubt in her mind that she was his.

As if the universe was tugging on his heart, he felt her, his head whipping toward the pull.

His eyes fell on her, and relief coursed through his veins, his shoulders sagging and his feet finally settling.

She was alright. She was here.

A smile broke across his face as he took her in. Her hood was drawn, her golden curls billowing out from under it, lighting the otherwise dreary day. A smile played at her lips, and the sight of it made his widen.

When her eyes fell on him, happiness settled on her face, and she raised her hand in a small wave.

It was as if the breath was being pulled from his chest as he watched her close the distance between them, only able to inhale again when she was by his side.

The way it was supposed to be.

He loved this woman, and he was going to tell her.

"I'm so sorry I'm late," the woman said. "Hopefully you weren't too worried."

"Not at all," he said, the lie rolling smoothly off his tongue. He didn't want to tell her how worried he'd been, how close he was to going out and searching for her.

His heart calmed now that she was near, and he wanted nothing more than to reach out and touch her with the same ease that he had for years. He'd only held back in recent years out of propriety, now that she'd become more a woman than the girl he's always known.

A dusting of pink kissed her cheeks, begging for him to brush his fingers over them.

They had plans, like every day, but after the torment of waiting for her, he couldn't hold it in any longer. He decided he had to tell her.

"There's something I want to—"

"You'll never believe what just happ—"

Their words clashed together, both of them too eager to get out what they had been holding in.

He smiled softly. Her excitement was palpable, and he wanted to see it, wanted to hear what she had been bursting to tell him before confessing everything to her.

"You first," he said. He extended his elbow to her, and she weaved her arm through it as he led her to the side, off the path of the other travelers.

They sat on a stone bench, secluded from the bustle of the city, in front of their favorite place, the place they spent hours every day.

Yes, this would be the perfect place to ask her to be his.

But first, he needed to know what she had to say.

"You'll never believe what just happened," she repeats, her face glowing as the blush deepens across her cheeks. "I'm still reeling. I can't believe it myself."

"Tell me," he says, leaning closer, pinning her with his eyes and hoping she sees how invested he is in every word that falls from her lips.

"I met someone…"

Her words trail away as her hand reaches up to cover her lips, and his world shatters around him. The cold of the stone bench soaks through his clothes and into his skin, sending dread seeping into his bones.

Her excitement was apparent as she recalled the moments that kept her from joining him, and the man that captured her attention, who was undoubtedly also captivated by her.

Who wouldn't be? She was everything.

But she was his.

Sour taste coated his mouth as tension roiled through his body, but he did everything he could to keep it off his face. He couldn't let her see the devastation her words caused, how he felt like he was imploding watching such happiness and excitement flitter across her face.

He watched her tell of her plans to see the man again. His focus faded in and out, and the humming in his ears drowned out her words, all while he kept his face neutral and locked on hers.

"Is that alright?" she said, weaving her face slightly closer to his and snapping his attention back to the moment.

"Is what alright?" he asked, keeping the smile tight on his face.

"I have to cancel our plans for tomorrow so I can meet him. Is that alright?"

No, it wasn't alright. It was the exact opposite. It was the worst thing that could happen. These afternoons were his, a constant in his life that was now being torn to shreds.

"Of course," he lied again.

Her smile grew impossibly wider, and she threw her arms around his neck, squeezing him tightly. He wrapped his arms around her, holding her back, soaking up the feel of her, the smell of her hair, and hoping he could hold on to it.

This man would never last. He could never be there for her like he had been. This new man doesn't have the history they do. The friendship. He would have to wait, bide his time, and when it was right, take back what was his.

She released him, leaning back and settling on the bench again, lacing her fingers in her lap atop one of her few simple gowns.

"What were you going to tell me?" she asks, the hope and excitement still shining in her eyes.

"Nothing," he said. "It's not important."

CHAPTER ONE

If someone tried to warn me about how many times I've almost died in the past few months, I wouldn't have believed them. I would have scoffed, or rolled my eyes, ignoring them and moving on with my pre-planned, monotonous day.

I'd never been outside my castle walls, and didn't expect that to change. I surely never anticipated living on the mythical island of Dawnlin, fighting to stay alive and searching for the healing waters to cure my mother.

Danger was not part of my reality in Blackwood, but danger is very real now.

It is especially real as I stand with a blade to my throat in the middle of a beach, surrounded by the Castaways, their weapons drawn and prepared to cause me harm.

As the future queen, my life had been filled with lessons on foreign relations and war strategies. If I tried hard enough, I could hear Edmond reciting them, lecturing me in survival tactics in case of an ambush or a mutiny. He made sure I knew the location of my safe room in the castle, and who to trust. Instructions on what to do if I was captured were repeated incessantly until I was sure it would never happen, and the time spent on it was wasted.

The masked woman who searched me moments ago stands in front of me, digging through her pockets, and my eyes track every movement. I know the lessons I spent so much of my life hearing are somewhere deep inside my mind, but as she lifts a blindfold toward my face, my mind is as blank as a new sheet of parchment.

I remember nothing.

Not one lesson, not one piece of physical training that was drilled into me as I stand frozen, hands bound, and staring my dangerous reality in the face.

This isn't the first time I've been captured on Dawnlin, but this is nothing like last time. My chest heaves with stuttering breaths as the rising fear threatens to suffocate me.

The first time, the fear dissipated quickly, the moment I realized it was actually Voyagers surrounding me, and I was in the midst of a huge misunderstanding. I knew I was safe, and everything would be easily corrected as soon as Dane returned.

This time, Dane is not returning, and I am not surrounded by Voyagers.

The Castaways are taking me captive, and no one once taken has ever returned.

"Let's move," Weston commands, and the statues around me snap into motion at his word.

"Close your eyes," the woman says as she smoothes the rough cloth over my face, tying a tight knot at the back of my head and casting me in utter darkness.

With my vision gone, my other senses become heightened, and my focus returns. Edmond immediately appears in my mind, and I remember his most important instruction.

Quiet.

I need to be quiet and observe anything and everything about where I am being led, and who is around me.

My skin prickles as I feel someone hover over me, and I stiffen, trying not to move. Without my vision, I do not know who it is or how close they are until he speaks.

"Can you be trusted enough not to scream, princess?" Weston says, his low voice causing an involuntary shiver as his breath tickles my ear. "I have no problem gagging you if you try."

Sealing my lips into a tight line, I don't answer; I refuse to acknowledge him.

He doesn't deserve it.

Dane warned me about Weston's motives and manipulations back on my first day in Dawnlin. He wants the healing waters, and now I know where they are and how to get them. Another spike of terror shoots through me as I imagine the lengths he may go to for that information.

I do not know the amount of torture and abuse it takes to convince someone that everything they know is wrong, to turn them against their friends and the truth. Wherever they are taking me, whatever their plans are for me, I need to be prepared to endure it.

I gulp down the panic and focus on my breathing, remembering Edmond's instruction to observe. I will endure everything else as it comes.

Shoulders press into mine on both sides as I am squeezed between two bodies, followed by fingers that wrap around each of my elbows to nudge me forward. I stumble at the sudden movement, but the Castaways at my sides hold me upright, almost lifting me to drag my toes across the sand. The complete darkness of the blindfold prevents me from seeing anything, with no clue where they are leading me, leaving me to blindly trust the enemies at my sides.

"Step up," a woman says on my right, her voice the same as the woman who bound and blindfolded me.

I lift my foot and bring my boot down onto solid ground, then follow with the other, trying not to lose my balance despite their support. We take another few steps forward before pausing, and I jump at the loud slam behind us, followed by complete silence.

Gone are the crashing waves and rustling palm leaves from the beach, replaced by the shuffle of footsteps and sound of movement from the Castaways ahead of us.

"Keep walking," the woman says softly, propelling me forward again with a gentle push of her shoulder.

I want to scream at her, to ask her why she is being kind and considerate to me, yet chose the side of a monster like Weston. I want to demand she release me and come back with me to the safety of Dane and the camp. I want to ask where she is taking me, and what they plan to do to me.

But I don't.

I stay quiet, fighting the mixture of rage and panic inside of me, all while staying alert.

Footsteps echo around me, and the fabric of clothing swishes as I walk with them into the unknown. Someone clears their throat, but not a single person speaks. It's almost as if they are trying not to give anything away, like they know I'm listening and cataloging every detail.

Dawnlin has never been this quiet before, and my mind races as I try to figure out where we are that all the noise would cease. It's as if the island swallowed us, like when Mara and I fell into the trap on my first day of searching.

Like we are *underground.*

It has only been days since I watched Weston disappear into the wall of the cave, but the thought never occurred to me. I was too focused on finding Fin and on discovering that the Castaway who saved me was actually their leader, Weston. I didn't see what was right in front of me.

Tunnels. The Castaways travel through underground tunnels. Which is why we can never find them, or any trace of them. Do they live underground too? Inside the heart of the island?

My spine straightens with a realization, and the fear I felt moments ago dissipates.

They are leading me straight to their base. If I survive and manage to escape, I will be the only one who knows how to find it, and I can tell Dane.

He can end the threat of the Castaways once and for all.

We keep walking, and I listen for any clues that might give away our location. The tunnel curves back and forth, with no distinct turns that I can memorize. Some movements seem so subtle, I can't really tell what direction we are traveling. Completely turned around, my sense of direction is gone.

"Stop," the woman says, as she and the other Castaway pull me to an abrupt halt.

We pause for only a moment before they nudge me forward again, and I feel the magic of a portal surround me.

How many portals are hidden on the island? And how do the Castaways find them?

The hands on my elbows fall away, and I wobble slightly. Trying to stay upright without my vision is difficult, and my balance is still off with my wrists lashed together.

Suddenly, I am hoisted into the air as firm, muscular arms hook under my knees and around my waist, carrying me forward.

"What the hell?" I screech as I try to wriggle free. The arms cinch down tighter, pushing me against a solid chest and holding me in place.

"Stop moving and be quiet. I said no screaming, remember?"

Weston.

"Fuck you," I whisper loudly in the direction of his face.

A low chuckle takes me by surprise, and I can't help the flutter in my abdomen at the sound.

"I can walk," I whisper angrily again, pushing my legs downward, trying to break his grasp, but his arms don't budge. He ignores my comment and keeps walking, taking me who knows where.

Then it dawns on me. My dagger is tucked into the front of his vest. If I can grab it, he's close enough that I can seriously injure him, giving me enough of a distraction and some time to slice through of these binds and escape.

I still, hoping my lack of movement doesn't draw his attention. A few seconds pass before I slowly drift my bound hands toward his chest. The blindfold is so dense, I can't see, but I know the dagger is in a slot near his heart. I watched him put it there back on the beach once he removed it from my throat.

I only need to get close enough to grab the hilt.

My knuckles brush the leather ties of his vest as I creep closer.

Slowly, slowly, slowly.

My fingers itch to grasp the jeweled metal, trusting only my memory and having hope that I am right.

"Don't even think about it, princess."

I freeze, caught like a mouse in a trap.

Fuck.

"I don't know what you're talking about," I grumble.

"You know exactly what I'm talking about." He hitches me in his arms, the momentum shifting my body and flinging my hands away from his chest and back into my lap. "Keep your hands to yourself."

I bristle at his words. It wasn't a brilliant plan, but it was the best I could do in the moment, despite being so quickly thwarted.

Silence stretches between us again as I fume in his arms. I'd been so easily distracted by him hoisting me up unexpectedly and my attempt to get the dagger, I stopped paying attention to my surroundings, and the details that could help me find their camp.

Waves.

We are back on a beach.

Weston lifted me before I could step onto the sand and feel that major tell under my boots, but the sound of the water is unmistakable. I don't know which beach it is, how far across the island we traveled underground, or where we are going now. There are no structures on the beaches besides the occasional Voyager safe house, and a beach seems too exposed to offer a secure hiding place for so many years.

Weston stops walking and turns, swinging me around and further confusing my orientation on the land, before he starts climbing or taking stairs, his footsteps loud beneath us.

I wish I could take this fucking blindfold off.

It isn't just his steps that are loud. The rest of the Castaways follow behind, their loud footfalls echoing over the waves, and I am thoroughly confused as to where we could possibly be. Suddenly, movement and voices erupt around us, and I try to pick up each one.

"Who'd you get?"

"Bring that over here!"

"Who's on tonight?"

I try to take in everything, but there are too many voices to keep track of, too much commotion to manage, until my attention is drawn back to the man holding me.

"I'm going to put you down now." Weston's chest rumbles against me as he lowers my feet to the ground, his other arm still wrapped firmly around my waist, steadying me.

My legs wobble before straightening again, and my fingers itch to push up the blindfold, but his hand still rests on my side. I don't want to make any sudden movements that might cause an issue. I'm in their territory, and I'm outnumbered, so I need to be smart.

"Sig!" he yells, the timbre of his call startling me.

"Cap?"

"Deal with this." His hand falls away, and I hear his footsteps grow quieter as the same fingers from before wrap around my elbow once again.

This. *Like I'm just an object to be dealt with. What an asshole.*

"This way, Lennox."

I whip my head toward the woman's voice, wishing I could see her, and trying to keep the shock off my face.

"How do you know my name?"

She stays quiet and leads me away from wherever Weston set me down.

I repeat the question, my voice more insistent. "How do you know my name?"

"There are stairs ahead. You can hang on to me."

I never told Weston what my name was, and all he's ever called me was that unnecessary nickname. So how does she know it? I think back to the first time in the cave. Did Mara call for me? Did he overhear it somewhere on the island?

I extend my arms, reaching out to feel for something to grab onto, when I find her other arm outstretched in front of me. Grasping it, I use her to steady myself as I slowly step down, counting each step as I go, noting how my boots pound on the floor. I can't tell, but it sounds like wood, just like the bridges and beams back at camp, the sound the same as the floor just before the steps.

She leads me on, and I work to memorize the way. Twelve steps. Flat landing. Straight for ten paces. Ten more steps. Left turn. Straight.

I repeat the pattern in my head, knowing I will need it when I escape. I can't risk getting lost wherever we are, so memorizing the way becomes my sole focus.

A handle rattles and hinges squeak in front of me; I assume coming from the door to wherever they are going to keep me locked away. I trip over the raised doorjamb as the woman leads me through a doorway, stopping just inside the room. It's quiet, the noise and conversations from above are completely gone, and I feel like we are alone.

Her fingers tug on the knot at the back of my head and the blindfold falls away.

My eyes flutter as they adjust to a different darkness and take in the surrounding room. It feels like a box. Wooden walls edge a wooden floor, the only piece of furniture in it a small cot shoved in the corner. A wooden panel sticks out from the wall across from the cot, hiding something behind it.

I don't move, I only take in the room and repeat the pattern of turns and steps in my head.

"Your cot is here. There's a washroom just behind the wall there. Feel free to get yourself cleaned up. Are you hungry?"

I miss the question, too focused on repeating the number of steps, and looking at the room that is about to be my prison.

"Lennox, are you hungry?"

My name startles me again, breaking the trance. How does she know it? Have they been watching me? Watching us? Did Fin tell them?

Fin.

There hasn't been one glimpse or mention of him since Weston's reference to the proposed trade back on the beach. I need to find him, to know he's safe, but most importantly, I can't escape without him. He can't stay here in the hands of a monster. I won't leave him behind.

"I know this probably seems like a lot at once, but it will all be fine," the woman says.

Turning to face her then, I'm shocked to find she is no longer hiding her face. Kindness fills her eyes and I relax slightly before quickly throwing my guard back up.

I can't afford to feel comfortable around any of the Castaways.

She looks down at my bound hands and steps forward, pulling a knife from her belt and sawing through the rope until it falls away. My arms pull free and I rub my wrists where the rope dug in, stretching the soreness from my muscles after being locked for so long in one position.

"I'll have someone bring you food soon. Try to get some rest."

She steps backward out of the room and gives me a small smile before closing the door in front of her.

I run to it, grabbing the handle and twisting violently, throwing all my weight into the smooth surface but getting nowhere. Locked. Almost instantly. I slam a fist into the dark wood and let out a frustrated grunt. Spinning so my back presses against the door, I sink down to the floor and wrap my arms around my knees.

I'm a prisoner.

My life in Dawnlin has just turned completely upside down.

I found the healing waters, and for a moment, the same hope that brought me to this magical place filled me once again, only to be destroyed as soon as I was deemed unworthy. Now, instead of returning to camp to help the others and tell Dane the location, I am locked in a room in the Castaway lair, with no weapons to protect myself, and no plan.

I'm at the mercy of the man who plans to manipulate me to get what he wants.

And all I can do is wait.

For what, I don't know. I have nothing but time to sit here and think of and prepare for all the ways he will try to get the information out of me, all before he tries to convince me he is right.

I need to stay strong, not just for me and everyone back at camp, but for everyone back in our world who would be exploited if he got his hands on the waters.

A tear falls down my cheek, and I let it. There's no one else here to see my weakness. The island may think I'm unworthy of the waters, but that doesn't mean I can't still protect them from him.

My eyelids droop, my eyes heavy with the weight of the day, and I let them drift closed. I can't make a plan if I am this exhausted. I need sleep, but I will not accept their false hospitality. The Castaways will not win by lulling me into a sense of security and comfort to turn me against people I love.

I won't let the mind tricks start now.

I nestle my head on top of my knees and recite the sequence of steps until sleep takes over, my determination the only comfort that Weston will not win.

CHAPTER TWO

The sound of something scraping across the floor startles me awake, and I look around quickly, before remembering where I am. I'm a prisoner, locked away in a room, taken by the Castaways. Letting out a deep breath, I look down to determine what made the noise, only to find a plate of food on the floor beside me. A moment later, a panel in the door opens, and a glass bottle of water rolls in behind it before the panel slams shut again.

Whoever delivered the food didn't speak, but I know someone is still there. The scraping of a chair on the wooden floor just outside the door, followed by mumbling I can't make out, confirms it.

I didn't realize I needed a guard in addition to an immovable locked door.

The aroma of roasted meat and vegetables immediately fills the small room, and my stomach gurgles loudly.

I ignore it.

I haven't eaten since this morning, before I left camp. The decision to risk angering Dane to take a chance at finding the healing waters feels like days ago now. After even just a brief rest, the shock of the day is wearing off and Edmond's lessons flood to the surface of my mind as if only to avoid the thought of hunger.

Observation is the first part, and I already know a good amount of my location. I'm near a beach, in a structure with three levels that seem to be made of wood. There's a guard at my door, and I am completely closed off to everything except for the slot in the door where they feed me.

And they're being kind. I can almost hear Edmond's voice warning me not to fall for kindness, as it is the easiest way to get someone comfortable and trusting enough to get what they want. The beating I'd take for information is almost preferable, instead of sitting and waiting to see how they are going to act next.

I glance over at the plate and push it away.

Don't trust the food.

Edmond would repeat the phrase randomly throughout our lesson. I can't rule out poison, especially since there is no one else in the room eating with me. Even if they do not intend to give me enough to kill me, it could be just enough to make me miserable, and eventually talk.

But I won't talk.

I ignore both the food and the sinking feeling in my stomach begging me to eat it while I look around at my prison. There are no windows, and the only door is the one I am leaning against.

Know your resources.

The room is barren, but there must be something in here I can use to my advantage, especially after they stripped me of all my weapons. I stand and circle the room slowly, looking for anything I can use. A loose floorboard, a nail sticking out from the wall, but otherwise there is nothing. Even the cot is bolted to the floor, so I can't try to break it and have a weapon.

I look back at my wooden plate when my eyes snag on the glass bottle. I snatch it off the floor and look around for something to hit it on. The guard would be alerted to the sound of the shatter, but at least I'll have a weapon to fight.

There's nothing in the room besides the bed and the wall, so I walk over to it and, with all my strength, slam the bottle into the corner of the bed.

It bounces right off.

"What the..." I mutter to myself and try again, the loud bang echoing through the room. It's still not breaking. I freeze when I hear the chair shift and footsteps approach the door. The bottle is too small to be used as a club. The only way it would be useful is if it had sharp edges, but at this rate, it won't.

I wait until the steps retreat again and the chair creaks as the guard sits back down.

Back to square one.

I toss the bottle back onto the floor by the plate and keep looking around the room. The woman was right. A small washroom is directly behind the panel, seemingly for privacy. A small wooden basin with a spout hangs off the wall, and I walk over quickly, placing my hands under it.

Clear water trickles into my cupped hands, and I greedily slurp it. The cool water slides down my throat, and I instantly feel refreshed. They can't poison what is coming out of the wall, especially since it seems like the same magic that runs camp. I can at least survive for a while with water. I just need to get past the initial hunger pangs.

After checking the rest of the room and coming up empty, I settle back down on the floor at the foot of the cot, my back pressed against the wall. I refuse to give them any satisfaction from using the comforts they offer, so sleeping on the floor will have to do.

I'm going to need to come up with a different plan, since all I have at my disposal is water. I may not be able to fight my way out, but I can still try to escape. Closing my eyes, I take some deep breaths and focus, hunkering down inside myself and steeling my emotions to the outside world.

I am not alone. I have a family waiting for me back at camp, and Fin somewhere around here. I have Dane. I will get through this, and I will get out. I have been overlooked and underestimated for most of my life. In the throne room, in the training rings, in our kingdom politics, but I am stronger than they think.

Weston will not break me, no matter how hard he tries.

Meals keep sliding through the panel in the door, but I leave them untouched from my spot on the floor. I can feel my body weakening as I lay here, trying to expend as little energy as possible.

The wooden boards are extremely uncomfortable, and my muscles scream at me with every movement, but I refuse to use the cot. The only time I get up is to take drinks of water and keep myself hydrated. I mourn for all the strength and endurance I built up over my time on the island as it disintegrates with my lack of food and movement.

Time passes, but I can't quantify it because I sleep most of it away. It's the best way to ignore the hunger, to preserve what little energy I have, and ignore anyone who might come in here.

They must know I am not eating. My plates get pulled back through the panel completely untouched. They are either trying to see who will break first, or weakening me as much as they can so that when the torture comes, I will break. Because there's no more kindness. There's no more contact, just complete isolation in this room.

At least I'm used to being alone.

But I always had Edmond and Brynne. I was extremely lonely, but never as overtly alone as I am now, except for the guard constantly stationed outside my door.

I lay on the floor in the dark, eyes closed but awake, with no way of knowing what time of day it is, whether it is day or night, or how many it has been. I could have counted the meals, but I don't know how many were brought and taken away while I slept. The number of days doesn't matter.

Remaining unwavering matters. My strength matters.

Noise outside my door catches my attention. I perk my head up, straining to listen, but I can't make anything out. Crawling closer and doing my best not to make a sound, I rest my head on the door, positioning my ear so it is on the seam, and try to hear through it.

Someone is talking. No, not talking. Arguing. But they are doing their best to stay hushed. I move to the other side of the door, pressing my ear against the other seam, hoping it is closer so the sound travels through it.

The low voice that I have become all too familiar with grumbles through the door.

"There is no reason for you to be concerned."

"Bullshit there isn't. You need a break." It's the woman who brought me here.

I stifle a gasp. Has Weston been the one on guard? Has he been the one sitting outside my door at all hours? Surely there's a rotation, or he's filling in. There is no reason the leader of the Castaways would guard a prisoner.

Unless he's waiting for the right time to break me.

"I'm fine," he snaps.

"You are not fine. I know what it's like when you are fine. This isn't it."

"I suggest you follow your orders, Sig."

"To hell with my orders. I'll take over, and *you* go do it. They need you up there."

"She hasn't eaten. At all," he grumbles, his voice rising slightly with anger so I can hear him better.

If I ever needed reassurance that I was doing the right thing, this is it. He wants me to eat, wants me to give in to my hunger, and he's sitting outside the door waiting for me to do it. Edmond was right. I can't trust the food.

"Sitting in this chair all day and all night isn't going to make her. Go. You need to take care of everyone else out there. Yourself, too."

There's a pause, and I hold my breath, waiting for his answer.

"I'll be back soon," he says finally, before his heavy footsteps trail away.

I slowly let out the breath I was holding, and my head spins with the lack of sustenance and air. A small shred of relief settles in my chest knowing he's gone, at least for now, but I know I need to hold out even longer. He could grow impatient at any time and burst through the door demanding answers. I need to prepare myself for that moment.

The chair scrapes on the floor again, followed by the squeak of weight settling into it. I am startled by her voice speaking again, breaking the silence of the room after I thought the conversation was over.

"You can stop listening to us now."

I freeze. I'd been silent. There is no way she could have known I was here listening.

As if she can read my thoughts, she calls out, "I saw you move under the door."

I scramble back to my spot, the movement and commotion giving me up, but it doesn't matter. I already heard their argument, and she already knows I did.

"You know, it would be better for everyone if you just ate something," she says, her voice raised so it easily carries through the door to where I rest back against the wall. "It's making him an asshole."

"He's always an asshole," I say without thinking, and am surprised to hear a chuckle from the other side of the door.

I can't help but smile slightly, even though I know I shouldn't. I shouldn't feel any sort of camaraderie or affection toward any of the Castaways, especially one who clearly has a great deal of sway with him. The first step of developing a connection to my captors is having something in common, and that is exactly what just happened.

It's exactly what they want.

I let myself have this one moment before shutting down again, turning off my emotions. His goal is to manipulate me, and he's clearly trying in different ways, but I won't give in.

My refusal of the meals is getting to him, and it gives me satisfaction that his plan isn't working. He probably thought I would be easy to break, a stupid young girl that would crack under a little pressure. Little does he know, I've been trained for this. I expected it, and I won't let him win.

My back aches as I curl onto my side and lay my head down. Thoughts drift through my mind as I let go and start to slip into sleep again. What is happening back at camp? Is Dane out looking for me? Will he ever find me?

The Castaways have stayed hidden for years, despite Dane searching for them every day. I know now how they've stayed hidden for so long, traveling through the island, not on it. Worry fills me as I think about being stranded here, the newest victim to the Castaway mind games, with no one to help me but myself.

Years of unsuccessful searching have proven the Castaways are invisible, so I can't sit around waiting to be saved. There are only three things that need to happen now.

I need to endure whatever torture, physical or mental, that Weston is about to inflict on me.

I need to find Fin.

And we need to escape.

CHAPTER THREE

"Lennox! Lennox! You're here! Wake up!"

Fin's voice echoes in my mind and I groan, squeezing my eyes shut tighter, trying to will away the image of him standing in front of me, waving and jumping excitedly. I don't need to endure any more pain right now. The nightmares haven't stopped, but instead have worsened since being locked in this room, fueled by starvation and isolation.

Because now I'm seeing Fin, and he's never been in one before.

I tuck my chin into my chest and curl into a tighter ball. This is the longest I've been without food in my entire life, and now my mind is clearly being affected.

"Why aren't you sleeping in your bed, Lennox? The floor is too hard."

The floor? We aren't anywhere near our bunks at camp.

My eyes fly open. His voice is too loud and clear to be part of my dream. Light and shadows dance across the wooden wall I turned to face in my sleep, a stark contrast to the darkness I've been living in for hour after hour. I push myself up onto my elbows, my head swiveling to look into the room.

I must be hallucinating.

Fin kneels next to me, eyes wide with a cheerful smile as he watches me look over him. A lantern sits beside him on the floor, the flicker of flames responsible for the light in the room.

He can't really be here. I hadn't heard him come in, which means he's either a figment of my imagination, my dream projecting into my reality, or I am so weak and unguarded that the sound of the door opening and closing, of him maneuvering into the room didn't wake me.

"Are you real?" I ask, hesitating to reach out and touch him.

"Course I'm real! Why wouldn't I be?" he says, his smile widening.

Slowly, I extend my arm. My fingertips brush the top of his knee and meet warm, solid flesh.

"Oh my gods, Fin!" I scramble onto my knees and all but tackle him with a hug. Dark spots appear over my vision and I heave breaths to keep my head from spinning. This is the most I've moved since I got here, and my stomach sinks as I realize how weak I have become.

I pull back and run my hands over his face and shoulders, my eyes assessing him for any marks or bruises. "You're alright. You're fine. They didn't hurt you?"

"Nope! They didn't hurt me. Don't be scared. I was scared at first, but everyone is so nice to me. You'll see."

I feel a pang in my chest at his youthful innocence. He is so pure, so loving. He isn't hardened to the world yet from the wicked motivations of others. I grieve for all of us who have already lost it. He doesn't understand how he is being manipulated, how the kindness they are showing him is only to gain his trust and compliance. It makes me want to protect him even more.

I shake my head. "No, Fin. I know it might seem that way, but they aren't nice. Remember everything Dane told us about the Castaways?

They try to confuse us to get us to believe them."

How did Edmond teach me these kinds of things as a child? How am I supposed to convey the severity and danger of the situation without scaring him, in a way he will understand?

"Oh," he says, his face falling slightly. "Well, when I asked if I could see you again today, mister Weston told me yes. He said I could have lunch with you. That was nice."

I huff a breath out of my nose. "Yes, I suppose that was nice," I say, keeping my voice soft. It isn't Fin's fault he's being manipulated by a monster. He's a child and doesn't know any better. He needs someone to protect him and teach him, but most importantly, to get him out of here.

"See?" he says. He spins on his knees and comes back around with a large wooden board piled high with food. Fruit and bread and chunks of cheese cover every inch, and my mouth salivates at the sight. My stomach feels like it is folding in on itself, and it takes a lot of focus to pull my eyes away from the food.

Fin shifts his body to sit down cross-legged in front of me, and I do the same as he slides the board between us. He reaches back toward the lantern and grabs a glass bottle and two wooden cups stacked inside each other, and sets them both down next to the board.

"I heard Sig say you were here, and I was so happy to see you! But then you didn't come out, and it was sad. I came out really fast, but you didn't. You just kept staying and staying and Sig told me I had to be patient. Being patient is hard. But then it has been lots of days, and I miss you." He rambles on, the disappointment from a few minutes ago already forgotten.

My attention catches on one statement, and I interrupt him. "Wait, Fin, how long has it been? How long have I been locked in here?"

"It's been so long. Days, Lennox. It was the longest wait ever. I had to wait like eight sleeps. I counted. But now you're here!"

Eight days. I have been lying here, starving, for eight days.

"Mister Weston has been really grouchy, but Eirlik said he'll 'get over it.' I dunno what that means, because he's not climbing over anything. Just sitting. But I believe him."

It's true then, that Weston is the one sitting outside of my door, keeping guard. If the argument from before hadn't been clue enough, Fin has all but confirmed it.

I hope he's uncomfortable.

He reaches toward the board and grabs a piece of melon, bringing it to his mouth, and my skin erupts in a cold sweat.

"Fin, no!" I snatch it out of his hand and toss it back on the pile. My hands shake as I take deep shuddering breaths, trying to calm myself. Is this Weston's new angle, using Fin against me? Force me to concede by threatening him? How low is this vile man going to sink, using a child to get what he wants?

My jaw aches from clenching it. I cannot wait to be rid of him once I get out of here and rally the Voyagers.

"Why'd you do that, Lennox?" Fin asks, his eyebrows squishing together as he looks between me and the piece of fruit.

"It could be poisoned," I urge, wiping the juice onto my soiled shirt. I've been in these clothes for eight days. I long for a bath and something clean to wear, but there is no way in hell I am going to ask for it.

"Is that why you aren't eating? Mister Weston says you aren't eating."

Of course he did. Leave it to the mastermind to tell the child more than he should know. Any child would be concerned if someone they cared about wasn't eating, so I am not at all surprised that Fin wanted to bring me food. But even though Weston is using it as part of his plan, that doesn't mean I need to lie to Fin about it.

"Yes," I breathe.

"It's not. See?" Before I can stop him, he reaches down and grabs the melon again, shoving the juicy fruit into his mouth. My breath catches as I watch him chew, waiting for a sign, any indication that he is going to fall in front of my eyes.

He swallows and smiles a big, toothy grin.

"See? Why would I bring you a poisoned lunch?" He plucks a chunk of bread off the board and starts ripping pieces off, popping bits into his mouth.

My body deflates.

There's no poison.

I've spent eight days starving myself, avoiding an attack I was sure was coming, but I was wrong.

Weston must have a longer game in play.

If poison isn't his tactic, then there's nothing stopping me from eating and regaining the strength I've let waste away over the last eight days. The decision not to trust the food might end up harming me more than it helped, but I guess if it was poisoned, the reverse would be true. What's important now is getting my strength back. If I am not strong enough to get out, or worse, to bring Fin with me, all the suffering will have been for nothing, and I'd be stuck here.

With Weston.

My hand shakes from the lack of use and hunger in my muscles as I reach toward the board. I choose a round, whole piece of fruit, already lowering the risk of poison unless it is on the outside. Juice drips down my chin with the first bite, and I let out a groan. My shoulders drop, the tension held there from my hunger finally able to release.

It's as if a dam breaks somewhere inside me with the one taste of the fruit, and I am suddenly ravenous. Poison is nowhere near my mind as I reach for more food, taking bites of bread and cheese, dipping it into a pot of jam, shoveling it into my mouth, and barely chewing before gulping it down.

"Here's some juice. I think it's apple," Fin says as he slides onto his knees and uses both hands to carefully pour liquid into both cups. Taking it from him quickly, I gulp the juice greedily before my stomach starts to churn. I need to slow down. I haven't had food in days, and my body might easily reject it if I don't pace myself.

Fin continues talking excitedly, while I take a few breaths, letting the food settle, then slowly take more bites. He tells stories about things that make little sense to me, naming people I don't know, as if he's known them for longer than just a few days. My mind is too foggy to focus on any of it, especially now that it is reeling from having access to food again.

"I'm so glad you're eating, Lennox! Now you just need to be good so mister Weston will let you out and I can show you all the stuff!" he says over a full mouth of food.

"Fin," I start, and then swallow my bite. "I can eat, but I can't be the way they want me to be. We have to get back to Dane and the Voyagers. That's where it is safe. That's where we belong."

"But I can't. I'm part of the crew! I have things to do! I don't get to leave, though. Mister Weston says it's not safe for me to. I heard him tell Sig that Dane was dumb and irresponsible for letting me go out all alone. But I told him I wasn't alone all the time because I had you! He said he knew that, but I still am too little and he would protect me here."

Blood pounds in my ears and I roll my lips together. How dare he? How dare Weston say those things about Dane, knowing that Dane is the only reason any of us have hope of finding the cure? How dare he believe Dane is the one in the wrong for helping Fin try to find the healing waters while he's the one trying to steal it?

Why shouldn't Fin have the same chance as all of us to search for it, solely because he's young? He's the true villain here, for thinking he can just take that away because he says so.

I close my eyes and take a deep, shuddering breath. Fin isn't the one I'm angry with, and I don't want him to believe I am. I lean closer and take his hands in mine.

"Listen to me, Fin. Weston is lying to you. He's trying to make you feel good, so you will help him find the healing waters." I pause and weigh the pros and cons of what I'm about to say. If I tell Fin, there's a chance that the information might get back to Weston, but if I don't, Fin might be less likely to follow along with my plan.

I lower my voice to barely a whisper. "Please don't tell Weston, but I found them. The healing waters. That's why we need to get out of here as soon as we can, so I can bring you back and you can help your sister. Then we can tell all the other Voyagers."

"Oh, I found them too!"

My spine straightens and I stare at him in shock.

"What do you mean you found them too?"

His shoulders hike up to his ears, and the tips turn pink. "I know you told me to stay away from the mountain, but I couldn't! And then I just felt like I should go behind the waterfall, and there it was! It was like magic, Lennox!"

My jaw slackens as I stare. Fin had found them. He found the entrance in the mountain. But was he granted them? Was he worthy? If he was, maybe Weston already took them. What does he want with me then?

"Did you get them? Where are they?"

His face falls and his shoulders slump. "No, I didn't. I guess I wasn't worthy."

Pressure fills my chest as my heart shatters. I reach over and wrap him in a hug. The moment the island refused to give me the healing waters, I was devastated, and I can't imagine how that same news affected this little boy.

I never want him to feel unworthy, especially risking everything to save someone he loves. I'd spent too much of my life feeling that way, and will do anything so he doesn't have the same experience. It doesn't matter what the island thought; he is worthy to me.

"I wasn't either," I say, as I stroke his hair softly. "Wait." I pull back to look him in the eye. "Is that when they took you? On the beach after you left?"

"Yeah, it was scary. And I lost your bow. I'm sorry."

"I'm not worried about the bow, Fin. Does Weston know you didn't get the cure?"

"I think so. But they were all still nice, even though I didn't."

I release him and fall back onto my heels.

So that's his angle. He's not trying to question us about where the cure is, because he already knows. He's simply waiting at the exit for someone to come out with it.

Was he unworthy too, and now his only chance is to steal it from someone who the island deemed worthy?

My fingernails dig into my palms, probably drawing blood. How does the island allow this evil, vile man to plot to take away the hope from someone else who had earned it? Who is deserving of it? Why hasn't he been swallowed up into the land like the rest of us? Why does it protect them and hide them away so they can take the hope away from someone else?

Tears prick at my eyes, but I blink them away.

"Fin, listen to me. I know you think they are all being nice, and maybe they are. But it isn't real. We need to get out of here. I will do my best to get us out, but if only I can at first, I promise I will come back for you. I will bring Dane and Storm and Mara and all the Voyagers, and we will get you out and get you home. Do you understand me?"

He nods, his lip puckering slightly, but says nothing. He hasn't been here more than a few days before me, and already Weston has him brainwashed and emotionally connected.

It's disgusting.

I push the hostile thoughts out of my mind and focus on Fin. We eat the rest of the food, clearing the board in silence. The mood in the room has changed after our conversation, and I don't want to do anything to upset him. Once everything is gone, Fin stands and gathers up the lantern and board, but leaves me the bottle of juice.

He stops just short of the door and faces me.

"Please keep being good, Lennox. I miss you."

My face softens and my chest aches. "I will do my best, Fin. I miss you, too."

He leaves me with a dazzling smile and slides out the door. It closes firmly behind him, and I don't even bother trying the handle. I know it will be locked.

Loneliness washes over me the instant the door clicks closed, and I scoot over toward it and press my ear against the seam, trying to soak up the last bit of Fin that I can.

His voice is easy to hear as his boisterous exclamations penetrate the wood.

"It's all gone, mister Weston! And she ate some too, not just me! She said she'll be good. Can she come out soon?"

Weston's response is harder to hear, and I have to strain to make out the low murmur. "We will see, Fin. We will see." There's a pause before he murmurs again. "You did good."

"Thanks, mister Weston! Maybe I can have a bow for when she comes out. She was teaching me how to shoot and I need to practice."

"We'll see if we can get you a bow."

Footsteps disappear up the stairs as the voices fade away, and the silence and darkness of my room feel stifling.

He is so convincing, the bastard. He has Fin wrapped around his finger, soaking up every word and praise for his actions, giving him gifts and telling him he is safe.

It's all a lie. And now I know his plan.

He might not want to poison me, or torture me for the location of the waters, but he has yet to ask me if Dawnlin deemed me worthy. I am going to hold on to that information as long as I can, and hopefully Fin doesn't tell my secret. He didn't seem to want to talk about it at all. He was more interested in whatever his new tasks were as part of 'the crew.'

Despite his manipulative tactics, I appreciate the fullness in my belly, which has eased much of the discomfort from the past few days.

I just hope I can keep it all down. Crawling into the cot is tempting for a second, but I hold my ground and curl up back on the floorboards, facing the wall.

Knowing Fin is safe and unharmed brings me comfort, but I know getting him to let go of the trust Weston has already won is going to be difficult. That comfort combined with the lack of hunger pangs makes sleep come easy, and I drift away, dreaming of finding my way back to Dane.

CHAPTER FOUR

My body jolts as I fall, a piercing scream ringing in my ears. My fingertips claw at the ground, only to find the wooden grain of the floorboards beneath me. Sweat covers my face, and my clothes are soaked through as I heave breaths, gasping and sobbing and looking around me.

Still locked away.

I try to focus on my breath to calm my erratic heart, but it's not slowing.

Another nightmare. This one wasn't like the first. I was falling, but there wasn't anyone chasing me off the cliffs. This time it was just me, falling into the center of Dawnlin, being eaten alive by the island as a punishment for being unworthy.

I roll to my side, facing the room, my ragged breaths broken up by a sob from all the emotions washing over me now that I am awake. The door slams into the wall behind it, and I jump at the sudden noise, snapping my head toward the doorway. Light from outside cascades in, slicing through the darkness, and I have to squint against it.

The silhouette of a body takes up most of the space, and I immediately know who stands there.

Weston.

My eyes adjust to the light as I squint up at him, only to find him looking around the room, head snapping back and forth. His eyes are wild as he assesses for the threat that caused my scream. Little does he know it's just my mind.

When he doesn't find one, his gaze falls to me. I can only imagine what he sees, what I look like now. Hollow, weak, and crumpled in a ball on the floor. Not the same person I was over a week ago.

Despite being fully clothed, my skin tingles as his eyes drag over me, and I suppress a shudder. His face hardens. Any concern that was there a moment ago is gone as soon as he lays eyes on me. A muscle in his jaw ticks, but he says nothing. He just turns away, slamming the door behind him, the force of it shaking the boards underneath me.

I'm once again shrouded in darkness as I listen to his loud footsteps stomp away.

"Signee!" he yells from somewhere far away, fury lacing his tone.

I lay my head back down on my arm, taking a deep breath and trying to prepare myself for whatever is coming next. I can imagine it won't be pleasant since his current tactics aren't working. He's going to have to shift to something else.

Barely a few moments pass before the door opens again and I turn toward it, but it isn't Weston. It's the woman. She is holding a lantern like Fin's, with a pile of fabric shoved under her arm. Setting the lantern down on the floor, far out of my reach, she crosses the room to the cot and tosses the pile on top.

"Come on," she says as she bends down and takes each of my hands in hers. "It's time to get up. Enough wallowing." Her voice is firm, and I immediately feel like I'm back in Blackwood getting scolded by Brynne during training.

"I'm not wallowing," I snap back. My voice comes out scratchy, probably from not using it for days and from the screaming moments ago.

"Could have fooled me. Now get up." She pulls me to a stand and holds firm when I wobble. "Take these off. I brought you new ones."

She gestures to my clothes and I hesitate a moment. She's trying to…dress me? Not lead me to the next phase of this prison sentence?

"I assume you're not embarrassed by undressing in front of someone?" She quirks an eyebrow in a silent challenge. She's right. I've undressed in front of Addy every day for years, as well as every other handmaid that has helped me since I was a child, but she has no way of knowing that.

"I'm fine," I grunt. Once I have my balance, I pull my hands from her grasp and start to remove my shirt. It's disgusting, and deep down I'm grateful for a new set of clothes, even though I won't admit it to her. First Fin, now this. I don't want them to think that any of their manipulations through kindness are working.

"You're washing too," she says firmly. She gestures toward the privacy wall with the washroom behind it. I take a step toward it until I'm hidden behind the wall and waiting for her next instruction.

The room behind the wall looks very similar to the showers back at camp, with a spout high above and a grate set into the floor. I shimmy out of my pants and toss them in the corner, feeling a slight relief to be free of the clothing.

"Do you need help with those?" She crosses her arms, nodding at my remaining undergarments, and waits for my response.

I muster the strength to roll my eyes and then peel those off as well. Something hits the floor, and I look around for the source of the sound. She bends next to me, quickly snatching something from under my feet, and my eyes track the folded piece of parchment clutched in her hand.

The map.

I'd been so focused on surviving and remembering my hostility training that I'd completely forgotten about the map. But now she has it. The Castaways are now in possession of a map that leads directly back to camp, and can use it to attack at any time.

She pockets it quickly, and I stop myself from reaching for it. There's nothing I can do about it now, other than get back as soon as possible to warn Dane. He will be pissed that I went against his orders and drew one, but he can't be too mad. The map helped me find the healing waters, so having it was worth it.

I step under the spout and welcome the warm shower of water that falls onto my head. A set of soaps appears in the basin next to me, and the woman reaches over to pick them up. She hands me a chunk of soap and a thick sponge and I get to work on my body, scrubbing my skin and ridding myself of all the grime I've built up since I've been trapped in here.

"I'm Signee, by the way. You can call me Sig."

I don't acknowledge her, keeping my eyes focused on scrubbing my skin with my mouth clamped shut. Assigning a name to her face makes her more human, more real in my mind, and that is the last feeling I need toward any of the Castaways.

I startle when I feel her hands reach into my hair and work up a lather to clean the greasy strands. When she came through the door and declared it was time to get cleaned up, I was expecting her to stand here and guard me, making sure I followed orders. I wasn't expecting her to help me.

The hint of kindness is disarming, and thoughts war in my mind. It isn't like me to be cruel to someone who shows me kindness, but I can't figure out if her kindness is real or not. I can't tell if it is all part of Weston's game, part of the mind tricks to win me over to his side. Part of me wants to believe that she is inherently kind, but my training tells me I can't trust it. I can't trust her.

I decide to give her a little back, just an acknowledgement with my words.

"I'm Lennox," I say.

But you already know that.

Recognizing her kindness may be part of their plan, but maybe I can use it to my advantage. I may look beaten down and weak, and to be honest, my body may be, but my mind is not. I need them to underestimate so I have the best chance to get home, and maybe accepting parts of the manipulation will make them think I am changing sides and make it easier to escape.

We continue scrubbing in silence until I feel alive again. The few times I lose my balance, Sig is right there, reaching out to steady me. Her actions say she cares, and it is too much for my undernourished mind to assess.

I don't even know her. There's no reason for her to care, except to win me over.

A towel appears, and she helps me dry off, squeezing my dripping hair until it falls in damp waves.

"I brought you some new clothes," she says as she reaches over to the pile on the cot.

She tosses me the undergarments, which I pull on quickly, covering myself up so I'm not still standing naked in front of a stranger. She hands me the shirt and I pull the linen garment over my head and slide my arms into the sleeves. The fabric is slightly thicker than the clothes Dawnlin gave us at camp, but still loose fitting. I look back up to see her holding a pair of pants out toward me, and I quickly grab them.

"These are going to be way too hot," I say as I stumble to get my feet into the correct holes.

"They won't be, I promise."

The pants are soft and flexible, tight fitting, but comfortable.

I can definitely run in these.

I stand upright and tuck the baggy hem into the pants, and feel sweat already dripping down my back. She is definitely wrong about the clothes. They are only going to make Dawnlin's heat worse.

"Your boots should be fine. Do you need help with them?"

"I can do it," I say and crouch down, sliding a small thin pair of stockings on my feet before slipping into the boots. I lace them up quickly and stand, waiting for the next direction.

"You good to walk?" She says, eyeing me suspiciously, as if I'm going to fall over at any second.

"What, are you going to carry me too?" I say, my words dripping with contempt. "I ate, remember? I'm fine to walk."

She nods. "Alright. If you start to feel dizzy, just let me know." We cross the room and she bends down to pick up the lantern. "I know this is a lot, but if you just—"

I don't stay to hear the rest of her sentence.

I run.

All it took was her looking away for a split second to put into play the plan I had been concocting the entire time I showered, because whether her intentions were pure or not, she made one crucial mistake.

She left the door open.

CHAPTER FIVE

"*S*hit!"

Sig curses behind me, but I don't look back. As fast as my weak legs will take me, I sprint through the gap in the door, fueled by sheer willpower. The pattern I spent the last eight days memorizing repeats in my head. I know it forward and backward, and backward is what I need right now.

I follow it, counting the steps and rounding the turns. Sig's footsteps pound behind me, but I have a few seconds head start. Hopefully, it will be enough.

"Cap!" she shouts, but I don't let it break my focus.

I keep running.

Ten, eleven, twelve.

The suns blind me as I step through the opening above the stairs, causing me to pause. Green and purple spots cover my vision and I try to blink them away. The sudden brightness is disorienting after being in the dark for days, but I can't let it stop me.

I lift my hand to block the light just enough to assess where I am and where to go from here. Figures stand around the area, unmoving, and I can feel their eyes on me. The scenery is completely foreign and I quickly try to make sense of it. Every surface is wooden, as far as I can see. The floor is the same familiar wood I just slept on for days, and the walls, the steps, the rails, are all the same. A large, round pole juts up through the center of the floor, with…sails?

Am I on a ship?

That's why we could never find them. The Castaways live on a ship, in the middle of the fucking water. We've spent all this time searching the land, and they aren't even on it.

I don't have time to figure out anything more. Sig is on my heels, and I can't let her catch me. Sprinting straight for the rails that line the sides of the ship, I glance around for Fin, but he's nowhere to be seen.

I warned him. I told him I might not be able to take him with me if I escaped, but I would come back for him and bring everyone else with me.

I can't throw away this opportunity. I need to get off this ship. Now.

Lifting my foot to the top of the rail, I hoist myself up and stand, throwing my arms out to keep my balance as I stare down into the rolling water below. My throat dries as I assess the risk of stepping off. I still can't swim, and the waves passing by the ship do not care about that at all. I don't have a choice. The only way to get off a ship is through the water.

Gods, please let me survive this.

Digging the toes of my boots into the rail, I leap into the air, only to be yanked backward sharply as powerful hands wrap around my waist and pull me in the opposite direction.

"Where," Weston grunts, "the hell do you think you're going?"

My back slams into his chest as his arms wrap around my middle. He pins me to his body and stumbles backward with the momentum.

"Let me go!" His arms tighten around me as I try to push them away.

"I don't really feel like jumping in after you again," he says, grunting from exertion. He fights against me as I kick and scratch at him, but he doesn't let me budge. Despite being weak and exhausted, I am still holding my own, not making it easy for him to keep me here.

"You don't need to follow. You could have just let me drown!"

"I'm still waiting for a 'thank you', princess."

My elbow slams into his stomach, and he lets out a loud grunt, before lifting me and shifting his arms so they are pinning mine down to my sides, preventing me from hitting him again. Movement catches my eye, and I remember we are not alone. Castaways stand around the deck of the ship, some moving in close to watch us grapple with each other.

I feel like a spectacle. It's worse than in the training rings at home.

"I told you already. You aren't going to get one," I grind out. I try to thrash, but his arms are too strong as they cinch tighter around me.

"You told Fin you'd be good," he says, his grumble low and in my ear so only I can hear him.

The heel of my boot connects with his shin and he sucks in air.

Good. Hopefully that hurt.

"I lied!" I shout, throwing my head back into his shoulder, missing the face I was aiming for. If he thought I was going to lie down and comply simply because I told Fin I would, he doesn't know me at all. I won't stop fighting him until I am free.

He groans loudly, the frustration of my resistance clearly wearing on him. "Enough!" he yells and lets go of me. I fall straight down and my ass hits the floor, hard. A couple snickers sound from somewhere around us, and heat creeps into my cheeks.

"Ow!" I yell up at him, glaring as I scramble to my knees, my tailbone throbbing from the fall. "That fucking hurt!"

He squats in front of me, so he's on the same level. His gaze hardens as his eyes pin me down to this spot. "If you want to act like a child, I'll treat you like one. You can either get it together, realize that your situation on this island has changed, and deal with it, or you can go back to that room."

"I didn't ask to come out of it!" I bark at him.

"Well, I didn't ask for you to starve yourself. I guess we all can't have what we want." He's still yelling, no longer caring that what he says stays between us, and I feel exactly like he described, like a child being scolded.

It is humiliating.

He stands then, towering over me, his shadow falling over my face so I can see the seriousness etched into his. "Now, will you behave instead of throwing yourself to your death? I won't let you put any of their lives at risk if they have to jump in and save you."

He gestures to the people standing around us and it is the first time I really turn to look at them.

The Castaways.

The people I have spent weeks fearing and avoiding all stare as Weston belittles me in front of them.

And they all look…normal. They look nothing like the images I'd conjured up in my mind of feral criminals out to capture us. They look just like me, like Mara and Dane, close to our ages, too. The group is significantly older than the Voyagers, and Fin is by far the youngest one here, just as he was with us.

Everyone wears garments similar to mine, with longer sleeves and thicker pants, and now I understand why. Living on the water is probably cooler than on the island. When Dane brought me to the beach, the wind coming off the water was cold, especially after I was already soaked from the waves. Now I understand why Sig wasn't worried when I said I would be too hot.

"I take your silence as agreement," Weston says, cutting into my thoughts. I bring my focus back and stand, crossing my arms, but refusing to look at him. Instead, I avert my eyes toward the feet of the people in front of me.

If I can't get over the rail now, I'm going to have to come up with a new plan. Now is the time to bite my tongue and get through it.

"Everyone, this is Lennox," Weston calls out over the deck. He turns back, addressing me directly. "You already know Sig, and Fin. That's Stassia and Jorn. Over there are Auralie and Fern." I look up to see who he points to, and each Castaway waves or acknowledges me when Weston says their name. He keeps naming them off until everyone has been introduced. "There are others. You'll meet them when they return."

The group is much larger than I thought it would be. How has he gotten this many people to sympathize with him? After they were all Voyagers, searching for the same healing waters we are?

I stay silent, my eyes scanning over all their faces, but the show is over. Everyone returns to whatever they were doing before I barged in from below. I look down at the deck, just as Weston's boots come into my view, lining up toe to toe with mine. I crane my neck up to meet his gaze, hoping my expression is dripping with the hatred I feel for him, made so much worse by the recent humiliation.

He juts his chin toward me and crosses his arms over his chest. "And I'm the captain. You'll obey my orders, princess. Understood?"

I feel like I am back in Blackwood, taking orders from my father, and I hate it. Dawnlin was supposed to be a fresh start with a new family once I decided I wanted to stay. But now, standing here on this ship, listening to this man bark orders at me, it's the same bullshit I have been dealing with for twenty-one years, just from someone new.

Someone who has no right to order me around.

Someone who, despite the stupid nickname he insists on using, truly has no idea that *I* am the one that gives the orders.

"Understood, *captain*." My voice drips with disdain, and I hope it wounds him, even just a little.

Neither of us break eye contact, and I have to bite my tongue to keep from yelling obscene things at him in the way I always wished I could to my father.

Sig steps up next to us, interrupting our stare down with her interjection. "Alright, well, if you aren't going to jump ship now, how about I show you around?"

"Fine," I say, finally breaking away from Weston's glare to look at her. "Where do we start?" I'll do anything, as long as it gets me away from him.

An older boy walks up to Weston and mumbles something to him before Weston nods and mumbles back. He turns to me and points to the floorboards.

"Your feet stay on the floor. That's an order." The low grumble is the same as it was back in the cave, and my stomach flutters at the memory.

Shall I disarm you again, princess?

I push away the feeling and focus back on my hatred for him. Dawnlin may feel like Blackwood now, but it isn't. I'm not talking to my father. I'm not talking to a king. I'm talking to a man who thinks he is important, but is manipulating and controlling everyone around him.

There's no hierarchy here, despite him calling himself the captain, so I don't need to hold myself back like I would to my father. I can make my time here as difficult as possible, while still looking for every opportunity to get off this ship and back to Dane.

Weston may have trapped me here, but he will not win.

I look back at him over my shoulder and smile sweetly.

"Fuck you, *Captain*."

A muscle in his jaw ticks before he strides away. The boy that spoke to him tries to hide a smile before he turns and follows.

"Ah," Sig says loudly, reminding me she is still standing with me, ready to show me the ship. She chuckles softly and shakes her head. "This is going to be fun."

CHAPTER
SIX

"Follow me," Sig says and waves over her shoulder, beckoning me forward.

My footsteps are heavy on the dark wooden boards as I rush to keep up with her, weaving through the bodies moving around the deck.

"We're on the main deck. You already know where to get below." She gestures to the set of stairs in the middle of the deck that disappear into the ship, the same ones I climbed moments ago. "Over there is the forecastle, and up the steps is the quarterdeck." I swivel my head to keep up with her pointing, my gaze snagging on Weston as he stands with the boy who pulled him away from us.

His eyes flick to mine, assessing, probably trying to determine if I'm going to make another run for it.

Not just yet, Captain.

I glare back before turning coldly toward Sig to focus on what she's saying. She talks about the ship as if it is a second skin, pointing out every feature that I undoubtedly won't need to know. Masts tower high over the deck with the sails rolled and bound, and ropes stretching across the space. I get slightly dizzy as I try to take in the crow's nest, the sheer height reminding me of the deadly mountain path and the ground falling out from beneath me.

"Stay off those until you learn how to scale them properly. We don't need any accidents," Sig says, tilting her chin toward the masts.

I nod. I have no intention of scaling them, now or any time in the future.

There's a break in the railing where the deck drops off into the open water, and I follow as she walks toward it. It's the opposite side of the ship from where I tried to jump. If I would have realized there was a side without a rail, I would have just run that way instead.

"This is where we disembark. Much easier than just jumping off the side of the ship." She smirks at me and crosses her arms as she leans on the rail next to the opening.

I step up to the edge of the deck and peer into the open water below. A strip of land parallels the ship, just far enough away that it would be a swim to reach it. Jumping to it would have been out of the question.

"How is this easier? There's no way across," I say.

"There's a gangway, but you don't have to worry about that yet. It won't come out since I'm sure the ship knows you'll take any opportunity to scurry back to Dane."

I ignore her jab because she's right, and I won't give her the satisfaction. Looking at the surrounding landscape, I want to see where off the island the ship is anchored. The strip of land looks familiar, and I lean out over the side to get a closer look.

My eyes trail over the jagged black rock, all the way to the black sand beach it connects to, and the memory of Dane and I tangled up on a blanket flashes before my eyes.

It feels like a lifetime ago now, but the emotions come flooding back to me. The only way to get through a week in the darkness of the prison below was to lock away all my feelings and harden myself, so the onslaught of the emotions returning is overwhelming. I try to swallow them down again, knowing full well I can't have them if I'm going to get through Weston's inevitable mind games.

But looking at the beach, I can't stop my cheeks from heating, not only with the memory of Dane's hands on my body, but also with embarrassment as I stare at the clearly visible stretch of beach from a ship full of people.

"How...I...did..." I stammer, trying to process all the thoughts sprinting through my mind.

"One at a time," Sig says. "I'll answer whatever questions I'm allowed."

A cool breeze off the water rustles my still damp hair, and I look up into the sky, trying to find the words for what I want to ask. The suns are on their way down, and the evening is coming quickly.

"We're on a ship, in a cove on Dawnlin," I say.

"That's not really a question, but I'll take it as one. Yes, we are." She hasn't moved, still leaning comfortably against the rail and watching me process everything.

"Why can't we see it? It's in plain sight. Why couldn't we see it?" I'm sure I sound ridiculous to her. The shock of my voice in my own ears is foreign, but I'm having a hard time wrapping my mind about how none of us, none of the Voyagers for years, could see this giant ship anchored right in the middle of the bay.

She shrugs. "You're gonna have to take that one up with Dawnlin. I don't have an answer for you."

Her response isn't enough, but there are so many things about Dawnlin that we can't explain. I'd just been a victim of the lack of explanation with the healing waters. My stomach turns at the memory, but there's something bigger bothering me.

I don't understand why the island is hiding the Castaways, protecting them from the eyes of the Voyagers, especially with Weston's intent to steal the water.

"Don't try screaming either," she says, interrupting my thoughts. "No one on the island can hear anything from deck, unless they're one of us."

I look back at the beach, and remember the glowing waves I watched crash through this cove. They rolled so smoothly, with no obstruction, only beauty, as the neon colors rippled and tumbled to the beach. In reality, there was a giant ship sitting right in the middle of them, but the magic kept us from knowing.

What else is it hiding from us?

"How long has it been here?" I ask, my head snapping back toward her.

"A long time. I don't have an exact amount of time, but since we needed it."

"Great, but I mean, how long has it been *here?* In this spot." I jab my finger into the wooden rail as my heart rate rises, the beats pounding in my ears and stifling her response.

Her eyes sparkle with understanding, like she knows exactly what I am asking.

"We haven't moved for…a while."

Oh gods.

I drop my head into my hands and lean over, resting my elbows on the railing, and let out a loud groan. From where I am standing, I can look out and see the exact spot Dane and I stood looking at the glowing animals in the rocks, where the waves crashed over us, soaking us to the bone. With just a little lean, I can see where we eventually went to the beach, back to the fire, and spent the rest of the evening before the thunder chased us back to camp.

My heart pounds in my chest as I gather the courage to ask the question I really want the answer to.

"Did anyone see…" I trail off, sheer horror and embarrassment at what all the Castaways could have witnessed preventing me from uttering the words.

"Yep," she pops the last sound. "We saw."

As if my time on this ship isn't already going to be repulsive, now I have to deal with the Castaways having seen me vulnerable and exposed. I don't need another challenge to overcome while I'm here.

"Well, that is mortifying," I say, letting out a long breath.

"You getting intimate with Dane? Nah. It was nothing most of us haven't seen or done before, though not with him, of course. But it made it real easy to see why he has you wrapped around his finger."

"No one has me wrapped around anything," I snap, my face still hot with humiliation. "But it doesn't matter what goes on between all of you. It doesn't mean I want everyone watching *me*."

"Relax. Cap made everyone go below before they could see too much."

I can't stop the look of surprise that comes over my face. Why would he do that? Why wouldn't he revel in something he could hold over me, especially when he seems to love making me feel as uncomfortable as possible?

"He's not a monster, you know."

I scoff. "Forgive me if I don't believe you," I say as I push off the railing. "It's fine. There's nothing I can do about it. Just finish the tour." The words came out more like a command than a statement, and it feels like I am back in the castle, short-tempered with Brynne. If Sig notices, she says nothing, only pushes off the rail and heads into the belly of the ship, not acknowledging me at all, just expecting me to follow.

The wooden steps creak under our feet as we descend onto the first level. Torches line the walls, casting the space in a warm glow. They stay lit in the main hallways, but just like back at camp, they light whenever we enter otherwise empty rooms, following us as we move through the ship.

"There are three levels, which you should know after your little escapade earlier. You were in the hold on the bottom. This is the first level, which is the crew's quarters. Cap's is that way," she says, pointing toward the back of the ship where a single door stands at the end of the hallway. "The rest of us are this way. There are bunks and a couple of shared rooms. I have my own. If you need me, I'm in here."

She knocks on a small door on the opposite side of the hall, just before the room for the rest of the crew. I peer inside and see an array of different beds, hammocks hanging from the ceiling, furniture pushed against the walls. Clothes hang haphazardly out of drawers, and swords and weapons litter almost every surface.

I make a mental note to grab one and hide it when I can.

"This way," Sig says, leading me back down the hallway.

We take the next set of stairs to the second floor, which is nothing like the first. It is wide and open and could easily fit everyone I saw on deck yesterday.

She points to a doorway on the back end of the ship. "That's the galley and mess where we eat. You can get food there any time of day. That door there is the infirmary if you ever get hurt. Armory is there. Don't even think about it." She eyes me over her shoulder and I roll my eyes, eliciting a smirk.

"You'll get there. I have no doubt." She spins to face the opposite side of the stairs. "Alright, over on this side is the lounge, and the bathrooms are right through there. Third floor is the brig, which you know well, and the hold. Any questions?"

I shake my head. Everything is straightforward, and just like camp, it has everything they need to live comfortably. Now that I've seen it all, instead of sprinting past everything, the size of the ship is deceiving.

Never having been on one back in our world to compare, it feels like the magic doesn't only hide the ship from the outside. The space below doesn't at all feel like we are shoved into the belly of a ship, but instead feels almost as big as if we were walking through the halls of the castle in Blackwood.

"Great. Everyone should come in for dinner in a few minutes. Feel free to head to the mess. I'll be in behind you."

Gurgles erupt from my stomach at the mention of food, and I don't fight Sig's suggestion. Now that I know they aren't poisoning me, and they're having me eat with the rest of them, I'm not afraid to have a meal. So much of my strength vanished in the last week, so I'll have to do what I can to build it back up if I want to have a chance of getting out. That means eating regularly, starting now.

As I start off toward the mess, I can't help but feel a sliver of doubt in my mind. Am I going about this the wrong way?

Weston wants to convert every captive Voyager to his side, and while I thought I had his methods figured out, it is clear that I don't. One thing is apparent though: they want me to trust them.

Instead of outright fighting at every turn, making them believe I trust them might, in turn, make them trust me. If I can pretend, and truly lead them to believe they are growing on me, and that I am converting to their side, no one will be suspicious. I will be able to do whatever I want, and can leave unscathed and unassuming.

But I can't change my behavior too quickly. Weston would pick up on that immediately. I have to play the game, letting them think I've changed. They have to believe I've softened to their cause, and that their mind tricks are working, and then I can bring everything I know about them straight back to the Voyagers.

It might take a long time, but fortunately *and* unfortunately for me, on Dawnlin, time is on my side.

CHAPTER SEVEN

The galley and mess are empty when I walk in and look around. They remind me of the tavern Dane took me to back in Blackwood with wooden tables and chairs scattered around the space, and a counter that lines the far wall. A stack of plates sits next to it and I walk over to pick one up.

Handles stick out of the counter's surface, and I reach to lift one. Steam rises in my face and I realize the galley is different from the tavern back at camp. I look inside each one, my stomach continuing to gurgle with the aroma that wafts out of the compartments before piling food high on my plate.

A small table shoved in the far corner catches my eye. I really don't want to talk to anyone, especially after what happened this morning, along with Sig's revelation about the beach, so I try to hide as best as I can in this open room.

I slide into a chair, my back to the door, and slouch over my plate, hoping my posture says 'fuck off' as much as I feel. Commotion from behind me echoes into the room a moment later as Castaways file into the mess, and laughter and yelling quickly overtake the quiet.

I set my elbow on the table and rest my head on my hand, turning to face the wall, trying even harder to deter anyone from sitting with me. After only a few bites, I'm startled by the chair beside me scraping along the floor before a body plops down into it. Apparently my body language attracted them instead of deterred, like a moth to a flame.

"Hello, new girl."

Peering to the side, I see a girl, adjusting herself in the seat, and watching me. She isn't alone. Another girl sits down across from her, heaping plates of food steaming in front of them. Both look about my age, and suddenly I miss Mara.

"Hello," I say warily.

"I'm Stassia. That's Auralie. You're Lennox," the girl next to me says. Her energy level is jarring for as unfriendly as I feel. She might even rival Edmond for the most chipper attitude.

"I am."

"It's nice to meet you," Auralie says. "Did Sig show you around the ship?"

I drop my arm down and readjust, so I'm sitting up straighter. Clearly my posture did nothing to deter them, so now I'm going to have to endure their company during this meal. As frustrating as it is, it might benefit me. This can be the first step in my plan.

I nod silently and take another bite.

"You'll get used to it," Stassia says. "It's hard to adapt at first, being so closed in and all, but now it just feels like home."

Home. She doesn't understand what that word means to me. No place has ever felt like home to me until camp. Until Dane. The castle was a prison. This ship is a prison. Camp is the only place I've truly wanted to return to, filled with people I care about. I don't care how long she thinks I will be here, no amount of time is ever going to make this place feel like home.

"I told you both to leave her alone," Sig says as she walks up to the table and settles into the empty space in front of me.

"And I ignored you," Stassia says. "Why wait? It's not like she's going anywhere. She might as well start getting to know all of us now instead of hiding in the corner."

I huff a laugh, eyes trained on my plate, and push the food around. Looks like she knew exactly what I was doing and sat down anyway.

"We wanted to make sure she feels comfortable. We know the transition is hard." I look up to find Auralie smiling sweetly at me. Her expression actually looks genuine, and I shift uncomfortably in my chair.

"So, Lennox, where are you from?" Stassia asks as she stabs a vegetable and pops it in her mouth, chewing daintily.

Sig looks up at me, waiting for my answer, the look on her face unreadable.

"I'm from Blackwood," I say flatly.

"Ooh, isn't that the kingdom with the really attractive king?" Stassia says, her eyebrows raising as her eyes widen.

Sig presses the end of her fork to her lips, trying to hide a smile.

"Uh, no, he's not. He's old and cruel." I make a face, trying to brush off this topic while also completely baffled at the ease of their conversation with someone they have never spoken to before. None of these women have any idea the king is my father, and I have no intention of telling them. I need to shift the focus away from Blackwood's royalty as soon as possible.

Stassia makes an incredulous noise. "Well, of course not now. At least he was when I left. I assume he's aged now," she says.

She must have been on the island for a while, if she remembers my father being a young king. I glance between the girls as they wait for me to respond. It makes sense now why they feel so comfortable with each other. They've been under Weston's trance for years.

When I offer nothing more, Auralie breaks the silence. "Stass and I are from Akarion. Sig's from Berrendahr."

"So that's why you know your way around a ship," I say, looking at Sig.

"I've also been here for a while, so that's mainly why. But yes, I grew up around ships. I know how to sail."

Blackwood shares a border with Berrendahr, a seaside kingdom whose ships are responsible for the movement of our lumber. They've always been an ally and partner in trade, yet I'd met no one from the kingdom. Sig is the first. The same goes for Akarion, though I should have met both at my ceremony months ago.

"How long have you been on Dawnlin, Lennox?" Auralie asks.

"Not very long. A few months, maybe?"

"Wow, and you found the healing waters that fast? Impressive. It took me a while, but I made it eventually," Stassia says, and Auralie nods along with her.

Ice slides up my spine and I do everything I can not to show any emotion on my face. How does she know I found them? Did Fin talk? Why would he tell them instead of Weston? Or is this just a tactic to get me to admit it, then pressure me into giving them up?

"What makes you think I found them?" I ask, keeping my face straight.

"We've all found them. Every one of us," Stassia says matter-of-factly, gesturing around the room.

"But none of us have been worthy," Auralie adds.

"So now we're here," Stassia says with way too much happiness for the heaviness of the statement. "That's why you're here."

My jaw drops, unable to hide my surprise. They've all found them, and no one has been deemed worthy? How could that be? Every single person here was a Voyager before Weston brainwashed them, so how could every single person be unworthy?

Or are they lying?

Sig focuses on her plate, not joining in the conversation but clearly listening.

I don't know how to respond, and I don't want anything I say to tell them more than they should know. So I remain quiet, my mind reeling at this new information, trying to pick apart how they delivered it to find the manipulation.

"Who did you come here for?" Auralie asks. She pushes her plate forward, finished with her food and leans her forearms on the table.

Both Stassia and Auralie seem so genuine, like they actually are trying to get to know me. The behavior takes me aback, because I'm not used to anyone treating me like I am anything but royalty, or accepting me so quickly and easily. Mara even gave me a difficult time at first. It makes me wonder if my interpretation is wrong, and the behavior is fake and part of Weston's long game to make me feel comfortable.

Either way, it's part of *my* game to make them think I am getting used to them, so I need to give them something.

"My mother," I say. "The healers told us it was time to give up hope, and I wasn't ready to yet."

Their faces fall, softening in understanding.

"What about all of you?" I ask, looking to Stassia first. This might be a game played to escape, but it feels like I can finally use the skills I've honed of politicking at court. Showing interest in them is one of the earliest lessons, and asking a simple question could help me learn a lot of information.

Learning more about them might be helpful, but I also risk making them seem more human. It isn't their fault that Weston has been deceiving them this entire time. They came here for someone just like I did. A good person may still live deep inside them, even if they are doing cruel things now. Maybe I can draw that good person out and remind them of the Voyagers they once were.

"My best friend," she says, the enthusiasm dropping from her voice slightly.

"My betrothed," Auralie adds. A tear falls down her cheek and she wipes it away.

I look at Sig last.

"My father," she murmurs.

Silence falls over the table at the admissions. Everyone sitting here found the healing waters and was deemed unworthy. The island gave us hope, then ripped it away. Was it simply because Dawnlin knew Weston waited on the other side, ready to snatch the waters from anyone who was granted them? Could that be the reason none of us got them?

And if that is true, how could these women stand to work alongside someone who continues to take the hope away from everyone who finds it? How could Sig stand on that beach and tie each of us up, when she knows what it feels like to come to terms with that loss? And it's not just for us, here now, but for anyone who may need Dawnlin in the future.

My blood boils but I stay quiet, willing the hardened emotions to come over me again. I try not to focus on the details that make these women seem more real, more like me.

"Is anyone on tonight?" Sig asks, breaking the silence.

"I am," Auralie says. "I need to go get ready."

"On what?" I ask, confusion replacing my anger from moments ago.

"On shift," Stassia says, as if it's obvious what she means.

I glance to Sig, and she shrugs it off. "You don't need to worry about it yet," Sig says. "Cap will explain later."

As soon as her words register, my stomach sinks. It's getting dark, the night fast approaching, and they're talking about leaving. They must be going to the island to hunt us, the exact reason we never leave at night.

And they think I'm just going to accept it blindly.

"If you think I'm going to kidnap my friends, you're crazy," I snap, the anger spilling over into my voice.

The girls fall silent and exchange looks.

Sig speaks first. "Like I said, you don't need to worry about it right now. Cap will explain when the time is right."

The time will never be right for me to bring more Voyagers here, no matter how hard I am working to make them think they're gaining my trust.

"You'll have a ship duty though. We all have them," Stassia adds.

"You'll get yours tomorrow," Sig says.

A ship duty. I've never had a job before, or a responsibility or chore, not counting all my lessons and training. There were no assigned responsibilities back at camp. The island took care of everything we needed so we could focus on finding the healing waters, but it seems things are different here.

My eyes start to droop with the comfort of a full belly, and I cover up a loud yawn. Sig notices and pushes her chair back as she stands.

"Let's get you a bunk," she says.

"I need to head out," Auralie says, following Sig's lead. "See you tomorrow. We're happy you're here with us, Lennox."

She smiles before grabbing her plate and heading toward the galley. I didn't get a chance to say or do anything besides stare at her, dumbfounded.

I'm not happy to be here, and it is absurd that they don't realize that. I don't care how welcoming they are trying to be. This isn't where I belong.

We gather our plates and drop them in a bin near the door before walking toward the first floor. By the time I reach the top of the steps, I'm a little winded, and I curse myself for the food boycott that weakened me so much. There was no way of knowing what Weston would do to me, so I had to stick to Edmond's training. I didn't have a choice, and I'm paying for it now.

I trail behind Sig as she leads me down the hallway toward the crew's quarters. We are barely halfway when I hear heavy footsteps approaching from behind.

"Princess."

Weston.

I stifle a groan and squeeze my eyes shut. Why can't this man just give me a break from him and let me go to sleep? Why can't he just let me blend into the crew and let Sig handle me? I don't want to see his face again for years.

Sig stops, so I do too, and both of us turn toward the voice.

Weston stands in the hallway, his hulking frame taking up so much space I can barely see past him.

"Where are you going?" He asks, his face passive as he looks between Sig and me.

"She's tired, so I was going to get her a bunk, Cap."

I stay quiet, waiting for him to dismiss us with Sig's completely adequate excuse.

Weston shakes his head before his eyes flicker to mine. He places his hands on his hips, and I stay focused on him, trying not to follow the movement with my gaze.

"No, princess. Your bed's not that way. It's this way." He quirks his neck over his shoulder, gesturing down the hallway behind him. "Follow me."

CHAPTER EIGHT

ig is absolutely no help as I look over, silently begging her to challenge Weston's statement. She raises her hands, palms facing forward, and gives me a look. "Sorry, Lennox. Cap's orders."

I roll my eyes and groan, then stomp toward him. Not being able to trust me around the crew yet is understandable, not to mention at night when everyone is asleep. I can't trust them either after only a day of semi-freedom. At least this time, when I'm locked up, I'll sleep on the cot. If this game is going to be long, I'm going to at least be comfortable.

Castaways come and go on the stairs and in the hallway around us, some shooting us funny looks as they watch Weston lead me away.

"Why can't I sleep with the crew?" I finally ask as I struggle to keep up with his long steps.

"Bunks are full," he says without so much as a glance back at me.

"That's a lie," I say. "And even if they were, the ship would just make me one, or give me a cot. I know how the magic works, Weston."

"Captain," he grumbles over his shoulder.

"*Captain*," I say sarcastically.

I glare at the back of his head. The least he could do is give me the respect of looking me in the eye when he lies to me.

"Why did you let me out of the brig if you were just going to have me sleep there, anyway?" We reach the stairs, and I take the first two steps, ready to make another comment, when I realize he isn't in front of me. I jerk to a halt and look back toward the hallway, where he continued walking.

He glances back at me over his shoulder. When he notices I am not behind him, he stops and turns, leaning an arm against the wall at the entry of the stairway. My eyes are immediately drawn to the curve of the muscles in his arms and shoulders as his shirt pulls tight over them, to the long plane of his body as he leans over me.

"You're not going back to the brig, princess. Not unless you need to." He glowers at me, hovering above from where I stand on the step. "I assume you will not need to."

I gulp down the lump in my throat, but my voice still comes out hoarse. "No promises."

He grunts and lowers his arm, turning quickly on his heel, continuing to walk down the hallway. I scramble up the steps, trying to ignore the rapid beating of my heart and the flutter in my stomach. I only make it a few steps before I realize where he is leading me. Sig said there was only one room on this side of the hallway.

Captain's quarters.

His quarters.

There is no fucking way I am sleeping in the same room as Weston.

The door to the captain's quarters is more ornate than the other plain wooden doors in the hallway. Carved filigree fills the corners surrounding intricate panels, complete with a golden knob that seems so out of place on the ship. Weston turns the knob and pushes the door into the room, holding his arm out across it and waiting for me to enter.

My feet stay planted on the floor.

"I'm not sleeping in there. I'll go back to the brig."

"You're not going back to the brig, princess. Your little escape attempt made it clear you need to be supervised, and I'm tired of sleeping in a chair."

My gaze flickers across his face, and I notice then how tired he looks. Dark circles fill the space under his teal eyes, and his expression is drawn, much angrier than he looked back in the cave when I first laid eyes on him. Sig did say he was being more of an asshole, but I'm not responsible for his decisions and how they affect his mood.

I cross my arms over my chest and hold my ground. "That's not my fault. I didn't tell you where to sleep. Aren't you the captain? You can order anyone else on this ship to guard me. It doesn't have to be you."

I take a step backward, which prompts him to release an aggravated sigh. His arm drops away from the door and he steps forward, crossing his arms and matching my stance.

"You have two choices, princess. You can either walk in here on your own, or I can carry you. But either way, you're sleeping in this room. Or sitting awake all night. I don't care what you actually do."

We're stuck in a standoff, both glaring and unmoving, when he breaks first, taking two long strides toward me. I startle at his sudden movement and throw my arms forward.

"Alright, fine! I can walk," I yell and stomp toward him.

Dane would be furious if he knew what Weston is doing, but I can't worry about that right now. This is all part of the game, part of the role I need to play to make him think I am becoming a Castaway.

And I will play it.

I push past him, slamming my shoulder into his abdomen as I go, and hear a low grunt behind me as I push through the opened door. His footsteps follow closely behind, and the door clicks closed once we are both inside the room.

Sconces flare to life around us, casting the room in a dim glow. The space is everything I would expect the captain's quarters to be. A large four-poster bed sits in the middle of the back wall, the posts secured on the roof to prevent movement when the ship is in motion. An opaque accordion screen stands off to the side, the end of a clawfoot bathtub peeking out from behind it. There's a trunk at the foot of the bed, and an armoire along the far wall, but unlike the crew's quarters, everything in here is tidy.

Except for the desk. Rolls of parchment, inkwells, and quills are scattered across the surface, all of them in complete disarray. A carved dark wooden chair with red velvet cushions is tucked into it, with belts and empty scabbards hanging off the back.

That is another difference between his room and the bunks. In here, there's not a weapon in sight.

Did he plan to bring me here and empty the room of anything I could use against him, to prevent me from slitting his throat in the middle of the night to escape?

The thought of actually killing someone has never crossed my mind, and deep down, I'm not sure if I could actually do it. Edmond discussed it in his hostility training, trying his best to prepare me for it, but the opportunity has never felt real before.

If my life was in danger, or Fin or Dane's, I could find it in me to do what needs to be done.

But in cold blood?

I clench my hands at the thought, hoping it will never come to that, and I can just stick to my plan and escape unscathed.

Weston breezes past me and starts unhooking his belt with the empty scabbard. He hangs it off the chair, then strides toward the back of the room.

"Did you eat?" he asks, his back to me as he fiddles with something on the bedside table.

"I'm fine," I say.

"That's not what I asked."

I don't bother trying to stop the irritation dripping from my voice when I answer. What is his obsession with me eating?

"Yes, *Captain*. I ate."

Items clunk as he sets them down on the table, emptying his pockets and vest. I try not to watch him, averting my eyes anywhere else, and settling on the intricate pattern of the rug under the desk.

My feet stay planted in this spot as the noises break the silence. Walking farther into his room feels too…intimate. While I need to work hard to make him think I trust him, intimacy is not part of that. No matter how good-looking he is, how much my body involuntarily responds to his actions, I will never fake intimacy to convince him to trust me.

I won't do that to Dane.

"In here you can call me Weston." His voice rumbles through the room, and the statement takes me off guard. Why the sudden revocation of formality, and why only here? Manipulating where I sleep, throwing me off so I am uncomfortable, then trying to make things more personal between us. It's all part of the game to get me to let my guard down.

"I'll stop calling you Captain when you stop calling me princess."

He chuckles. "That won't happen, princess."

"Well then, *Captain* it is."

"Whatever you want, princess."

Folding my arms, I strain to see what is on the desk when I'm distracted by the singing of a blade being unsheathed.

So there is a weapon in here.

Abandoning the desk for another time, I look toward Weston's back and immediately see the cause of the sound.

My dagger.

The blade catches the light as he slides it beneath the pillow on the bed, then moves to untie the laces of his vest.

He just made a crucial mistake, showing me where he keeps my dagger. All he's done is give me a better chance and more motivation to get it back. I need to wait for the right time, which definitely isn't tonight, not after I already tried to escape once today. I know everyone, especially Weston, will be waiting for me to do it again, and I need to keep him guessing.

He hangs his vest inside the armoire next to the bed, and I look around the room, alarm rising in my chest.

"Where are you going to sleep?" I ask as I look around the room again, willing new furniture to appear.

He looks toward me, his expression unreadable, and holds my gaze as he points to the bed right next to him.

"Where's my bed?"

Unfazed by my question, his eyes refusing to leave mine, his hand flicks as he points to the other side.

No, absolutely not.

I will not be sharing a bed with Weston. A room was bad enough, but a bed?

"I'll go back to the brig." I turn on my heel and head straight for the door.

"You aren't going back to the brig. You can sleep on the floor here if you're that desperate to prove a point. Or you could actually get some sleep."

I turn back toward the room and feel my body grow heavy as I take in the huge pillows and fluffy bedding. It reminds me of my bed back in Blackwood, and I long to curl up in soft sheets and just sleep.

But my bed doesn't come with an evil captain sleeping an arm's length away.

"I won't touch you, princess." His face stays blank, and my insides start to squirm.

As much as I hate him, and as much of a monster as he is for robbing us of our hope, I believe him. I don't think he will touch me. I know he's using statements and promises to manipulate me into doing what he wants, but everything he has said so far has been true, even as far back as in the cave. He hasn't tried to hurt me with his own hands. Fin was safe. The food wasn't poisoned. He even had Sig search me when he could have himself. He's been straightforward, even if everything he utters has an ulterior motive.

Can I trust he won't take any liberties if I am in his bed, just because he says he won't?

I don't think I have a choice.

If I am going to play the game and convince him I am on his side, this is a big step. Besides, the closer I am to my dagger, the easier it will be for me to get it.

"Fine. But if you touch me, you won't just have Dane to deal with, you'll have me, too." I narrow my eyes at him and bristle when all he does is chuckle.

"I can handle that."

What an asshole.

I walk to the opposite side, the side he indicated is mine, and kick off my boots. Peeling back the bedding, I start to climb in when he stops me.

"What are you doing?" His eyebrows draw together as he tilts his head slightly.

"You just told me to sleep here," I say with a huff, gesturing toward the mattress. "Does getting into bed really need an explanation?"

My body lights on fire as he trails his gaze up and down it. I clench my jaw, angry at him but also at my stupid body. Clearly I miss Dane, and the attention of anyone is sparking something inside me.

"Not in outdoor clothes, you aren't."

"I'm not sleeping naked, *Captain.*" The thought makes my cheeks heat, and I hope he doesn't notice in the dim lighting.

"Thank the gods for that," he grumbles with a shake of his head. He walks to the trunk at the end of the bed, pulls the lid open, and digs through it for a few moments before shutting it with a loud thump. He rounds the end of the bed and holds his arm out to me, a dark crumpled piece of fabric in his hand.

"What's this?" I ask, eyeing the lump warily.

"Something to sleep in."

I don't know what I was expecting when I opened it, but I watch as the form of a large long-sleeved shirt falls into place. It's shorter than any nightgown I've ever slept in, probably only hitting me mid thigh. No man has ever seen me in such a state of undress, and Weston will not be the first.

Besides, it's *his*. Back at camp, I just slept in the clean clothes the island provided after my shower, making it easier to get up and search at first light.

"I'm not sleeping in this," I say, dropping my hand to my side.

"Then I guess you can sleep on the floor."

It baffles me how he can go from seemingly kind and thoughtful, straight back to annoying asshole in the blink of an eye. Now that I've got it in my mind how great a night's sleep will be on the soft mattress in front of me, the thought of sleeping on the floor again doesn't seem worth it enough to prove a point.

"Ugh!" I groan before snapping at him. "Turn around!" I spin as well, turning my back to him as his steps retreat to the other side of the bed. Peeking over my shoulder to make sure he isn't looking, I quickly undress.

I lift the hem of my shirt and slide it over my shoulders, tossing it onto the ground at my feet. Slipping the new one over my head, my senses are instantly overwhelmed with fresh air and salt, and something earthy that makes my stomach flutter. I stop myself from pressing my nose into the fabric and inhaling deeper, refusing to believe his scent is this tantalizing. Instead, I focus on sliding out of my pants and socks, and making sure the shirt doesn't ride up as I move.

Fabric rustles behind me, and I assume he is doing the same. Without turning, I lift the covers and slide between the sheets, keeping my back to him.

Weston blows out the lantern on his bedside table, and the rest of the sconces in the room extinguish, casting us in darkness. The bed is so comfortable, arguably better than mine in the castle, and I want to relax into it, but I can't. The mattress shifts underneath me as he climbs onto it, and I curl up on my side facing the wall, so near the edge I might fall off in the middle of the night.

My body hums as I lay there, trying to relax and not pay attention to every single noise and movement, anticipating anything and everything. I try not to focus on how close to him I am, and how scantily clad, but I can't.

Sleeping next to Dane hadn't felt as intimate as this, and we aren't even touching. I stare at the wall until I hear Weston's breathing slow behind me, and then let out a long breath, finally able to relax even just a little.

After fighting exhaustion for hours, I drift off at some point in the night, once I am convinced this all isn't just a ploy to get me comfortable, then surprise me with an interrogation. It isn't until I wake the next morning that I realize how rested I feel, and I know exactly why.

For the first time since being on Dawnlin, despite sleeping next to the enemy, I didn't have any nightmares.

Not a single one.

CHAPTER NINE

The room is empty, and the door is ajar when I wake the next morning, feeling like a new person after a night of uninterrupted sleep. My muscles ache as I stretch, arching backward and trying to straighten out the curve from sleeping curled up all night. I hadn't moved an inch from where I fell asleep, subconsciously afraid to brush against Weston in the night, but despite the soreness, I feel good. I'm ready for a full day of fooling the Castaways into letting their guards down.

Sig and Stassia mentioned a job at dinner last night, so I expect I'll learn all about that this morning. Having a responsibility that signals I'm part of the crew doesn't feel right. I am a Voyager in my heart, and I always will be. There's nothing anyone here can say or do to convince me otherwise.

I slide out of bed and Weston's shirt brushes against my thighs. For once, I am thankful he is so much larger than me, and I'll never admit that the shirt is actually comfortable. Scanning the floor, I realize the clothes I left there last night are missing.

Is Weston messing with me? Did he do this on purpose? I can't wear only his shirt all day, and I can't even leave the room to go yell at him about it.

I scan the room, looking all over the floor and on the furniture, hoping my pants are folded somewhere else, when a squeak from Weston's side of the bed catches my attention. The door of the armoire slowly opens on its own, the hinges responsible for the noise. I walk over and peer inside. A new stack of clothes sits on the bottom shelf, identical to the ones Sig brought me yesterday.

"Thank you," I whisper to the island, and grab the clothes, happy to escape from Weston's scent following me everywhere. Falling asleep immersed in it was enough for the day.

"You awake?" Sig's voice calls into the room as the crack in the doorway widens.

"Yes," I say as I finish tucking my clean shirt into the waistband of the pants.

"Great, follow me."

Shit.

It is the first time I'm alone in this room, and she gave me no time to look around. I eye the desk from where I stand, the rolls of parchment calling to me. I doubt Weston would even notice if I moved anything, but with Sig waiting for me, I will have to try at another time.

"Coming," I call, quickly lacing up my boots and striding toward the door to find Sig standing just before the steps that lead to the deck.

"Sleep well?" she asks, eyes trailing over my face.

"Sure," I say, refusing to give her any more than that.

We climb the stairs and step onto deck, the warmth from the suns enveloping me quickly, but the hint of a cool breeze comes off the water. Castaways are already milling about, everyone seemingly busy with their tasks for the day. I look around for Stassia and Auralie, but don't see them amongst the rest of the crew.

Laughter breaks out above us, and I look up to find Weston leaning on the quarterdeck railing, smiling with a bunch of the boys around him. One of them is telling a story, acting something out, and Weston throws his head back, grinning as a boisterous laugh erupts from his lips.

"Looks like someone got some good sleep," Sig says as she watches the scene above us. "Finally."

I ignore her comments and turn my back to them, facing the front of the ship. The vision of Weston grinning and laughing and the muscular column of his neck is the last image I need playing through my mind all day.

"You said I have an assignment?" I say, not doing anything to hide the scowl on my face.

"Yes," she answers. "Everyone in the crew has an assignment to be done daily. Captain assigns the tasks, but if you have a problem, you can talk to me about it and I will bring it to him." She strides over to a stack of supplies sitting on the deck and reaches down, grabbing the rope of a wooden bucket. "You," she stops in front of me, extending her arm as the bucket dangles, "get to scrub the deck."

My fingers grasp the rope handle, and my teeth hurt from clenching my jaw. Looking around the ship, I realize at this moment how truly large the deck is. I'm expected to scrub this entire thing by myself? I peer inside the bucket, empty except for a handheld scrub brush.

"You've got to be kidding me," I say and meet her gaze again. She doesn't look like she is kidding at all, and ignores my statement.

"Water and soap are in the bathroom on the second level, so you'll need to make trips up and down to fill the bucket and switch out the water. Don't slosh too much water on the steps. Cap will get pissed if someone slips."

"I'm supposed to do this every day? Just scrub around everyone?" I ask, seething.

It's not the fact that I have a job that is upsetting me. I may be a princess, but I'm no stranger to hard work. Just ask Brynne. It's the manner of the work that is making my blood boil.

He expects me to be on my hands and knees, scrubbing this deck every day while everyone in the crew watches, undoubtedly treating me like a spectacle.

Fuck him.

Sig winces slightly. "Cap said to tell you it is your 'punishment for the starvation stunt.' His words, not mine."

"He wasn't man enough to tell me that himself?" I snap back.

Her head bobs in a slow nod. "I will tell him that was your response."

I groan loudly. "Being forced to sleep in his room isn't punishment enough?"

"There are probably a lot of women out there who would not consider that a punishment."

"Well, I'm not 'a lot of women,'" I say. I let the bucket dangle at my side and look out over the water, the waves rolling in, giving me a small sense of calm. It isn't Sig's fault. She's just the messenger for the cowardly captain who apparently only wants to deal with me behind closed doors.

"Does every new Castaway need to be *supervised*, or am I just the lucky one?"

"Nope. Just you." She smiles sweetly, but gives no further explanation.

I roll my eyes and fish the brush from the bottom of the bucket. "Well then, I better get started."

Spinning on my heel, I head toward the stairs. Something moves in the corner of my eye, and I glance up toward the quarterdeck to find Weston, elbows resting on the railing and hands clasped out in front of it, watching me. A ghost of a smile sits on his lips, and I glare back at him, before picking up the bucket and disappearing into the ship below.

My knees dig into the hard wooden deck as I sit back on my heels. My lower back feels like it is on fire, and pain shoots up my spine as I dig my fingers into the muscle at the base. I have been scrubbing the deck all morning, dodging the feet of the Castaways coming and going, and as I look around I loose a ragged sigh.

I am barely halfway done. My body aches and my back is screaming. I don't even want to look at the skin on my palm. My hair is a sweaty mess, the moisture in the air doing nothing but making my waves knot as I fling them out of my way while I work. I would kill to have something to tie it back out of my face.

But I don't want Weston to see the pain I'm in. I won't let him think this is breaking me. Instead, I will take a few breaths, then get back to work.

Relief washes over me when I hear a cheerful voice call out behind me. I drop my head back and smile at the sky, before turning to find a joyous face smiling back at me.

"Hi Lennox!" Fin says as he skips across the deck, straight toward me.

Shifting my body, I slide my feet out from under me and lower myself onto the deck. The muscles in my legs pull and my knees ache as I stretch them out in front of me.

That's it. Time for a break.

"Hey Fin," I say. "How's your day going?"

"Great! I've been hiding from mister Weston, and he has to come find me. I get to see all kinds of things on the ship. He found me real fast last time, though."

Fin is playing with Weston? The thought of him doing anything for fun, let alone playing with a child, doesn't line up with everything I know about him. Maybe Fin is mistaken and there's another reason he's sending him off into the ship.

"That's alright," I say. "I'm sure you can find a really good hiding place next time."

"Can you play with me soon?" he says, excitement and hope etched across his face.

"I don't think I can today. I still have a lot of work to do."

He looks at the bucket beside me, then around at the deck.

"Yeah. Ryum is real happy he doesn't have to scrub the deck anymore now that it's your job. He used to use a mop, though. How come you're doing it with your hands?" Fin cocks his head to the side as he waits for my answer.

I clench my teeth, my jaw popping with the pressure.

I was right. That asshole is doing this on purpose, humiliating me in front of the rest of the crew, and trying to literally keep me down and bend me to his will.

I clear my throat so Fin doesn't detect the hatred in my voice. "The captain didn't give me a mop, he only gave me this." I raise the brush so he can see it.

"Oh, okay. Wanna see me do my job?"

His rapid change in conversation helps soothe my anger in the moment, although I will not forget it. I'll need to hold on to it, and use it as fuel to get me through my time here and keep moving me forward to my goal.

Fin doesn't need to see it.

"Sure," I say, and he smiles a toothy grin.

"It's really fun, and mister Weston says it's a super important job."

He runs to the mainmast and wraps his arms around it, his small body shimmying up the pole and scaling it. I jump up off the floor and yell, remembering my warning from Sig on the ship tour.

"Fin, no! What are you doing?" I scamper over, pain flaring in my legs as I run, and hold my hands aloft, trying to be there if he falls.

"It's okay, Lennox! Jorn taught me! He says I'm a real good climber!"

"The kid's right," a voice calls out from high on the mast. I startle when I see a man sitting on one of the beams, lounging in the sun.

He grabs a rope and swings down to the next level, descending the mast as if it is the easiest thing in the world. He stands on the lowest crossbeam, holding onto the mainmast on the opposite side of Fin.

"He's a natural," he says before he jumps down to the deck, feet slamming into the floorboards, causing them to vibrate under my boots.

"Name's Jorn," he says and extends a hand out to me. I take it warily and shake it.

"Lennox."

He nods at the bucket and brush I left in the middle of the deck. "What'd you do to piss Captain off, huh?"

I shrug. "I don't know. Exist?"

That elicits a laugh, and I find myself unable to contain a smile for the first time with one of the Castaways.

"I'm sure there's a reason. Captain has a reason for everything he does."

"Just because he has a reason, doesn't mean it's a good one," I counter.

"Point taken," he says, bowing his head slightly to me. "Maybe if you're nice, I'll tell you where he hid the mop." He winks, and I can't tell if that's just the way he is or if he is trying to shamelessly flirt with me. Either way, I ignore it.

I cross my arms over my chest. "How about you just tell me, so I can get done and stick it to him?"

"Lennox! Look at me!" Fin calls from even higher on the mast, interrupting our conversation. I shield my eyes and crane my neck to see him climbing into the crow's nest at the very top.

"Is he really supposed to be up there?" I ask, not taking my eyes off the structure with a wildly waving Fin sticking out of the hole in the bottom.

"He doesn't need to be right now, but yes. It's his job to use the helio when Captain tells him to."

"What's the helio?" I ask. I've never heard that word before, and am curious what it is and why it needs to be all the way at the top of the mast.

"They haven't told you yet?"

I shake my head.

"Makes sense if you aren't on shift yet, you have no reason to know. But you're asking, so I'll tell you." He leans his back against the mast and crosses his ankles in front of him. "It's how we communicate with anyone who isn't on the ship. It's Fin's job to send out the signal when Captain gives the order."

He ticks off his fingers as he recites, "Stay put, come home, and meet…somewhere." His eyes dart away from me, a clear tell that he is hiding something, but I don't ask. He's offering so much already, I don't want to seem like I am prying for more.

"So how does it signal?" I ask.

He points to the sky. "See the suns? Each one reflects a different color. So each signal has its own color."

"That doesn't make sense. You said there are three signals, but there are only two suns."

He claps his hands loudly, and I jump at the sudden sound.

"Mix 'em together," he says, his voice lilting in a singsong way.

I file the information away in my mind, not for when I need to know it, but to bring back to Dane. Knowing how the Castaways communicate on the island is a tremendous advantage, especially if we can't see the ship.

A question pops into my mind, something that doesn't make sense with his explanation. If what he said is true, that means there are Castaways on the island, right now, in the middle of the day.

"Wait, I thought you only went out at night?"

"That's what they want you to think." He winks at me again and turns back toward the mast, looking up at Fin hanging over the side of the crow's nest.

That's why the ship seemed a little empty today. The Castaways travel through tunnels, so they don't have to only be out at night, and if Weston needs to communicate with them, he uses light signals.

It's all actually really well thought out, but I still can't understand why the island is helping them accomplish it without being caught. I hope it is only a matter of time before I find out where they hide.

"Well, it was nice officially meeting you, Lennox. I'm going to go get the bird in the nest up there, but we'll talk soon. Just make sure not to piss Captain off too bad. We don't like it when he's grumpy."

"I'll do my best," I say and watch as Jorn jumps up and grabs the cross beam, hoisting himself over it then scaling the central wooden pole.

Standing alone on the deck is the cue I need that my break is over. I drop back down on the deck next to the bucket and reach for the brush. My body protests strongly, and a wave of exhaustion crashes over me before I have even started again.

It suddenly dawns on me what Weston is trying to do with this stunt. Sure, he told Sig it was to punish me for my hunger strike in the brig, but there's more to it than that.

He's trying to exhaust me, to work me as hard as he can without being conspicuous, so I will be too tired to try to escape. He wants me to fall into bed and go right to sleep, unable to move from the manual labor he forced on me today and every day in the future.

If he thinks this manipulation is going to work, he's wrong. If anything, it makes me want to do something about it even sooner. If he thinks I'm too exhausted, then maybe this is the best opportunity to try.

Right when he least expects it.

I shift to all fours and scrub the wood until it is sudsy. As I stare into the bubbles, I realize that Jorn never actually told me where Weston hid the mop.

CHAPTER TEN

arkness shrouds the room. Only a sliver of moonlight shines through the row of small windows above the bed. I've been lying awake for hours, not moving a muscle, and waiting for the noises outside the room to cease and Weston's breaths to slow.

Scrubbing the deck took me the entire day, and the suns were setting when I finally stowed the bucket away and headed to the mess to fuel my growling stomach. If his goal was to exhaust me, he accomplished it. I can barely move. My neck and back ache, my knees are stiff and rubbed raw. I can hardly close my hand from grasping the scrub brush all day.

But I refuse to be deterred from my plan. I will fight through the pain.

After I washed and changed in the crew bathrooms, I went straight to bed, well before Weston returned, and was already curled up and feigning sleep when he undressed and settled on his side.

Then I waited.

And waited.

And waited.

I kept the sheets drawn up over my shoulder so my clothes weren't visible. Fuck Weston's rule. I can't waste any time for this escape, and I won't leave without my dagger.

He stole it from me, and I am going to steal it back.

Now, I lay here waiting for the right time. I send a quick prayer to the gods to let this go smoothly so I can get back home.

Weston hasn't moved for a while. His rustling and shifting ceased as he fell into a deep slumber. It's time to make my move.

Lifting it slowly, I peel the bedding back, trying to be silent and avoid the rustle of the linens as I set it down between us. I pause, straining to hear any indication that the movement disrupted him, but he still lays completely unmoving, the rise and fall of his chest the only sign he is still alive.

My limbs shake as I slowly shift on the mattress, propping myself up and biting my lip as the fatigue threatens to let me fall. With every large movement, I pause and check that he's still asleep until I'm lying on my stomach. I slowly lift to all fours and move closer, crawling across the space between us, heading straight for the pillow.

This is the first time I've actually looked at him in this bed since I lay facing the other direction. I sneak a glance at his face and can't help but notice how different he looks. It's nothing like the grumpy and angry Weston I see every day. The muscles in his cheeks and jaw are relaxed. His brow isn't bunched in the middle or downcast with disapproval aimed at me. His lips are parted slightly.

I squeeze my eyes shut.

Focus, Lennox.

I move closer until I'm right alongside him; the pillow concealing my dagger within reach. Another quick glance tells me he's still asleep. His hand rests low on his chest as his breathing stays steady, and the glint of metal catches my eye. A thick gold band sits on the third finger, marring his otherwise empty hand.

Is Weston *married*?

What woman could put up with this incessantly irritating man enough to marry him? Something deep inside me squirms at the thought, and I ignore it before realizing it can't be true. This band is on the wrong hand.

No more reason to feel sorry for that poor imaginary woman.

Yanking my eyes away from the ring and trying to ignore the bare muscular chest beneath it, I focus back on my task.

There's no sign that my dagger is under the pillow, but I know it's there. I heard him unsheathe it again tonight and slide it between the sheets when I was faking sleep.

I need to be careful. The blade could be pointing in either direction, and I don't want to slice open my hand. The last thing I need is an injury to tend to on my way off the ship.

Holding my breath, I extend my arm slowly, trying not to shift the bed as I reach. My fingers slide under the cool sheet, flat as possible, so I don't jostle his resting head. They slide over the metal, and I try to avoid the sharp edge as I move toward the hilt. I stretch a little farther, my balance wavering slightly on my one shaky arm.

I stop short as my fingertips brush against something warm.

Fuck.

Everything happens so quickly, I don't have time to process that Weston's other hand is under the pillow, wrapped around the hilt of my dagger. I am suddenly flipping in the air, my back slamming down onto the bed as a heavy weight lands on top of me.

Weston hovers, his face so close to mine we share a breath. His forearm presses against my chest, his hips lining up square with mine, pinning me beneath him. Heat pools between my thighs as I gape up at him until I feel cold metal digging into my neck. I lift my chin to avoid being sliced open, but my eyes don't leave his. He stares right through me, his glassy gaze unblinking, his disheveled hair falling over his forehead.

I don't move. I don't say a word. He doesn't look like he's awake, but I'm scared to break his trance and have him move against me, slicing through my skin before he knows what he's doing.

Maybe he'd mean it.

His eyes flutter as I stare into them, his pupils widening as he slowly comes to. My cheeks heat as his gaze trails over my face, then down to the blade he holds to my throat. I watch as the realization strikes him barely a moment before he speaks.

"What are you doing, princess?" His voice is deep and gravelly with sleep.

"Nothing," I lie. He caught me, but I'm still not going to admit to my plan. The word comes out breathier than I intended, but I don't break the eye contact as his search mine for the lie. I ignore the throbbing between my thighs as I feel every plane of his body pushing me down, and instead try to focus on slowing my heaving breaths.

The cold press of the dagger is gone instantly as he flips the blade away from my throat and tosses it across the bed, out of my reach. Even without the threat of breaking skin, I don't move. I stay frozen beneath him as he shifts his weight, lifting one side of his body off mine as he looks down toward our feet. His eyes rake over me and my skin burns beneath my clothes. My gaze lowers, following his, until he snaps his head toward me, his stare intensifying.

"You were trying to escape again."

It isn't a question, so I stay silent, pressing my lips together, and breathing through my nose, trying to slow the rapid pounding of my heart.

His arm lifts off my chest and I feel like I can breathe again, until he sits back on his heels, his knees between my thighs. I almost choke on my breath as the moonlight illuminates every hard angle on his shirtless torso. My mouth dries as my eyes graze his skin, snagging on a large gnarled scar that slashes across his abdomen, just above the defined muscles that disappear into his low hanging waistband.

This isn't the first time I've had him pressed against me, but it is the first time I can actually see it. I can understand Sig's statement about women being happy to be in my position because Weston looks like someone straight out of Tila's books. I've been around training men all my life, and no one has looked anything like Weston. Even Dane, with his height and broad frame, doesn't feel like this.

His hand wraps under my thigh and he swings my leg over his knees, dropping it on the other side of him, only to plant his hand on my hip and push me off the side of the bed. My knees hit the floor with a loud thud and I snap back up to glare at him.

"Hey! What the fuck was that for?"

"What did I say about outdoor clothes in my bed?" he says as he snatches the dagger back up and swings his legs over the side to stand.

That's it? Is he going to ignore the part where he held my dagger to my throat and pinned me to the bed?

I scramble to my feet and snarl at him, "That's all you have to say right now? No apology for almost killing me?"

His loose linen pants are distracting as they hang low on his hips. He strides over to the desk and opens the top drawer before dropping my dagger inside. The drawer slams and I hear a click before he pulls a key. He stares me down as he lifts the key and slides it right into his pocket, his eyebrow lifting slightly, as if challenging me to try to take it.

"What else do you want me to say, princess? I didn't kill you. Didn't even nick you. There would be no need for an apology if you hadn't been trying to leave."

"Can you blame me? Why would I want to be around you?"

With all the emotions welling up inside me, I don't even think before I hurl those words at him. I don't feel even a sliver of guilt, though, because they're true. Why would I want to be here? I didn't come here on my own. He captured me. He's a grown man. He can take a little dose of truth.

He lets out a huff. "You're not going anywhere."

"I don't belong here, *Captain*."

He crosses his arms over his chest, his muscles rippling in the moonlight. "You do, but that is beside the point. You still aren't going anywhere."

"That may be what you believe, but I will get out of here," I grind out, matching his stance and crossing my arms, too.

This is not part of my plan. Admitting that I still want to leave is only going to undo any progress I had made over the past two days. But he just caught me trying to leave. That alone clued him in to how I feel, so voicing it won't change anything.

He jerks his head toward the door. "Go try it."

I pause, waiting to see if he is serious, but his face stays stoic. Walking to the door, I feel his eyes on me the entire way. The handle turns as I twist it, but when I pull, nothing happens. The door doesn't budge. I pull harder, quickly scanning for a lock I had missed when I hear his footsteps padding up behind me.

I release the handle and step back from the door as he stops next to me. His gaze holds mine as he reaches out and turns the handle, pulling the door open with ease.

My jaw drops.

His lips turn up in a smirk as he pushes the door closed again.

"See, princess? You aren't. Going. Anywhere." The grumble in his voice sends shivers down my spine, and he brushes past me, heading back to bed.

I silently curse the island and the magic, and a seed of doubt sprouts inside me again. Why is it keeping me here? Why won't it let me go home? Why is it subjecting me to this monster?

I spin around, scowling at the room, hoping the island knows how much I hate it right now.

Weston slides beneath the covers, resuming the position he was in before I tried to take back my dagger. I stomp to my side of the bed and kick off my boots, ready to curl up and sleep away the defeat.

"Clothes," he calls out, clearly annoyed.

"Ugh," I groan and grab the shirt from where I had hidden it under my pillow. I quickly undress, sliding his shirt over my head and pulling it down so it doesn't reveal too much.

Not that he's looking; his eyes are closed.

I curl onto my side and pull the blankets back over me. My body hums with energy, hyperaware of his proximity, and I readjust every few minutes, trying to find a comfortable position. I'm still way too tense after being pinned underneath him. I squeeze my thighs together, trying to stop the throbbing that has only barely subsided, and let out a frustrated breath.

I need to clear my mind, focus on something else, not every tingling nerve in my body.

Weston sighs heavily from his side of the bed, but says nothing.

I finally find a comfortable position and stare at the wall. If I stare long enough, hopefully the exhaustion will eventually overtake me.

Minutes pass and I can tell he isn't asleep. He should be able to relax now that the threat of me getting my dagger and escaping is crushed.

I don't know what makes me ask it, if it's the energy or the defeat, a moment of insanity brought on by my eyes gawking at his body earlier, or just pure curiosity, but once the words are out of my mouth, I can't take them back.

"Where'd you get your scar?"

The question hangs in the room between us, and I wonder if he actually is asleep.

A few beats of silence pass and I nuzzle back into my pillow, relieved that he didn't hear me ask it, and it's as if I never did.

His response breaks the silence a moment later. "I'll answer your question if you answer mine."

The words give me pause. I have no idea what he wants to ask me, and it feels like his curiosity is coming out of nowhere. He hasn't asked me hardly anything except if I've eaten since I've been on this ship, and

I wonder if now is the time. Is he going to use my vulnerable position to get information out of me?

I can always lie. He can't see my face, so if it is something I don't want him to know, he won't. But if this is it, the inquiry about the healing waters, why would he give me the option to say no?

My curiosity wins out.

"Fine," I agree.

"Your boyfriend gave it to me," he grumbles. No explanation, just the statement. I didn't realize he and Dane had any interaction, and I'm surprised. Especially because I feel like this is something Dane would have told me.

Is Weston lying?

"You must have done something to deserve it," I say.

Like kill the last Guardian.

A soft chuckle echoes in the otherwise silent room. "Keep telling yourself that, princess."

Silence falls again as I wait for my question. I wonder if he changed his mind when he doesn't speak, and my impatience is too much to handle.

"What's your question?"

He doesn't answer right away, just shifts and adjusts the blankets, pulling them slightly tighter around me.

"How old are you?"

That's what he wants to know? My age? On an island with no time, my age shouldn't matter at all, especially since every person on Dawnlin is of varied ages. All of us deserve to be here, no matter how old we are. I can't believe he didn't ask me something he truly wanted to know, something that would help his cause.

Maybe he thinks showing a personal interest will soften me. He's wrong. I answer him anyway. If he squandered a perfectly good chance to find out information, that is his mistake.

"Twenty-one."

He looses a soft sigh before speaking again, the words barely a mumble, "That's what I thought. Goodnight, princess."

The mattress shifts underneath me as I assume he turns away.

My mind reels with what he could need to know my age for, but I decide I don't care. How do any of the Castaways even know how old they are? They've been stuck at this age for as long as they have been here, and no one truly knows how time moves here compared to the real world.

I shrug it off as a mere curiosity and close my eyes, praying for another night without nightmares.

"Goodnight, Captain."

CHAPTER ELEVEN

Images of Weston hovering above me flash through my mind all night, making sleep near impossible. It's like I can still feel his hips pressed into mine, his breath brushing my lips, the grumble in his chest as he questioned me.

I should not be this attracted to him, and I can't make sense of it. How could someone as beguiling as him have such a cruel heart? My body can't seem to control itself when it comes to Weston, and I blame it on pent up sexual frustration from stopping Dane so he didn't find my map.

I toss and turn all night, giving up on staying hunkered close to the edge. Sleep is intermittent, an unsatisfied ache preventing any true rest for my body or my mind. I need it to go away, and there's only one way to do it. My eyes stay closed as I bite my lip, heart pounding in my ears, blocking out all other noise.

Fingertips brush over the soft shirt as my hand wanders slowly over my body, moving to fill the need itself. Part of me doesn't care if I rustle the bedding, as long as I don't make any other noises. My solitary focus is to get rid of this need.

I feel the edge of my undergarments and slowly slide beneath them, my hips wiggling in anticipation of the touch, when I freeze. The brush of lips on the tip of my shoulder startles me, followed by a callused palm sliding over my elbow, down my forearm.

"Let me."

The voice grumbles in my ear and heat floods my entire body, the space between my thighs turning molten. My chest heaves as my hand quickly abandons its plan, instead grasping the sheets beside me as his lips trail light kisses across my collarbone.

I nod quickly, squeezing my eyes shut tighter. I know if I open them, I might stop this from happening, even if my body is screaming at me to let it. I feel his smile on my skin as he shifts over me, hovering, driving me wild without any contact except for his lips. He trails his nose up the column of my neck, kissing and licking his way up to my jaw.

A hum fills my chest, and I lift my chin, giving him more access.

He slides his hand down my side, settling at the crease above my thigh. His fingers flutter, bunching my shirt until the hem is balled up in his hand. An involuntary shiver courses through me as the shirt slides up higher.

I know what he wants, and I arch my back, lifting off the bed, helping him slide the shirt over me until I'm left in only my undergarments.

His hands press into my skin, more insistent than before, grasping my waist as his lips find my neck again. He trails kisses down my chest before reaching up and freeing my breast from the lace. His large hand covers it, kneading and pulling, before sucking my nipple into his mouth.

I moan quietly, and he switches to the other, his hand covering the one he just left, tugging gently.

He releases me with a soft pop, then his lips find mine, slow but strong, coaxing my mouth open and brushing his tongue against mine in long languid strokes.

His hand moves then, trailing circles over my pebbled skin toward the place I am throbbing for him. I writhe under his fingers, my hips shifting, urging him on, begging him to touch me where I need him to.

He slips beneath my undergarments, cupping me and kneading the heel of his hand into my most sensitive spot. I groan against his mouth, and it encourages him, the kiss becoming more eager as his fingers explore and tease.

I gasp as he presses inside me, and my knees slide wider, the wet heat of my core begging him for more. My hands find his shoulders, his chest, and I pull him closer as he slowly pumps his finger into me.

I cry out as he hits something deep inside, and my eyes fly open, staring directly into his soft, gentle amber eyes.

"Come for me, Lennox," he grumbles above me.

"Dane," I moan as his pace increases, my hips wriggling to meet his motions. The pressure builds, tingling rising through my body as he pushes in and out, his eyes never leaving mine, watching the pleasure he is pulling from me.

"Oh, Dane," I call out as it rises higher and higher, his palm now working me in tight circles.

SLAM.

The noise jolts me awake, my eyes flying open to find the early light of morning shining in through the windows. My chest heaves, and a light sheen of sweat covers my body. Wrestling the blankets off me, I try to pull away the damp shirt that sticks to my skin. I need to cool down. Everything inside me is still wound up as tight as when I fell asleep, and maybe even more.

I glance around the room, trying to find the source of the sound, when my eyes fall on Weston standing at his desk, sliding my dagger into his vest. He isn't looking at me, and his expression is unreadable.

My cheeks heat as I take him in, remembering my dream from only moments ago. I feel like it is written all over my face, but there's no way he could know. It was all in my head, and I'm the only one who is uncomfortable about it. I just need to pretend like nothing happened, and figure out a way to get it off my mind.

I clear my throat and slide off the side of the bed, pulling down the shirt that had bunched up around my hips in the midst of my dream.

Weston fiddles with something on the desk as I pad over to the armoire, and pull out a new set of clothes. I refuse to look at him. My face is still warm with embarrassment and desire, and I don't want him to see my flushed cheeks.

Once I am back on my side, my back to him, he breaks the silence.

"You talk in your sleep."

I freeze, one leg halfway in the pants as I process what he just said, and I'm frozen for so long I almost tip over.

Horrified.

That is all I feel right now.

Throw me off the side of the ship and let the ocean take me, mortified.

"I-I don't know what you're talking about," I stammer, my limbs finally regaining the ability to move. I shove my legs in the pants and pull them up under the shirt, tying them quickly and tightly.

He has to be lying, trying to ruffle my feathers after my escape attempt last night, just like he does when he calls me princess. He's toying with me, trying to make it seem like I'm a burden to share a room with. There's no way his comment has anything to do with my dream.

"Oh, I think you might." The rumble in his voice makes my breath catch.

He knows.

He definitely knows.

I refuse to look back at him. Instead, I intently focus on getting dressed underneath his large shirt and ignore his scent filling my senses.

Right when the nightmares have disappeared, and I'm grateful to finally get solid sleep, I have a sex dream.

In front of Weston.

I silently plead for him to leave, so I can have a moment to sit in my humiliation before having to go out onto the deck and be demeaned by the rest of the crew, scrubbing the boards by hand so everyone can gawk at me.

He doesn't leave.

The clink of his belt buckle is the only sound, and I wonder why he needs to wear an empty scabbard all day. I don't actually care what he does with it. I just need him to get out of this room.

Right now.

"Most men who have a woman in their bed aren't exactly happy if she calls out another man's name."

"Oh gods," I groan and drop my face in my hands. "Please stop talking," I beg, a growl lighting on the last syllable. His boots pound on the wooden floor as he heads toward the door.

"Sounds like you need to work out some frustration," he says, the words harsh, almost threatening. "Get dressed and meet me on deck. You have two minutes."

He steps out the door, leaving it open for me to follow behind him, and I listen as his boots stomp down the hall. There's pounding on a door, some muffled voices, then another door closes.

It is only moments before Sig's voice calls out repeatedly, as she moves through the belly of the ship. "All hands on deck!"

Now that I'm alone, I pull the damp shirt off and slide mine over my head before Sig's head peeks into the room. "Hurry and head up to the main deck."

"Yeah, I know," I huff, bending down to lace my boots.

She steps in closer and leans against the doorjamb, crossing her arms over her chest.

"What's up with you?" Her eye trail over me and land on my face, and a single eyebrow raises as she takes in my flustered appearance.

"Nothing." My foot slams into the other boot.

She tries to hide a smile with pursed lips and nods. "You better move faster than that." She disappears back down the hallway just as I stand and straighten my clothes before following her to the main deck, unsure of what I am going to find when I get there.

Weston is right. I do have a lot of frustration I need to work out, but now most of it is directed at him. He's humiliated me repeatedly, both publicly and privately, and he will not get away with it. I may be just anyone here in Dawnlin, but I'm still a fucking princess, and I will not tolerate him treating me like I'm deserving of indignity.

I just hope he keeps his mouth shut. I don't need anyone else's judgment, and I definitely don't need Weston telling anyone what happened in that room.

Breathing out some of the anger in prolonged exhales, I step out onto the deck, standing with the rest of the crew already assembled there.

Something tells me this morning is only going to keep getting better.

CHAPTER TWELVE

Energy hums through everyone gathered on the main deck as we wait for word of what is happening. Weston and Sig aren't on deck, having disappeared somewhere below. I stand alone off to the side, as the Castaways nearest me chatter amongst themselves. After the morning I've had, I don't feel like interacting with anyone.

"Lennox! Lennox!" Fin's call catches my attention, and I look up to find him bouncing toward me, a small bow and quiver in his hands. He is the only exception to my current mood. There's nothing that could keep me from wanting to be around Fin.

"Look what mister Weston gave me!" He waves it up at my face and grins.

"Wow, Fin. That's even better than the one you had before." The bow is the right size for his body, probably the right tension too. It won't be as difficult to handle, unlike when he tried to shoot mine.

"Yeah, but that one was yours. This one is *mine*." His face lights up and his eyes sparkle as he brings it closer to his chest. "I wish I could show Roley. He would want one too." A brief glimpse of sadness flashes over his face, before he is right back to happy Fin.

I tousle his hair with a smile. "I'm sure he would."

"I asked mister Weston if he had one for you too, but he said you can't have one yet. He said he can't trust you." He looks up at me, confused. "Why can't mister Weston trust you, Lennox? I trust you. You always take care of me."

I crouch down to his level. "He probably doesn't trust me because I've tried to get out of here too many times," I say.

"But you said you'd be good!" he whines.

"It's not that easy, Fin."

He thinks for a minute. "Maybe you shouldn't do that anymore. Maybe you should stay, so that mister Weston will give you your bow and we can practice together."

"We can't stay, remember? We have to get back to Dane, back to the Voyagers." I plead with him to remember, but I know he is just a child. He doesn't see the situation like I do, and he never will. At least not while we are in Dawnlin.

Maybe when we get home, once he's grown, he will look back and understand that everything I did was only to protect him and keep him safe from this man who tried to take advantage of him.

A loud crow gets my attention, and I stand, looking around the deck only to see Jorn swinging down from the mast. A cheer rises among the Castaways as Weston and Sig step out onto the deck, arms piled with swords.

They're not just any swords, they're dull training swords, just like Brynne and I used back in Blackwood.

"Partner up!" Weston calls out before the deck erupts into more cheers, followed by the scattering of bodies.

Fin tries to crow like Jorn, and I suppress a giggle. "Come on, Fin. We can find something for target practice."

"Not so fast, princess." Weston's eyes gleam as he saunters up to us. "You're with me."

As if he hasn't tortured me enough this morning, now I have to spar with him too?

My mouth drops open, but the 'no' dies on my lips. My first reaction is to resist, to cause a fight on deck again, but I don't. Maybe it isn't a bad idea, fighting him and letting out the aggression that has been building up since Fin was taken.

I snap my jaw closed and snatch the practice sword he tosses at me out of the air. A look of approval flashes in his eyes, but as quick as I notice, it disappears again.

"Sig set up a bale for you to shoot, Fin. It's right over there." He points toward the bow of the ship, where a small bale sits near the rail, positioned so Fin won't hit anyone if he misses.

Which is likely.

Fin runs over excitedly, and starts nocking an arrow, his feet and hold nothing like what we practiced back in camp.

The crew has come to life around us. Most pairs are already in the middle of a match, the clash of swords and laughter ringing out over the deck. Stassia and Auralie stand off to the side, swords balanced against the railing as they stretch their muscles before getting started. Jorn and another boy I haven't met have already taken their fight to the floor, grappling and tossing each other about, laughing and taunting as they go.

The training session on the ship feels vastly different from what I'm used to back home. It doesn't feel like work, or something everyone dreads going to. Everyone seems to actually enjoy it, like it isn't a responsibility and more of just part of who they are.

Weston weaves through the practicing pairs, and I follow closely. He stops just shy of the far rail next to the opening for the gangway. Goosebumps prickle my skin when I look at how close we are to the open deck. The threat of falling into the water is very real.

Maybe if that happens, I'll have a chance to escape.

"Now," Weston says as he readies his dull training sword. "If you're going to try to steal your dagger back from me, you're at least going to learn how to use it. But first, let's see how poorly you were trained."

"What makes you think I don't know how to use it?" I sneer as I raise my sword in front of my body.

"I know you don't know how to use it. I watched you try to use it against me, remember?"

A smirk lifts his lips as he waits for me to attack, taunting me with his insult. I taste blood from biting my tongue. I don't want to give him any satisfaction in knowing he's getting to me.

I focus on everything Brynne has taught me through the years, trying to visualize the movements that used to be second nature. If there is a time I need them, it's now. The sword is heavier in my hands than usual, and I know I'm going to have to compensate for my newfound weakness in the fight.

Just another reason I need my strength back.

I step toward him and strike, which he blocks easily. My movements are rough, not smooth and quick like I was trained, but I follow the strike with a backward swipe, a combination Brynne and I worked on for hours one day until it was fluid. He sidesteps it easily and shoots me a look that says, 'Is that all you've got?'

He's clearly unimpressed.

Fuck him.

I try again, moving quicker than before as my muscles loosen and get used to the feel of the sword. The motions come back quickly, but he matches every one with a complete look of boredom as he swats my sword away.

He doesn't say a word, not like Brynne, who constantly yells commands and adjustments while we are training. Instead, he just watches me, his eyes never leaving my body, and it fuels my desire to best him. On the next blow, he knocks the sword from my hand and it clatters to the ground between us.

"I was right," he says as I bend to snatch the sword off the ground. "You were trained poorly."

"You don't know what you're talking about," I say. He doesn't know the highest ranking guard in the kingdom trained me, that I've spent years of my life devoted to being able to protect myself. He might think whatever man in my town I wanted to secure with a betrothal taught me how to fight, but he'd be completely wrong.

When his eyes are nowhere near my sword, I try to catch him off guard with a quick swipe across his abdomen, but he steps back lazily, as if he expected the move. His sword slaps the back of my calves and I cry out, shocked at the sting.

"Hey!"

"Fix your footwork. You're giving away your next move."

He did expect it.

I visualize my footwork and feel the way I am standing holding the sword, and as much as I hate to admit it, he's right. I'm leaning on my lead foot, giving away which side I'm moving toward, and it is making me slightly off balance.

Stepping back and resetting my feet, I'm barely ready before he charges me, his strength sending vibrations through my hand as I block every one of his strikes. Our blades clash, locking us together in a stalemate before I push him away. The force pushes me backward, and I stagger, trying to steady myself. My eyes widen with panic as I look down at my feet, realizing how far we've shifted across the deck. The heels of my boots are now hanging off the edge of the ship, begging to tip over.

My arms windmill as I try to right myself, feeling my weight pulling me toward the water below. A scream catches in my throat and my stomach bottoms out before I feel Weston's hand wrap around my waistband and yank me forward. I fall into him, but even with my weight and the momentum from my almost fall, he doesn't budge.

"Careful, princess," he grunts, and I shove out of his grasp.

"You should have let me fall," I snap.

"I could have, but I didn't think you wanted to get wet again this morning."

I don't need a mirror to know my face is bright red, not only with embarrassment, but with fury. Weston doesn't need to be thinking about me wet in any sense of the word. He makes me want to stab him, and suddenly I'm wishing these were real blades, not training swords.

"What do you know about making a woman wet, *Captain?*" I seethe, wiping the sweat on my palm on my pants, trying to do anything to keep my hands busy so I don't throw a punch.

"I know enough, princess."

"Fuck you," I spit out and spin so the opening is alongside me, no longer at my back. There are Castaways fighting near us, and I hope they were too preoccupied to hear.

"I've seen all I need to see, anyway."

His dismissal feels worse than being scolded by Brynne on her worst day. My confidence is low when I fight with a sword. If given a choice, I'll always choose a bow, and hearing him confirm my inadequacy makes me bristle.

Coming after his inappropriate comment, the words make me hate him even more.

He takes the sword from my hand and leans it against the rail, along with his. The jewels on my dagger hilt gleam in the sun as he pulls it out of his vest, then flips it so the blade rests against his palm.

"Can I trust you to practice with this?" he asks, his eyes meeting mine. Any humor I may have found there from before is gone now, as he considers handing me an actual weapon.

No.

I don't speak, just nod. A thrill hums through me as he extends his arm and my hand clasps over the metal hilt. I feel safe again, my dagger back where it belongs.

Weston pulls a different blade from his belt, the dagger slightly larger than mine.

"Now let's see what bad habits I need to train out of you."

He's doing this on purpose. Antagonizing me, trying to get me to react to him. As if having to endure this morning wasn't punishment enough, he feels the need to take whatever he's feeling out on me here.

Is he jealous? Angry?

Was he *excited*?

No, absolutely not. If Weston enjoyed whatever he thought he saw this morning, there would be no way I could sleep in that room with him ever again, let alone in the same bed.

I look down at the sharpened edge of the steel and watch as my fingers close tighter over the hilt.

"Eyes on me, princess."

My eyes flick up to meet his, as if I can't disobey his command. He waits, his gaze not leaving mine, until I strike, swiping at him, but I'm met by his blocks every time.

I groan in frustration as we reset.

"I think I've heard enough of your moaning for one day."

It's almost as if something physically snaps inside me. He's punishing me, and I've had enough of it. I want to beat him, to be done with this stupid exercise, but I don't want to just walk away. He wins if I walk away.

Ignoring the heat burning in my face, I charge at him, letting my rage take over my actions. I thought the anger and humiliation I felt when I was in the training ring with Brynne being mocked by the guards was bad, but that was nothing compared to this. The last time I felt *this* was the last time I fought him, when he took Fin.

My training takes over, the movements the same as with a sword, only with the shorter weapon. Much closer, more personal.

Because he's made this personal.

With every blow he dodges or blocks, my frustration escalates.

How is he this skilled? He's been hidden away here for years, with no one to fight. Why is he making me look like I can't touch an opponent?

A grunt escapes my lips as I slice at the air, until his fingers wrap around my wrist, squeezing tight and jerking it to an odd angle, just as he did in the cave. My grip loosens on the hilt, and I cry out and grab my wrist, pain lacing from it up into my arm as he slides the dagger out of my hand.

"You're fighting with too much emotion. You'll never win that way." The dagger clatters on the wooden deck as Weston tosses it at my feet. I bend over, snagging it quickly and ready myself again.

All I have is emotion right now. So many mixed negative emotions flooding my mind, day and night, and I want them all to stop. I just want to feel good, happy. Like myself. Or, at least the new version of me I became once I found a home here.

I inhale deeply, trying to settle the emotions, and realize the noise on deck has dulled. Many of the Castaways have stopped their duels to watch us, and it gives me even more motivation in this moment to beat Weston.

We slowly circle each other, each of us stalking our prey, waiting for the other to make the first move. It feels like a dance, not that I have ever danced with anyone outside of lessons.

He watches me intently, and his eyebrow quirks in a challenge. I barely wait a second before I feign a strike to his left side, only to step back to his right, and swipe at the arm he's moving to block me.

My blade meets his skin, and deep red blood blooms across his forearm before his dagger drops to the floorboards.

Pride rises inside me, not at making him bleed, but at besting him. After all the taunting, the jabs, the embarrassment, the criticism, I won. An uncontrollable smile breaks out across my face, but before I can celebrate my victory, he grabs the wrist of my dagger hand, and descends on me, invading my space until my back hits the railing and my own dagger is held to my throat.

By both of us.

I arch my back, leaning as far away as possible, bending over the rail, but he follows, towering over me, his strength fighting my own and keeping the blade in place as I try to lower my weapon.

My eyes widen as he leans in, closing the space between us until I think his lips might actually brush mine. His expression is more serious than I've ever seen it, the intensity bordering on hatred as he snarls at me.

"Don't *ever* let your guard down."

I hold his gaze, my eyes flitting between his, trying to figure out why he doesn't seem to be angry about me cutting him. Why is he concerned I didn't protect myself? Is there a hint of worry in those teal eyes?

My lips part slightly as I suck in a sharp breath before I nod quickly, barely moving my head so I don't draw blood on my neck. He releases my hand, his other wrapping around my back and settling between my shoulders before he pulls me upright. He steps away quickly, leaving me to stagger back onto my feet before looking down at the wound on his arm.

The ship comes back to life, and I'm aware that there are other people around us as the dull roar in my ears starts to subside. Bodies shuffle away and training resumes, as if the fight between the captain and the newest victim hadn't ever happened.

Weston rolls his sleeve up to his elbow, and my eyes fall on the slice that is much larger than it felt.

He scowls at me, then reaches back and snatches the dagger from my hands.

"Go get your scrub brush. There's blood on the deck."

He stomps away and I'm left stunned. I shouldn't feel guilty for hurting him, but deep down, I do. I've never actually harmed anyone before, and Weston is the only person who's been on the other side of my attempts. Now that I have, I don't like the way it feels.

I know my kingdom has the tradition of giving the royal family a dagger for protection, so if we need to, we can use it. I've been trained to use it, but being trained and actually harming someone are very different experiences. Now that I have, now that I've hurt someone who has repeatedly sworn he will not hurt me, even though he is my enemy, it feels harrowing.

Like I have blood on my hands.

CHAPTER THIRTEEN

After the incident in training, I avoid Weston like I avoid my father, and it seems he does the same. Days pass without a single word exchanged between us. Instead of using the healing salve from the island, he walked around the ship with a bandage wrapped over his forearm; his sleeve always rolled to his elbow, as if he wanted me to have a constant reminder of what I'd done. Otherwise, he pretended it never happened, and so did I. I never apologized for hurting him, and he never apologized for his behavior.

But his message was well received.

I have not let my guard down once since our fight, since he growled the warning in my face. If anything, I am on guard more now than ever before, even if it is mostly around him.

There hasn't been another opportunity to escape. Dawnlin locks me in the room at night, and there's never a moment alone on this damn ship. I'm trying to blend in, to seem like they are growing on me and I'm accepting my position among them, becoming a Castaway.

That will never happen.

I won't stop trying to get back to Dane, bringing all my knowledge with me and finally righting the wrong Weston has inflicted on the island.

A dull ache settles in my chest when I think about Dane, remembering how he was wild with concern when I was missing as I searched for Fin. The memory of us standing in the clearing, worry etched on his face as he confessed it all to me, flashes in my mind.

I can't let anything happen to you. You're too important.

I miss him, and if he was going crazy back then, I can only imagine how he is feeling now. All the more reason I need to get home to him.

It isn't just missing Dane that is bothering me, though. I spent every day for months with full reign over the island, able to go anywhere and do what I please, but now I'm stuck. I'm trapped on this floating prison, and even though I'm no longer in the brig, not being able to see anything but wooden walls and glaring sunlight as I work is starting to get to me.

The Castaways come and go around me, but no one has given me any indication of when or if I will ever be let off the ship. Sig mentioned I would, but she hasn't brought it up again, at least not since training.

Is keeping me under constant supervision another punishment for besting him?

At least I'm grateful my strength is rapidly improving, and my body is becoming used to the tedious chore. I'm finishing faster each day, leaving the rest of my afternoons open to sit in the lounge, or chat on the deck with Stassia and Auralie. Sometimes Sig and Jorn join us if they aren't on shift.

I still haven't figured out what that means, and no one says anything about it. They just...go.

No matter where I go on this ship, or what I am doing, I am constantly listening, waiting for someone around me to give up a piece of information I can bring back to Dane. Back at camp, we often talked about the Castaways, the only other regular topic besides finding the cure, but it doesn't seem like anyone here talks about the Voyagers.

So far, besides my conversation with Jorn about the helio, I've discovered nothing new, so I need to bide my time. When they trust me enough, they will at least tell me, and hopefully include me, in whatever is going on here, so I have another chance to get out. I'm trying to stay patient, but something gnaws at me. Will the rest of my life, all of eternity on this island, be spent scrubbing the deck and fighting with Weston?

Today, I decide it won't be. I'm going to make the best of it, spending time with the one person on this ship who brings me joy.

I stow the bucket and brush away in the supply closet before heading below deck to find Fin. His feet kick up and down, as he lies on his stomach playing with a set of wooden blocks he has constructed into a castle.

"Nice castle you built there," I say as I plop down next to him, folding my feet under me.

"Do you like it?" he says, his face brightening with a smile.

"It's great. Is it like the one in your kingdom?"

His shoulders touch his ears in a shrug. "I dunno. I've never seen it before. I want to! I bet it is huge!"

I chuckle softly. "Yes, it probably is," I agree, setting a block down on top of a tower.

"Have you ever been inside a castle, Lennox?"

I nod once. "I have."

"Really? You have? How come? What was it like? Did you see the king and queen?"

If only Fin knew.

I am more familiar with the walls of a castle than the outside world. He looks at it with a sense of wonder, and I see it as the same kind of prison that I'm locked in here, run by a tyrant who doesn't care about me, only wants to control me. I've kept my title a secret this long, and I don't plan on letting it slip. Fin doesn't need to know me as anything other than Lennox. That's who I want to be while I'm here.

"That's a story for another time," I say, watching his face drop slightly. "I actually had a different question for you." I lean in closer and whisper loudly, "Do you want to play?"

The light in his eyes is back in an instant, and he jumps up off the floor, knocking the castle down and sending blocks scattering.

"Yes! Yes! Let's play!" He jumps up and down with each word, a huge grin on his face.

"Let's clean this up first," I say, reaching over to pile the wooden blocks into an empty basket next to the crumbling castle.

Fin is still bouncing with excitement once the floor is clear and immediately launches into initiating the game.

"You can hide first, Lennox, since you haven't played before. I should go tell mister Weston so he can play too!" He runs for the steps, but I stop him.

"No, Fin, how about it's just you and me today?" I still want to be as far away from Weston as possible during waking hours. Fin hasn't picked up on the coldness between us, but it is obvious everyone else has. As soon as Weston and I are remotely close to each other, whoever happens to be around gives us a wide berth.

"Alright!" he yells and hops off the step.

"Tell me the rules," I say.

"I have to count to one hundred, and while I'm counting, you go hide somewhere. You have to stay real quiet until I find you."

"What happens if you don't find me?" I ask.

"That won't happen!" he giggles. "Mister Weston always finds me. That's how the game ends!"

I try to hide my smile. "When can I come out if you don't find me?"

"You can't. I have to find you." His eyebrows crunch together, like he can't fathom the game ending any other way.

I guess I am not moving all day.

"Alright, let's do it."

"Ready, set, go!" Fin dives face first into one of the cushions and covers his eyes. Numbers ring out into the room as he counts.

"Seven, eight, nine, twelve, eleven, fourteen."

I stifle a giggle and tiptoe out of the lounge. There will be plenty of time before he searches for me, so I don't rush.

Spending time with Fin isn't my only motivation behind the game today. Searching for a place to hide gives me a perfectly innocent reason to wander around the ship. Sig said nothing was off limits, but there has to be something more they aren't telling me.

I can't shake the feeling they are hiding something. Whether it is physical, or just being elusive about their motives and plans, I don't know. But there's a secret somewhere. If there wasn't, I'd already know everything about having a shift.

The Castaways are mainly on deck today, or tucked away in their quarters. Not many are roaming below deck, and the few I heard are in the mess. Checking over my shoulders to make sure I am still alone, I pull open a door in the hallway and peek in, only to find a small supply closet. I continue looking behind every door, but there's nothing out of the ordinary. Closets, supplies, tools, bedding. Everything is neat and tidy, and I wonder if it is someone's ship duty to stock them, or if the island does it.

The bottom floor with the brig wasn't included on Sig's tour, but I don't want to go back down there yet. I spent enough time down there for now. I can check it another day. Heading back toward the lounge, I can still hear Fin counting. His numbers are quickly approaching the end, so I need to think fast.

The infirmary is the closest door to me, so I quietly turn the knob and slide in. Choosing somewhere so close to him puts me at risk of being discovered quickly, but it's fine. It's only the first round.

The room is small, with only a stool and rectangular table, I assume for injuries that may require someone lying down to be treated. Looking around for a hiding place that will give Fin a little challenge seems of no use in the sparse room until I spot a tall cabinet door on the wall. I peek inside, finding enough room to sit comfortably, so I climb in quickly and shut the door behind me.

Fin's counting drifts through the air, and I listen as he finally finishes.

"I'm coming!" he shouts loudly, and his footsteps pound on the wood as he climbs steps to the first floor.

So much for thinking he was going to find me quickly.

I sit inside the small cabinet, and it is the first time I have truly been alone with my thoughts since being let out of the brig. There's no Weston, or Sig, or even Fin, to distract me from the tidal wave of emotions and thoughts about how my entire situation has changed. With all of my time spent plotting a way to escape or fighting with Weston, I have barely had a chance to process everything and let the change settle over me.

The weight of my situation feels like it is crushing me in this small, dark corner of the ship. Everything I came here for, I've been denied, and everything I found was taken from me. I have no healing waters, no friends, no family. No Dane.

Silent tears fall on my cheeks and I don't stop them. None of Edmond's hostility training had prepared me for this, nor the finality of it. Succumbing to the enemy was never part of the training, but you can't really comprehend how it feels unless you are in it.

If there's one thing I've learned from Dawnlin, it's that I can't lose hope, no matter how hard things feel. I have to trust that things will work out in the end, and if they haven't yet, it isn't the end.

I am determined to make it back to the Voyagers, but I haven't dealt with the possibility of never going back to the real world. Dane and I never got a chance to find out how to replenish the dust before I found the waters and was taken captive. I left that mountain convinced that I no longer wanted to return to Blackwood, but was that a decision in the heat of the moment? Is staying here truly what I want, or was it just a result of my failure? I'm scared I won't have the choice. I also have no way of knowing how many trips Dane has had to make since I've been here, or how many people he's had to bring back to the island.

The dust could already be gone.

I suck in a deep, shuddering breath and push the thought from my mind. I can't worry about what I can't control. My focus needs to stay on getting back to camp before deciding whether or not I will stay here.

Forever.

The tears dry on my cheeks. I refuse to wipe them away, but need to move forward. I don't want Fin to see me crying, so everything I dealt with in this tiny box needs to stay right here, for me only. I breathe deeply, clearing my mind and listen for Fin, but don't hear the patter of his little feet anywhere close.

Time ticks on, but I don't hear Fin again. My body aches from being crunched in this cabinet for so long, and I really want to take a walk around the deck to stretch my legs. Fin told me to stay put, but something tells me this is the first time *he's* doing the finding. It doesn't surprise me at all that Weston always finds him. This is his ship, but it is probably the best way he can think to keep an eye on Fin and keep him out of trouble.

He told me Fin was safe. I guess he wasn't lying.

My knee bounces uncontrollably as I sit, waiting. I'm getting impatient, but I promised Fin I would play the game the right way. So I don't move.

I don't know how much time has passed when footsteps pound above me, the echo of doors slamming follows in their wake. They get louder as they move through the ship, and I know they don't belong to Fin. Who the hell is searching for something so frantically?

My spine stiffens as the answer to my question comes in the form of a voice booming through the body of the ship.

"Where the fuck is she?" The words reverberate through the room as if he was standing next to me.

More sets of footsteps join in now, pounding up and down the stairs on the other side of the wall. I can almost feel his wrath in the air, and gods help whoever pissed him off, because he sounds murderous.

It can't be me. I already finished my task for the day, and it isn't my problem if anyone's sandy or muddy boots already messed it up. I'm not redoing it.

Curiosity gets the best of me and I want to peek outside to see what the fuss is about. Pushing open the door to the cabinet, I crawl out of the tight space, my legs tingling as the blood flows back into them. I jolt as the door to the infirmary flies open, knocking into the wall next to me. Light from the hallway pours into the room, but it is blocked by Weston's broad frame.

His head whips around the room, searching, until his eyes fall on me, half hanging out of the cabinet on the floor. I push to stand just as he steps into the room and slams the door behind him.

Wait, is he mad at me?

I open my mouth, ready to fight, my explanation tumbling out of my mouth.

"I already fin—"

"What the hell do you think you are doing?" His voice echoes through the small room, surrounding me, his temper making my blood start to boil in retaliation. The first words he's said to me in days, and he's yelling at me? No. I'm won't let him try to intimidate me like this, so I fire right back.

"If you didn't interrupt me yo—"

"I thought you'd have this out of your system by now. How many times are you going to try to get away before you accept the fact that you aren't going anywhere?"

My mouth falls open and a short laugh bursts from my lips. "*That* is what you think I'm doing?"

"No one could fucking find you!" He gestures wildly to the cabinet I emerged from.

"Because I'm playing with Fin! Hiding is the whole point of the game, *Captain*, and I'm pretty sure you're the one who taught it to him!" I match his tone, his volume, both of us yelling at each other, anger seeping from our pores.

"How do I know you aren't lying to me? Were you waiting until you thought we wouldn't notice? I'll always fucking notice, princess." He takes a half step closer, but in the small room, it seems like he's right on top of me. I have to crane my neck to keep glaring, showing him I am not backing down.

"Because I still can't get off the ship! I can't swim, remember?"

"Didn't stop you from trying to jump last time."

I let out a frustrated groan. "Not everything I do is a personal attack on you, *Captain.*"

He scoffs, like what I said is just another lie. "You could have fooled me."

"Listen," I yell, poking a finger into the center of his chest repeatedly. He barely glances down at it before looking back at me. "If you're going to keep me here, you're going to have to learn to trust me. Otherwise, let me go home!" I school my face, hardening my stare, doing everything I can not to give away the secret I am hiding.

I still can't be trusted.

Our eyes stay locked on each other, neither of us willing to let the other win. My chest rises and falls rapidly, my breaths heaving with emotion as I wait for an answer. This feels like a pivotal moment, where he will either choose to move forward, or make me work harder for it.

Weston doesn't speak or move, continuing to tower over me. His jaw clenches and unclenches, then clenches again as he stares me down.

Maybe I wasn't doing as well as I thought of convincing them they can trust me. If he can't, despite explicitly telling him I had no intention of leaving today, then my attempts haven't been enough.

I tear my eyes away from his and push past him, shoving him with my shoulder as I try to leave this stifling room. He barely budges, and I don't hear the pounding of his steps behind me, so I know he isn't following.

Pulling the door open, I slip through the gap out into the hallway. I'm finally able to catch my breath now that he isn't trying to prove I am lying.

I stomp through the hall and up the stairs, to the only other place on this ship I have to go, even though I still share it with him.

It isn't until I'm at the top of the steps about to turn down the hall that I hear Fin's voice call out, "You found her, mister Weston! You're so good at this game!"

CHAPTER FOURTEEN

All my focus is trained on getting as many barriers between Weston and myself as possible, but the moment the door slams closed, I realize I'm now trapped inside the bedroom. *Shit.*

I stomp over to the desk and throw myself down in the chair, trying to calm down from the standoff between us. A groan of frustration rumbles in my throat and I let my head fall back into the soft cushion.

My efforts haven't been working. Weston still doesn't trust me, and I have no one to blame for that except myself. My early escape attempts got me nowhere and ended up hindering any progress I needed to make with the Castaways.

How am I ever going to get out of here?

Glancing around the empty room, I realize that I've never been in here, alone, in the middle of the day before. Sig has always come to collect me almost immediately after I wake up, and I've avoided the room otherwise for fear of running into Weston. I also never wanted to tip him off that I was trying to find information if he were to come in and catch me in the act. That would not bode well for building trust.

But now, an idea strikes, one I've been trying to find the right time for, and it's sitting right in front of me.

His desk.

Chaotic and littered with every type of paper and writing utensil, I can barely see the wood surface underneath. Rolls stacked haphazardly, crumpled balls and flattened packets give me confidence that if I move anything, he won't notice.

I stand, pushing the chair out from under me with the backs of my legs and crouch down to try the drawers first. My hopes rise as I try every drawer, only to have them catch at the last second, the lock clicking behind it. I know exactly where the key is, because it is sitting in Weston's pocket. He never takes it out unless he's using it. After my last attempt to take something from him while he's sleeping, I won't be trying it again.

Moving on quickly, I focus instead on the piles stacked on the surface. I scan everything quickly, trying to figure out where to start, when a familiar folded piece of parchment catches my eye. Snatching it from the pile, I unfold it as fast as I can without ripping it and smooth it out on the surface. My eyes scan the contents, only to confirm it is exactly what I thought.

My map.

Sig must have given it to him when she took it from me back in the brig, and it has been sitting on this desk right under my nose ever since.

Ice runs through my veins as what I feared is confirmed. Weston has known the exact location of our camp for days, weeks. My map has everything spelled out for him. Why was I so stupid to draw camp, including the portal? He could have attacked at any time, and for all I know, he already has.

There's no way to know the fate of everyone back at camp, especially with the secrets Weston and the Castaways are keeping from me. The only thing I can do now is hope that his focus has been elsewhere. Maybe being a pain in the ass has kept him preoccupied, so he hasn't executed an attack on the Voyagers. That would be one good thing that came from this whole fucked up situation.

I set my map to the side and rifle through the parchment underneath. There's a large flat piece that spans almost the entire length of the desk, and I start there. Shuffling everything off it, I gasp when the image underneath is revealed.

It is a map...of Dawnlin.

My eyes trail over the intricate details, beautifully inked on the page, much nicer than anything I could have drawn, and my breath catches in my throat as my gaze falls on the lower part of the island.

Camp. Weston's map already has the location of camp. My eyes fly up to the next most important part of it, the location of the healing waters, which is also inked in.

The Castaways have known the exact locations this entire time.

It didn't matter at all that he had my map. Dane's reason for forbidding maps is moot. It didn't matter if they fell into the wrong hands; the wrong hands already had them.

I feel a pinch of resentment, thinking back about how much damage that rule has done. How many Voyagers could have found the waters sooner if only they had a map? How many of them could have gotten home long before this issue with Weston started? Has Dane done more harm with the rule than good? I understand he made it because his job as the Guardian is to protect everything here, but it's also his job to help people find the waters and bring them home. No one has been able to do that.

The rule was made out of fear of what the Castaways would do, but the fear was unwarranted. They already knew, but they did nothing about it.

My vision blurs slightly as I try to reason through what this means.

Weston knows where camp is, but hasn't attacked us. He knows where the waters are, but hasn't gotten them.

So what does he want?

I lean closer to the map, focusing again and finding markings I hadn't drawn into mine. They look like structures scattered around the island, similar to the Voyager safe houses. But I've never seen any of these before, and I've been all over this island.

I must have walked right by some of them and had no idea they were there.

My fingertips trace over them in disbelief. Why is the island hiding them? Why is it helping harbor the people who want to bring harm to others?

"It's not polite to look through someone's things."

I gasp and spin toward the door to find Weston leaning against the frame, his arms crossed over his chest.

How long has he been standing there?

I hadn't heard the door open, too focused on my discovery and the slew of questions it unleashed.

"That doesn't apply if everything is sitting out in the open, especially if the person is being forced to live in the room against her will." I lean back on the desk, gripping both sides and trying not to let my anger from before get out of hand again. Starting another fight so soon will not help with trust.

A hint of a smirk lifts his lips before they fall back into his normal scowl.

He saunters over to the desk, rounding the corner to the opposite side, and stops, resuming the same stance, and I spin around so he doesn't have my back. This may not be a physical fight, but the same guidelines apply. Don't give your enemy your back.

His anger seems to have dissipated, at least on the surface, and maybe that is a good sign. I'm thankful for whatever calmed him down so quickly, especially if it worked in my favor. As much as I don't mind fighting with him, my mind is too full of questions to hold my own in another one this soon.

"I'm sorry I yelled at you," Weston says, as he stares down at the desk between us.

Shock hits me like a blow to the chest.

Weston is apologizing?

My jaw falls open, but I stay silent, not wanting to interrupt him and knock him out of whatever stupor he's in.

His jaw ticks, and he looks like he is trying to decide what to say next.

"You were just playing with Fin, and I see that now. I know you two have a friendship. You were concerned about him before…" His voice trails off, and I remember the day I searched for Fin, back when everything started spiraling out of control. Finding his things broken and scattered in the sand, fighting Weston. Him offering a trade.

It wasn't necessary, because now he has us both.

But why does he want me?

"You're right," he continues, bringing my attention back to him. "I need to be able to trust you, but trust goes both ways."

My mouth dries a little and I have to focus really hard not to let my body shift in excitement. This is it. What I said to him worked.

He is opening the door, letting me in and giving me some trust. All I have to do now is make him think I am doing the same.

He finally meets my gaze, and I nod slightly, agreeing to his truce.

Leaning forward, he spreads his arms out across the map between us. I try not to notice how the motion makes his shirt pull tight across his shoulders, how the top buttons of are undone, exposing more of his chest as he leans forward. Where the hell is the damn leather vest he normally wears that keeps it hidden?

"You found my map," he says, and I snap back into the conversation, clearing my throat quietly.

"If you didn't want me to find it, you should have locked it away," I say. "Besides, it's not like it was really that hidden."

"You're right, it wasn't. Yours is pretty good too." He nods at the piece of parchment I had pushed off to the side.

He's apologized *and* said I was right, all within a few minutes? This can't be genuine. It has to be part of the plan. Are we both playing each other?

I narrow my eyes at him. "You looked at it."

"I did."

"Why? If you already had this one," I gesture to the map underneath his palms, "then why would you need to look at mine?"

"How was I supposed to know it was a map until I looked at it?"

"I thought it wasn't polite to go through someone else's things?"

"That rule doesn't apply to prisoners on my ship." Challenge sparkles in his eyes and I scoff, ignoring it.

"Having the map helped me find the healing waters. Dane has a no map rule, but I knew I needed it, and the island gave me what I needed."

I don't know why I'm explaining myself to Weston. He doesn't need to know why I had the map, or about Dane's rule, but once the words are out of my mouth, I can't take them back.

The corner of his lips turns up. "I guess the island didn't agree with him."

"Yeah," I sigh. "I guess it didn't." Since it happened, I haven't been able to make sense of that fact. Dane is the Guardian, the protector of the island and the healing waters, and has a rule for that purpose, yet the island went against it. Why?

I still don't have an answer. I can't seem to make sense of anything Dawnlin does, but all I can do is trust it will one day be revealed.

Silence falls between us, and I realize Weston is waiting for me to speak. He must know I have a million questions about the map, and is giving me an opportunity to ask, and an opportunity to show his trust by answering.

I think for a moment, prioritizing what I want to know before speaking again.

"You already know where camp is." It isn't a question.

He nods. "We do."

"How?"

His head quirks to the side, his eyes narrowing, like he doesn't know why I asked this question. "Everyone here was once a Voyager, remember?"

Exactly as I thought, but I needed to hear him confirm it. I didn't understand why Dane never saw this obvious fact, or if he had, why he explained it away. Weston had an entire crew of people who once were Voyagers. Every person on this ship would have known everything about us, including where we lived. Having a map never would have mattered.

"But you never attacked us." Again, another statement, not a question.

"I had no intention to." I try to analyze his tone, his expression, to find the lie, but I can't. This seems like the most authentic Weston has ever been with me. There's no air of authority or fury. The only other time I've seen or heard him this real is when I watched relief flash over his face back in the cave, back when he was assuring me I was alive.

Goosebumps erupt over my skin at the memory and I ignore them, grateful they are hidden under my long sleeves.

"Why?"

"There's nothing I need at camp anymore." His eyes find mine, and I feel a flush of heat creep up my neck.

Anymore.

That means he managed to get whatever he was searching for. But if he didn't attack camp, how?

"What did you need from camp?" I take a chance asking, trying not to be obvious I'm prying. Hopefully, he is caught up in the conversation and will just answer without thinking.

"Any other questions, princess?" he grumbles, completely ignoring what I asked.

Fine. Still keeping secrets.

I move on to the obvious question in front of me and hope he doesn't dodge it.

"Why do you need a map?" I ask. "You aren't searching for the waters. You already know where they are. Stassia told me every Castaway has found them." I eye him curiously. "What are you looking for?"

He rolls his lips together, and I hold my breath, waiting for a response. I can tell he is trying to decide whether to reveal his secrets, despite the entire conversation about trust earlier, and I see the moment in his eyes that he decides to.

"We're looking for a way home."

His words crash over me, followed by a flicker of doubt.

Home.

Are the Castaways only trying to get back to our world? They aren't trying to steal the healing waters, not trying to use them for their own gain. They're simply trying to return, after being denied the help that every one of us came here seeking?

Have we been wrong about them the entire time?

No. We can't be. If he was telling the truth, he wouldn't be capturing everyone as soon as they left the mountain. Why would he need to take every Voyager as soon as they left, if his only motivation was to leave?

This is a manipulation, another mind game, and Weston doesn't think I see it.

He's trying to get me to sympathize with him, to keep pushing me onto his side, to turn me against Dane by directly contradicting everything Dane has told us. He doesn't know that we're both playing the same game.

"The Guardian is the only way on and off the island," I say. "He is the one with the dust. Why haven't you just told him you want to leave?"

"Dane and I don't see eye to eye," he says. My eyes flick down to his abdomen, where the large scar I saw marring his skin hides beneath his shirt.

There is reason for their animosity, caused entirely by Weston's actions. Of course Dane won't help him if he is trying to steal the healing waters, but would he if everyone on this ship wants to leave empty-handed?

"Why haven't you just sailed the ship and left?"

"We've tried. It will only go so far, then just stops."

So, the dust truly is the only way on and off Dawnlin.

I gaze down at the map once more, thinking through this new information, when my face snaps back up to his, my jaw slackening slightly.

"You're trying to find the dust." It's almost a whisper, but with as close as we are, he has no trouble hearing it.

He nods slowly, confirming my guess.

Satisfaction explodes in my chest. I know what their goal is now, even if I don't know the exact details of a plan. I've still won. I convinced him to trust me, and now I can use this knowledge to plan my escape. Now that I know about the dust, it is only a matter of time before he trusts me with more.

And by the time I am ready, I will be so engrained in the crew, they will never see it coming.

"Thank you, you know, for trusting me." I look away, my insides squirming. Was this what he felt like when he apologized earlier? Gratitude toward Weston is not something I thought I would ever feel, even if it isn't exactly for the reasons he thinks.

"You're welcome," he grumbles softly.

He straightens and strides back toward the door. Before he reaches it, he pauses and turns back to me.

"Now that you know about the dust, you can have a shift. We leave at dusk. Get some rest."

He leaves me alone, my thoughts reeling. No one has outright said what a shift is, but after everything he just admitted to me, I can only assume it is when they go search for the dust.

The Castaways are out looking for the dust every night, trying to get home without the healing waters. They say the island deemed everyone unworthy, but what if that isn't true? What if someone lied? What if they have been trapped on this island, holding the cure, but unable to leave without tipping off Weston? And if so, who could it be and why haven't they tried to get back to Dane?

So many possibilities spin through my mind, and I feel like there is more I don't know. Who is lying? Because what I know from Dane and what I'm being told by Weston and the Castaways is not adding up.

There is one thing for certain, though. Tonight, after weeks of captivity, I'm finally getting off of this ship.

CHAPTER FIFTEEN

Resting is impossible, despite Weston insisting I get some. Excitement and anticipation of finally getting off this ship courses through my body the entire afternoon, and it is all I can think about. I hope the energy is enough to get me through the night, through whatever constitutes a shift.

Just before we finish dinner, Sig tells me to check the room for a new set of clothes. Sure enough, in the armoire I find a lighter version of the clothes I have on, as if the island is prepping me to be back in the heat and away from the cool breeze off the water.

The sky is a light purple and the suns are almost set as I step out onto the main deck to find Sig, Stassia, and Auralie waiting for me. Each of them is strapped down with their own choice of weapons, just as the Voyagers always are, but none of them look as eager or tense as I feel. To them, this is just another shift, but to me, this is the start of my return home, as well as a pause in my captivity.

A wave of vulnerability washes over me as I take in everything they've chosen to arm themselves with, and remember that I have nothing. I never left camp without at least having my dagger, and I promised Brynne I would always be armed. I start to speak, to beg Sig for at least something small, but I haven't gotten a word out before she's looking past me, shaking her head aggressively.

"No. Absolutely not," she says firmly, and I glance over my shoulder to see what she is talking about.

Weston steps out onto the deck, his vest tied tightly over his dark shirt, a variety of blades tucked into the front. A hilt sits at the top of the normally empty scabbard, and it sways as he saunters over to us, his expression completely neutral.

Sig brushes past me and meets him halfway, her arm extended as she points toward the entrance below deck.

"You better turn back around. You're not tagging along on my shift," Sig says, pinning him with her glare.

"You can't tell me what to do, Sig," he says as he comes to a stop in front of her.

"Oh yes, I can Cap. You aren't coming."

He shoots her a look, but she doesn't back down, only widens her stance and slams her fists into her hips.

"I have this," she motions with her hand to the three of us standing behind her, "completely under control."

"I'm coming, Sig. Don't make me give you an order."

"Don't throw orders around at *me*, Cap. We both know this is my shift. It's my call. You aren't on tonight, so you aren't coming."

I've never seen anyone on the crew talk back to Weston like this, especially Sig. She usually has no problem following his orders, so what changed now? Whatever it is, I'm silently applauding her.

"Some space will be good for you," she continues after he doesn't respond. "Maybe she'll actually start to like us without you around."

Stassia giggles and I look down at my feet, trying to hide a smile.

"Sig," Weston growls in warning.

"*Cap*," Sig snaps back.

They stand in silence, staring each other down, having a silent conversation that I can't decipher, until Weston huffs and breaks away from her.

Wow, he really gave in. What power does Sig hold over him?

There's no time for me to wonder before I realize he broke away, only to head straight toward me.

The girls shuffle a few steps away as he stops directly in front of me, his brows drawn in and his jaw tight. He reaches to his side and pulls something from his belt.

"Can I trust you to carry this?" His voice is a quiet rumble, as if he doesn't want them to hear. He extends my sheathed dagger toward me, and I reach out and take it, my chest swelling with happiness once it's back in my hands.

"Yes," I breathe, and slide it in the back of my waistband, right where it belongs. Neither of us moves. The weight of his stare is heavy, and I'm glued to this spot, waiting for whatever he's planning to say next. It feels like at any moment he's going to tell Sig he changed his mind and come with us, even if it causes a fight.

His throat bobs and his jaw clenches. "Stay alert, princess."

He steps away quickly, snapping the tension between us. His sudden lack of proximity is jarring, but I feel like I can breathe again the closer he gets to the stairs.

"Go keep Jorn and Eirlik company," Sig yells. "Oh, and Fin is ready for bed. He's asking for the next part of his story."

I glance at Sig, then back at Weston in shock.

Has Weston been putting Fin to bed every night?

My heart swells at the thought, but I quickly push it away. I want Fin to have every kindness in the world, especially if he is going to be a child forever in this one, but how is it coming from *him*?

She walks toward the opening for the gangway before calling back over her shoulder, "And get some sleep!"

Weston rolls his eyes before turning his back on us and crossing the deck. I expect him to disappear below, but just before he does, he spins again, and crosses his arms, waiting. I can see the tension in his shoulders and arms from here. It's obvious he is not happy about staying on the ship while we leave. His eyes flicker to mine for a moment, and I turn away to join Sig and the girls.

I don't know what he is so worried about. I've been on Dawnlin for months, searching for the healing waters alone every day. I know the island; I know the dangers, and I'm not alone. Just because they took me captive doesn't mean I lost all of my experience and need to be coddled on this shift. Besides, the weapon is more for my comfort. The Voyagers would never hurt me.

"Let's go, ladies," Sig says and steps up to the edge.

The boards under our feet rumble and I watch as a gangway appears out of nowhere, extending out from the side of the ship directly to the slip of rock that juts out creating the cove. It stops extending with a thud, and everyone bounds down it toward the rocky land on the other side.

The back of my neck tingles, and I know Weston is watching me as I follow behind the group, down off the ship for the first time. It takes a lot more effort than I want to admit to stop myself from glancing back, but I don't. My boots pound on the gangway as I jog to catch up with them, muddling my way along the jagged rock toward the beach.

Moonlight brightens the clear sky, lighting the way along the rocks. The glowing waves roll through the cove, and the memory of the last time I stood on these rocks pops into my mind.

Life has changed so much. Then, I felt carefree and happy, excited for the possibility of a future, and now? Now I'm trying to survive, battling with a horrible man daily, all so I can make it back to the person who brought me here.

Once we are on the beach, Sig falls into step beside me, letting Stassia and Auralie lead the way. Stassia walks up to the cliff face, on the opposite side of the beach from the steps Dane and I took to get down here, and steps right through the rock.

Auralie follows right behind, and Sig gestures me forward. "After you," she murmurs.

If I didn't already know that portals existed on the island, watching them disappear into the stone would be shocking. Using a portal is the same way we got into camp, but the shocking part is that there is an entire system of tunnels under the island that none of us have ever found.

But now I know the entrance, or at least one of them.

The portal magic surrounds me as I step through it into a dim tunnel carved into the earth. Auralie and Stassia wait patiently, and I glance back to watch as Sig steps through, the space around her transparent as if there is a hole that leads out to the beach. The only other place I've seen a portal look like that, transparent on one side and completely hidden on the other, is at the exit of the mountain.

I look around, trying to pick up on any details, but the carved land is plain. There's enough space to walk side by side, maybe even with three or four people, and torches that line the walls throw off light. I peer past Stassia, trying to see anything farther down, but all I can see is a split, and then darkness.

"Phew! Now we can talk. I'm so glad you're with us tonight Lennox! It's about time you got off that ship," Stassia rambles.

Auralie leads us down the tunnel and we turn off to the right. Just like in the mountain, the torches light as we move through the carved space, but everything looks exactly the same. There's no way I could do this on my own. My sense of direction is completely gone down here, despite knowing the island extremely well.

"How do you have any clue where you're going without getting lost?" I glance back to where the tunnels branched, the light already extinguished.

"Years of practice." Auralie smiles over her shoulder.

"Where are we going?" I ask.

"Far side of the island," Sig says. "We don't have a ton of ground to cover today, so it'll be a good first time."

"So, is this just the same as looking for the healing waters? We just...search?" I ask.

If Dawnlin was a person, I would have a few choice words to say about the amount of time we have spent searching for things that should be obvious on the island. Why are things so damn difficult? The purpose of getting to the island is to get the healing waters, and the purpose of the dust is to come and go. So why do we have to spend years looking for both? If we're supposed to have hope to get here, why is it ripped away from us the second our foot touches the ground?

"For the most part, yes, it's the same," Sig says. "The big difference is we didn't come here for dust. We knew we were searching for the healing waters, but we didn't know we'd be trying to find a way to leave. We don't know if Dawnlin even has it concealed like the waters, but we have to try."

"Do you know how boring it is to just sit on the ship and do nothing all day? *Forever?*" Stassia says.

"I do, actually," I say.

Auralie gives me a sympathetic smile.

"But you're out now! That's what matters!" Stassia cheers.

Stassia's enthusiasm is contagious, and I find myself smiling softly. None of them know I wasn't only referring to the ship, although somehow, being trapped and isolated without a purpose seems to follow me wherever I go.

We keep moving through the tunnel, following curves as they wind around and dip low, and I blindly follow the group. With no landmarks or clues as to where we are, it doesn't matter if I try to escape right now. They'd find me lost and wandering in no time.

Traveling underground is actually very convenient. We are moving quickly, straight through, with no barriers or winding paths. There are no trees to cut through or bridges to cross, and I doubt the island is going to swallow us farther down when we are already here. Once we get out of the tunnels though, I have a feeling things will go back to normal.

"Captain is being so serious lately. I wish he would knock it off," Stassia says.

"I'm just glad he's back. It was weird not having him around," Auralie says.

Sig clears her throat loudly. I sneak a glance at her, but I can't read her face.

"Back around?" I ask. "Where did he go?"

Sig sighs when Stassia turns around and stops in the middle of the tunnel. She quirks her head to the side, her eyebrows drawing together. "He was following you."

I jerk back slightly and shake my head in disbelief. "What do you mean, he was following me?"

"You know," Stassia says. "Up there." She points to the roof of the tunnel. Sig's gaze drops to the ground, and she kicks the toe of her boot into the packed dirt.

Suddenly it makes sense.

Weston saved me from the sirens in the lagoon. I couldn't have been in there for long, or else I'd be dead. He had to have been nearby to make it in time. I was too focused on figuring out who he was and feeling guilty for keeping it from Dane to ever question that he was nearby.

The noises.

Every time I heard them, I'd attributed them to the island. It makes sense that I would hear noises as new traps came to be, or a piece of the land shifted, but it wasn't the island. Not every time, at least.

It was Weston.

He was watching me, following me every day as I traipsed across the island, searching for the waters, but only when I was alone.

"But why?" I ask incredulously.

"Let's keep moving," Sig says, brushing past my question and starting down the tunnel again.

I clamp my lips shut. I was not expecting this conversation when I pictured how the shift would go tonight, and I don't know what to think about it. Why did he follow me? Why didn't Sig want Stassia to tell me? What else are they hiding from me?

The more time I spend with the Castaways, the more questions I have, but I can't just ask them. I have to find the right time to get them answered, and tonight's excursion is all part of setting that groundwork, developing that trust. Asking too much too fast might make them suspicious and cause them to question their trust in me.

Stassia chats as we walk, filling the silence and keeping the mood light. Glancing between them, listening to Stassia talk and laugh every so often, I wonder...Is this what it is like to have friends? To just spend time together out of enjoyment, not out of any sort of obligation or duty?

Mara and I are friends, but we didn't spend a lot of time together. Not like this. Our days were separate, our evenings short. But it actually seems like this group enjoys each other's company and seems like they want me to be part of that. I don't know if Stassia has a manipulative bone in her body, and Auralie seems too kind for her own good. Sig showed today that she could fight back against Weston's orders when she didn't agree with him.

Are they...real? Is this not part of the manipulation, the mind tricks? Or am I already in too deep and starting down the exact path of sympathy they want me on?

A roaring noise gets louder as we walk, and I realize exactly what it is.

The river.

We are walking under the river. The other side of the island shouldn't be far now, but I'm thankful we don't have to cross the water, especially in the dark.

"Almost there," Sig says to me as Stassia and Auralie pull ahead of us slightly.

"Can I ask a question, Sig?" I say.

"Sure."

"Why are there so many of us on a shift? Wouldn't it be easier to cover more ground alone? That's how we always look."

She shakes her head. "We don't go anywhere alone. It is safer in pairs."

"But Weston was alone, when he was following me," I counter.

"He's the captain. He makes his own choices. Plus, he didn't want to put any of us in danger in the daylight."

I'm just going to outright ask what I want to know. I could tell Sig didn't want me to find out about Weston's stunt, but now that I know, maybe she'll give me a reason.

"Why was he following me, Sig?"

A few beats pass before she finally responds. "I told you before I would answer whatever questions I am allowed. That's not my answer to tell."

I groan. "I don't want to talk to him. I'd much rather talk to you. He's an asshole, remember?"

She laughs. "See? I told him you'd like us when he isn't around."

It's the second time she's said it, and despite my worry that this is all part of their plot to turn me, deep down I somewhat agree with her. It is nice having people to talk to during the day, who seem to care about what I have to say and what is going on with my situation. It feels like a void I've had since I was a child is slowly filling, even more than it had back with the Voyagers.

And that terrifies me.

I have to remember, it isn't their fault that they've also been manipulated. The person at fault here is Weston, and I can't take my anger out on them.

"Everyone ready?" Stassia calls out.

The tunnel takes a sharp turn, then elevates to a set of steps carved into the dirt and rock. Auralie climbs them first, each of us falling into line behind her. She creeps to the top and sticks her head straight through the ground, waving us forward a moment later with her hand that is still visible. She climbs the last steps and the rest of her body disappears through the portal.

Stassia goes next, and Sig motions me forward again, taking up the rear herself.

When I push through, I immediately know where we are.

The bridge I crossed with Mara is nearby, the tunnel letting us out between a mound of boulders near the edge of the forest. Stassia and Auralie are already looking around, assessing for any threats when Sig steps through behind me.

"Is there anything specific we are looking for?" I ask Sig.

"Our best guess is the same as the healing waters. Patterns, hiding places. The waters were marked with the Dawnlin symbol, so we look hard for that."

I nod. "Sounds easy enough."

Auralie and Stassia each draw their swords and start toward the marsh.

"You don't need to be on edge, you know," I call after them. "Dane doesn't let any of us out at night. He says it's not safe."

"Not safe from who? From us?" Stassia says with a giggle.

"I guess so…" I trail off.

Were the Castaways only armed to protect themselves? They weren't out prowling the island looking for camp. They don't seem to want a run in with the Voyagers as much as we don't want one with them. Finding the dust is their goal, not hunting or hurting anyone. They are only protecting themselves from an attack the other way.

My head starts to hurt as, once again, I feel like I'm questioning everything I know.

We spend a few hours searching the marsh, checking every surface of tree trunks and bushes, feeling for carvings or signs in the land like the chalice in the waterfall. We flip boulders so large it takes all four of us to get it to budge from where it is sunken into the ground.

Now I understand why no one goes out alone. This entire search is a team effort, each person working together to do their part searching for what they need to get everyone home.

I don't know if I believe the island is hiding the dust somewhere like the waters for anyone to find. I still believe the Guardian is the only way on and off the island, and that there is a way to replenish it. I won't voice my opinions, though, no matter how much I like these girls.

We tromp through the marshes, and I am grateful that my boots are in such good shape. The dirty water seeping in through worn spots would make the rest of this night miserable. Squelching through the mud, my eyes are on the floor when Auralie's voice breaks through the quiet.

"Get down!" she hisses.

My head snaps up, looking for the threat. There shouldn't be anyone out here this late at night, and my mind conjures up everything else it could be.

I hear it before I see it, a voice coming toward us in the darkness.

No, not just one voice. Two voices.

I strain to hear, confused and wondering if there is another Castaway shift out tonight when I realize what is happening.

Both voices are familiar, but one stands out to me. It's the one I've been longing to hear, the one that sends shivers down my spine. The one that brought me here and asked me to stay.

A voice I'd recognize anywhere.

Dane is walking toward us.

CHAPTER SIXTEEN

My heart pounds in my ears as I stand, completely frozen, staring in the direction of his voice. Dane is coming this way, and this could be my chance to escape.

But is this the *right* time?

Different scenarios race through my mind, and I have a split second to decide. I could make a run for it, trudging my way through the marsh as fast as the mud will let me, and hope the girls don't follow. I could call out to him, which would draw him straight to me and, in turn, straight to them.

Or, I could do nothing.

Something doesn't sit well in my stomach at the thought of leading Dane straight to Sig, Stassia, and Auralie. If I got away from them right now, I doubt Dane would believe that I was alone. If I was, then I would have gone straight back to camp, not wandered around in the mud. He and Storm or Mara would likely search the area, and it would be a slim chance if they weren't spotted.

If I call out to him, they definitely would be found, and I don't know what manner of questioning Dane is willing to do back at camp. I feared for what Weston would do to me as his prisoner, but would Dane be the same to them?

The choice is paralyzing, but I'm running out of time. The girls have been kind to me, and without ever having genuine friends to compare them to, I can't discern if they are part of Weston's trickery. My problem is with him, and I don't necessarily want to condemn them to the same fate I just had to endure, or worse.

I could play this game a little longer. Doing nothing would help solidify their trust, and make it easier to leave when the time is right, when I can bring Fin. If I don't use the first chance I have to go back to Dane, it could help prove that I am on their side. They would never expect when the moment comes that I'm not anymore.

I'm still frozen, weighing the decision in my mind when the chance gets taken from me, as Sig clamps her hand over my mouth and drags me into the mud.

Her body covers mine, pushing me down into the muck. She stays silent, holding me firmly, so we stay as still as possible.

I decide then to go with the third choice.

I do nothing.

Weeks ago I would have fought, struggled, tried to roll her off me. I'd done it enough with Brynne that I knew I could hold my own with Sig, especially now after feeling stronger again and more like myself. But I don't fight her. Instead, I wait, peering through the reeds and leaves hiding us, watching to see if we will be discovered.

I hope this is the right decision.

Dane comes into view, and he isn't alone. I place the second voice as soon as I see Storm walking beside him. They carry no torch to light their way, only illuminated by the glare of the moon off of them. Their voices carry as they get closer, and I strain to hear what they are saying over Sig's breathing in my ear.

"We have to get her back. We can't have him turn her against us!" Dane roars.

"Do you really think he can? She's pretty taken with you. I don't think she will listen," Storm says.

"I can't risk it. We have to find her."

They take a few steps in silence, and I can see the tension in Dane's shoulders from where we lay in the reeds.

"Maybe he'll use her as a bargaining chip," Storm says, and my breath catches in my throat.

A bargaining chip.

Is that why Weston has been so protective? So he can keep me safe and use me to get what he wants from Dane? He's told me repeatedly he won't hurt me, or touch me, that he wants to trust me. Yet he followed me, he captured me, and he imprisoned me.

To use me to bargain for a way home.

"He can try, but he won't get anything from me."

My chest swells and warmth washes over my body.

He's looking for me. He hasn't given up on me. The Voyagers never seemed to have hope of rescuing previous members who fell victim to the Castaways, but Dane hasn't given up hope for me. He wants me back, and I hope he knows that I'm trying, too.

"And if he dares to show his face on my island, he won't make it out alive," he growls as he rounds the corner, disappearing down the path.

My breath hitches slightly and the warmth I just felt from the realization he is searching for me runs cold. The hatred in Dane's tone brings me back to the other night, trying to steal my dagger from Weston, contemplating if I could kill someone in cold blood.

Could Dane?

He'd never shown me that side of him before, but now, hearing his words, his voice, I can't help but picture it.

There was a moment when Sig dragged me down that I thought I made the wrong choice, but now I don't think I did.

Not only has my action, or inaction, given them something to trust, but I have learned important information about Weston's motives. It may have shown me a side to Dane I didn't know was there, but that isn't a priority right now. I'll deal with that if I need to.

Weston's mind games won't have any hold on me now that I know he's trying to use me, and that is why he's keeping me safe. It isn't out of concern for me, or for my well being. What makes me so special? What else would make him follow me around the island, pull me from the water, and keep me alive?

He needs me to get to Dane.

But Dane won't let him.

Unlike Weston, I actually trust Dane. I trust him to do what is best for me, and I need to get back to him.

Sig lifts her hand from my mouth and rolls off me, falling onto her back and letting out a loud sigh.

"You didn't scream," she says. She stares up at the sky, waiting to hear my explanation.

I shake my head. "No. I didn't."

"Why?" She turns her head, and her eyes meet mine. It reminds me of the night back on the beach, when she was searching me for weapons. Her eyes held her apology then, even though her face was covered. Now they are filled with curiosity and doubt, and maybe a little hope.

My lips turn up in a small smirk, even though my insides tumble with uncertainty. "Maybe I do like you three after all."

A smile lights up her face and she chuckles softly. "See, I knew getting away from him would get your head on straight." Pushing up from the mud, she sits and looks over her shoulders for Stassia and Auralie.

I push up and rock back to my knees just as I feel something shift under me. My head swivels around as I stare down at the mud surrounding me and watch as it starts moving.

Not moving, sinking.

Oh shit.

"Sig," I say, trying and failing to hide the panic in my voice. I throw out my arms for balance as the unstable ground threatens to knock me over.

"Fuck! Stass!" Sig hisses out to the darkness, her voice low enough that Dane and Storm wouldn't have heard.

I try to get onto my feet, yanking my limbs from the sticky muck, but the more I move, the faster I sink.

"Stass! Auralie!" Sig hisses again, the urgency rising in her voice as she slowly starts sinking, her legs disappearing underneath her.

I hear a splash nearby, followed by Stassia whisper yelling, "Oh fuck. Hang on!"

My chest sinks below the surface, and the deeper I go, the harder it is to move. The thickness surrounds me, pressing in and sucking me down. Sig is up to her waist as she tries to lean closer to me. She reaches out for my hands and grips my wrists, squeezing so tight I'm sure I'll have bruises.

"Do not fucking let go," she growls.

I nod quickly, the jarring motion only making me sink faster.

If I had been out here, alone, or got caught in this mess when I was searching the island with the Voyagers, I wouldn't have survived. Now, we have a chance, all because of Weston's order never to search alone.

I squeeze Sig's arms back, as tight as she is holding me, and look into her face. The fear I feel is reflected at me, and I squeeze even tighter, hoping she can sense how thankful I am she is here.

Something hits the ground near us, and Sig releases one of my arms.

"Don't let go!" I squeal. The muck rises up my neck, dripping into my clothes. It's going so fast now I lean my head back, trying to keep my face above the surface as long as I can. I suck in rapid breaths, but the pressure around my chest is constricting, and I can barely breathe.

"Sig!" My voice is a squeak, the air trapped in my chest as I flail the arm she released around, searching for her other hand.

"Lennox, listen. I'm going to scoop you out. You have to trust me, alright?"

I don't answer. I can't. I've run out of time. All I can do is gasp in one last breath and trust she has a plan.

Sig releases my other arm and my hands fly free above the surface, fingers grasping the empty air. I slam my eyes and mouth shut as the mud engulfs me, and I can't stop the panic.

My breath is running out and I can't feel Sig as my shoulders sink lower, my hands now the only part of me still free above the surface. I try to calm my mind, but I can't. There's no air. There's no Sig. Did she abandon me, even after telling me to trust her? Did she sink just as fast as me?

Somewhere deep inside, I thought after finding the healing waters, the island would have no need to protect them from me anymore. I was wrong. Maybe this is the punishment for being unworthy. Who knew that I could drown without even being in water?

My thoughts grow hazy, and the worry starts to dissipate when I feel something. An arm, wrapping under mine and clasping around my back.

Sig.

She didn't abandon me.

Pain erupts in my chest as she squeezes tighter than anything I've felt before, and suddenly I'm being pulled from both sides; a war between the Castaways and the mud. I move my arms and wrap them around her, holding tight right before my face breaks the surface.

My mouth fills with mud as I suck in a breath, and I splutter, spitting out the sludge, then heaving in air as the rest of my body is yanked from the marsh.

I fall on top of Sig as we're dragged away from the sinking pit through the pools and reeds. We stop on solid ground and I roll off of Sig, throwing my arms out to my sides, chest heaving and unable to speak.

Stassia collapses to her knees just behind my head, and I look up to see Auralie doubled over, breathing deeply. A rope lays at their feet, and I follow it, to find it tied under Sig's arms. One of them must have had it on their belt. I hadn't realized they came prepared with anything more than weapons.

Thank the gods they were, because if they hadn't been, Sig and I would be dead.

I swipe the mud from my face, tossing down large chunks of it onto the ground. My entire body is caked in a thick layer, and I look over to find Sig looks the same, though only from the neck down. She lies on her back, her chest rising and falling rapidly, and she stares at the night sky.

I look between each of them, and say the first thing that comes to my mind.

"Thank you, all of you."

Just like when the bridge broke with Mara, none of them had to help me, but they did anyway. Sig threw herself into the sinking mud to save me, when we both easily could have been pulled under if Stassia and Auralie hadn't gotten to us in time. They barely know me, and they don't know I'm plotting against them, but they didn't hesitate to be there when I needed them. My chest swells, and my vision blurs with tears that I'm glad are hidden by the darkness and mud.

"Cap is going to fucking kill me," Sig groans toward the sky.

Stassia walks over and reaches down to her, taking her hand and pulling her to her feet. "No, he won't. If we leave now, we'll be back before he wakes up. He can't kill you if he never finds out."

"I won't tell," Auralie says as she rounds Stassia and reaches down to me. I take her hand and pull to stand.

All three of their heads swivel toward me, and I scoff.

"I barely want to talk to him. There's no way I'll tell him about this."

A quiet chorus of laughter fills the space between us, and my chest warms.

This is what friendship feels like.

It's different than with Brynne and Edmond, or even Fin. These three saved my life when I'm basically still their enemy. I know some part of it is because Weston would probably have Sig's head if his bargaining chip is harmed, but in this moment, conspiring to hide something we endured together from Weston, it feels like more than that. It feels real, and something deep inside me doesn't want to lose it.

The laughter in Sig's expression disappears as her brows draw in and her eyes grow serious again. "We need to get back *now*. Stay alert. We don't know how many others are out there."

We fall back into pairs and hurry through the marsh, back toward the portal.

My mind wars with itself after everything that happened tonight. My feelings toward Weston and his motives haven't changed. Arguably, they are worse than before I set out on the shift tonight, now that I know he is using me. I still want to get home to Dane, even though I didn't take the opportunity tonight, and I can't imagine how he feels looking for me every day.

But I also can't deny that I'm starting to grow fond of some of the Castaways, who clearly care enough about me to put themselves at risk. How can I turn on them, simply because I have to turn on Weston?

Just before we reach the entrance to the portal, I stop short and quickly reach back to my waistband, feeling around for my dagger. I breathe a sigh of relief when I feel the hilt, still secure and not sucked into the mud and lost to the island forever. At least if I have to endure feeling uncertain about some things, I still have the familiarity and comfort of my dagger.

Please gods, don't let Dawnlin take that away from me too.

CHAPTER SEVENTEEN

Sunrise quickly approaches, and the edges of the sky lighten overhead as we step out of the portal onto the beach. I hadn't expected the shift to last all night, and exhaustion hits me like a wave as we trudge through the sand. The mud has hardened on my skin and clothes, and I've done nothing but fantasize about the shower and scrubbing myself clean during our entire walk back.

Eyes trained on my boots as I stumble along the jagged rock, I almost slam into Sig's back as she stops abruptly in front of me.

"Oh gods," she groans, throwing her hands to her head.

"Oh gods, indeed," Stassia says, her voice lilting and very different from Sig's inflection.

I peek between them, following the line of their gaze to see what is causing the pause. My jaw slackens as I take in the scene on deck.

A few torches burn, a flickering glow casting shadows near the mainmast, but that isn't what catches my attention.

Skin.

Weston's glistening, bare skin, to be exact.

His hands grip the mast as he hangs above the deck. His forearms are taut, his biceps bulging as he rhythmically raises and lowers his chest to the beam. The muscles in his broad back and shoulders ripple, and I can't stop my eyes from taking in every inch of them. My mouth goes dry at the sight.

Stassia throws her arms out to the sides wildly, blocking anyone from passing her.

"Can we stay here just for a few minutes?"

Flutters fill my low stomach as we stand in silence watching. Hatred for him aside, anyone would be distracted by his hard curves, the way his body moves, and the feelings that stir at the sight of it. I know it isn't just me, even though I hate the way I respond to him.

Stop it, Lennox.

Stassia makes a low grunt of appreciation and Auralie lets out a tiny giggle.

"This is going to be bad," Sig says with a sigh. "He was supposed to be asleep."

She pushes past Stassia's arm, causing her face to fall into an exaggerated frown. He hasn't seen us approach yet, his back still to us as we follow Sig, closing the distance to the gangway.

"How do you know?" I say, clearing my throat after my voice cracks on the last word.

"He only does this when he's stressed," Sig says.

"The last time was when you showed up," Stassia says, a wistful smile on her lips. "Ah, that was a fun day to be on deck."

Stassia's comment is confusing. What about me showing up would make him stressed, and how did he even know? I was with Dane all day, and there was no way he was following me already. Dane and I hadn't really talked about the possibility of us yet, so there would be no reason to capture me to use against him that early on.

"I'm sure it will be fine," Auralie says. "We're all back."

"He can't be mad that the island attacked us," I say. "He's always pissed at me, anyway. I'm not afraid of him. I've dealt with worse."

"I warned you," Sig says, her shoulders pulling back in anticipation of facing whatever mood Weston is in.

As we climb the gangway, I try to keep my eyes off of Weston.

I fail.

His rhythmic movements haven't stopped or slowed, and the closer we get, the more clear his body becomes. Sweat covers every exposed inch of his skin, the light from the torches making him glisten. Soft grunts and heavy breaths with every pull break the silence, and I ignore the flicker of flame that ignites in me at the sound.

He must hear our footsteps, because in the next moment he's dropping to the deck, the boom of his landing followed by a snort and loud yawn. Just next to where Weston hung a moment ago, Jorn sits on the mast, rubbing his face with both hands. They must have kept each other company, like Sig suggested when we left.

"Signee," Weston growls, and my gaze falls back to him. He barrels toward us, his eyes flying over our group, taking in the mess from our shift.

"Everyone is fine," Sig says, her hands raised slightly like she is trying to calm a wild animal.

I see now why she warned us. Weston has worn many emotions since I met him, but this is anger like I haven't seen, not even when he was yelling at me in the infirmary. Outrage burns in his eyes, his jaw clenching and unclenching as he glowers at her.

"You said you had this under control," he grinds out, brushing past her and weaving through the group.

Straight to me.

She spins to follow him. "I did. We're all back in one piece. Just a little dirty."

His eyes meet mine, the fire in them still blazing and I am caught up in the intensity. I can't look away, can't think, can't even process what is happening as his hands are in my hair, working through the thick, dry mud until his fingertips reach my scalp. They roam over me, sliding down the back of my neck and over the curve of my shoulders. A shiver runs down my spine that has nothing to do with the cool breeze coming off the water.

My throat bobs with a hard swallow as my focus falls away from his stare down to the glistening bare skin in front of me, so close I could barely move and reach out to touch it. A bead of sweat trickles between the muscles of his chest, heading toward the defined bulges of his abdomen, toward the scar Dane gave him. I'm too stunned to do anything but gape at him, everything happening so quickly but also feeling like it is in slow motion.

When his fingertips brush my palms, turning my hands over to inspect them, it's like I'm doused with cold water. The movement feels more intimate than any of the others, and I suddenly remember who he is and what he's doing.

I take a step back and slap his hands away.

"Excuse me? Get your hands off me," I snap.

Who does he think he is, just walking over and putting his hands on me, treating me like an asset he has to inspect to make sure it still holds its value? It's obvious, now more than ever, why he is so overbearing with me. He knows Dane won't agree to a bargain if I'm harmed. That's why he didn't want me leaving the ship. That's why he wanted me to eat.

I'm just a means to an end.

He steps back like I've burned him, lifting his hands away and pinning his arms to his sides. The fury is gone in an instant, but he looks away, keeping me from seeing what replaces it.

"I apologize, princess," he mumbles and runs a hand through his sweaty hair, mussing it even more than it already was, before turning on his heel toward the rest of the group. "Is everyone alright?"

"Yep," Stassia says, a smile on her face and her voice as cheerful as ever. She's probably still enjoying the view that she wanted so badly.

"Yes Captain, we're alright," Auralie says.

His head turns back toward me, but his eyes stay averted, falling to the ground next to me.

"I'm fine," I say flatly, and his chin dips in acknowledgement.

"Like I said," Sig says, "all under control."

"What happened?" he says, his voice calmer, but still hard.

"We ran into Dane," Sig says.

"What?" Weston barks, the calm gone in an instant as his head snaps toward Sig.

"He and Storm were out walking. We hid in the marsh. Once they were gone, we started to sink. Stass and Auralie pulled us out." Sig glances around at us with a hint of apology in her expression. We all agreed not to say what happened tonight in order to protect her, but that was before Weston caught us the moment we stepped onto the ship. There was no way of keeping what happened tonight from him now.

"Did you see what they were doing?" he asks.

She shakes her head. "They were just walking."

There's no mention of the conversation they were having, and I can't be the only one that heard it. Is she going to keep that from Weston? Or does it not matter for whatever he has planned?

He nods and places his hands on his hips, the motion drawing attention to the carved out muscles that dip below his belt. This time I'm the one averting my gaze.

"We won't stop the searches," he says finally. "But make sure that everyone is aware of what happened and on high alert. Smaller search areas, back well before sunrise. We don't need any more run-ins."

"Aye, Cap," Sig says with a nod.

"Go get some sleep, all of you," Weston says, dismissing us but not moving a muscle. Sig walks to the mast, shaking Jorn's foot to wake him before he hops down to the deck. Auralie and Stassia head toward the steps, Stassia stealing one last look at shirtless Weston before raising her eyebrows at me with a smirk. I fight to not roll my eyes before following behind them.

"I'll stay out of the room so you can get cleaned up," Weston says just as I am about to walk past.

"I'm more comfortable using the crew's showers, thank you," I say, without even a hitch in my step. I won't take his offer as considerate in any way, not after he manhandled me only moments ago. He didn't consider how I felt about it then, apology or no apology.

He doesn't respond and I almost make it to the stairs before I whir back around, facing him. I want to call him out, let him know I know his plan, his motives, even if it tips my hand that I'm still not completely on his side.

"Am I just a bargaining chip to use against Dane? Is that why you were following me around the island?"

Surprise flashes on his face, probably at divulging I know he followed me.

"That's what you think?" he asks, his face stoic and his voice even once more.

I raise an eyebrow and fold my arms across my chest. "Tell me I'm wrong."

"No, princess. You aren't just a bargaining chip." His throat bobs as he swallows whatever else he was going to say, and silence stretches between us.

"How do I know you're not lying to me?"

"You don't," he says, cocking his head to the side. "You're just going to have to trust me."

I huff and turn back around.

Trust goes both ways.

I'll never be able to trust him, not after everything that has happened, every Voyager he has stolen. But despite my mind screaming that he's lying to me, manipulating me and trying to keep me unsuspecting, something deep down feels like his words are genuine.

I only make it one step before I hear him speak again behind me.

"Give it back, princess."

I drop my head back with an aggravated sigh before turning back toward him to find he hasn't moved. "Give what back?"

He drifts across the deck, stopping a few steps from me.

"Do you think I forgot?" His eyebrows raise in a challenge, and I keep my face trained.

"I don't know what you're talking about."

"The dagger," he says and extends his hand toward me. I glance down at it, the same hand that was tangled in my hair minutes ago, before looking back up at him.

Narrowing my eyes with a scowl, I reach behind me and yank the scabbard out of my waistband, chucking it as hard as I can at his chest before stomping down the stairs.

Tonight may have been valuable for my relationship with the girls, but it definitely wasn't enough time away from Weston.

So much for trust.

CHAPTER EIGHTEEN

*D*ried mud is caked so thickly to every exposed inch of my skin and hair, that it takes multiple rounds of scrubbing to get it all off. I don't rush, though, instead taking my time under the relaxing water.

I'm still fuming after Weston took my dagger back, so the more time I stay away from him, the better. Questioning whether or not he can trust me with it before I left was obviously just a show, because if he actually trusted me, I would still have it.

I let the water fall over my head, tilting it back so it rinses the third round of soap out. The heat from the water feels amazing, loosening the tension that built up in my muscles after everything that happened tonight, as well as days of pent up anger. Steam hovers in the room, making it feel more solitary than it is, even though I can still hear Stassia and Auralie chatting happily in nearby stalls. An uncontrollable yawn brought on by actually being able to relax halts their conversation mid-sentence.

"I'm not sure if Sig told you," Auralie says into the room, "but we get the day after our shift off. No need to rush to do your assignment."

"No scrubbing the deck today!" Stassia calls out. "We can sleep the day away."

I breathe a sigh of relief. Now that all the anticipation and excitement have died down, I don't know if I could make it through my task after only an hour or two of sleep. I would have forced myself if I needed to. I don't want to give Weston any more ammunition to use against me, especially since I'm still scrubbing by hand in his attempt to keep me manageable.

"I don't know about you, Lennox," Stassia starts up again, "but I had fun tonight. Hopefully Captain lets you go out again."

"How often are the shifts?" I ask, ignoring any mention of fun, so I don't admit that I didn't entirely hate the shift tonight. Being on the island again felt amazing, and having my dagger back made me feel like myself. I want to do more shifts, mostly to keep up with my plan and get off this damn ship, but I'm not going to jump to calling it fun so soon.

"We have a rotation of every nine days," Stassia says as she steps out of her stall, stark naked without a care in the world for anyone shuffling in and out of the room getting ready for the day.

"There are enough of us that we can all rotate and have the next day off to recover," Auralie adds.

I stifle another yawn. "Good, because I think I need it." Grabbing my towel off the door of the stall, I dry quickly before dressing in a clean set of clothes I snagged from the room before coming down. "I guess I'll see you both later on then?"

"Meet for dinner?" Auralie says.

"Sure," I agree before slipping from the room and heading to the galley to grab a quick snack.

Life on the ship is beginning to feel too familiar, too normal. Add in the fact that these girls were willing to risk their lives to save me, someone who they barely know, and it didn't seem to phase them at all.

Life just went on; back to the routine, as if nothing happened. As if it was just part of being a Castaway.

Mara saved me too, and I won't ever forget the danger she put herself in, but Sig, Stassia, and Auralie didn't hesitate. Mara admitted she questioned it before deciding that it wasn't like her to let me go. I can't help but wonder if any of the other Voyagers that I considered family would make the same decision.

The contrast of life as a Voyager and life as a Castaway is more obvious every day. As a Voyager, most of our days are solitary, searching the island alone with our own plan and own goals. The Castaways do nothing alone. They are a unit, a crew, bound by their joint fate of being unworthy and trapped. It feels different from the Voyagers, bound only by a shared goal of finding the waters.

Castaways sit around the mess, eating and talking as I walk in and grab a pastry before going straight back to the stairs. I hope Weston kept his word and left the room alone so I can get to sleep.

Hopefully he found a shirt.

Taking a bite of the fruit filled roll, I round the corner at the top of the steps, and slow my pace.

The door is closed. It's never closed unless Weston is inside, mostly because if it is, I can't get out.

So much for leaving me alone.

But why is it closed? What is he doing inside?

I slow my steps, setting my boots down softly as I creep toward it, pleading with the ship not to creak and give me away. Hovering close, there's no sound from the other side, so I inch closer, pressing my ear to the crack and straining to hear.

The soft lilt of voices falls on my ears.

Someone else is in the room with him, the words barely above a whisper, preventing eavesdroppers from being able to make out much. I squeeze my eyes shut and stop chewing, focusing on the noise and praying that the door doesn't open suddenly.

Sig's hushed tone creeps out as she gets a little louder. She wasn't in the showers with the rest of us, but something must be important enough to need to speak to the captain behind closed doors.

Her voice rises again, enough that I can make out her words. She seems upset, or worried, but I can't tell without seeing her face.

"They're looking for her, Cap." I listen harder, my attention piqued. When she didn't mention anything about hearing Dane was searching for me, I didn't think she cared, let alone that she would tell Weston.

"That's no surprise," Weston grumbles from the other side of the door.

"No. You didn't hear Dane. He was adamant. Threatening. He will not stop until he gets her back."

"You know I won't let that happen."

Won't let that happen? Was Weston actually telling the truth when he said I wasn't a bargaining chip? His plan isn't to use me to get what he wants from Dane?

Then what does he want from me?

"But what if it should?" Sig says, a question pleading in her voice.

"Careful, Sig," he grinds out.

"I'm serious. Listen to me. Let me explain."

The voices fall silent, and I press my ear to the door even harder, trying to make sure I don't miss anything. Despite not knowing her very well, I can already visualize Sig's face, pleading with him to listen in that silent communication they have.

She continues, "She may be the best chance we have. We've been here over twenty years, Cap. It's time to go home."

Twenty years?

How does she know how much time has passed? I can barely wrap my head around the days passing, much less keep track of them. Even Dane didn't know how long it had been since he was the Guardian.

"No," Weston says firmly. "There's got to be another way."

"We've tried," Sig says, her voice still pleading. "We've been searching, and we haven't found it."

"We'll keep looking. We're not giving up hope."

"I'm not saying to give up, but what if she is our new hope?"

The screech of his chair dragging across the floor startles me, and it's followed by a heavy sigh.

"She's not on our side, Sig. She'll go running right back to him."

Weston isn't wrong, although I need this to change. I need him to believe that I am with them, part of the crew, but his words make me squirm. It's as if he can see right through me, like he knows I won't turn on Dane, even if I do care for people on this ship, like Sig. My feelings for them won't change my hatred for him.

"Then maybe you need to stop being such an asshole to her so she will stop thinking we're all evil," Sig says, almost yelling now.

"It's not that simple, Sig, and you know it."

"It is that simple. Be nice! Let her see! If she understands, if she sees our side, she's the best way to get one of us close enough to Dane to take it. That pouch has the only dust on this island, and it's the only way out of here."

I press my hand to my lips, trying to stifle a gasp. Sig wants me to take the dust from Dane. She wants me to sympathize with them, then send me back to take it and end their searching, but Weston doesn't seem to agree.

"I can't just send her off to him and hope she comes back," he says, his voice rising now too.

"Well then, help her understand why she should! You're the only one who can."

"The answer is no, Sig." The chair squeaks and footsteps pound across the room. My body shrinks away from the door. If he opens it, he'll catch me, but I don't want to miss anything they say.

I'll take that chance. He's the one forcing me to stay in his room. He's accepted the risk I might find out something he doesn't want me to, and he can't be his angry self about it if it happens.

I press my ear back to the door and hear Sig's lighter steps cross the room.

"Cap, think about this—"

"I said no Signee," he says, cutting her off.

"Argh! You are infuriating, you know that?" Sig yells.

"Thanks for reminding me."

My breath catches and my chest swells. This is it. This is how I can get back to Dane. Getting the Castaways to trust me is just the beginning, but if I can do it, the next step in my plan can unfold. If Weston can trust me to come back, I can convince him to let me leave. I can convince him I am going to steal the dust, but instead, come back for Fin with Dane in tow. Sig is right. I am the best way to get close to Dane, but there is a huge flaw in Sig's plan.

They don't know the dust is almost gone.

Even if they get ahold of it, there isn't enough to get all the Castaways off the island unless Dane has figured out how to replenish it since I've been gone. By the sound of the conversation between him and Storm, though, replenishing it isn't his focus. His focus is on finding me.

I can use this.

Weston might be convinced to send me if I let slip that the dust is running out, and he might be willing to send me sooner. Not to mention that telling them this crucial information will give me more reliability, letting them trust I'm on their side. If I play this correctly, they'll never know I heard this argument, and it will feel like their idea all along.

By the time they realize I have been lying to them the whole time, it will be too late.

I'll be back where I belong.

CHAPTER NINETEEN

The days until my next shift are long and slow. Since that night together, it has been easier to spend time with the girls, either on deck or in the lounge, in the evenings. Weston never brings the shifts up to me again, and after his reaction to our return, part of me is waiting for him to take back his permission for me to leave.

But it never comes.

Instead, I wake up the morning of the shift to my dagger waiting for me on the bedside table, and complete avoidance for the rest of the day.

Dusk is falling when I head to Sig's room to see if she's ready to leave. She wasn't at dinner tonight with the rest of us, I assume to get some extra rest before we are out all night. I knock a few times and wait, sliding closer to her door as a few of the Castaways trudge down the hall from the crew's quarters, carrying a big crate between them with a smile on their faces.

There's shuffling from behind the door before it opens wide, and I pull back, shocked to be looking up into Jorn's smiling face.

"Ready for your shift?" he says.

"Uh, yeah?" I answer, confused why I'm answering him and not Sig.

"Have a good one," he says as he slips out the door and past me, heading toward the stairs.

I peer inside the doorway to find Sig, tucking her shirt into her pants, and raise my eyebrow at her.

"What's that look for?" she says as she reaches for her belt and wraps it around her waist.

I shrug one shoulder. "Nothing, nothing. Just…observing," I say innocently.

It never occurred to me that any of the Castaways were *together*, but by the look of Jorn's smile and Sig's state of undress, I am rethinking that assumption. Maybe they weren't actually together. Maybe it is just what happens after being stuck here so long, but either way, it's definitely different from the situation back at camp.

She stands and strides toward me, grabbing her sword and sliding it into the scabbard on her belt.

"Let's go," she says as she brushes past me. I hide a smirk before turning on my heel and following her up the steps.

The torches are already lit on deck, the sky now fallen dark as Stassia and Auralie wait for us at the gangway. They stroll down it as Sig and I cross the deck, and my skin tingles with the weight of eyes following me. Glancing over my shoulder toward the quarterdeck, I find Weston, arms crossed and jaw clenched, as he watches me leave. Fin bounces around his legs, talking animatedly until he sees me and runs up to the railing.

"Bye Lennox! See you in the morning!" He stands on his toes and waves wildly at me, and I wave back with a smile.

My eyes flicker back to Weston's, waiting for him to comment or challenge me leaving like the last shift, but he doesn't move, doesn't say a word, and I can't read the emotion behind his stern face.

His emotions are not my problem tonight.

I turn my back and amble down the gangway, but I can still feel him watching me the entire way to the portal.

Sig's comments must have gotten to him, but truthfully, I don't care what made him let me leave without creating a fuss. I need to get off the ship and feel like I am doing something productive again, not wasting away scrubbing the deck and letting time pass for eternity. Besides, tonight is the night to enact the second part of my plan and find the right time to tell Sig about the dust.

The tunnels drop us out in the canyon near the end of the river, the stone bridge Dane walked me across on my first day off just ahead of us. Goosebumps cover my arms as I scan the water, remembering the monsters up the river that wanted to make me a meal, but when I ask, Sig assures me they don't come down this far.

We traipse over the slick, moss covered river rocks, searching the bank for any sort of symbol or clue. I press my hands onto surfaces and take wary steps. With as many portals as the Castaways travel through, I'm even more cautious than before that I might stumble onto a new one.

The rushing water and chirping insects are the only sounds tonight, the conversations between us like last shift nonexistent. It's too quiet. Stassia isn't her usual rambling self, and I need everyone talking in order to have an opportunity to bring up the dust without seeming suspicious. I decide on the first thing that comes to my mind, and honestly, something I *am* curious about since the moment I saw him open the door.

"So you and Jorn," I say to Sig. She's become my shift partner, so while we hover around each other searching on our own, she stays fairly close. She stands from a crouch and dusts her hands off.

"Me and Jorn," she says.

"How long has that been going on?" I ask.

She shrugs. "Who really knows? A while. Even though we're all together on the ship every day, and it can feel small and stifling some days, the thought of spending eternity here is hard. Having… someone…makes it a little easier."

I feel a pang in my chest. Getting to know the Castaways has made hating them harder and harder each day. I'm starting to really see them as people, Voyagers who are trapped here because of Weston and his deception, and my heart breaks for them. They have to live here forever, knowing that they can't say goodbye to their loved ones, and were denied the ability to help them. But this isn't only a Castaway issue. This very soon could be the reality for every person on this island.

"Why don't you just go back to Dane? Ask him to send you back? Why are you staying with Weston if you really want to go home?" Years of manipulation might not let her answer this question the way she would have before, but I ask it anyway. I watched Sig push back against Weston; she's the only one who has. If anyone can think through the situation and see that following Weston's lead isn't the only way, it's her.

"It's not that simple," she says, her gaze falling to the ground at her feet.

Why isn't it that simple? Why can't they go back to the person who brought them all here, the one who helped them and housed them, who cares about them finding the cure?

I think about Auralie, here to save her betrothed, and Stassia, who with her attitude probably had suitors lining up at her door. They don't have a Jorn, and who knows if they ever will. They don't have someone to pass the years with and, like Sig said, make it easier. Keeping them on Dawnlin is depriving them of the ability to be loved like they want to be, and is just another thing on the list of what Weston is taking from everyone in his crew.

"I think it's really simple," I say, a twinge of irritation in my voice. "You found the healing waters, and you weren't granted them. You just need to tell Dane you want to go home, and he will bring you. He's the Guardian. His entire purpose is to protect the waters and bring people to and from the island. He can't keep you captive like Weston has been."

She heaves a sigh and reaches down, picking up a rock and chucking it into the river, keeping her eyes averted the entire time. I'm not trying to upset her, but I can tell she doesn't want to talk about it anymore. I can't lose my opportune moment, so I need to drop it and move on to something she can talk about.

"Does everyone know about you and Jorn?" I ask.

"Of course," she says. "Can't hide much on a ship. Especially after this long."

"Are there more? Couples, I mean," I ask.

"I think Fern and Eirlik have been together on and off for a while. Some of the others do the same. It's not serious, but it tends to be committed. It's not like we can escape each other."

Not Weston, though.

"That's all?" I ask, my curiosity getting the best of me.

"Are you asking about anyone specific?" she says with a smirk.

I roll my eyes. "Well, I mean, I'm sleeping in his bed. I think it might be pertinent information to know if I'm making enemies on the ship for something that's completely out of my control."

She chuckles and shakes her head. "No, Cap hasn't been with anyone. At least not since I've known him."

"That doesn't mean they don't want to. Stassia is clearly interested," I say, glancing down the riverbank toward where she and Auralie are searching.

Why do I sound jealous?

I'm not. I'm with Dane. It's just odd that if the Castaways don't care about having relationships on the ship, that he hasn't. Maybe the thought of having a woman is too distracting from his need to be in control of everything.

Sig shrugs. "Don't know. You'll have to ask him."

I huff a laugh. I will never talk to Weston about relationships, let alone any women he's taken to bed.

I don't need that mental picture.

"So how are there not, you know, babies running around everywhere?" My cheeks heat and Sig breaks into a smile at my obvious embarrassment.

"There's no time, remember? We're frozen here, and that includes making babies. At least there hasn't been a baby in twenty years, and there has definitely been enough fucking to make one."

Intimacy isn't openly talked about back in the castle, so Sig's blunt remarks take me off guard. My responsibility as the future queen is to produce an heir, and I'm well aware of how that happens, but I guess when it isn't a transaction to seal a marriage alliance or produce that heir, it is a more accepted part of life. More normal. Definitely less scandalous discussion. Sig doesn't seem to mind at all, which must be why she was so willing to tell me that everyone saw Dane and me on the beach.

"Speak for yourself!" Stassia calls out, spinning on one foot until she is facing us.

A laugh bellows from my chest. The rushing water next to us is loud enough that I needed to raise my voice when talking to Sig, but I didn't realize they could hear us from where they stand.

Which means they heard our entire conversation.

Including me asking if Weston has ever been with anyone before.

Shit.

"Stassia, I have a hard time believing that you have trouble with men," I say, hopefully diverting the conversation away from any of my previous inquiries.

She leaps from boulder to boulder toward us. "What can I say? I'm an acquired taste. How about you, Lennox? Are the men lining up to court you back home as much as they are here?"

"There's no one lining up, at home or here," I say.

Stassia laughs her high-pitched giggle, and spins back around, heading over the boulders in the other direction. "You're so funny, Lennox."

"I'm with Dane, remember?"

"Oh, we remember," Stassia says. "How could we forget after that *warming up* by the bonfire?" She looks back and wiggles her eyebrows at me before cackling again.

Sig wasn't lying when she said the Castaways had seen what happened on the beach. After getting to know her for weeks, it doesn't at all surprise me that Stassia was probably front and center to observe.

"Alright, that's enough. Get back to searching," Sig calls out.

"You're no fun, Sig." Stassia giggles before bending down and feeling between the cracks of two large boulders. Auralie shakes her head with a smile and heads down the river, leaving Sig and me alone again.

This is it.

This is my chance to tell her. Dropping my shoulders and lowering my voice, I try to look as genuine as possible. I don't want her to suspect that I overheard the conversation between her and Weston.

"I've already made my peace with never leaving Dawnlin, anyway," I say with a deep sigh as I stare out over the rushing river.

"You want to stay here?" Sig says, a hint of surprise in her question.

She took my bait, and now I just need to drop the most crucial piece of information. When Dane trusted me with the knowledge about the dust, he didn't want any of the other Voyagers to know. Telling Sig, and eventually Weston, goes directly against his wishes, but if it helps me get back to him sooner, I don't think he will be upset. With as frantic as he was to find me over a week ago, I hope escaping sooner will bring him nothing but relief.

I shrug and look toward her, keeping my face as neutral as possible. "I never intended to stay, but I don't really have a choice now. You all have been searching for a way off the island for years, and Dane's dust is almost gone."

Sig's jaw slackens. "I'm sorry, say that again?"

"Dane's dust? It's almost gone. The pouch is almost empty, and he doesn't know how to refill it."

Sig's face draws in as her shoulders pull back. Her eyes flutter around, never settling on any one place for more than a second as her thoughts reel, processing everything I just said.

It's exactly how I want her to react.

She needs to see the severity of the situation, needs to know how important it is for me to go back. I fit right into her plan, the plan she pitched to Weston that he immediately shot down. But now, time is of the essence. It's now or never, because once it is gone, it could be gone forever.

"What do you mean, he doesn't know how to get more?"

"It was full when he became the Guardian, and he never had any instruction on how to replenish it," I say and step onto a new rock. "We were trying to figure it out before I found the waters, but now I'm here. By the sound of his conversation the other night, I don't think he's made much progress."

She shifts on her feet, glancing down the bank toward Stassia and Auralie. She stays silent, her jaw working, before looking back at me.

"We need to tell Cap," she says finally, her voice lower than before.

"I can imagine he doesn't really want that to get out amongst the crew. I didn't want to say it in front of Stassia and Auralie, but I don't know. I just…felt like you should know."

Something inside my chest pinches as soon as the words leave my mouth. I feel conniving and manipulative, exactly how Dane described Weston to me all that time ago, and I don't want to be like Weston. We are the same, though, having to make moves to get what we want. The fundamental difference is I'm not harming anyone else with mine.

He is.

It hurts watching pain flash across Sig's face. I've actually come to like her, and even though she is crucial to my plan to get back to Dane, I deep down don't want to hurt her. Sometimes I think I'll actually miss her when I leave, but I push those thoughts away the second they come up. I don't need any distractions.

She clears her throat, breaking my train of thought. "Let's just keep searching. We'll talk to Cap tomorrow. Like you said, please just keep it to yourself. For now."

I nod, the feeling of success making my limbs feel lighter, but there's something tugging at me, and I can't explain it.

Is this the right choice? If it is, then why do I feel bad about it at all?

We head back to the ship shortly after, having covered our small patch of search area unsuccessfully. I'm thankful for a calm night without the island attacking because there were no distractions stopping me from telling Sig. She was quiet the rest of the night, and I know she was thinking about what this means for everyone on board.

Unlike last shift, Weston isn't on deck when we ascend the gangway, and I'm grateful not to have to put up with his mood tonight. We each go our separate ways once we're below deck, the quiet of the ship so different from the constant bustle I'm getting used to. Weston had ordered smaller search areas and earlier return times after the incident with Dane, so the sky is still dark and the hour still too early for anyone else to be awake.

The room is dark and quiet when I enter, the only sound the quiet repetitive lap of the waves on the side of the ship. Weston's prone form is hanging off the side of the bed, face down, so all I can see is the steady rise and fall of his bare shoulders.

He's asleep, thank the gods.

Now that things are moving forward exactly how I want them to, I need to fall in line with getting Weston to trust me, which means giving back my dagger. I reach back and pull it from my waistband with a twinge of sadness at handing it right back to the enemy.

It's necessary. I'll get it back.

I walk to his side of the bed and set it down on his bedside table lightly, so as not to wake him. Just before I turn around, my eyes snag on his face, relaxed in sleep, and I can't help but pause.

His hair is tousled, even more than normal, his lips slightly parted. He lays so far away from my side that his arm hangs over the side of the bed. For someone who is so deceitful, so power hungry, and such an asshole, he sure doesn't look like it when he sleeps.

Breaking out of whatever trance had pulled me in, I walk back to my side, kick my boots off, and change into my shirt. I curl onto my side, my heavy eyelids fluttering closed the second my head touches the pillow, but they fly back open a second later when Weston lets out a long slow breath, as if he'd been holding it.

Maybe he had been waiting up for me after all.

CHAPTER TWENTY

Early afternoon sun shines through the windows, illuminating Weston's room before I wake, the anticipation of finding Sig and telling Weston the development rushing through my veins. The other side of the bed is already empty. I don't know how long he has been gone, despite possibly being awake all night waiting for me to return. I wish he wouldn't have, because I don't need to be wondering if there are other reasons besides not trusting me to return.

Sig is walking down the hallway toward me as soon as I emerge from the room.

"Hungry?" she says as she turns down the steps to the second floor.

"Starving," I say and take the steps close behind.

We walk through the doorway into the seemingly empty mess, and I startle when I see Weston sitting alone at a corner table, the plate in front of him almost empty.

"Oh good, you're here Cap," Sig says.

This is it.

My stomach tumbles as the moment I've been waiting for approaches. Telling Sig made me nervous, but once it finally happened, it felt easy. Telling Weston feels different, like he will be able to see through my motives the second I utter the words.

I still have to try.

Following closely behind Sig, we fill some plates, then weave through the mess toward Weston's table.

"What's up, Sig?" he says, as she drops into the seat in front of him. I slide in next to her, trying not to look as anxious as I feel.

"We need to talk to you," she says.

He leans back in his chair, draping his arm over the one next to him. It's almost as if he's trying to put as much space between us as possible, not acknowledging me until his eyes flick toward me quickly before returning to her.

"Both of you?"

"*I* need to talk to you. But she needs to be here too," she says.

"I'm listening," he rumbles.

She leans over the edge of the table, lowering her voice despite being the only ones in the room. "Remember what we were talking about before? About the thing you said no to?"

"I'm not sure why she needs to be here to continue that conversation, Signee." A flicker of anger is his only tell before his face falls back into the stoic mask he wears daily.

"Trust me, Cap, she does. You remember, right?" she urges.

His eyes don't leave her as he answers. "I do."

"I need you to reconsider."

"I'm not changing my mind, Sig," he says.

"I think you might." She looks at me, her eyes shining full of hope that what I have to say will change his mind. "What did you tell me last night?"

His stare slowly shifts to me, as if he's having to pull it away and it isn't going without a fight. I squirm in my seat, readjusting and clearing my throat before I speak. Getting him to understand the risk of inaction and ignoring time is crucial to getting back to Dane, and I'm already going in at a disadvantage. He doesn't want to change his mind.

And he's a stubborn asshole, so I really need to convince him.

"The dust is almost gone."

Weston's eyes flash to Sig before settling back on me as he shifts forward in his seat, leaning his distracting forearms on either side of his plate.

I have his attention now, his desire to pretend I'm not part of this conversation disintegrating quickly. It's the next part that is the most important, more so than the dust being almost gone. The next thing I say should convince him, because it is the true deciding factor for all of us being stranded on Dawnlin for a timeless eternity.

I hold his gaze as I say firmly, "Dane doesn't know how to replenish it."

Tension pulls between the three of us as the words settle. Weston's face hardens and a muscle in his jaw ticks as we sit in silence, waiting for him to say something.

"How do you know this?" he says, his voice gruff, his words cut short.

"Dane told me," I say and shoot him a look, "before you took me."

That probably wasn't the smartest way to answer, at least for the progression of my plan, but I couldn't help it. I wanted to take a stab at him, reminding him of what he did, the life he upended, and the risk that he potentially put everyone in.

If I hadn't been captured, if I had been back at camp, I may have been able to help Dane find an answer by now. The reality of being trapped here may have just been a fleeting worry if we discovered how to replenish the dust. Since Weston captured me, though, Dane's focus has been entirely on getting me back. I hope he realizes how much his actions have affected his goal.

Weston breathes through his nose and his eyes fall down to the table.

"See, Cap?" Sig says, pushing harder, taking her opportunity to make him see the urgency. "We need to do something now."

Ignoring her completely, he looks back up at me, his teal eyes piercing. "What made you tell Sig?"

The question catches me off guard. Why does it matter what made me tell Sig? Why is he not focused on the actual information? Is this a test of some kind, trying to feel me out to see if I'm telling the truth?

"Huh?" I say. I can hear Edmond in the back of my mind, scolding me for my very unregal response.

"You've been here for weeks. What made you tell her? Why bring this up now?"

I shrug. The last thing I want is for the conversation to feel planted, but just as I expected, he seems wary. I hate how much he can read me, like he knows my every move. It's almost as if we're using the same arsenal of tools against each other with every battle that we fight, and waiting for the other to surrender first.

"Sig and I were talking as we searched," I say. I refuse to give him any details about the rest of the conversation. He doesn't need to know I asked if he was with anyone, or has ever been. I can't even believe I asked it myself, and I try to ignore the little feelings the question still stirs up deep inside me.

I continue, "I told her I'd already made peace with living on Dawnlin, especially after being denied the healing waters, because the dust is almost gone, anyway."

Sig leans farther over the table, inching closer to him, but he's still staring at me, trying to read me. "If we don't send her now, Cap, it'll be too late." I've never heard Sig sound this desperate, not even when they spoke about this before.

"Send me where?" I ask, looking between them to prevent holding any eye contact that might give away that I already very much know where Sig wants me to go.

"This doesn't change anything," Weston says, finally breaking away from me and looking back at Sig.

"What are you talking about, Cap?" she says, her hushed voice cracking with her attempt to keep from yelling.

"It doesn't, Signee."

She slams her hands on the table, the bang ricocheting off the walls of the empty room. "Bullshit it doesn't! We always thought we had a chance, that time would never run out. It's running out, Cap. She's our last chance. Whether that fits with all your other…" She pauses, and he tilts his head slightly, and I watch another one of their silent conversations happen before my eyes.

"Motives," she says finally. "It's all moot."

"Enough, Signee," he snaps. "I said it isn't happening. That's an order."

"You can't make that choice for the rest of us," she says, her eyes turning to glass and her voice quivering. Sig is always strong, Weston's second in command of everything, and while she sheds the responsibility when she's relaxing with the rest of us, it's back on in an instant if she's needed. I've never seen her this vulnerable or upset, and I can't help but wonder who is waiting for her back home.

But it is obvious she and Weston don't see eye to eye.

"I'm the Captain. I have to make the best decision for everyone on this ship. *Everyone*, Sig."

She sniffs slightly, then clears her throat. "I hope you know what you are doing."

He stands, his chair scraping the wooden floor behind him, snatching his plate from the table and stepping away before stopping next to her. "I'm having hope."

Without another word, he storms out of the mess, his plate clattering in the return before leaving Sig and me sitting in silence.

"I really thought he would listen to you," she says finally, dropping her head into her hands.

"He never listens to me," I say. "I'm not sure why this would be different."

She gives a half-hearted chuckle, before leaning back in her chair and staring down at her untouched food. "I think he's afraid."

Weston doesn't strike me as the kind of person that ever experiences fear. He's too in control of everything, too demanding. Like he just said, he gives an order, and that is the way it will go. What's there to be afraid of when you are the ultimate authority? Especially if you're the ultimate authority with no emotional attachments or relationships to anyone else here?

"Afraid of what?" I ask.

She looks at me and rolls her lips into a tight line, as if she's trying to decide if she should say what is clearly on the tip of her tongue. She gives in with a small shake of her head.

"He's afraid that if we send you back to Dane to take the dust from him, you won't come back."

Why would Weston have any fears about me? What does it actually matter to him if I go back to the Voyagers, to Dane, or stay here? If he's just trying to eventually have everyone on his side, then it makes sense that he would be afraid to lose one person.

But why do I feel like it only has to do with me?

Have I not been convincing enough, and he just doesn't trust me yet?

"That was your plan?" I ask, looking for the confirmation so I can stop pretending I don't know. "To send me back and take the pouch from Dane?"

She nods. "You're the only person who can get close enough to him to do it."

I pause for a moment. If I need to be more convincing, I have to start with Sig, and I need to mitigate the fears.

"I would come back," I say, dropping my voice low and serious.

"You would?" Her eyes narrow and a single eyebrow raises.

I nod. "Yeah, I would."

"Why? You wouldn't stay with Dane?"

The words are tumbling out of my mouth before I can even process that I'm saying them, and it isn't until they hang between us that I realize I actually mean them. This isn't part of my lie.

"No one deserves to be trapped here if they don't want to be. I'd make Dane see that, and he'd let me come back."

I remember feeling trapped the moment Dane told me he didn't know how to replenish the dust. Immediately my thoughts went to my fellow Voyagers, who didn't know the choice was going to be taken from them. The same worry applies to the Castaways, especially the ones I've gotten to know. They've already completed their goal, they found the healing waters, and now they are trapped.

But Weston is the reason for that. He's the one who is refusing Sig's plan to let me go, and give everyone a chance to get off the island. He's the villain here, not me, or Sig, or Dane. He's the one saying no and controlling the fate of everyone around him.

"Then we need to get Cap to understand that, and change his mind. The only way he'll say yes is if he can trust that you'll come back."

"I can work on that," I say, and again, I'm telling the truth.

Maybe Sig's advice the other night wasn't just for Weston. The best way to gain his trust may be to stop being an asshole to him, even though it feels like he draws it out of me, challenging me at every moment. He says he wants to trust me, and he's taken some steps to show me he's starting to, but just when I think I'm making progress, something sets it back.

Changing my method might be in my best interest, and maybe instead of fighting, I need to start befriending. Being friends with Weston might just be his weakness, as long as I can keep from blurring the lines and falling into his trap.

With as little friendship experience as I have, I'm not sure how I'll accomplish that, but I need to try.

My life on the island depends on it.

CHAPTER TWENTY-ONE

Keeping the lines from blurring is turning out to be a lot harder than I expected.

The moment I decided to stop fighting back and to try to be his friend was the moment life on this ship became tolerable, like when the tumblers in a lock fall into place, and a door opens. I still avoid him as much as possible, but it is easier to exist in the same space when we aren't at each other's throats.

Whenever it is necessary to interact, we do, and it is…fine. Which is confusing, and I have to repeat the mantra that this is all part of the game constantly in my head. But now that I am not trying to sneak away, and he is not trying to keep me under tight control, we can move in the same orbit and I don't have a constant feeling of hatred clouding my every move and word.

Otherwise, I spend my time elsewhere, running my shifts, playing with Fin, talking with the girls. I still feel like there are eyes on me constantly, watching my every move and hopefully deeming me trustworthy, but the days here have become so normal, so familiar, that it is hard to vilify the people I'm spending all this time with.

One night after dinner, Auralie and I decide to pull out some games and activities in the lounge to break up the monotony. She had taught us a card game she played growing up that can easily include all of us, so we move the cushions around and spread out on the floor to play.

Eirlik, Veck, and Ryum lounge in the chairs off to the side, passing a bottle between them and talking quietly, while laughter and noise softly echoes through other parts of the ship. Fin lies on the floor next to me, looking at a stack of picture books that appeared on the ship after he arrived.

It feels so comfortable and ordinary, it's almost...enjoyable.

I never thought I would actually feel any positive emotions on this ship, and it's pleasant and terrifying at the same time.

Sig flips a card over and Auralie groans, passing one from her hand across the circle to me. I smile and shuffle my cards around when a door closes behind me and multiple sets of footsteps approach from down the hall. I glance over my shoulder, my eyes falling on Weston as he walks toward us, Jorn following closely behind, their bodies strapped down with weapons.

Something that feels too much like worry fills my stomach. Weston never leaves, and I've never seen him this armed before.

Did something happen that we should know about? Was there another Voyager who found the waters?

Before I can stop myself, words are spewing from my mouth, betraying my feelings of unease.

"Where are you going?" I ask, the question making them stop just in front of the stairs.

Weston stands facing us, his hand resting on the hilt of his sword, and I focus on his face, fighting the urge to run my eyes over the rest of him.

Don't get comfortable. This is part of the game. This is part of the game.

"Out on my shift," he says, directly to me, as if no one else in the room exists.

Of course, Lennox, because you're the one who asked.

"Bye mister Weston!" Fin yells, as he jumps up, running to wrap his arms around Weston's legs and squeezing them tightly. Weston finally pulls his gaze away, his chin dipping to look down at Fin as he rustles his hair. My chest tightens at the movement, and I take a deep breath to clear it before Fin is sprinting back to my side, plopping back down with his books.

I set my cards down in front of me and spin so I'm facing him.

"You've never had a shift before." It's not a question, but he answers what he knows I'm asking.

"Veck took over for me," he says, nodding toward where Veck sits across the room.

"But now he's back!" Jorn cheers, shaking Weston by both his shoulders. He lets out a loud crow, then steps around him, closing the space between him and Sig, and dropping down to plant a quick kiss on her lips.

"Let's go!" he yells, before turning and running up the stairs.

Weston plants his boot on the first step, but pauses. His eyes catch mine and one corner of his lips turns up.

"Don't wait up for me, princess."

My skin is on fire as I hold his gaze for a moment too long; long enough for his smirk to deepen and laughter to sparkle in his eyes. He turns away and jogs up the steps, leaving me staring after him.

What was that?

Was Weston *joking* with me? Does he know I suspect he stays awake every night when I'm out on shift, pretending to be asleep and only relaxing as soon as I am locked back in the room? And why were his words laced with challenge?

I'm still staring at the now empty space where he just stood when Stassia breaks my daze.

"Whew! I need to go up to the main deck to cool off because that was hot."

"I don't know what you're talking about," I mutter, spinning back around and picking up my cards. I stare down at them, hoping my face doesn't give away the fire that is still smoldering under the surface. Shuffling the cards in my hand, I wait for Auralie to take her turn.

"That eye contact," Stassia says, fanning herself with her cards. "What I wouldn't give to have a man look at me like that."

"There was no look. You must be seeing things," I say as Auralie sets down one of her cards with a giggle. Stassia stares at me, eyes wide and mouth open in an exaggerated look of disbelief.

"I can see your hand, Stass," I say, as she slams her mouth shut, pulling her cards to her chest.

I smile down at my hand. This is the first time I've rendered Stass speechless, and it feels better than winning a spar in the ring back home. Movement catches my eye, and I look over to see Sig smiling at me. I assume I'm going to have to defend myself again about whatever that was, when I realize that's not why she's smiling.

I used Stassia's nickname without thinking, and it felt normal.

Easy.

Shaking my head, I try to push away the guilt I have actually been happy amongst everyone here, and focus on the game. We play a few more rounds until most of us are yawning, and Fin lies sprawled out across the floor at my side, softly snoring. Sig and I wake him just enough to walk him to his bed and get him tucked in, since Weston isn't here to do it before everyone disperses for the night.

Once I'm back in the room, it's as if all of my drowsiness disappears and restlessness takes its place.

The room feels…empty.

I haven't slept alone since they let me out of the brig, and while I should be overjoyed that Weston is gone, it doesn't feel right, even though I know I shouldn't care.

I shouldn't be thinking about being alone here. I shouldn't be thinking about falling asleep without his steady breathing on the other side of the bed.

It shouldn't feel like this.

My sigh comes out more like a huff, and I walk to my side of the bed, changing quickly before sliding between the sheets. The desire to glance over to his empty space pricks at me, so I stare at the wooden ceiling as the flames in the sconces dim around me, casting the room into darkness, ready for sleep.

But sleep doesn't come. My mind won't stop cycling through, trying to decipher everything that has happened tonight.

You're just pretending to be close to them, Lennox. You aren't actually close.

I repeat the words in my head as I stare at the dark ceiling, listening to the lap of the water against the ship, but the more they cycle through my mind, the more it feels like I'm not only lying to all of them.

I worry that I'm lying to myself.

What feels like hours pass as I lie awake, tossing and turning, unable to get comfortable because of the constant reel of thoughts flying through my mind.

I sit up with a groan, shoving the lush pillows behind me and propping myself against the headboard.

This is ridiculous. I shouldn't be lying awake like this. There is absolutely no reason I should be worried about Weston on his shift. He's the captain. He will return when he returns.

Staring out over the room, I'm contemplating getting dressed again and going to see if anyone is still awake when I hear a small thump beside me. I turn toward my normally empty bedside table to find a book and a small candle.

Reaching over, I pick it up and run my fingers over the worn leather cover.

The Maiden's Moonlight Venture.

I've read this book before. It's one of my favorites from Tila's shelf, about a woman who gets caught up in a quest, and meets a handsome prince along the way. I smile up at the ceiling and thank the island for giving me this small form of comfort.

A flame flickers, lighting the candle and casting my space in a soft glow. I open the cover and immediately relax as my fingers brush the thick pages. It feels like ages since I've read. The last time I opened a book was with Dane in the library, and it isn't until this moment that I realize how much I miss it.

I turn to the beginning and gobble up the text, turning page after page as my mind plummets into the familiarity of the story. Sinking down into the pillows, I ignore the world around me: the empty room, the emotions, the conversations, and immerse myself into one of my beloved stories.

CHAPTER TWENTY-TWO

"What are you reading?"

The book nearly falls from my hands when I hear the voice, and look up to find Weston standing at the desk, dropping his blades into the drawer. I hadn't latched the door in case I needed to leave, so there was no turn of the handle that would warn me when he came in.

Even so, I'd been too engrossed in the love scene after the maiden and the prince finally admit their feelings for each other to even notice him walk into the room.

"Nothing," I say, my cheeks warming as I close the book without marking my place, and set it on my lap.

"Doesn't look like nothing."

"It's just a book," I say, a little too quickly. My body is too warm under all this bedding, and I'm trying to focus on what he's saying and the fact that he's back, not the pounding of my heart in my ears and between my thighs.

He cocks his head to the side, and a smile plays at his lips. "Is there a reason you don't want to tell me what is in your book, princess?"

"It's not my book. It just appeared. When I couldn't sleep. Right there," I say, my statements stuttered, as I try to hide how flustered I am. I set the book on the bedside table, like having it out of my hands will stop this conversation.

He looks down at the drawer, his smirk deepening, and I feel the burn of embarrassment flare in my skin.

"If you want to avoid the question, you can just say so. I think that gives me a pretty good idea, anyway."

I cross my arms over my chest, wishing I could slink down and hide. Why does Weston seem to always catch me in compromising situations, like he's drawn to me as soon as he can make me feel uncomfortable?

Maybe it's just him that makes me feel uncomfortable. I've never felt like this before, back when I was reading the same book alone in my castle rooms.

Silence stretches between us, broken only by him closing the drawer and locking it with his key.

"Were you waiting up for me, princess?" I can hear the smile in his voice, the same challenge as before when he told me not to.

I scoff. "Absolutely not."

Was I though? Was something deep down not letting me fall asleep because this pattern we've created was broken? Is that why he doesn't sleep too?

"Sounds like you were worried."

I can't tell from here with the shadows and darkness hiding his face, but there might be a playful glint in his eye, like he's teasing me. If getting him off the ship put him into a good mood, one that isn't snapping at me every second, then he needs to get off the ship as much as possible. But a princess isn't teased, no matter how much of a good mood he's in, so I need to stop this immediately.

An abrupt laugh bursts from my throat. "Worried? The only thing I'd be worried about is being trapped in this room forever if Dane finally got hold of you."

He chuckles softly, as he unties the laces of his vest, then disappears behind the screen next to him. A moment later, the sound of running water fills the room, and panic fills my chest.

Oh gods. He's filling the damn tub.

I sit up a little straighter and clear my throat so my voice doesn't come out the same way my insides feel.

"What are you doing?" I ask, raising my voice so he can hear me over the sound of the rushing water.

"Taking a bath."

"Why?" I shriek, cringing at how I must sound and praying the water covers it up even just slightly.

He steps just beyond the edge of the screen at the end closest to the bed, his hands at his hips, slowly undoing the buckle of his belt. He's still completely clothed, but the motion still feels indecent.

I swallow hard.

"Do I really need to explain why people take baths, princess?" he says with a smirk.

I keep my gaze trained on his face, trying to keep my expression as neutral as possible. "You know that's not what I meant. I mean, why do you have to right now?"

"I'm not getting into bed sweaty and dirty." The buckle on his belt clinks before the leather strap falls away. He tosses it on the floor before disappearing behind the screen again. The running water stops abruptly, followed by the rustle of fabric and the familiar sound of clothing hitting the floor.

Oh my gods.

Weston is naked. In this room. And I'm in this room.

Before coming to Dawnlin, I'd spent plenty of time around dirty and sweaty men in the training rings, but never in a way that required anyone to remove clothing. The showers in camp were combined, just like on the ship, but I did a good job of avoiding being in there at the same time as any of the other men in either crew.

But this, this is unavoidable.

My eyes dart to the door, only to find he shut it behind him. I couldn't get out even if I tried.

"You can't take a bath with me in here!"

"Then close your eyes, princess. You were supposed to be asleep, remember?"

Water sloshes and hits the floor, followed by a low groan that resonates through the room. Indecent images flash through my mind, and heat pools between my thighs. I've never been in a room with a naked man before, let alone one who looks like Weston. My pulse is hammering again, my body affected the same as before, and I squeeze my thighs together at the way his groan hits me.

Stupid book. Stupid tub.

From where I sit in bed, he's completely hidden behind the screen, but I know what he looks like beneath his shirt, which makes it easy for my mind to conjure up the images.

Water darkened hair, tousled with droplets falling down onto his skin. The long column of his neck leading right into round, muscular shoulders. The muscles in his back rippling as he reaches up to rest his bulging arms on the rim of the porcelain. His powerful hands massaging suds into his glistening skin.

"Ugh!" I grunt to myself, pulling the pillow out from behind my back and fluffing it with my pent up aggression. Leaning over, I blow out the candle, and slide farther down into the sheets, pulling the bedding up to my shoulder and curving in on myself, as if I've transported back in time to my first night being forced to sleep in this bed.

This is wrong. I should not be thinking about him this way. I blame Dawnlin for sending me one of Tila's books and Weston for provoking me all night.

Please, don't let me have another dream for him to overhear.

Squeezing my eyes shut tight, I try to focus on taking deep breaths, but I barely get through a few when the water sloshes again, bringing me right back into the room.

"Is this us being friends?" Weston says, taking me completely off guard.

"We're not friends," I answer automatically.

He chuckles but doesn't argue.

Befriending him was my new strategy to get him to trust me, and after tonight it seems like it is working, but my answer was for me, to remind myself that I shouldn't be friends with him, not truly, despite how normal and comfortable this feels. No matter how much he jokes with me and provokes me.

I can't *really* be friends with Weston.

"I'm going to sleep!" I call out and pull the sheets tighter around me again.

"Good. I'm taking you somewhere tomorrow. I'll wake you when it's time to leave."

"Where are we going?" I say, suddenly curious. He shouldn't have another shift, since he had one tonight. So does that mean we're going to the island during the day?

Splashes and the sound of scrubbing distract me from my questions, and I squeeze my eyes shut again.

"You'll find out tomorrow. Goodnight, princess."

I let out a sigh and try to clear my mind. Any relaxation I'd achieved from reading completely reversed once he returned to the ship. I take another deep breath and try to remember what it felt like to sleep at camp, to have Dane's arms wrapped around me, but all I can conjure up are flashes of the nightmares I had every time I closed my eyes.

So instead, I drift off to the soft sounds of rippling water.

CHAPTER TWENTY-THREE

"Princess."

My eyelids flutter open, despite my eyes feeling heavy and grainy. Weston stands beside the bed, shaking my foot lightly, and I groan loudly, pulling the bedding higher up on my face.

"We need to leave," he says, his voice low as if he's trying not to wake anyone, even though I'm the only other person in the room. "I let you sleep as long as I could."

That small kindness makes something in my chest ache. With all the other ways he's tried to make me uncomfortable since capturing me, he could have done the same this morning, waking me early so I was miserable for the rest of the day. But he didn't. After all the friendship talk last night, it makes me think he actually listened to Sig and is trying to not make me hate them.

It's too early to be feeling so many things.

"I'm coming," I mumble as I throw the sheets back and slide off the side of the bed. As I stand, Weston's shirt falls over my thighs, from where it had pooled around my hips in sleep.

He clears his throat and tosses my dagger down on the bed as I bend down to grab my pile of clean clothes.

"Meet me on deck."

I'm too tired to care about what he might have seen, so I just nod and cover my mouth to stifle a yawn. Footsteps ring through the room as he heads out the door, leaving it cracked so I can follow.

He hasn't told me where we are going, but by the way he's talking, I assume it will just be the two of us. I've avoided spending as much time with him as I can, but this may be an opportunity to play nice, especially if he already is.

The suns have not risen when I step onto the deck. The early morning is still, the only sound being the slow crashing of waves in the cove. Weston stands alone by the gangway, his body covered with weapons just as he was last night, but my eye catches on something he didn't have before.

A bow.

Why does he have a bow this time?

I clasp my hands behind me, stretching my arms and shoulders as I walk over to him. He doesn't spare me a glance before he's bounding down the gangway, calling out over his shoulder.

"We need to move fast. We're running out of time. Follow me."

I bound down the boards behind him, wondering where the fuck he got all this energy after having a shift last night, but I feel dead. Regardless of my fatigue, my steps have become more sure of the uneven land and beach during my time on shift, and I'm not as worried about falling into the water as I was weeks ago.

Weston steps to the side of the portal, waiting for me to pass through before him and following a breath later. Now that we're safely in the tunnel, he doesn't seem as rushed, his steps slow and measured, so I can easily keep up with him.

Neither of us speaks, and after his prodding and teasing last night, it feels like a step backward. If I'm going to make strides befriending him, I need to do something about it.

"Did you find any clues last night?" I ask.

"Nothing out of the ordinary."

Silence.

I try again, brushing off his non-conversational answer as the effects of the early morning.

"Where did you look?"

"We were out in the dunes," he says, short and clipped.

My teeth worry my lower lip. I don't think he's upset with me. I had done nothing between now and falling asleep last night after his teasing, so it must just be from a severe lack of sleep.

Or he regrets saying we are friends.

I try again. "Did you see anyone?"

He glances down at me before looking back at the tunnel ahead. "I didn't see your boyfriend."

I can understand that he would think I was asking about Dane, but honestly, the thought hadn't crossed my mind. I don't know how many Voyagers Dane has allowed out after dark now that he and Storm were patrolling, and my question was out of pure curiosity, not out of seeking any morsel of Dane that I could.

"That's not what I asked."

"That's what you meant, though." His gaze is unmoving, but his jaw tightens slightly.

I roll my eyes, knowing he won't see it, and shut my mouth. If he doesn't want to talk, then I won't talk. We can spend the rest of the day in silence wherever we are going.

The tunnel ahead splits, and we veer to the left, opposite of the direction I have gone with the girls on our shifts. After a few more minutes in silence, Weston takes an abrupt turn into a short tunnel that looks to end just ahead. As we get closer to the packed dirt wall, I spot the way out. Handholds carved into the wall lead up into a circular passageway with no light at the end.

Weston steps to the side and motions toward the wall.

"After you, princess."

I start to climb, too aware of Weston following right behind me, until I reach the top of the tunnel. The roof overhead is wooden, so I press my hand to the boards and they move, flipping up and opening a trapdoor. The boards clatter on the other side as I climb through and look at the structure around me.

A wooden, circular space surrounds the trapdoor, with large windows open to the surrounding island. Hooking my knee over the lip of the opening, I pull my body up and crawl across the floor, leaving enough space for Weston to follow. I grip the half wall railing and pull myself up, looking around for the first time.

The balcony railing runs along the entire structure, and light pours in through the open sides. We're surrounded by tropical trees, but hidden from the beating suns by a wooden roof that looks to have the seams of another trapdoor.

I spin slowly, taking in this new spot on the island I never knew existed, just as Weston lifts himself through the opening. The already comfortable space feels even smaller with both of us occupying it, his hulking frame taking up much of the open space with the hole in the middle of the floor. He rectifies that quickly, bending down to flip the boards back into place so there's now a little more room to walk. I clear my throat and turn toward the railing, peering through the thick trees to determine where on the island we are.

We're inside a lookout, like the stone turrets at the edges of my castle, somewhere high in the trees. The loud crash of water booms around us, and I circle around the railing until I see it. From here, there is a perfect view of the waterfall and the lagoon below, but we're positioned out of the way just enough that I can see down the path on both sides of the bridge and watch anyone coming toward it.

They surveil the entrance.

I spin to face Weston, my jaw slack as my mind reels. He's leaning against the railing opposite me, arms crossed over his chest, watching me piece things together.

"This is how you take the Voyagers? You watch to see who goes in?"

He nods.

All this time, the Voyagers have feared being outside of camp at night, assuming the Castaways never were on the island during the day, but in reality, they were. Someone sits here, day after day, watching them walk past the one thing they came here for.

"So it's not just nighttime shifts. Someone sits here all day and waits?"

"Yes."

"You dragged me out of bed before dawn but won't speak. Are you ever going to say anything more than a few words at a time?" I say, not bothering to hide my annoyance any longer.

The corner of his lips tip up. "We'll see."

"Ugh, you're infuriating," I groan, rolling my eyes and angling back toward the waterfall.

He chuckles. "Sig tells me that all the time."

"Well, she's right."

"Something tells me if I tried to explain anything, you wouldn't believe me. It's better you just figure it out yourself."

My head snaps back toward him with a glare. "Excuse me for not being able to trust someone who takes us against our will."

"I know that's what you've been told, but I'm not out to get everyone. I have my reasons."

My eyebrows raise. This is the first time Weston has ever brought up anything about his reputation or interactions with the Voyagers, and he's outright denying it. But is he telling the truth? If he is, he wouldn't have to hide his reasons.

I narrow my eyes at him. "Seems like something anyone would say to get people to side with them."

He doesn't say anything more, his face a neutral mask as he watches me. If he won't explain or give me any answers, I'm going to ignore it. He might be trying to get me to believe him, but I'm also trying to get him to believe me, and that is what I need to focus on.

"So I'm just stuck here with you all day?" I say.

"Fortunately for you."

I snort and immediately picture the appalled look that would be on Tila's face if she were here. "Was that a joke?"

His eyes sparkle with laughter and I can't tell if it is at his attempt at a joke, or my snort.

"Maybe."

"It wasn't funny," I say, but have trouble hiding my smile.

Maybe there is hope that he isn't regretting this budding fake friendship if he's joking with me again.

He pushes off the rail and walks over to my side of the lookout. "I can take the first watch. I know you're probably still tired. You can sit and get some rest."

I step out of his way, putting as much space between us as possible in the close quarters, and slide down the wall to sit across from him. I am exhausted, but this is too good of an opportunity to let go. Spending all day with only each other could help me learn more and convince him I'm warming up to his plot.

"What happens if someone finds the entrance? What do we do?"

Weston gestures to the trapdoor on the roof.

"Did Fin tell you about his job?"

I nod. "Jorn did."

"There's a helio here too. If someone finds it, we signal the ship and make our way back. Then we go meet them at the exit."

"That's it?" I ask.

"That's it."

"I can't believe you just sit here, every day, watching. Doesn't it get boring?" I ask.

At least when the day's searching felt the same, I was seeing something new, interacting with the island, never knowing what challenge was going to come at me. But this? Staying in this small room day in and out for who knows how many years seems like it would make the time on Dawnlin pass so slowly.

He shrugs. "I don't do it every day. It rotates, just like the shifts."

"How long did you have to wait on the beach for me?"

"Not long. Maybe an hour. Once you're inside, you won't come out until some time after dusk, so we have until nightfall to get into position."

"It didn't feel like it took that long at all."

I found the waters early in the morning, but by the time I stepped through the portal onto the beach, it was already dark. I'd never thought about it before, but now that I know the Castaways wait it out, all day is too long to hide unnoticed by any of the Voyagers out in the daylight.

"That's part of the island's magic. It feels like it goes by quickly, but really you were walking through the mountain all day." He looks back out over the trees toward the mountain, and I hop back up, crossing over to his side and leaning against the railing next to him.

"No one can see us?" I ask, leaning forward, looking down at the ground below us. "Does the island hide this, too?"

I can feel him tense at my side the farther out I go over the rail, but I ignore it.

"We think so," he mumbles. "No one has seen us yet."

Straightening again, I lean my hip against the rail and look up at him. "Were you here the day you pulled me from the water?"

There's a long pause before he answers, his gaze still trained on the mountain ahead.

"No. I wasn't up here that day. Sig and Jorn were."

Of course he wasn't. He followed me around the island. He'd been the noise I heard in the trees, right before I got the courage to approach the bridge. It's the only explanation for how he got to me so quickly; how he kept me from drowning.

"So they saw you jump in after me."

He nods. "They watched the whole thing."

After being with the Castaways for weeks now, Sig hadn't ever told me she saw what happened. She barely wanted me to find out Weston had been following me. Maybe she didn't want to divulge that there was a lookout, especially if that piece of information wasn't one she could tell me. Weston obviously had to be the one to decide it was time to trust me with it.

"Why'd you do it?" I ask.

He finally peels his gaze away from the entrance as his head swivels toward me.

"Do what, princess?"

"Save me," I say. "It was broad daylight, and other Voyagers were in the area. You could have been seen, or captured, and that would have changed everything for everyone back on the ship. If I'm not a bargaining chip, then why'd you do it?"

My mind flashes back to that moment in the cave, his teal eyes and hard expression softened by relief when I opened my eyes and gasped for breaths, completely ignorant of who was hovering above me.

I am not asking to further my plan. I'm asking because deep down, I truly want to know. Why would he put everything in jeopardy for just another Voyager?

A muscle ticks in his jaw as his eyes flicker between mine. "I couldn't let you die."

"But how'd you know I couldn't swim?"

"Lucky guess," he grumbles, then seals his lips shut.

So we're back to barely speaking.

It's my turn to look away and stare at the mountain.

The Weston I know who is trying to steal the hope away from every single Voyager and taking the cure to benefit himself doesn't seem like the same Weston standing in front of me, who would risk his crew being discovered, having their leader taken, to save someone he's never met. If he is the monster that Dane says he is, the life of a random person on Dawnlin wouldn't have mattered to him.

Edmond always taught me to take in all the information and see the truth, and something is not adding up.

Would a monster put a stranger's life in front of everyone they know and care for?

Has Dane been wrong about Weston this whole time?

Or is this just another manipulation?

Confusion and uncertainty war inside of me, yet some sliver of certainty buried deep underneath them tells me that Weston isn't lying to me. I don't know if it's his tone, or the look on his face that said he was trying not to say too much, but I think he is telling the truth. He didn't want me to die. His protectiveness since being part of the crew has confirmed that.

The question is, why?

"You've never asked about the other side, the Voyager side. Don't you want to know what we think about you and the Castaways?" I ask. Maybe if he doesn't want to answer why, he'll answer something else I've been curious about.

"I don't need to know the exact words being said to know they aren't true."

"But *I* don't know they aren't true. You keep telling me to trust you, but I can't. Not when you're still plucking us off the island against our will."

He lets out a sigh through his nose. "I hope one day you'll understand."

"I won't understand why you're rounding them up and turning them against everyone else. You're taking away their chance—"

"I didn't take anything away from them. The island already did that. I don't turn anyone against anyone, princess." His voice is tinged with frustration, but he doesn't raise it. "Have I once said anything to turn you against them? Have I tried to make you hate Dane? Despite everything being said about me?"

My mouth opens, but no words come out. He's right. He hasn't ever said or done anything besides acknowledge the Voyagers exist. He's never coerced me to change my mind about anyone, or said anything about Dane, other than they don't see eye to eye.

Have I been believing he is manipulating me, simply because I was told that is what Weston does? Was my reality tainted by my previous perceptions?

Every thing that has happened, that I thought was a manipulation, was only because my mind saw it as such.

And I saw it that way because Dane told me I should.

Now I don't know who to trust, Dane or Weston.

But there's one piece that I can't write off, that I need to know the truth. If Weston wasn't actually trying to take the waters for himself, stealing it from anyone deemed worthy, that means he came here for someone he wanted to heal, and he is trapped like the rest of us. But if he didn't, then I know this entire conversation has been a game.

"Did you even come here for someone?"

Tension fills the small space between us as I wait for his answer. I turn and watch him intently, trying to find any clue or tell that he's lying to my face.

When he does finally speak, his voice is thick with emotion.

"I did truly come here for someone. I came for a friend."

He drops his gaze to the rail, then back out toward the mountain, looking anywhere but at me. His normally emotionless face has faltered, his lips curved down in a slight frown.

Is Weston sad?

The thought seems so foreign for this grumpy, overbearing captain.

"A woman friend?" My heart beats a little faster as I wait for confirmation.

"Technically, yes."

"She must mean a lot to you if you are willing to sacrifice everything for her."

"She does." His throat bobs with a hard swallow and my heart sinks, but I choose to ignore it. Who Weston has waiting for him back home is none of my concern.

"How do you know she's still waiting for you after all this time?" I ask.

"I just have a feeling." He stays fixated on the waterfall, and I know he isn't avoiding my eyes out of dishonesty. He doesn't want me to see the emotion hiding behind them.

I think Weston is telling the truth.

What it must be like to have a love last this long, over time and space, through magic and uncertainty; to be so thoroughly connected to another person that you would know they are still alive.

I'd always hoped for a love like that, like the love in the stories I read, but that kind of love isn't written for me. That kind of love doesn't exist for a princess with a duty to her kingdom.

I swallow down the lump forming in my throat and look down at my boots, hoping he, too, doesn't see the emotion in me.

"I hope you make it back to her," I murmur.

We stand side by side for a while, neither of us moving, only staring out at the entrance to the mountain. I wait, anticipating the same question, but he never asks it. He's never asked who I sought Dawnlin for, or if the island deemed me worthy.

It's almost as if he doesn't care, or rather, it isn't necessary for him to know.

Which makes me wonder yet again if the story that Weston is out to get the healing waters for himself is just that.

A story.

I don't know how I could ever confirm it, but once again I find myself doubting everything I knew since stepping foot on Dawnlin.

But now the bigger question that I can't seem to shake is, if Weston is being honest, then why is Dane lying?

CHAPTER TWENTY-FOUR

Silence between us stretches on for hours, the only sound the roaring of the waterfall and the chirping of wildlife after the heaviness of our conversation settled. When he said we'd be going somewhere today, I did not expect to have my world turned on its axis yet again, or to have an entirely different perspective on Weston.

I don't completely; I can't with only a few truths and the snap of fingers. A sinking feeling creeps over me, as I wonder if I blindly followed someone else's beliefs without making my own judgments. I didn't look at all the information and find the truth.

Edmond would be disappointed in me.

Yes, Weston took me and the rest of the Castaways captive after finding the waters, and he still won't give me an adequate reason for that, but since then, he's been nothing but be extremely protective of his people. He claims he is trying to find a way home, and seemed truly distressed when he found out that opportunity might be coming to an end.

Maybe he only wants to get home to the woman he came to save. But if that is the case, why didn't he just go to Dane? And why did he kill the last Guardian?

The sliver of hope I keep clinging to is my trust in the island. If Dawnlin trusts Dane as the Guardian, why can't I? I'll admit, the island and I don't see eye to eye on everything, namely not being worthy of the waters and keeping me trapped on the ship, but it seems to be all knowing, and I need to remember that.

My head hurts from all the questions cycling through it when Weston finally breaks the silence.

"I can hear you thinking, princess."

"No, you can't," I say. I lean my hips back, bending forward and hanging off the railing to stretch out my spine. My muscles are tight everywhere with the intensity of the morning, and my entire body feels like one large knot. "What do you normally do to pass the time up here?"

"I don't think I want to know the answer to that question." He chuckles, and I remember he said Sig and Jorn were on duty the day he saved me.

I make a face and shake my head. "I didn't need that mental picture, thanks."

He laughs, a full, hearty laugh that feels like warm honey. My eyes snap to him and my jaw drops as I take in the smile lighting up his face. My stomach tumbles. I've only seen him laugh one other time, but it wasn't with me, and I was seething with hatred at the time. Now, after our conversation this morning, I see it differently than before.

Only a little differently.

"What?" he asks, quirking his brow.

"Nothing," I say, quickly looking away and straightening my body.

"How about we make a bet."

"A bet?"

He's caught my attention. What could Weston possibly want to bet, and why? Is it just a way to pass time, or is he serious about it?

"A bet, a wager, a game. Call it whatever you want."

"What's the catch?" I ask, eyeing him skeptically. Playful Weston is still uncharted territory, and I haven't gotten used to it yet. The idea of him proposing a game now makes me a little wary.

"If I win, I get a truth, no questions asked, whenever I call for it. But if you win, you can have your weapons back."

I all but stand at attention with the wager.

My dagger.

He's offering to return it to me; no more allowing me to have it whenever he deems it necessary. He's showing he trusts me, at least enough not to slit his throat in his sleep.

"What are the rules?" I ask. My skin prickles with excitement. The worry from a few moments ago is completely forgotten, and all I can focus on is winning.

"You pick the weapon." He gestures to himself and everything he's got strapped to his body. "I pick the task. Fair is fair."

"The bow. I want the bow." The words spill from my mouth, and he smirks, lifting it over his head and extending it toward me.

"Fin said you wanted one."

My fingers wrap around the grip and a thrill hums through my body.

"More like Fin wanted me to have one so he could shoot with me. I was teaching him how before…" I trail off.

Neither of us acknowledges Weston taking Fin, and how distraught I was when I discovered he was gone. The last thing I want this morning is to talk about more heavy and confusing things, because now, if I try hard enough, I could probably see Weston and my fight in the cave in an entirely different light.

"What's the task?" I ask.

He wraps his hands around my shoulders and leads me to the other side of the lookout, facing deep into the forest. The back of my neck tingles as he leans over me, pointing over my shoulder, so close our clothing brushes together.

"See that tree over there?"

I nod tightly, trying to ignore his proximity and the images conjured in my mind from last night.

"Three arrows. Whoever hits the most coconuts wins."

The tree is deep in the jungle, far off the main path, so anyone passing by the mountain wouldn't see the flying arrows or falling fruit unless they were right under it.

Weston sets the quiver against the rail and steps away from my back, giving me space to breathe again. He pulls an arrow from the quiver and extends it to me.

"Ladies first."

"If you think I'm going first, Captain, you're mistaken." I step aside so he can take my place in the opening. "Your task, you first."

He holds out his hand, and I place the bow back in his palm. He moves into position, and I stand behind him, giving him enough space so he can shoot, but not enough that I can't see the target.

He sets up his shot, turning sideways and nocking the arrow before pulling back the string and taking aim. His form is good, which shouldn't be surprising based on how well he can handle weapons otherwise. A few moments pass, unmoving, until he releases the arrow. It whizzes from the lookout, straight toward the target tree, before slamming into the trunk, just beneath the coconuts.

A smirk forms on my lips.

"Shit," he murmurs under his breath, and pulls another arrow, going through the same motions. He looses it and it slices through a coconut, splitting it and sending pieces falling to the ground.

He pulls his last arrow from the quiver and lines it up, taking a moment longer than previously before he lets go. The arrow flies right at the tree, then whizzes just past it, disappearing into the forest.

"Fuck."

I laugh and step toward him, holding my hand out for the bow. "Are you letting me win, Captain?"

"Gloating doesn't look good on you, princess. Especially since you haven't shot anything yet."

It sure feels good, though.

"You can pull my dagger out now. I'll be taking it back." I push past him, and he huffs a laugh as I set up my feet, analyzing the target, the wind, all the other factors that might affect my shot. I try not to focus on anything but the tree, but my skin tingles with Weston's attention.

Maybe he'll stop underestimating me now.

Pushing out my breath slowly, I release the arrow, and it slams right through a coconut, knocking it to the ground. I smirk at him over my shoulder as I grab another arrow from the quiver, nocking it quickly and lining up the next shot.

"I'm about to lose this, aren't I?" he grumbles.

"Don't feel too bad, Captain." I pull the arrow back and release, watching as it slams into another coconut, slicing it in half.

I've already won, but I can't help sticking my victory to him after all the ways he's pushed me over the weeks. I grab a third arrow and let it fly, knocking a third coconut right from the tree. "I was trained poorly, remember?"

I hook the bow over my chest and turn toward him, my hand extended expectantly. He is already smirking, and my insides tumble, but I can't stifle my own beaming smile.

It's probably just the excitement from beating him.

He slides my dagger from his vest and hands it to me. "I'm trusting you not to stab me. Again," he says.

Trusting me. He's just admitted he is going to trust me, and this wasn't just a way to pass the time. He's actually letting me have my weapons back, without a question.

"No promises."

My chest swells the moment I hold my dagger again, my fingers grasping the sheath tightly. I turn away so he can't see any hint of my vulnerability before sliding it into my waistband where it belongs.

"Who taught you how to shoot?" he asks.

"No one taught me. I watched the guar—men…in town…practicing." I catch myself before saying the wrong thing, and risking giving my title away. Coming off the excitement of beating Weston at his own game caused me to get too comfortable, and I almost revealed too much. I push past the stumble and hope he didn't catch it. "I picked up a bow one day and really liked it. It helped me clear my mind and focus on something I could control. So I just kept doing it. I got better with practice."

"Your parents didn't teach you?"

I pause for a moment, trying to find the right words and determine how much I want to give away. Knowing a little about my family shouldn't give him any power over me, no matter which way I look at it, so I decide to go with a partial truth.

"I lost my mother, and my father and I don't really speak."

"At all?" His brows draw together.

"Only when he needs something from me."

He doesn't seem happy about my answer. His only response is silence as he looks back toward the waterfall.

"I'm sorry you had to go through that," he says. "I'm sure that was not an easy childhood."

"Are you, or *were* you, close to your parents?"

It's only fair that I get to ask the same question of him, especially since I'm still trying to determine if he is really being genuine or if it is all just an act.

"My father and I were close, but obviously not recently. I lost my mother too. That was a long time ago." He leans forward, resting his forearms on the rail, his hands clasped out in front of him, but it's his stoic face I watch.

He answered the question, but didn't give up anything else, the same as me. Having something in common with Weston makes me feel off balance, like I'm teetering toward belief and trust instead of the vast hatred I felt when I was first taken. The tiny voice in the back of my head still wonders if he is being authentic, or if he concocted this commonality just to tug at my empathy.

I kick the toe of my boot into the floorboards, anything to get rid of this nervous energy from his revelation. I have no way of knowing how much time has passed, and I don't want to sit in uncomfortable silence until we return to the ship. I clear my throat, and try to return to the light-hearted unexpected emotion welling up there and change the topic again.

"You could have just given me the dagger back, you know. You didn't have to embarrass yourself in the process."

His smile returns, but his eyes stay trained on the mountain. "I could have, but it was more fun this way."

"I just can't wait to get back and tell everyone what a horrible shot you—"

"Quiet," he hisses, holding out his hand toward me.

I stop talking automatically and walk over toward him, leaning in to see what made him so on edge.

Storm stalks down the main path, heading to the stone bridge, his crossbow loaded and drawn, as if he's waiting for some kind of confrontation. He seems more on guard today than he did when we saw him and Dane a few weeks ago. I wonder if he is still searching for the healing waters, or if he's searching for us.

Us.

Am I included in that collective now?

Weston and I watch as Storm hops off the bridge on the other side and follows the path around the lagoon before he disappears into the forest.

Neither of us moves once he's gone, and I let out my held breath slowly.

"Is that why you wanted me to have my weapons back?" I ask quietly.

He nods. "You need to be able to protect yourself."

"They won't hurt me."

He stands upright, and turns, towering over me, and I have to crane my neck to meet his gaze. His eyes darken as they roam my face, and my cheeks heat under the scrutiny.

"I'm not willing to take that chance."

I'm too aware of the breath of space between us, and the fire low in my abdomen at his words. My eyes scan his, and he doesn't shy away, just stays gazing intently at me, as if he has more to say, but won't.

Why does he care this much? Is he this protective of everyone in the crew? As the captain, I know he feels responsible for everyone's well being, but he saved me before he knew me, before I was anywhere near his ship and his crew.

Blinking rapidly, I break out of his trance and step away, turning to cross the lookout again and plopping down on the wooden floor. I pull the bow off and set it next to me, extending my legs out in front of me and crossing my ankles.

I'm exhausted, both physically and mentally. I didn't expect to have to pick apart every word that Weston uttered today, but that is all I've done, and I need a break. I need to get my mind straight and figure out what is really going on.

This is the first time Weston has actually talked to me. Not commanded me, or made comments. Actually talked, and it feels like it came out of nowhere.

Taking him up on his offer to rest, I close my eyes and lay my head back on the boards, trying to piece together everything I know with everything I learned today. Seeing Storm walking around Dawnlin like he was hunting something makes me uneasy.

The Castaways have never spoken of harming anyone. Weston has only ever talked about protecting and defending themselves. But seeing the way Storm was ready to shoot, and knowing the beliefs back at camp, I can't help but wonder if maybe I am making the wrong decision, trying to get back to them.

What if I'm not on the right side after all?

CHAPTER TWENTY-FIVE

On the days Weston and Sig bring out the training weapons, the mood on deck is always light and playful. Everyone can learn something new and blow off a little steam, which builds up in a group of people that only leave the ship once every nine days.

When I stepped back on deck yesterday with my bow slung over my chest, Fin was so excited that he started begging Weston to let us practice. The moment he saw the training swords in their hands this morning, he let out an enormous cheer and started running around the deck in circles, only amplifying the excitement among everyone.

Weston doesn't demand I partner with him this time, and instead works with Eirlik on his footwork, so I grab a couple full quivers and find Fin. After setting up the target bales at the bow of the ship and getting Fin in position, Auralie wanders over and asks for a lesson.

I demonstrate for a few minutes, then hand her my bow and start moving her around in the proper stance to get her started. Stassia comes along a few moments later, plopping down on the deck next to us before laying flat to soak up the sunshine.

Fin's shots are all over the place, and arrows fly everywhere, but he isn't deterred. Auralie takes to the bow quickly and starts hitting the bale after only a handful of attempts. I stand over Stassia, making sure not to shade her as I watch Fin and Auralie, offering comments when I need to.

"So, Lennox," Stassia says from below. "How'd you convince Captain to give you your weapons back?" Stassia asks as Auralie's arrow strikes the target on the second ring. I shoot her a smile as she excitedly grabs another arrow and lines up her next shot.

"I didn't have to convince him," I say, glancing down at her. "He bet me for them, and I won."

"He *bet* you? What was the bet?"

It sounds like Weston doesn't make bets very often, and I hide that away in my mind as just another thing he's done with me and not everyone in the crew.

"I showed him I wasn't completely inept with a weapon. Did you know he's a terrible shot?"

I feel him before I hear him, and I know he heard me, but that doesn't make my statement any less correct.

"Careful, princess." His voice rumbles behind me, sending involuntary shivers down my spine. "I still can take them away." Weston steps up beside me and crosses his arms over his chest as he surveys our practice.

"I won fair and square," I say. "Besides, I'm not wrong. You completely missed the target once."

"The tree was far away. It was supposed to be hard." He sounds defensive, but in a playful way.

A friendly way.

"Well, *I* didn't miss."

Stassia smirks up at the sky as she listens to us, her eyes closed against the rays. Weston looks down at her and chuckles.

"Looks like you're getting a lot of good practice in, Stass."

She gestures to her supine body with both arms. "This is important work, Captain. I can't be rushed." She drapes an arm over her eyes, blocking them from the suns, and he smiles again.

We stand side by side in silence for a while, watching Auralie and Fin shoot with Stassia laying at our feet. Fin jumps and cheers when he strikes the target, and the sounds of training and laughter still ring out across the deck. After yesterday, and everything Weston revealed to me, this silence and proximity feels oddly comfortable, and I don't want to know what that means.

Suddenly, I get an idea. I'm nervous to ask, because I don't want to do anything that will force us to be closer together, but I want to learn. It shouldn't feel different from sparring with any of the guards back home.

Fuck it.

I turn toward him quickly so I don't go back on my decision.

"Can you teach me how to do that thing? That you did in the cave?"

He glances down at my sudden movement, and his lips curve into a smirk.

"You're going to have to be a little more specific than that, princess."

"When you took my dagger. Can you teach me how to do that?"

My face heats when I remember back to the fight, so similar to when I tried to escape in the night, yet so different, so much having happened in the time between.

Shall I disarm you again, princess?

My spine tingles, and I stare up at him, waiting for an answer.

"I'm not sure it's in my best interest to teach you how to disarm me." His eyes flicker with mischief and I roll mine. It feels good to be more like myself, more how I would act with Brynne, even though my first reaction is to fight back at him or challenge him whenever I can.

"I have a feeling you're going to teach me anyway." I rest my hands on my hips and stare up at him, waiting for the 'yes' I know is coming. He hasn't turned down anyone's request to learn how to defend themselves, and even during the last training session, he told me ways to improve. Those suggestions could be used against him, just like this.

He beckons me with a flick of two fingers. "Come this way."

We move into the center of the bow, far enough away that if something goes wrong, we aren't going to accidentally injure someone. I reach in my waistband and pull my dagger from the sheath, holding it out for him to take, but he shakes his head.

"I'll show you a few times, and then we'll practice, alright?"

I nod quickly and watch as his fingers close around mine, wrapping them firmly on the hilt and adjusting my hand position so I'm ready to strike. Tingles erupt on my skin everywhere we are in contact, and I refuse to look at him, keeping my eyes trained on my hand so I can pick up the movements.

"I'll start slow," he says. Shifting his hand, his fingers wrap around my wrist, pressing into the tendons there, then angling my hand until my fingers become slack. I can't keep my grasp on the hilt, my hand loosening just as his moves again, quicker this time, fingertips sliding slowly against my palm.

My chest shutters with a sharp intake of breath, as the trickle of heat following his fingers on my skin makes me squirm. I hope he didn't hear it.

The dagger falls into his palm and he pulls it out of my hand, then flips it in his fingers so the blade is facing the right direction, ready to stab his opponent.

I watch the whole thing, my mouth agape at how easy the moves are for him.

"Do you want me to show you again?" he mumbles.

I slam my mouth shut and swallow hard. "Nope, I think I got it."

That didn't feel like sparring with the guards back home.

"Your turn then."

Inhaling a deep breath through my nose, I focus on the task, trying to remember each of the movements in order. He points the dagger at me and I fumble through the steps, each one more difficult than it looked because of the sheer size of his hands. I have to learn how to adjust my grip, all the while trying not to think about how intimate this feels.

Unlike the last training session when I was too flustered and too pissed off to focus on anything other than beating him, this time Weston is a good teacher. He doesn't get frustrated or impatient. When I struggle, he shows me the movements again and again, or offers constructive words until I get the feel for it.

After countless tries and a mediocre performance, my hand starts cramping, so I take the excuse to step away from him.

"Now I just need to learn how to do the flippy thing you do at the end," I say.

"I would highly recommend you try learning that with a practice dagger, not this one." He flips it again, so the blade lays across his palm and extends it toward me. The skillful way he handles a blade shouldn't surprise me, with the years of practicing in Dawnlin under his belt, but sometimes I wonder if there is more to it than that.

"Thank you for teaching me," I say as I slide the dagger back into its sheath. "I'm sorry I kept you to myself today."

When his lips turn up in a smirk, I realize what I said.

"I mean, not you, just your instruction. You didn't have to spend so much time with me," I stammer, trying to dig my way out of the embarrassment that is consuming me.

"You don't have to thank me, princess," he says, smiling softly. "It's my job."

The crew around us has calmed after spending hours beneath the blazing suns training. Many sit around in groups in the shade, eating and laughing, and weapons litter the floor.

"It's not really a captain's job to teach everyone how to defend themselves."

"Maybe not, but it is mine."

"Captain!" someone calls from behind him.

Weston steps backward, his eyes locked on mine until the last moment, before he turns on his heel and heads across the deck. There's a small flutter in my stomach at his attention, but I turn away and walk back toward Stassia, who has barely moved. I lay down next to her, Auralie and Fin having disappeared in search of some lunch, so we are alone. I close my eyes, letting the heat and sunlight soak into me and let loose a sigh at how amazing it feels.

"I could lie here all day," Stassia says. "Especially once the shirts start coming off."

A giggle erupts from my throat, and I reach my arms up, stretching out my forearms.

I'm going to be sore later.

"Yours included?" I ask with a smile.

"You're lucky it isn't already," she says, and something tells me she is not joking.

"We don't get any sun in Blackwood," I murmur. "It's one part of Dawnlin I will definitely miss when we get home." Light dances over my closed eyes as the sails rustle in the light breeze. Returning to my cold and wet kingdom isn't enticing, despite knowing I need to get back home for my people.

"*If* we get home."

"Yeah, if."

"I have a feeling we're about to get a heat wave," she says after a few moments.

"You mean it gets hotter?" I say, popping up to look at her.

"Oh yeah. It's going to be glorious."

I lay back down with a groan. Though it took me time to get used to the heat, I've grown to enjoy it, knowing that if we ever do make it home, I likely would never experience heat like this again. The thought of it getting even hotter, however, is not something I am looking forward to.

We fall into silence, enjoying the calm of the deck and the break from our daily tasks. Even though my arms are heavy and exhausted, I feel good. Strong. Like how I felt after a great training session with Brynne.

It's been a while since I felt that way, especially since being here.

"Why do you hate us?" she asks suddenly.

Her question takes me off guard. I didn't think I'd have to explain myself, that I don't really hate them, especially her and Auralie and Sig. Friendly feelings toward all of them have been developing more and more each day, despite still having deep-seateded reservations.

"I don't hate you, Stass."

"Obviously, you don't hate *me*. But all of us. Why did you? I was a Voyager too, remember? We all were. We know what Dane tells people. But I still saw the good in us."

"Do you expect me not to question it when people are being taken against their will and hidden away? You all were taken, and you just choose to ignore it because people can still have good in them?" I push up onto my elbows and look over at her, but she still lays unmoving, eyes closed.

"Captain has his reasons," she says.

"But no one will explain them to me, Stass. I don't understand why he is keeping everyone here. He says he is looking for a way home, but he won't let anyone go back to Dane and just ask to be sent home."

"You're smart, Lennox," she says. One of her eyes opens and squints at me against the light. "I have a hard time believing that you never had the thought that maybe Dane is the one trying to keep everyone here. Maybe the person in charge of who comes and goes is the reason people come, but never leave?"

I shake my head. "It's not about the dust. It's about Weston wanting to steal the healing waters. That's why he's taking everyone."

She closes her eye again and straightens her head, looking back up at the sky.

"If all he wanted was to steal the healing waters, why would we be looking so hard for a way home without them? Don't forget, none of us have them. Does that explanation even still make sense?"

Her words settle between us.

She's right.

Why would he want to help everyone leave empty-handed, if he was just trying to bring the waters back to our world to use for his own gain? Especially if he was telling the truth that he came here for someone. He doesn't seem like he wants to get home, just to have money or power, at least not how he's been acting recently.

"But Dane said that Weston killed the last Guardian," I say, forgetting that important detail.

"It seems to me like you're getting to know him a little better. Ask yourself, does he seem like the kind of person who would just kill someone?"

My jaw slackens as I sit, stumped, but Stassia continues on.

"Dane says Weston did, and you believe him. But if Weston said he didn't, would you believe him?"

"I don't know who to believe anymore," I whisper.

"The island," she says. "We always trust the island. It hasn't steered us wrong yet."

Stassia is right. Dawnlin hasn't been wrong, even if I don't agree with it and question the magic. Dawnlin gave me the means to make a map, which helped me find the waters, but after leading me to it, deemed me unworthy. It doesn't make sense.

If empty handed you leave by dust, in the magic of Dawnlin, you must trust.

Every one of the Castaways left empty-handed, but the island specifically told us to trust it, and if it has been hiding them for all this time, maybe not trusting them is wrong.

The island led me here, led me to the Castaways.

Led me to Weston.

Is this where I was supposed to be all along?

Sometimes I catch myself thinking it feels like…home.

"Can I be honest with you, Stass?" I murmur.

"Hmm?" She hums in response.

"I don't really have friends back home. Being here, on Dawnlin, is the first time in my life I haven't been lonely. Whatever happens, you and Sig and Auralie, you all are important to me. I just wanted you to know that."

She turns her head and smiles at me, reaching over to squeeze my hand.

"Careful Lennox. You're starting to look like you actually like it around here."

I chuckle and squeeze her hand back before she releases.

"Don't worry," she says. "We all care about you, too. And your secret is safe with me."

CHAPTER TWENTY-SIX

*S*leep is hopeless in this heat.

Stassia was right, a heat wave was on its way, and I was not prepared for it. At least on deck there was a breeze off the water making the heat tolerable, but the captain's quarters are hot and stifling, and I cannot relax.

Laying under the bedding is out of the question, so instead, I'm sprawled out on top, the sleep shirt sticking to my skin. Sweat dampens my scalp and my waves are wild as I toss them off of my neck. Staying still is impossible, and I'm constantly having to readjust my limbs, seeking a cool spot on the sheets.

Nothing is comfortable.

I roll onto my back and let out a frustrated sigh into the quiet dark before jolting to attention when the silence is interrupted.

"You're going to rock the entire ship and wake the crew if you don't stop tossing and turning," Weston grumbles from his side of the bed.

"It's too hot," I groan. He hadn't moved for a while, so I didn't think he was awake, yet it wasn't implausible that he was awake too. He must be suffering as much as me in this humid room.

"Maybe if you try not moving, you won't be as hot," he says.

"I tried that. Doesn't work."

He rolls onto his back and it's then I notice he isn't sleeping under the bedding either. The pants he normally wears to sleep are gone, replaced with some that are cut off at the knees. Otherwise, he's unclothed, and it's easy to see the sweat on his skin glistening in the moonlight.

He lets out a deep sigh. "I have an idea, but you don't have to agree."

"If this involves me taking my clothes off, that's never going to happen."

He chuckles. "Good to know, princess. But that wasn't what I was going to suggest."

"What then?" I ask.

He throws his feet over the side of the bed and stands before turning to face me. "I could teach you how to swim."

"*Now?*" I say, sitting up.

He shrugs his shoulders. "What better time than when it's too fucking hot to function?"

"I'm terrified of the water."

"That's the entire point," he says. "If you learn how to swim, you won't be scared anymore. There's nothing to worry about. I'll keep you safe, princess."

My belly stirs and I blame the heat.

"But it's dark. We won't be able to see."

He nods at the line of windows above the bed. "There's a lot of moonlight tonight, and it's not like we can do it during the day."

I slide off the bed and bite my lip. Learning to swim is a skill I should have, especially living on a ship, but do I really want Weston teaching me? I'm sure Sig would, if I asked her, but he's offering now. He already spent the day teaching me how to disarm someone, so what is another lesson?

And it's so fucking hot.

All I can think about is cooling down, and that outweighs any negative arguments about being alone with him again so soon.

"Alright. What do I wear?"

He grabs a loose shirt and slides it over his head. "What you have on is fine."

"But I sleep in this. And I need pants."

"I have more shirts you can sleep in, and if you want to force yourself into pants, be my guest."

He pads to the door on bare feet, grabbing his belt with his sword as he passes the chair.

My pants stick as I try to yank them on, and I curse him under my breath. It takes a few minutes of tugging before I get them up, and once I do, I immediately regret it. The heat is amplified. They pull with every step, and all I can think about is getting them off again.

I grab my dagger and follow Weston, our bare footsteps silent on the wooden floor. The night is still, and the ship is quiet. The only sound is the rustle of sails and the creak of the boards, indicating no one else is awake. Rumbling fills the air as the gangway extends from the edge of the ship, and we bound down it quickly.

The jagged rock on my bare feet slows me down. The softness of my soles is not acclimated to the points that poke into my skin and throw off my balance. Weston extends his arm to me as I wobble, and I reluctantly grab hold of it.

He keeps me steady as I slowly amble along, gaze trained on the rock in front of me to dodge holes. As soon as my toes hit the sand, I release him and step away. I don't need to touch him any more than necessary, and I deem preventing myself from falling into the sharp rock of the cove necessary.

"Where do we go now?" I ask, looking around at the empty beach and scanning the cliff above. After seeing the way Storm patrolled yesterday and knowing he isn't afraid of being out at night with Dane,

I'm a little wary of being beyond the safety of the ship, even though I still don't believe he would hurt me.

"This way," he says. "We should walk in the surf so our footprints get washed away. Are you alright with that?"

I nod and swallow the lump in my throat. I have never willingly been this close to water, but I know I am about to get a lot closer. Learning to swim has been in the back of my mind for a while now, and I feel relieved finally being able to get it over with. I'm ready. And because it was Weston's idea, I don't have to deal with the consequences of asking and having him think it is so I could safely escape.

Foam covers the sand as we step into the surf, the water lapping at our ankles while Weston positions himself between me and the waves rolling in. The moon is bright tonight, and reflects off the surface of the glowing water, making it easy to see where we are going. We follow the curve of the beach, the water on my feet already cooling me down, but making these dreaded pants stick to my legs even more than before.

Large boulders form the other side of the cove, and I follow behind Weston as he climbs over and weaves through spaces between them. The cove behind us is completely out of view as we follow the shoreline, until another cove, much smaller than where the ship is anchored, appears before us. The water inside it is calm, only rising and falling with the swell of distant waves that crash into large rocks that guard the space. It's the perfect wading pool, and I assume where he's going to teach me to swim, outside the reach of the waves.

It's also tucked away enough that if someone were to be out walking tonight, they wouldn't be able to see us.

Weston sets his belt down on top of the boulder before reaching over his head and pulling off his shirt. He drops it next to his sword before sliding down the side of the boulder and landing in the water below.

My breath catches as he disappears beneath the surface, and I scan the water, waiting for him to emerge. I shouldn't be afraid for him. He isn't scared of the water like I am, but I can't stop it from happening.

He breaks through the surface a moment later, his hands pushing his hair back out of his face as rivulets of water cascade down his chest and abdomen.

"I thought you said this didn't involve taking my clothes off," I say, crossing my arms over my chest and suddenly feeling very vulnerable.

"I lied."

I make a sound of shock, which makes him smile. "Finally admitting you lie? What else are you going to admit to?"

He smiles and his face glows in the moonlight. He must be feeling better after being in the water, because it seems like the grumpy, overheated captain is nowhere in sight.

"I'm kidding, princess. You don't have to take anything off. It might make it more difficult, but it's your choice."

I set my dagger next to his things and crouch down, scooting my body toward the edge of the rock. The water sits at Weston's waist, but that will be significantly higher on me. My stomach rolls as I scan the water, trying to find the courage to jump in like he did.

"You'll be able to stand just fine."

I nod quickly, and suck in a breath, keeping my gaze on the water below. Extending both legs out over the side of the boulder, I slide down slowly until I fall, feet first, into the water. Somehow I remain standing, but push up on my toes so my chest stays as far out of the water as possible. I suck in a breath, overwhelmed by the sudden change in temperature, doing exactly what Weston expected, cooling me down and making me more comfortable in this heat

But just as I expected, panic rises in my chest as my breaths shorten.

"You're alright, just get used to it. You can walk around." He hovers barely an arm's length from me, I assume for reassurance and hopefully not because I'm going to drown.

Holding my arms up above the water, I take a step away from the boulder. The water holds me upright, the slow swell from the waves making me sway back and forth as I try to move. My clothes drag around me, heavy with the weight of the water, and I now understand why Weston took his off. They feel like they're tugging at me as I trudge through the pool, my stance loosening up slightly the more I move.

"What do we do now?" I ask. Addy always told me that my voice gets high pitched and squeaky when I'm scared, specifically when I found a spider or insect she always took care of in my rooms. I hope the squeak isn't present now.

"Nothing for a few minutes. You need to feel a little more comfortable in the water first." He sinks into the water and disappears, before resurfacing again a second later, and running his hand over his face and wiping the water away. Dropping lower again, his body disappears until I can only see his face watching me.

"It won't hurt you, princess. You can put your head under. Just hold your breath."

I narrow my eyes at him. "If I die, it's your fault."

He chuckles. "I think I can save you again if that happens."

I take a deep breath and lower my arms, then sink my body into the cool water, letting it surround me before panicking and pushing myself back up again. I splutter uncontrollably, then gasp for breath. My hair is soaked and plastered to my face, and I shove it out of the way, only to find Weston laughing, the sound filling the little cove as he watches me cough from sucking in too much salty water.

"Relax," he croons. "You're thinking too much. Try it again."

I try a few more times, taking in a large breath and holding it before dropping into the pool. The more times I do it, the more in control I feel, and I can sense the unease and fear subsiding.

"Alright, what's next?"

He glides closer and extends his arms, resting them on the surface of the water.

"Hold your arms out like this. Do you feel the water, how it holds you up, pushes your body around?"

"Yes," I say, mimicking his movement and resting my arms on the surface.

"It will do the same when you swim, so you need to practice letting it."

"How do I do that?"

He steps closer, eyes not leaving my face. "You have to trust it," he says, rising so he's at full height and towering over me. "I'll show you," he says and reaches out toward me. "But you have to trust me, too."

CHAPTER TWENTY-SEVEN

*T*rust Weston.

That's the real question.

Can I trust him?

He doesn't give me a moment to overthink it, he just moves, bending forward and hooking his arms under my knees. My muscles tense as his other arm presses across my back, just below my shoulders, and then I'm off the ground.

I shriek and flail at the sudden loss of security, despite his arms holding me firmly. The water pushes me on all sides, and I feel like I'm going to drop beneath the surface.

"Relax," he murmurs. "Just focus on the water, and keep your body as straight as possible."

I follow his instructions, straightening my body and feeling the water underneath me, supporting me, and completely ignoring the fact that he's holding me in this shirt that is probably plastered to my skin and leaving little to the imagination. I don't think about it. Instead, I suck in slow, deep breaths and try to let go of my fear, feeling the water pushing me up like it had on my arms only moments ago.

Trust it. Trust it.

"Good. Keep going," Weston says, but his voice sounds far away. My eyes fly open, only to realize he isn't actually holding me anymore. He's stepped away, his hands no longer on me, and I'm doing it on my own.

"Wait, wha—" My focus snaps and I sink like a rock. I find the floor and push to stand, coughing and spluttering water all over again.

"What the *fuck*?" I yell between coughs.

"You were fine, princess. But see what happened when you started thinking too much and stopped trusting? Try again, but do it yourself this time."

I shoot him a glare, but follow his direction. Again and again, I try to float, falling into the water most of the time, but floating often, too. Once I feel comfortable enough on both my stomach and back, he shows me how to paddle myself around, using the water to stay above the surface.

I haven't thought once about my fear of the water since my determination to master a new skill kicked in, but now that I'm moving around and not just floating, my water logged clothes keep pulling me down, slowing my movements and tangling up my limbs.

"Ugh!" I grunt in frustration and yank at the heavy fabric, trying to untwist myself and adjust my pants so I can move my legs.

I don't care if it isn't fitting for a princess. Rules don't apply here.

I slog my way over to the boulder with our things and clamber up it, which is much more difficult than before, with my movements restricted by the wet cloth.

"Turn around," I say, narrowing my eyes at him.

He does so without question, and after waiting a moment to make sure he isn't going against my command, I pull the shirt over my head and plop the sopping mess down on the rock. The pants are much more of a challenge, fighting me as I try to peel them down my legs.

Standing on the top of the boulder in nothing but my undergarments makes me feel freer than I ever have in my life, but at the same time, too conscious of exactly how little I'm wearing. No one other than Tila and Addy has ever seen me show this much skin. The dark lace undergarments cover everything essential, but are much smaller than the layers of gowns and corsets I am used to at home.

And Weston is *right there*.

He hasn't come near me at all since I've started trying to swim on my own, so I should be safe from lingering eyes as long as I stay mostly under the water. I drop back in with a small splash and crouch down so my shoulders only peek through the surface.

"Alright, you can turn around now."

He sinks farther into the water and backs away, staying on the side opposite of the pool, giving me enough space to practice. Now that I'm not fighting the clothing and constantly being pulled down by the weight, focusing on the strokes as I make laps back and forth is much easier. With each pass, I'm becoming more and more comfortable in the water, knowing I can at least keep myself above the surface.

It feels like no time has passed at all when Weston finally speaks.

"We should get back. It's going to be light soon."

I finish a lap and stand, panting with exertion. A quick glance at the sky shows he's right. The edges are changing colors, so it is time to get back. Despite getting no sleep, I don't feel tired yet. Energy thrums through my body, along with the excitement of overcoming a fear that would have made my time on the island completely different.

Would things have turned out differently if he didn't have to pull me from the lagoon?

Weston rises and wades closer to me.

"How do you feel?" he asks.

"I feel great, actually," I say. "Maybe the water isn't so bad after all." I skate my hands over the surface and notice the change in his face softening with relief.

"I'm not as afraid anymore," I continue. "I know it will be different when it isn't as calm as this, but at least now I know how."

"You're a fast learner," he murmurs.

I don't respond right away, trying to find the right words to express all the thoughts flickering through my mind. Weston has now taught me skills that will help keep me safe on three separate occasions, more than anyone else, since being on Dawnlin. I know the dagger skills I never got to learn from Brynne will be valuable eventually, and I'm sure my father will be happy I know them, but learning to swim feels more personal than that.

He pulled me out of the water, saved my life, and now is teaching me how to keep myself safe, so an entirely new world opens up to me here.

It means more than he knows.

"Thank you for teaching me," I breathe, the words rushing out of my mouth before I regret saying them. "We don't have water like this back at home, and knowing how just...It just makes me feel a little safer here now. So thank you."

His throat bobs with a swallow, and his voice is low and quiet.

"You're welcome."

A small shiver tickles my spine, despite the overbearing heat, and I look away, my gaze fixed on the water between us.

"Besides, now that I know how, aaahhhh!"

My discomfort is immediately forgotten as something brushes the back of my legs, eliciting a sharp scream from my throat. Even after having interactions with the other life on Dawnlin, I'd never considered what else lived in the sea, and this feels like an entirely new fear I'm having to process in this exact moment.

I don't think. I just act.

Flying through the water, I try to put as much distance between myself and the invisible threat as possible. I clamber up a slick boulder, my neck craning as I look over my shoulder to make sure whatever monster lurks beneath the surface isn't chasing me.

"There's something in the water!" I shriek. "Something touched my legs!"

I cling to the boulder, hoisting myself up so I'm completely out of the water. My eyes scan the surface, but the pool remains still, with nothing visible except the glow of the moonlight. I strain to see, waiting for something to pop out from below, like the fins of the sirens that lured me in so long ago.

But there's nothing. The water is calm and continues to swell and fall calmly with the movement of the sea.

Then I feel it.

Heat radiates off the rock, warming every speck of skin I have pressed against it. It's comforting against the panic from the unexpected attacker.

Until it moves.

Strong hands flex under me, gripping my backside and holding me above the water, and I realize what I have done.

It isn't a boulder I clambered up to escape.

It is Weston.

And I'm essentially naked, every exposed surface of my body pressed against his, clinging to him like the moss on the bark of the trees back home.

I squeeze my eyes shut, as if being unable to see what I did will somehow reverse time. My neck turns painfully slowly, and I gently lift my gaze. The monster in the water is completely forgotten as my eyes trail over everywhere our skin touches.

I'm hyperaware of the press of my soft curves against the hard planes of his body. My arms wound around his neck, pulling my body and breasts flush against his bare chest, so the delicate lace is the only separation between us. My feet clasp around his back as my now throbbing core settles against him.

Pressing against his, my chest rises and falls with shallow breaths. My eyes lift to his face, only to find his chin tucked, his gaze downcast, as if he too is trying to avoid this forced entanglement.

Until he isn't.

Teal eyes meet mine, holding them for just a moment before they slide over my skin, caressing my face, and settling on my lips. My breath hitches, and my mind empties of everything except the feel of him against me, firm and smooth and real. The muscles in my arms tighten involuntarily as my eyes flicker to his lips, pulling me closer until we're barely sharing a breath. The air is intoxicating, and as if it's affecting him too, his arms move, his effortless hold changing as he crushes me against him.

His throat bobs when my hips shift in his grasp, pressing the heat between my thighs into him. I suck in a breath; the sound breaks his trance and sends an imaginary bucket of cold water tumbling over my head.

What the fuck am I doing?

This is Weston.

His chin drops again as he turns his head away, while I still sit, chest panting against his, with my heart pounding in my ears. He's moving again, shifting one arm underneath me and dropping the other to his side, before leaning sideways into the water. When he straightens again, his arm extended out next to him, a long, rope-like plant dangles from his hand, its huge leaves protruding in all directions.

He looks back to me then, his lids hooded and eyes still darkened.

"Are you afraid of plants now too, princess?" His voice vibrates in his chest, and I feel it reverberate through mine.

"Oh," I say, thankful for the darkness hiding the heat in my cheeks as I look away, trying to settle my gaze anywhere but on him. "I'm sorry I didn't know."

"No need to apologize."

Tilting to the side again, he drops the rope plant back into the water, then straightens with a deep breath through his nose.

"We should, um," I clear my throat. "We should probably go back."

He nods. "We should."

A moment passes, but neither of us moves. His eyes are pinned to my mouth again, and my lips part at the thought of what I would do if he leaned in and closed the distance between us.

I can't find out, no matter how much my entire body feels like it has been engulfed in flames under his attention and touch.

"You can put me down now, Captain," I finally whisper, my eyes trailing down to his lips once more, and I catch the quick clench of his jaw before it relaxes again.

His shoulders barely tense under my arms as he lets out another slow breath. I unhook my arms and legs, and he shifts me to his side, slowly lowering me until my feet splash into the water below, but not before my thigh brushes against the front of him, long and firm.

Oh gods.

Was Weston just as affected by the touch of our bare skin as me?

I step away quickly, turning in the direction of our belongings, and he does the same, putting more space between us as we wade slowly to the boulder.

He reaches it first and pulls himself up before leaning back down and offering me a hand. Without a second thought, I take it, letting him hoist me up onto the warm dry surface. Weston keeps his eyes averted as he bends to pick up his shirt and belt, but instead of sliding it over his shoulders, he extends the dry clothing out to me.

"Thanks," I murmur as I slide it over my head, his scent immediately overtaking the smell of the sea and the fragrance of the trees on the wind. Leaning over, I wring the excess water out of my hair, the salt making the waves spring into shape, and pick up my dagger and still sopping clothes.

We amble along the rocks, weaving through them back to the beach, the silence thick between us, broken only by the rolling waves in the cove. The ship is still dark and quiet as we climb the gangway and pad across the deck, but being back around the other Castaways, no longer alone in an isolated cove, brings me a little relief.

"Are you hungry?" Weston mumbles, his question so simple but so jarring after what had just happened in the water.

"I'm fine."

We start down the stairs, and his voice remains low.

"I'm going to the galley to—" He stops abruptly, and I almost crash into his back. I lean to the side, peeking past him to see what is blocking his path, and shift on my feet when I see what caused his quick reaction.

Sig stands at the base of the stairs, arms crossed, fully dressed and strapped down with her weapons, with Jorn striding up beside her.

"Signee," Weston says.

Her eyes narrow, gliding between us and taking in our state of undress: Weston shirtless in soaked cut off pants, and me wearing his shirt, both of us still dripping on the wood at our feet.

"Cap," she says, with a lilt in her voice. I can't tell what she is thinking. The glint in her eyes unreadable. She nods at me. "Lennox."

Jorn glances between us, a casual smile on his face. "See you later!" he says before taking the steps two at a time and passing by us.

I bite my lip, feeling like I've been caught doing something wrong, when in fact that's exactly what happened.

Except nothing *actually* happened.

Teaching someone in the crew how to swim is probably something Weston has done countless times.

But according to Sig, what he hasn't done countless times is spend time alone with a woman, especially when that involves rubbing her almost naked body against his and looking like he was going to kiss her at any moment.

Shit.

He brushes past her, heading down the second flight of steps, and disappears below. I watch him go the entire way, the glow of the few lit torches casting shadows across his muscular back.

Sig clears her throat and my attention snaps back to her.

"What?" I ask when we are alone.

A hint of a smile graces her face before she says, "Nothing." She jogs up the steps and just before she passes me calls back over her shoulder, "Hope you had fun," then disappears through the opening, her footsteps echoing over the deck as she catches up with Jorn.

Fun isn't really the right word to describe it, is it? I'm glad Weston taught me how to swim. I thanked him for it. I'm happy to be out of the sweltering room, but the rest of it is more confusing than fun.

I can't deny the reaction my body has to Weston, and tonight was the worst it has ever been. Call it the heat, the proximity, the confusion at his complete change in behavior, it doesn't matter.

It can't happen again, and it won't.

My time on this ship started out with pretending enough to convince Weston and the Castaways that I trust them, only to get what I wanted: a way out. It shifted to befriending them, but in the process, so much has changed and I feel like the only person I am convincing is myself.

Goosebumps erupt on my skin, and I know they aren't from spending so much time in the cool water.

It's from the reality that after so much time fighting it, maybe I am actually starting to trust Weston.

CHAPTER TWENTY-EIGHT

Heat pounds on my skin as I work, and I need to take extra breaks just to stay hydrated and cool. Jorn finally showed me where Weston hid the mop, so at least I am not scrubbing on my hands and knees any longer.

The heat wave is still in full force, and after passing out for only a few hours this morning, I'm exhausted. The wall of the quarterdeck provides a block of shade, so I huddle inside it and take a swig of cool water from a bottle I snagged from the galley. Only a few Castaways have been out on deck today, most staying below, away from the direct sun with nowhere else to escape to.

The solitude is broken a few moments later as Fin comes bounding out from below. He takes off across the deck, running circles around it, his little voice rising in a yell then trying to crow like Jorn.

"What's going on, Fin?" I call out. He spots me then, skipping over and stopping just before my extended feet. Something has gotten him excited, but with as quiet as the ship is, I can't imagine what it would be.

"Hi Lennox! Guess what? I get to do my job! I get to do my job!" He spins around in circles and then tumbles to the ground.

My spine straightens. Did something happen? Is anyone in trouble? Jorn and Sig are on the island today, but how would Fin know if something had happened to them?

I try to remember what Jorn said about the helio signals and what they stand for, because this is the first time since I've been on the ship that they're going to be used.

"Is everyone alright?" I ask Fin calmly, trying to hide my concern so he doesn't get scared.

"Everything is fine," Weston says as he steps on deck, looking more casual and relaxed than his typical buttoned up, firm captain role requires. His loose shirt falls open over the chest I was intimately acquainted with just last night. He's probably still suffering from the heat down below, with the way his sleeves are rolled and the hem is haphazardly tucked into his pants. But he's not alarmed, not as he would be if someone in the crew were in trouble.

Fin runs to the mast and starts climbing, and I shade my eyes, craning my neck to follow his ascent. He disappears inside the crow's nest for a few moments before dropping out of it and shimmying back down the mast.

"What's he signaling?" I ask Weston, who stopped to watch Fin's progress, too.

"It's too hot for anyone to function, so we're going to the Oasis."

"The Oasis?" Was this the 'somewhere' Jorn spoke of? He didn't tell me details, probably because back then, the crew didn't trust me. That time has passed now.

"You'll see," he says. He shuffles down the stairs, disappearing below before his voice rings out.

"Oasis! Everyone get ready!"

Cheers erupt from all over the ship, and the previously quiet and relaxed atmosphere is suddenly buzzing. I bring my mop and bucket down to the storage closet as Stassia and Auralie come bounding down the hall.

"What exactly am I getting ready for?" I ask as Stassia weaves an arm through mine and drags me toward the steps.

"We're going to the Oasis. It's the only time we leave the ship during daylight hours, so it's a little stressful at the beginning. But once we're in the tunnels, the fun begins."

Within a few minutes, everyone waits on deck for Weston to give direction. He stands at the edge of the ship, blocking the entrance to the gangway, sword drawn and looking severe, before he addresses the group.

"Everyone remember, move quickly, but wait for my signal," he says, and looks up to the top of the main mast. Ryum stands in the crow's nest, a spyglass pressed to his eye as he scans the island.

"All clear, Captain!" he calls down, and Weston turns on his heel, striding down the gangway and making his way to the beach. As I watch him traipse over the jagged rock and onto the beach, my chest flutters with worry at his exposure to an attack. I know Ryum is watching over him, and he has the best vantage point in this scenario, but after seeing Storm with the determination and readiness to fire his crossbow on his face, I can't help but feel nervous.

But it's not just about Weston. It's about every single one of us that is about to leave the protection of Dawnlin.

Weston is alert as he walks, his head swiveling side to side, prepared for any threat. At the entrance to the tunnel, he waves toward the ship, and the group in front of us barrels down after him on the same path he just tread.

I take Fin's hand in mine, and we follow behind Stassia and Auralie. My shoulders tense as I continue to look around, eyes flickering to the ridge above us, all the way to the top of the steps Dane and I took so long ago. As I watch the Castaways ahead of us disappear into the portal, my mind flickers to Mara, when she thought she saw someone down at the beach during the daylight hours. Had she *actually* seen someone? Were the Castaways heading to the Oasis that day, and she caught a glimpse of someone just before they disappeared?

I shake the thoughts away and focus back on getting Fin through the obstacle ridden terrain until we reach the entrance. Weston stands to the side, ushering everyone in. His gaze catches mine for an instant before I step through the portal. Fin and I bring up the last of the group, his small steps making it difficult to keep up.

Weston waits just outside the opening, and I look back to watch as Ryum sprints across the rock and over the sand, before ducking through the portal. Only once everyone else is safely inside does Weston cross through, and his shoulders visibly release the tension they held.

"Everyone alright?" he calls out, and is met with a chorus of affirmations. "Let's go then."

People break out into a run and disappear into the tunnels ahead of us, probably eager to finally be free of the confines of the ship and inside the cool tunnels. Fin lets go of my hand and tears after them, and before I can call out, Weston is brushing past me, his long strides catching up to him easily.

"I've got him," he mutters before he's charging down the tunnel, following the pounding little footsteps and leaving Auralie, Stassia, and me alone.

"Anyone ready to tell me what the Oasis is?" I fall into stride with them as we weave through the land in a direction I'm mildly familiar with after going on so many shifts.

"It's our sanctuary, well, besides the ship," Auralie says.

"With the Voyagers hunting us during the day, we can't really go anywhere and enjoy the island," Stassia adds. "The Oasis is just ours, somewhere we can enjoy on days like this."

We wind further into the tunnels, going down a few I have yet to pass through. A light appears just ahead and gets larger as we approach. I watch it, confused. We haven't ascended, and there don't look to be any steps or ways to get to the surface, so I have no idea where this portal is going to open up to.

The closer we get, the more I see it isn't a portal.

The tunnel ends, the opening in the rock leading to an enormous cavern, and my mouth drops open as I soak it in.

It looks like we are out on the surface, but we aren't.

Light pours into the cavern from a fissure in the earth above, the glow from the suns the same as it was on the beach moments ago. Vast pools of water are scattered, edged by white sand beaches and rock formations. Leafy palm trees grow around the edges, casting shade in places and rustling in a wind that can only be explained by the magic of the island.

Dawnlin created a mini-Dawnlin, an oasis for the people who are trapped and unable to experience the beauty of the land during the day.

"Where does that open up?" I ask, pointing to the crack in the rock above. "How has no one found this place?"

"Our best guess is it's between some of the dunes," Auralie says. "But we've never seen it on the outside, and you can't get through it. It's not a portal. It's more like a window."

I stare at it in disbelief. Just when I think I'm getting used to the island, we find something new and even more amazing.

The Oasis is already full of chaos and laughter. Water splashes as the Castaways run through the beach, diving into the water, causing waves to waterfall into other pools. The cavern isn't immune to the heat wave, and I'm glad to be a little more comfortable with the water now because the thought of cooling down is enticing.

"I'm so glad Captain decided on this today," Stassia says as she peels her shirt over her head and tosses it onto the sand before shimmying out of her pants.

Auralie follows suit, and I balk. Neither of them show one shred of consciousness about stripping down to their undergarments amongst everyone in the crew. Their clothes and weapons pile up at their feet and they stride away, wading into the water.

"Are you coming, Lennox?" Auralie calls back at me as she lowers herself down.

"Don't be shy," Stassia says, gesturing around to everyone else who has also shed similar amounts of clothing. "Nobody cares."

I look around at the rest of the Castaways, and Stassia is right. No one cares. All of them are similarly dressed, and because of last night's lesson, I now understand why.

As the future queen, I've never been around anyone this undressed, partly because the weather and lack of swimming in Blackwood wouldn't allow it. Only my handmaids had ever helped me bathe, as well as Sig when I first was released from the brig, but I didn't consider that scandalous.

Last night, I'd been so concerned with Weston seeing me with almost no clothing in the dark, but little did I know that this was comfortable and familiar amongst the Castaways. He probably didn't care at all.

Yet he still kept his eyes averted, respecting my request to look away, even when I hadn't said it again. My chest squeezes and I fight the unexplainable urge to look around to find wherever he is in the cavern.

If we're unable to replenish the dust, and this is what my life ends up being, I'm going to have to let go of the feeling that it is improper and disobedient.

I'm not in Blackwood.

Before I can talk myself out of it, I breathe deeply and lift my shirt over my head, tossing it on top of the pile beside me. My pants go next, and I stride toward the pool where they are wading. I feel like every eye is on me, even though I know they are not, and my skin tingles under the imaginary scrutiny. I'm hyper aware of every inch, feeling more exposed than ever before in my life.

Except last night.

I bound into the water, and any lingering hesitations after my lesson last night are gone when I see that the pool is similarly shallow. The cool water is an instant relief, and I sigh, letting my shoulders relax as I approach them. It's surprising how comfortable I feel; such a huge contrast to the fear I felt only days ago.

Most of the Castaways are swimming in the pool just above us, and the frolicking and movement sends waterfalls cascading down the rock wall. The trickling of the water intermingles with the shrieks and laughter as everyone lets loose, enjoying their time. Someone cries out, and I glance over to see Fern cascading down a slide carved into the rock before she falls into the water, spluttering and laughing once she resurfaces. Others are climbing up a set of rugged steps to a platform and flinging their bodies off before crashing down and splashing everyone below.

This may be the first time in my entire life that I might actually have fun. There never were gatherings, or plays, no balls or competitions. The closest might have been the time in the tavern, but back then, I wasn't partaking in any of the merriment.

I can here.

There's no one to remind me of how a princess should act, no lesson to get to, or orders to obey.

It's just a group of people enjoying a slice of the endless time that they have together.

Fin screams, and I turn to see him fly through the air and splash into the water on the other side of the pool. He surfaces, gasping for air before yelling, "Again! Again!"

Weston's deep laugh cuts through the noise and I realize he and Eirlik are tossing people through the air.

"I love it here," I murmur, not talking to anyone in particular.

"I live for Oasis days," Stassia says, arching backward to dip her hair below the surface before she wades back toward the beach. She sits down in the damp sand so only her legs are covered by the lapping water.

Fin's cry peals through the air again, followed by an enormous splash. "That was so high!" he screams a moment later, and I giggle, imagining the huge smile on his face.

Water splashes everywhere as Sig comes sloshing toward us, her arms pointed over her head as she cuts through the surface, diving below and popping up far away.

"What took you so long?" Stassia calls out to her.

Jorn runs along the beach behind Stass, shedding his weapons and clothing as he goes. He takes a running leap directly into the larger pool, crowing as he flips through the air and soaking everyone around him.

"Some Voyagers were milling around in the area," Sig says. "We didn't want to leave until it was clear. Doesn't seem like anyone is around now, so we left."

I wade to the beach and sit down next to Stassia as Sig swims up to us.

My eyes dart over to the large pool and snag on Weston. It looks like the Castaways surrounding him are fighting, but laughter rings out as they try to dunk each other under the water. His face is bright with a smile as he watches them, all the anxiety from getting everyone to the tunnels safely completely gone.

His eyes flash to mine, and I look away instantly. Heat rises to my cheeks, as images of last night flicker in my mind, brought on by how similar he looks now, bare skin and wet, tousled hair. It's hard to do on the ship, but I know I need to avoid him and get my bearings back. After last night, this facade of a friendship is starting to feel less fake and more charged than it should be.

I can't start to care.

The day passes luxuriously. We spend it resting in the water, sleeping on the beach, everyone talking and laughing completely carefree. A large blanket piled high with food and drink appears on the beach at some point, and everyone meanders to and from it all day, the pile constantly refilling with different options as the hours go by.

The Oasis is a perfect remedy for the heat. I actually enjoy laying on the beach, my legs extended out into the water as it slowly laps back and forth. I could get used to this kind of water, but the thought of going into the larger pool or anything deeper still makes me a little uneasy.

While I have the basics down after my lesson, I'm still not confident, and with all the ruckus and waterfalls, I'd rather keep it calm.

The suns beat down on my skin as the four of us lay lined up on the sand. I close my eyes and feel myself drifting off, still exhausted after barely any sleep, and truly relaxed for the first time in a while.

"Alright, time to spill," Stassia says.

My eyes remain closed, but I listen, curious what her next rant is going to be about. I'm always amazed at how she can have so much to talk about with people she sees all day, every day.

"I'm talking to you, Lennox," she says.

I don't move a muscle. "What do you want to know, Stass?" I say lazily.

"Please tell me that man is good in bed."

Laughter erupts from my chest, as her statement takes me completely off guard.

"Oh my gods, *Stass*," Auralie says.

"What? Everyone wants to know. Except for Sig."

"Ew, he's like my brother. Please stop," Sig says.

My laughter calms into a giggle, still shocked that she would even ask something like that. I shouldn't be, not with the way she has implied things in the past, but I wonder if Sig or Jorn said anything about how we returned to the ship last night, or if this is just Stassia assuming. There's no way she or anyone else knows how heated things got between us, how aroused he was at our bodies pressing together.

"You can't tell me you've been sharing a bed all this time and nothing has happened. I don't buy it," Stassia says.

"Nothing has happened," I say with a straight face, finally able to calm down my laughter.

"You're being serious," she says flatly, and I open my eyes and turn my head to see her, lifted onto her elbows and staring at me like I just grew another face.

"Yes, I'm being serious."

"Damn," she says as she lays back down in the sand. "I thought maybe that's why you weren't at each other's throats anymore."

"Sorry to disappoint you, Stass." I close my eyes again and focus on the heat beating down on me and the cool water over my legs.

Not on the firm shoulders and hard chest. The muscular arms hoisting me up and pulling me closer. Gaze trained on my lips.

"Ugh, Lennox! If you don't want him, can I please have him?"

"He's all yours," I say.

My fingertips tingle and I fist my hands into the sand, squeezing tightly to make it go away.

Of course I don't want Weston. I want Dane. But giving permission to Stassia doesn't sit right, and I don't want to think about what that means. Maybe it would get Weston off my back and loosen him up a little if they were together. I'd finally get to sleep in my own bed.

Stassia makes a dissatisfied sound and I try to hide my smile, but it disappears quickly as shouts, unlike the earlier playful ones, erupt from the larger pool. My eyes fly open and I sit up, peering over at the commotion in the water.

Something is wrong.

All of us rise quickly and scramble across the beach, trying to see what is causing the frenzy, when Weston and Ryum burst through the surface of the water, hurrying toward the beach.

"Move!" Weston shouts, and the crowd of Castaways parts, giving them a straight shot to the sand. They bound up it, and it's only then that I see what they are dragging, or rather, who.

"Jorn!" Sig screams and pushes past us, sprinting toward them.

Small arms wrap around my leg and I look down to find Fin, pale and wide eyed.

"It's alright," I tell him, and squeeze him closer to me.

Once they're on the beach, they drop him into the sand. He lies completely motionless, his eyes closed and lips blue, and my stomach falls at the sight. Sig drops to her knees when she reaches them, pushing Weston out of the way.

The silence is deafening as everyone watches with bated breath.

"Do you know what happened?" I whisper to Fern standing next to me.

"They were holding their breath, trying to see who could stay under the longest."

I look back at them and watch, feeling like time has slowed. Weston moved to his other side, kneeling next to Jorn's lifeless body the same as Sig, but she is not still. She pushes into his chest, repeatedly, before pressing her mouth to his, breathing her air into him. She repeats the pattern over and over again, and Weston watches, his eyes hard and his face grim.

The moments feel like an eternity as I watch Sig never let up. I've never truly seen death before, and despite my life being threatened multiple times on the island, I haven't known it. My mother doesn't count, not yet anyway.

But Jorn… Jorn would.

My eyes well with tears at the thoughts of what the ship would be like without his presence, his crow echoing through the sails, his laughter and joking nature lightening any conversation.

How will Sig handle his loss?

I cover my mouth, trying to hold in this fear that I'll never speak to Jorn again, wondering how I'm going to help Fin through the loss of his friend, when a gurgling sound breaks the silence.

Jorn moves, his body expelling the water. His coughs and gasps eliciting startled reactions among everyone on the beach.

The tension breaks, and my tears fall as relief floods my body.

He's alive. He wasn't, and now he is.

Coughing, gasping for air, burning.

Nothing.

Is that what happened to me, back when Weston saved me?

Sig throws her arms around him as he tries to sit up, tackling him back to the ground.

He wraps an arm around her weakly, still coughing.

"I knew you'd save me, babe," he says, his voice creaking with a small chuckle.

Sig's body stiffens, and she leans back. "You're an idiot, Jorn Whitehollow!" she screams as she slaps his shoulder and chest repeatedly.

"Never argued with that," he says. He captures her lips in a quick kiss before she pushes him off her. He erupts in a fit of laughter mixed with more coughing, and the terrifying moment of losing one of the crew has disappeared.

Everyone disperses, heading back to different places in the Oasis, but the mood is less jovial.

Sig leads him up the beach, away from the crowd. She is already looking him over and probably scolding him some more.

Fin still clutches my leg, and I bend down and peel his arms off. He still looks stricken, and I wonder if, like me, he also hasn't seen death, despite enduring his sister's illness.

"Hey," I say, crouching down to his level. "Jorn is alright, see?"

He looks past me to where Jorn and Sig sit, and nods.

"I know that was very scary. I was scared too. But it's alright now. We don't have to be scared anymore. We just need to make sure we stay safe in the future, alright?"

He nods solemnly. "Can I go back and play now?"

"Of course. Come find me if you need me, alright?"

"Thanks, Lennox." He throws his arms around my neck and squeezes me tightly before running back toward the rock slides.

I watch as he climbs the stairs to the top, tracking him until he's with someone else. The last thing we all need is another incident.

My eyes snag on someone still on the beach, and I look over to find Weston sitting alone, staring out over the Oasis, watching everyone get back into the activities from before the interruption. His forearms rest on his bent knees, and I can see how tight his shoulders are from here.

Without thinking, I traipse through the sand and sink down next to him, crossing my legs under me. I don't speak. No words feel right, so I just sit and watch everyone as he does.

Finally, I say the only feeling that I can put into words. "I'm glad Jorn is alright."

He doesn't answer. The only acknowledgment that he's heard me is the tick of a muscle in his jaw.

"Does that happen often? Not with Jorn, specifically, just in general?"

"No."

His gaze stays trained ahead, his body still wound tight as he sits with whatever is going on in his mind. Heavy breaths heave through his nose, and I feel like his teeth might crack under the tension of his jaw.

"It doesn't happen often," he finally murmurs, "but it isn't easy when it does."

Vulnerable Weston is not a side of him I've seen. The closest instance may be the first moment we met, but other circumstances kept me from noticing it any more than in hindsight. I don't think he shows it often, and even when he feels it, it still seems like he tries to hide it from the crew.

I lean to the side slightly, enough that our shoulders barely touch. I don't really know what it is like to be there for someone when they need it, but it feels like Weston needs it. Our skin barely brushes and I feel him let out a breath, his shoulders relaxing a bit before pressing a little more firmly into mine.

I feel a pang in my chest, and a lump forms in my throat. Weston is constantly putting up a show of strength and leadership for the crew. He's there when everyone needs him, but who is there when he needs it? From the way I found him sitting alone on the beach, it doesn't seem like anyone.

I clear my throat. "Where did Sig learn to do that?"

"She's from Berrendahr. Spending so much time on the water, it's something they all learn to do."

"Did she teach you?"

He nods, eyes still trained straight ahead.

I glance down at my fingers in my lap, nervously winding them together. I want to know, but I'm afraid to ask, so I keep my eyes trained on my fidgeting fingers so I don't have to look at him.

"Is that what you did for me?"

My lips start to tingle, thinking back to how Sig saved Jorn, pressing into his chest, breathing breath into his mouth and I remember back to that day.

Teal eyes searching mine, water dripping off his soaked face and hair as he hovered over me.

You're alive. Just breathe.

Weston was just as worried about keeping me alive then as he was with Jorn today, and he didn't even know me then.

"I did what I had to do, princess."

I'm starting to feel like these are the words Weston lives by. Everything he does is for everyone around him. Maybe he truly doesn't have an ulterior motive, some hidden plan that he's coercing everyone to be part of. Every decision, every action is what he believes he has to do as the captain, to keep everyone safe.

"You don't have to take responsibility for everyone, you know," I say.

"If I don't, who will?"

I glance back up at him then. His face is still drawn, not as harshly as it was before, but it's clear he doesn't see any option other than him bearing the responsibility.

"And what would happen to them?" he continues, nodding toward the crew all around the Oasis. "Every single one of them is my responsibility, even if they don't necessarily want to be. I can't count on someone else to do what is best for them."

Words escape me. He doesn't know I understand that responsibility more than anyone here, the kind that is thrust upon you, and you don't know if you are capable of it. The responsibility for the well-being of everyone, even if it is at the detriment of yourself. The selfless responsibility, to put everyone else's needs before your own.

Maybe Weston and I understand each other a little more than I thought.

Now that I've seen what happened with Jorn, what was so close to being my fate, and knowing he threw himself into danger to make sure I survived, I can't keep the words in any longer.

"Thank you for saving me."

He finally looks over at me, a small smirk turning up his lips. "I thought you said you were never going to thank me for that."

I roll my eyes. "Will you just accept it and stop being an ass about it? I'm trying to be nice."

He chuckles softly, then turns back toward the pool. "You don't need to thank me, princess."

"I am anyway."

We stay sitting in companionable silence, bare shoulders pressed together, watching everyone around us enjoy the rest of the day, until Fin comes running back over, begging me to watch him try to flip into the pool. It feels like an excuse to leave Weston's side, and I know it has been long enough to confuse all my thoughts all over again. Fin drags me by the hand off the beach, and I perch on a rock with my feet dangling into the cool water.

Maybe eternity won't be so bad if this is what it looks like, surrounded by a bunch of people who watch out for each other, and generally want to be with one another.

I thought my time as a Voyager was everything I ever wanted in life, but looking around now, I realize how different it is. Their time on Dawnlin is full of fear and purpose, but so much of it is solitary. The Castaways try to make the best of their time, living the stagnant life as best they can, while still having hope that they can return home, despite being empty-handed.

I've listened to everything Dane says, heard his stories and arguments, and I believed them. But after living among them, being brought into their crew, treated as an equal and trusted, I just don't know if I believe it anymore. I'm getting the impression that the monster Dane painted Weston to be is the exact opposite, and instead he's a man who truly cares about the well-being of every single Castaway, and wants to make sure that their time here is enjoyable and safe.

Because none of us really knows how long forever will be.

CHAPTER TWENTY-NINE

After the events yesterday, I volunteered to cover Jorn's lookout shift so he could rest and recover, but I'd be lying to myself if I didn't also need the time away from Weston. He agreed to let me switch without an argument, so Sig and I head to the lookout just before dawn.

Watching everything unfold at the Oasis, and sitting with Weston after, knowing now exactly how he saved me and how close to death I was, kept me lying awake in bed well into the night, unable to quiet my mind. I just can't make sense of how someone who would risk themselves to save a stranger matches up with Dane's warnings. Weston would have to be playing a game so deep and so manipulative if his motivations back then were solely to have one more chance at stealing the waters.

Deep down, I just don't think that is true.

I also can't help but wonder what happened between Weston and Dane that caused such friction that Dane's perception would be so skewed. And what happened to cause that scar?

Would my mind change about either of them if I find out the truth?

I hoist myself through the trapdoor behind Sig as she sits on the rail with the direct view of the mountain, feet crossed out in front of her.

Now that we're alone, I can finally make sure she's doing alright. She's never shown that much emotion before, and quickly buttoned it up just like Weston does as soon as everything was back to normal. But just like with Weston, I want to be there for her the same way she's been there for me.

"How are you doing after yesterday?" I ask, and hop up on the rail across from her.

She lets out a deep sigh. "Fine. It's never easy, but I'm sure you won't be surprised to hear that this isn't the first time it's happened."

I huff a laugh and shake my head. "I haven't known him very long, but with Jorn, I am not at all surprised."

She shakes her head and rolls her eyes, the hint of a smile on her lips.

"What's going to happen with you two? You know, if we get back."

"I don't know," she murmurs quietly. "Probably nothing. He'll go back to his kingdom, and me to mine."

"Would either of you change your mind and follow? You seem like you care about each other. Why would that change just because we make it home?"

She stares off toward the mountain. "It's not that simple," she says, her head swiveling toward me, her eyes filled with sorrow. "Not when you aren't the one that can decide who you marry."

I search her face, confused. "Why wouldn't you be able to marry Jorn? The only time I've ever heard that happening is if..." My voice trails off as what she said clicks.

Sig is royal.

Just like me.

My mind reels, and I grip onto the railing tighter. Names of the ruling families shuffle through it until I remember.

Berrendahr.

The seaside kingdom that shares a border with Blackwood. The kingdom Sig is from.

"Otin," I whisper. "Signee Otin."

She nods slowly, watching me figure it out.

"My father is the king. Well, I assume my brother is now."

Zyke Otin, the king that stepped into power after his father fell ill, is her brother. He isn't much older than my father, still a young king in the spectrum of our world.

"Zyke is king now." I don't explain how I know. The lines and names of the royal families of other kingdoms isn't common knowledge for someone who is a maid in the castle. I thought I was the only one, but now I know there could be others hiding among not only the Castaways, but the Voyagers too. Keeping the royal lineage hidden wasn't only my decision, Sig did too. And there could be more.

She nods solemnly. "I knew, deep down, but hearing it isn't easy." A tear falls down her cheek, and I cross the space to wrap my arms around her. She squeezes me for a second before releasing me and swiping her hands under her eyes.

It wasn't my intention to bring her more pain after what sh dealt with yesterday, but I'm glad it happened. Sig trusts me enough to tell me more about who she is back home. I thought I would feel elated when that happened, like I'd finally accomplished my goal, but it hasn't been on my mind at all.

I can't even remember when I stopped thinking about it. I've just been living, and learning, and truly getting to know everyone, and it's just... felt right.

"Why not stay here, then?" I ask. "Why go back when you can be happy with Jorn and live in paradise?"

She speaks slowly, choosing her words carefully. "I've been here a long time, and while I love every person on that ship, living stuck in time for eternity isn't the way I want to live. I don't want to be deprived of what it is to actually *live*. I want to experience what it is to be human.

I want to know what it feels like to grow old, and have a family, even if it isn't with who I would choose."

Her words hit me like a slap across the face, but she continues before I can say anything.

"If my fate is to remain here, with all of you, then I will live the best life I can, and mourn the loss of what I thought I would have. But when it comes down to it, I wouldn't choose it. I don't think any of us were truly meant to stay here forever. This place is meant to help us save someone we love, which means we return home. That's why I have hope Dawnlin will let us."

When I'd been deemed unworthy, my first decision was to remain here with Dane. If I didn't have my mother, I had nothing else to return to. My life in Blackwood was not better than the one I had found here, filled with all the experiences and relationships I'd only dreamed of.

Sig's perspective shocks me back into reality. My life in the castle is unfulfilling because I didn't have any of the experiences I wanted, and didn't think I ever would. But here, I truly wouldn't.

My life as the future queen may not have been exactly as I hoped, but it was still my life, and I could live it.

And I could change it.

I'd already proven that to myself, seeking the island, and finding the impossible.

I understand now more than ever why Weston wants to help everyone get home, even if it is empty-handed.

"Hopefully, we all can live the lives we dreamed of." I swallow the lump in my throat and fight back my own tears.

Sig is right. The Castaways are making the best out of a situation they cannot control, trying to live happily every day, but how long can you live without actually living? Is eternal life worth living without purpose?

What about all my dreams of seeing the kingdoms, forging relationships, and becoming a fair queen? Like Sig, love may never be in my grasp, but a family can be, and not just one that I've chosen here.

A scream breaks through the air, piercing the sound of the waterfall and falling straight into my ears, distracting me from my thoughts.

I know that voice, and my blood runs cold.

Roley.

The shrill scream sounds again, and I run around the lookout, peering through the trees, trying to find where it is coming from.

"Where is he?" I cry as I scan the space around us, to no avail.

"I don't see anyone!" Sig says as she circles around the lookout, leaning over the rail to get a better look.

On the third scream, I can't stop myself. I need to get out of here and find him.

"How do we get down?" I yell to Sig.

She shakes her head. "We don't, Lennox. We can't leave the lookout."

"I'm going down there, Sig. I'm not going to abandon him."

I step up onto the rail, hanging on to a pillar for balance as I reach out and grab the nearest tree branch.

"Shit! Lennox, wait!"

I barely think as I descend the wooden beams that hold the lookout in the air. I don't wonder about the magic that keeps it hidden, or prevents anyone from stumbling into it. I don't think about the danger I'm putting myself in.

All I can think is that Roley needs help.

Jumping off the last rung, my feet slam into the ground and I take off in the direction of the screams, trying to stay just inside the line of the trees, off the main path.

"Help!" Roley cries again, from deeper in the forest. Turning toward the sound, I push the foliage out of my face as I crash through the dense trees. By the sound of his voice, he can't be far.

"Roley!" I scream, hoping he will hear me and respond so I can follow his voice again. The trees thin out just ahead as I charge forward, heading for the open space, when I hear another cry for help.

Movement catches my eye and I stop, pulling my bow off my chest and nocking an arrow. I creep forward and my eyes fall on Roley, suspended in the air by thick green vines, covered in long, sharp thorns. They don't just hold him, though. They slither quickly through the space, wrapping around trees, writhing across the ground, twirling around themselves to get to him. He's in a cage, no weapon in sight, and no way out.

He sees me then, and a sob escapes him. "Lennox! Help me!"

"Don't move!" I yell. Footsteps pound behind me and I gasp, spinning and raising my bow, only to lower it a moment later as Sig bursts through the leaves, sword drawn and scanning our surroundings.

"Shit," Sig hisses as her eyes fall on Roley, suspended in the air.

"We have to help him," I say. I don't care that we aren't supposed to interact with the Voyagers, he's my friend. He's a child. I won't leave him here to become a victim of the island.

"Of course we're going to help him." She jogs around the perimeter, staying just out of reach of the vines.

"Lennox, look! Right in the middle, there's a stalk where they're growing from."

I dart over to her side to follow her point. From this side of the cage, I can see it clearly, a thick trunk growing from the ground, with branching ropes extending out the top in all directions.

"We need to cut it, but there's no way to get in there," Sig yells.

Roley whimpers above us, and my heart pounds louder in my ears. I need to get him out *now*.

I raise the bow and line up my shot. This might be the only way, and I have to work fast.

"Roley, listen to me!" I yell. "I'm going to try to kill it. You might fall, and it might hurt a lot, alright? But we're going to get you out!"

"We have to take him back after this," Sig hisses in my ear.

"I know. He saw you," I mumble, and let out a breath. Releasing the string, I watch as the arrow sails through the air and hits my mark, tearing a huge gash into the stalk. An ear piercing squeal erupts from it, and Sig and I throw our hands over our ears. Vines lash out toward us then, as the others shake Roley in the air. Sig lets out a cry as one wraps around her leg, and she hacks at it with her sword.

I grab another arrow and let it fly, following quickly with a third. With the last arrow, the stalk starts to turn brown and shrivel. The thorn covered shoots unwrap from Roley's limbs, flinging him to the ground where he lands in a heap. The vines retreat into the stalk, hissing and squealing as they go, until it disappears into the ground, as if it were never there.

I run, dropping to my knees in front of him, Sig close behind me.

"It's alright Roley," I say. "Anything hurt?" I grasp his shoulder, turning him from the curled position he landed in so I can assess him.

"Just the cuts," he whimpers. His clothes are torn, and puncture wounds cover his entire body. He needs the salve immediately. We don't know if the thorns had any poison in them, and we can't risk taking too long to find out.

"It's alright. We'll get you all cleaned up," I say.

"Lennox, we have to go," Sig says. Her unease is palpable, and I nod quickly and turn back to Roley.

"Roley, you're going to come with us, alright?"

Terror fills his wide eyes, and he shakes his head roughly.

"No! She's a Castaway! I can't go!" he cries and tries to crawl backward away from me, wincing in pain as he moves.

"I promise it will be fine. You have to trust me."

His head swivels between Sig and me, and I see reflected in him what I believed before, that the Castaways were monsters and being with them would change who we are.

"Come on, Lennox," Sig grumbles.

"I'm going to carry you, alright?" I lean toward him as a rustle of leaves causes his eyes to flick over my shoulder.

I spin around, looking past Sig, and my breath catches in my throat.

Sword raised to strike with fiery hatred in her eyes, Mara charges right toward us.

CHAPTER
THIRTY

"Mara! No!" I scream, as she lifts the sword over her shoulder. I leap forward, tackling Sig, and pushing her out of the path of the sword that comes swinging down over us, right where Sig had been standing a moment ago.

We land on the ground in a heap, but quickly scramble to get back to our feet. Mara's sword is embedded in the ground, her strike so fierce it pierced through the soft dirt. She yanks on the hilt, grunting and screaming before it releases, and she turns on her heel, stalking toward me.

"You!" she screams, the tip of her sword pointing directly at me. "You were trying to take him!"

"Mara, please, listen to me!"

"You fucking traitor!"

Her sword slices through the air, aimed right at my head, and I duck under it.

"Mara, stop!" I yell as she charges at me. I stumble backward, almost falling to the ground, trying to keep my eyes on her when I feel Sig grab the shirt at my shoulders and yank me away and back to my feet.

"We need to run!" she yells, and I don't hesitate.

I turn and bolt.

Sig is steps ahead of me, her longer legs giving her an advantage. Leaves and branches tear at us as we push through the forest toward the open path, in the opposite direction of the lookout. We can't go back to it; it would lead Mara straight there.

"Shit, we left Roley!" I yell to Sig. Mara's steps pound behind me, and I push myself harder, trying to stay out of reach of her sword.

"It's too late! We need to get out of here!" Sig yells. I can barely hear her from the pounding of my feet and heart, the swish of the leaves as we fly past. We weave and dodge, trying to throw Mara off, but she knows Dawnlin as well as we do, if not better. We burst through the tree line and sprint across the main path into the grassy plains that lead to the cliffs.

"Where do we go? We need a portal!" I scream at Sig's back. She stumbles in front of me, then picks herself back up.

"They're too far, and we can't lead her right to one. We have to lose her!"

Fuck, she's right.

If we lead her to a portal, she will know exactly where we can enter and exit. She'll know how we get across the island. There's no way of knowing how long she or others would wait for someone to use it. We'd be putting Castaways in danger. We—

Pain erupts in my arm and I scream, the intensity so strong I fall to my knees. The tip of a blade pokes through the front of my arm, and bile rises in my throat. I reach behind and pull the knife out, dropping it to the ground as another wave of pain comes over me and my mind spins.

Sig skids to a stop in front of me, her eyes wide as she yells at me, but her voice sounds far away. My ears ring and my stomach rolls. Squeezing my eyes shut, I shake my head.

Focus. You'll die if you don't.

Sig's scream cut through the fog. "Behind you!"

I can't think. I clutch my arm and blood oozes through my fingers as I roll to the side, just as another knife sticks into the dirt where I knelt.

"Castaway scum!" she screams as her sword drives down toward my head again. My eyes snag on my bow laying in the grass, and I reach for it, scrambling for some way to protect myself from her next strike.

My fingers wrap around the wood and I shove it above me, just as her hands come down again. The metal blade hacks into it, splintering the wood, and jarring my limbs, weakening me enough that I don't know if I'll be able to ward off another strike.

I have to get through to her.

"Mara, listen to me! We don't hurt our own, remember?" I yell as I crawl backwards, the heels of my boots slipping on the slick grass under me.

"You aren't one of us! You chose them!" She pulls a knife from her belt, eyes blazing down at me. "And now I'm going to bring you back to Dane, and he's going to see you for the traitorous bitch you are."

My arm slips out from under me and I fall, slamming my other into the ground with a cry. I can't fight her off. My bow is broken and useless without both of my arms. I let go of it and try to move, try to scramble back away, when suddenly Sig is there, her fist slamming into Mara's cheek.

The force of Sig's blow whips Mara's head to the side, and her knees hit the ground. Sig stumbles forward, catching herself before she's on me in the next breath, yanking me up to my feet as I scream in pain. Our feet pound on the ground as we get farther away from Mara. I hope Sig's punch was enough to give us time.

"Cap taught you how to swim, right?" Sig says as she runs alongside me, not ahead any longer, her hand gripping my arm and urging me faster.

"Uh-huh," I say, and her plan clicks in my mind.

We sprint through the grass, straight toward the edge in front of us. Mara is behind, screaming and giving chase.

Pain sears through me with every pump of my arms, but we don't slow down. All I can see is the edge, the expanse of water below. My nightmare flashes before my eyes, the first ever I had here, with the Voyagers and Dane chasing me off the cliff. The fear I had then, so different from the fear I have now, but it's as if the island knew.

Was Dawnlin warning me?

"Don't slow down! We need to clear the rocks!" Sig yells, and lets go of my arm. "Point your feet and take a breath. Do you hear me, Lennox?"

I can't respond to her. I can't do anything but run and think about hitting that water below. The edge gets closer with every step. I don't think. I don't stop. My foot hits the edge and pushes me into the air.

I'm weightless.

Wind whips at my clothes and hair as my arms and legs flail, running without purchase into what just days ago was my biggest fear.

The surface gets closer with every second, and I slam my legs together, pointing my feet and sucking in all the air I can before I crash into the abyss below.

The world goes dark.

My flailing arms are now sluggish, fighting against the thick force around them. What I thought was searing pain before is only worsened with movement and the salt of the sea.

This is nothing like the pool. There's no ground under my feet, no way to stand when I feel overwhelmed, no Weston to save me. Rough currents flip my body over it self, and I can't determine which way is up. I kick and kick, hoping it's the right way.

Please be the right way.

My chest burns and squeezes. It's too far. My vision blurs, and panic takes over my body as I fight the treacherous water.

Air.

I need air.

Kicking and fighting the urge to breathe in, remembering Jorn only yesterday, his lips as blue as the water I'm immersed in. I kick harder, toward the space above me, the space that is lightening.

The gasp that erupts from my throat as I break the surface hurts, and I heave the air in and out, the tears seeping from my eyes mixing with the rivulets running down my face. Before I can get my bearings, waves crash over me, rolling me under again. I flail, trying not to lose sight of the surface when fingers grasp mine and tug. I squeeze them and hold tightly until I break the surface again, to find Sig bobbing next to me and clutching me to her.

"We need to get to the rocks," she yells over the crash of the waves around us.

The weight of my soaked clothes pulls me down, and my arm is useless. Sig swims to the side with perfect strokes and I try to follow, kicking and paddling slowly behind her, trying to make it before the next wave comes crashing down on us.

We reach a large sharp rock jutting out of the sea, and I grab hold, clinging as hard as I can with only one arm as my chest still heaves breaths. I dare to glance up at the top of the cliff and find Mara pacing back and forth, scanning the water below.

"Shit, Mara's still up there. She's looking for us," I say.

Sig walks her hands around the back of the rock, gesturing for me to follow. We sink low into the water, trying to stay hidden. I don't know what she can see from her vantage point, but maybe she will think the water took us. She probably still thinks I don't know how to swim.

Mara continues pacing until she lets out a feral yell, the sound muffled by the crash of the water around us. We wait a few moments longer after she disappears from the edge, pulling our shoulders farther out of the crashing surf.

"How's your arm?" Sig asks.

"Pretty bad. I can't really use it."

Her jaw ticks and she looks past the rock toward the island. There's no beach under the cliffs, the sheer face extending directly into the sea.

"We need to make it back. The entire way, I want you to think really hard about needing safety, alright?"

I nod. Is that how portals appear? Have the Castaways figured out how to ask the island for help? Is that how Weston snuck through the back of the cave when I couldn't?

I'll have to ask Sig later, because right now, I need to focus on safety. I won't be able to swim around the island like this, so I have no choice but to beg Dawnlin to help.

Sig starts toward land and I paddle behind her with one arm, struggling to stay above the surface. I focus on safety, just like Sig told me to the entire way. The last bit of distance disappears as the waves push us into the cliff. We cling to the rock as waves pound at our backs.

We're barely there a moment before the rock above us begins to shift, disappearing where we clutch it, forming a rock ledge that leads straight into the wall.

"Thank the gods," Sig breathes.

She reaches over and yanks me up, my feet kicking for purchase to pull my body up into the opening. I gasp and grunt as I fall down onto my arm, rolling quickly to my other side to get the pressure off it.

Sig pushes herself over the edge, her upper body falling into the opening until she can crawl forward on her elbows. The moment we are both inside, the wall seals shut again and we're cast in darkness. Neither of us moves, the sound of our panting filling the tight space.

I don't regret anything that just happened, although my body is screaming otherwise, and I know I'll have to answer to Weston later.

Roley is safe, and hopefully relatively unharmed. But Mara?

This is not at all how I expected this shift to go.

"We need to get back to the lookout. We shouldn't try to get back to the ship in the daylight."

I manage a grunt. The pain in my arm is escalating again now that all other threats are gone and I have nothing else to focus on.

"Alright," I say and sit up, hissing with even the slightest movement of my arm. Blood drips down my fingertips and splatters on the floor.

"We need to move. That needs to be bound until we can get to the infirmary." She grips my good arm and pulls me up, and we walk. Torches light with our every step as we follow the path, which quickly connects to the Castaway tunnels. Sig recognizes where we are and leads us back in the right direction.

Climbing back up into the lookout is rough, and tears run down my cheeks by the time I flop onto the wooden floor.

Mara threw a knife at my back. More than one. After everything we bonded over, after she saved my life, she forgot it all. I'm the enemy now. A Castaway. Nothing in our shared history or friendship mattered enough to even listen to what I had to say.

The thought makes a pit in my stomach threaten to swallow me whole.

I'm thankful it was just my arm, but *fuck*, I cannot wait for the healing salve. The bleeding hasn't slowed, and Sig drops to her knees next to me, urging me to sit up. She rips my sleeve off at the shoulder and ties it around the gash tightly, eliciting an aggravated groan from my lips.

"Fuck, Sig, that hurts," I growl.

"She got you good. We need to stop the bleeding because I'm not carrying you back to the ship."

The sleeve is soaked through already, so we rip another strip off the hem of my shirt and tie it tighter, then she uses my other sleeve to make a sling to keep my arm from moving and restarting the bleeding. Once I'm situated, she rolls up her pant leg, and I notice why she was limping as we ran. The vine that had Roley caged must have gotten her when it lashed out. Her pants are covered in blood from a ring of deep gashes all the way to her knee. They've mostly stopped bleeding, but she keeps the pants rolled up, letting the wounds breathe.

The air is buzzing. Even though I'm not looking anywhere but at the wooden roof of the lookout, I can feel it. It feels like the island is awake, like it was watching everything that had just happened and is paying attention.

It feels like there's more coming.

"You could have let her get me," Sig says, and I drop my head to the side, looking toward her. "Why didn't you? You would have been free to go back."

Sig is right. It would have been easy to let Mara take her out and go back to camp without anyone knowing until we didn't return that night. It would have been easy to return with the news of the healing waters' location.

That has been my plan since I was captured, to find the right time to get back to the Voyagers.

But it doesn't feel right anymore.

The thought of Mara harming Sig makes my stomach sink. In that moment, I didn't think, I just acted, and I don't regret my decision.

I settle on an easy answer. "You saved me, and now we're even."

"I think there's more to it than that, but I'll accept it. Thank you." She looks down at my soaked bandages and winces. "Besides, now it's your turn. Cap is going to kill you."

I can't help but chuckle, remembering what she said after she pulled me from the sinking marsh. It seems like so much time has passed since then, so much has happened.

Because it has.

Everything feels different now, and today proves that.

"I can handle him," I say with a laugh and look back up to the roof.

"Of that, I have no doubts," she says quietly.

Voices sound in the distance, and our stares snap to each other instantly.

"They must be hiding near here! I swear, Dane, it was her!"

Mara.

We scramble to our feet, crossing the space to the rail overlooking the main path. Sig grips it tightly next to me and we both peer out, looking for the source of the sound.

"Tell me what happened exactly," Dane's voice says, just before they step into view.

Mara, Dane, and Storm all walk along the packed dirt, scanning their surroundings. Mara still has her sword drawn, and Storm has his crossbow loaded, the same way as before, when Weston and I spotted him.

Mara proceeds to recount the details to Dane as they walk around the area, cutting in and out of the trees. When she gets to the part about striking me with her knife, he whirls on her.

"You did *what?*" he yells, his face contorting with anger.

"She's a traitor, Dane! She's one of them now!" Her voice rises, matching his tone.

"She's being tricked, Mara! Once we get her back, we'll convince her again. She'll see reason. But not if she's maimed in the process! No one is to lay a hand on her, got it?"

His words make me squirm. In the depths of my being, I don't believe them anymore. I don't feel tricked, or convinced, or manipulated. For the first time in my life, I finally feel like I can make my own observations and decide for myself. I've lived among them, been accepted as part of them, been trusted. It can't all be part of a sinister plot. It can't be fake.

They round the curve in the path, and my heart speeds up.

"They can't see us, right?" I murmur to Sig, my body frozen.

"No, they shouldn't be able to, but we never had them look for us like this," she whispers back.

Neither of us move so much as a finger. I can barely breathe as they walk directly in front of us, scanning the area below the lookout, touching trees, moving leaves.

They're trying to find a portal.

Dane steps backward into the open path and looks around. His gaze moves over the trees and I hold my breath as it falls right on us.

And sees nothing.

He looks straight through me, without so much as a blink until his gaze moves past us and they continue down the path.

I let out the breath in a deep sigh. I thought I might feel doubt when I saw Dane again. Despite changing my mind about the Castaways and not believing Dane's stories any longer, a small part of me wondered if all those feelings would turn back again the moment I looked into his eyes.

I wanted to. Everything I had worked to build, to gain trust, to find a way back, was to get home to him. I wanted him to look at me and remind me of everything that was between us, of the future he wanted together.

But just like he looked through me, I looked through him, too.

He may not have known it was happening, but I did look into his eyes, and I can't help but feel that everything has changed.

CHAPTER THIRTY-ONE

arkness creeps over the sky before we finally leave the lookout. Dane and the others lingered in the area for hours before giving up and going elsewhere, and I felt a sense of relief wash over me once they were gone.

It has disappeared now though, as we head back through the tunnels to the ship, and dread slowly fills me. I know I told Sig I could handle Weston, but it is significantly worse this time around than after my first shift. If he was angry about some mud, I don't want to see his reaction to this.

Hopefully, the gods are looking down on us and Weston is below deck, so Sig and I have a chance to sneak to the infirmary and get rid of the evidence. My blood-stained shirt with missing sleeves isn't exactly inconspicuous. That's not even considering all the other grass and dirt smeared over us, and my wild waves from the salted water.

Sig doesn't look much better.

After Mara saw us and brought Dane and Storm to search the area, we can't take any chances that they aren't still out looking. We take extra precautions when we exit the portal before hurrying to the gangway. The deck is dim and quiet, and relief floods me as my feet hit the boards, until the soft sound of voices carries to my ears.

I hear Weston before I see him. Stopping in the middle of the gangway, I drop my head back, closing my eyes and bracing myself for what's about to happen.

"Oh fuck, here we go," Sig grumbles under her breath.

Our steps drag as we take our time to get to the deck, but once we crest the top, my worries are realized. Weston sits perched on top of a barrel, his back to us, as he talks with some of the crew. Auralie and Stassia are among them, everyone lounging on the deck or other crates and barrels, enjoying the balmy, clear night.

He hasn't seen us yet, and I glance toward the entrance below and consider making a run for it. The opportunity disappears when Auralie spots us, her eyes and mouth growing wide. Silence falls over the group as all eyes shift to us. Weston turns to look over his shoulder, his smile dropping quickly, only to be replaced by a hardened jaw.

"Clear the deck. *Now*," he commands and springs to his feet. Everyone in the group jumps up and scrambles, disappearing below deck without a word or a glance in our direction. Weston charges toward us, a look of fury on his face that I haven't seen since we came back from my first shift.

"Someone better start fucking explaining," he growls, as he looks back and forth between us. He jerks to a halt, barely an arm's length away as his eyes trail over me, up my slung arm and over my blood-soaked clothes to the dressing. His knuckles turn white as his fists clench at his sides. Shoulders pulling back and stiffening, he looks like he's ready to pounce, but holds himself back.

He's not touching me like last time, not after I told him not to.

Sig starts to speak, but I cut her off. She isn't responsible for what happened today. I am, and I won't let her try to take the fall for me.

"We were attacked. It was my fault. Sig had nothing to do with it."

He looks sharply at her. "They found the lookout?"

"Not exactly." Her words trail off and he stares expectantly.

"I climbed out of it. Sig followed, so I wasn't alone. We were found, and we escaped."

"What possessed you to climb out of our safe hold?" he grinds out.

I know my reason will soften his anger. At least I hope it will. He knows what it is like to protect people he cares about, and that is all I did today.

"My friend was in trouble. He's close to Fin's age. There was no other option. I had to help him."

Just like you helped me.

"She saved his life, Cap, and mine." He glares at her, but she continues, "She pushed me out of the way when Mara attacked."

"Who saw you?"

"Only Roley and Mara," I say.

"She brought Dane and Storm back to the lookout to search for us," Sig explains. "They looked right past us. The island kept us hidden."

"Why didn't you come straight back?" His eyes darken as he looks down at my arm again.

"We couldn't risk coming back in daylight, not with them searching for us. We went back to the lookout and waited until nightfall," Sig says.

His glare settles on me again. "You didn't go back."

It isn't a question, but I can hear the word left unsaid.

Why?

I don't have an answer for him, because I honestly don't know the answer myself. So I take the easy way, just as I had when the questions got tough earlier.

"I stayed with Sig."

"Leave, Signee," he growls, his gaze fixed on the floorboards.

Sig glances at me, and I give her a small nod. She knows I can handle his wrath alone, especially when I did exactly what Weston would have done. Despite how it turned out, we came back to the ship. Both of us. That must mean something to him, after all this time.

"Aye, Cap," she says, and steps around him, limping toward the steps until she disappears below.

Once the sound of her footsteps fades, he steps away from me, hands on his hips, and begins pacing.

"Can you please explain to me why you keep putting yourself in danger?" His voice is still harsh, full of anger and frustration, but he refuses to look at me.

"I'm not doing it on purpose."

His head snaps up as he shoots me a glare, and I retract my words.

"Alright, today was on purpose. But I had a good reason."

"No reason will ever be good enough to put yourself at risk."

"You're wrong, and you know it."

He halts, his body turning toward me as he speaks. "I'm not wrong, princess. You disobeyed my orders, you put yourself and Sig at risk, not to mention those of us that would have had to come get you if they had captured you."

"He's a child! He's barely older than Fin! He could have died, and I wasn't going to let that happen. You would have helped him too, just like you helped me. You wouldn't have done nothing and just let him die. I know you wouldn't have, because despite everything that I've been told, deep down you're not the monster you've been made out to be."

"It's different with you." He brushes past my declaration like my changing beliefs about him are the most meaningless thing in the world.

"Why is it different with me?" I snap.

"Because I'm responsible for you."

"You're responsible for every one of us, yet you clearly treat me differently. I'm the only one that gets yelled at for facing the dangers out there. I'm not fucking breakable!"

He steps forward, gesturing at my bandaged arm. "Clearly, you are. You were reckless. No one else comes back to my ship having put themselves in danger."

"Every time we leave this ship we put ourselves in danger."

"You let your guard down!" he yells, throwing his arm up wildly toward the beach. "I told you to never let your guard down. That girl shouldn't have been able to *touch* you with all your training, yet here you are, wounded and bleeding on my watch."

"She threw a knife at my *back*, Weston. What did you expect me to do?"

His eyes fly to mine at the use of his name, and I flinch, surprised myself at how easily it slipped out.

He looks away again, his face sobered, the wild anger from moments ago hidden away back under the stern facade of the captain.

His voice is dangerously low. "You're off shift duties until I say so."

Turning abruptly, he stalks back toward the steps, but I chase after him.

"You can't do that! You can't just trap me here!"

"It's my ship princess, I can do whatever the fuck I want."

All the old feelings of being trapped in the castle, hidden away and isolated from the world, come rushing back, and I do everything to stomp them down. I won't let him do that to me, not here, not without an explanation.

"Why are you doing this to me?"

"To keep you safe!" he yells over his shoulder.

"Bullshit! Stop being a coward and tell me the real reason!"

An angry growl erupts as he spins back toward me, and before I can even process his change in direction, his hands wrap around my face and his lips crash into mine.

My mind is a blank void.

The fight.

The pain.

The chaos.

It's all gone.

There's only Weston.

His lips move against mine, hard and desperate, like I'm the only source of air and he can't breathe.

Oh gods, Weston is kissing *me.*

And I don't want him to stop.

His hand moves off my jaw, weaving through my hair and cradling the back of my head, angling me to deepen the kiss and causing my eyes to flutter shut. My head spins and my knees buckle, but he doesn't let me fall. One arm releases me and wraps around my waist, pulling me tighter to him, so the toes of my boots barely touch the floor.

Desire rushes through my veins, and I sigh into him, my mouth parting slightly, and he doesn't waste it. His tongue slides along mine, stroking and savoring and igniting an inferno inside me. I reach up and fist his collar, pulling him closer, the pain from my arm that's trapped between us completely forgotten.

All I can feel is him.

His grip tightens, his fist clenching in my hair and I moan into him, the sound only fueling him more. He bends, not breaking the kiss, as he picks me up so we're on the same level, wrapping my legs around him and pulling me against his body.

A memory from the night in the pool flashes in my mind. It was the last time he held me this way, and now there's no doubt this was exactly what was on his mind. As fast as the thought came, it's gone again, replaced by the need to get even closer.

I clutch his jaw, his closely shaven beard prickling my palm and scraping against my chin as his lips and tongue continue to move against mine, sending chills down my spine with every movement. His grip tightens on my ass as he hikes me higher, and I tilt my hips into him, pressing myself against the ridges of his muscles.

Every previous thought I had about him, every worry, every perception, is shattered, only to be replaced with his feelings. Worry, protection, concern. He pours it into the kiss.

Is this why he's been so domineering? Because he cares about what happens to me?

I weave my fingers through his hair, my nails scraping the back of his neck, which is met with a low grumble in his chest.

Then he tears his lips away.

As quickly as it started, he's gone, and lowering me down until my feet hit the deck as he abruptly steps away.

"Fuck!" he yells as he turns his back to me, throwing his arms up and tugging at his hair. I stumble slightly, my balance thrown from the lightheaded daze that kiss left me in.

What the fuck just happened?

My chest heaves as I try to catch my breath, my mind still reeling as I watch the tension ripple through his arms and across shoulders. Lacing his fingers together behind his head, he stares out across the ship. He doesn't move; he doesn't speak. There's only the rolling of the waves and the creaking of the ship in the silent night.

"Fuck," he mutters under his breath, before he stomps toward the stairs and disappears below. Not a word or even a glance back as I stand here reeling, my lips swollen and tingling, and my stomach flipping over.

"Jorn!" His yell comes from somewhere in the ship, followed by muffled voices, then Jorn's crow.

The solitude of the deck grounds me, and every part of this day rushes back. Now it's my turn to pace.

Once again, my world on Dawnlin has been completely turned upside down. Everything I thought I knew, thought I understood, thought I felt, is brought into question yet again.

And then he does this.

He kisses me, then immediately regrets it.

The sinking feeling in my stomach tells me *he* may have, but I didn't, and that somehow makes it all worse.

I looked into Dane's eyes today, watched as he and the others searched for me. I heard the way he spoke about getting me back, and convincing me again that he is right. There's no doubt in his mind that I will come back to them, to *him*, and that everything I've learned and experienced here is all a lie.

But I didn't.

I didn't go back.

I could have jumped out of the lookout again, ran straight into his arms, and been back at camp minutes later. Sig wouldn't have followed that time.

I didn't move.

The pull I felt to return to Dane when I was first taken by the Castaways has dulled, almost completely disappeared, the only remnant one tiny sliver of doubt from unanswered questions.

My mind spins as I pace, and my emotions are so overbearing that I'm starting to feel numb, except for the throbbing pain starting up again in my arm.

Footsteps pull me out of the reverie, and I look up to find Sig slowly approaching. Her clothes are changed, her limp gone. She takes in my face, which I'm sure looks as stricken as I feel, but there's no judgment or question there, just a friend standing to support whatever I'm going through.

"Come on," she says quietly. She extends a hand to me and I reach out to take it. "Let's get that arm cleaned up."

CHAPTER THIRTY-TWO

ig and I walk straight to the infirmary, ignoring the stares and questioning looks aimed at us the entire way. I can't wait to wash all this grime off and crawl into bed and shut my exhausted mind off from the constant onslaught of thoughts. Mara's attack, seeing Dane, and now Weston. I just need this pain to go away so I can start over tomorrow, and hopefully figure out where to go from here.

"Sit," Sig says, pointing to a chair tucked against the wall. I plop down on it and start to remove the sling, wincing with even the slightest movement. The wound stopped bleeding hours ago, but has rendered my arm almost completely useless. I'm grateful for Dawnlin's magic, so I don't actually have to let this heal. The pain will be gone in moments, but the memory will last.

Commotion erupts on the other side of the door and it sounds like something is happening in the mess. Muffled shouts and laughter float through the air, followed by the scraping of tables and chairs on the wood.

"I'm sorry I'm keeping you awake after the shit day we had," I say. She's already cleaned herself up and healed her leg, but instead of joining the rest of the crew or heading to her room, she stayed with me.

Even after all the danger I put her in.

"Don't worry about it. We need to get this taken care of," she says. "Besides, with all that," she tilts her head toward the galley, "we'll be lucky if we get to sleep anytime soon."

She crosses the room and opens a cabinet filled with supplies before scanning over them and pulling out specific items. The familiar jar of salve catches my eye and I almost heave a sigh of relief at the sight. She sets everything down on the chair next to me and sits on a stool in front of me, angling herself so she can better see the puncture that goes completely through my biceps.

"What are they doing in there?" I ask as I watch her practiced hands move across my skin, cleaning and dabbing with a linen bandage.

"Playing games. Probably drinking."

"You don't want to join them?" I grumble as she moves my limb, trying to better access the other side, biting my lip and trying to remember the pain is almost over.

"Someone has to keep their wits about them," she says as a chorus of roars erupts outside. Her movements are gentle but firm, and I hiss when she douses the opening with some liquid. She doesn't flinch at all, and no one would guess that this strong woman tending to wounds is a princess like me. It makes me wonder if she learned it all here, or if this is part of who she was back home, too.

"I probably should have offered you a drink before I did this," she says with a chuckle.

"No, I'm fine," I grunt out. I don't want to do anything that might loosen my inhibitions, not after what happened on deck. Not after how that kiss made me feel, especially knowing he regretted it before it was even over. I still have to sleep next to him tonight, and adding alcohol to my already muddled mind won't result in anything good.

"Why didn't the captain use this stuff when I cut him in training?" I ask. He walked around with his arm bandaged for days before a dark pink line took its place on his skin, but I never asked why. I was avoiding him then, and I wonder if Sig will tell me, or if she even knows.

"He doesn't like using too much of the magic. He says he's thankful enough for everything Dawnlin does for us. He doesn't need to ask for more of it."

I must have made a face because Sig laughs.

"I think it's stupid too."

"Is that why he has that big scar? He refused it then too? I'm sure you gave him a piece of your mind about that one," I say.

She hesitates, and I can see her thinking, choosing her words carefully. "We actually didn't have it when he got that one. He probably would have taken it then. That was a nasty slash."

Her lips press together like she wants to say more, but stops herself. She leans in to look at my arm a little closer, so I don't pry.

Someone shouts 'no', which is met by a chorus of laughs and cheers, the sound so loud it feels as if we're in the same room.

Once she's satisfied with her cleaning, she grabs the salve and smears it over the opening on both sides. At the first touch, the pain disappears, a cool tingling left in its wake, followed by the warmth of healing.

I breathe a sigh of relief and drop my head back against the wall.

"Why does he treat me like this, Sig?" I murmur.

I can't let it go. I have to ask. It is blatant that Weston treats me differently than the rest of the crew, and after tonight, I thought it might be because of some repressed feelings. But after watching him walk away, without so much as a look back or a word other than cursing his actions, I don't know what to believe.

Sig knows him better than anyone else. She isn't afraid to challenge him, and he clearly trusts her. Maybe she knows something I don't.

Her lips form a line, and she stays focused on her task, wrapping a clean bandage around my healing arm.

"Cap has his reasons."

I sigh heavily. "That's all everyone ever says. He has his reasons. What are the damn reasons, Sig? Why won't anyone tell me?"

She looks me in the eye, her face serious. "I'm not trying to keep things from you, but it's not my place. I understand what you're saying, and I'm not saying I don't see it. I know he doesn't treat you like the rest of us. I just hope you can be patient and trust him enough to accept it."

The fabric constricts as she pulls the knot tight, and I try to wiggle my fingers, the movement already coming back painlessly.

I don't know how to respond to her, so I stay quiet. I know I'm coming to trust Weston and everyone else in the crew, but I don't understand why he doesn't trust me enough to give a reason. Why will no one tell me the truth?

We clean the infirmary quickly, the strain between us evident after her continued secrecy. The noise from the game has not let up and instead has only escalated to the boards shaking under our feet. Once we're in the hallway, she gestures to the galley.

"I'm going to grab some food to eat in my room. I don't want to listen to their shouting in that proximity. You've got to be starving, too. You should grab a plate."

Sig is right; with all the developments of the day, food hasn't even crossed my mind. I'm starving and exhausted and confused, but the last thing I want is to be in the same room as Weston.

"Sure," I agree and follow her into the galley. A resounding cheer rises from the group as soon as we enter the room, followed by a yell from Jorn.

"Sig! Lennox! Come play!" There's a chorus of agreements, but Sig shakes her head.

"Go back to your game, Jorn," she calls as we fill up plates.

I keep my gaze trained on the food, refusing to look over at the crowd, at Weston. The back of my neck tingles as I feel like one particular set of eyes is on me, watching me move through the galley behind Sig.

"Boo!" the group yells at our response.

Sig waves them off and we walk straight back to the door, just as Stassia walks through it.

"Stass!" Everyone cheers.

Is part of the game saying everything in unison?

I must be hungry, or flustered, or both, because something as simple as that doesn't usually grate on my nerves like it is right now.

"I want in on the fun!" Stassia yells and saunters over to the group. "Scoot over!"

Chairs scrape and bodies shuffle, but I keep my eyes averted, my shoulders relaxing the moment I step back into the hallway. Another round of laughter sounds behind me and I ignore it, instead bidding Sig a good night and heading to my room. The sconces brighten as I enter, and the lantern on Weston's desk lights as I set my plate down and slide into his chair.

I want answers, and I feel like I deserve them. I can't keep being treated differently without knowing the reasons. So many of my feelings have changed based on my time here, but there's still a sliver of doubt that I can't get rid of, especially with all the secrecy.

What if how I'm feeling is wrong?

What if it really is all a trick?

Do I really believe that?

It feels like there's something looming, something that Weston doesn't want me to know, because maybe it would change everything.

More than the kiss did.

I shake my head and squeeze my eyes shut. The kiss changed nothing. It was obviously a mistake, nothing more than a release from the tension of the other night. A roar erupts from below, and the room shakes with the noise. Sig was right, again. Sleep is going to be futile until whatever is going on down there dies down or breaks up.

My eyes roam over the maps spread across the desk as I pick at my food. Since I'm going to be awake, I might as well try to do something useful with the time. I think back to my map, and how the island gave me the tools to create it when I wanted to be methodical.

There's got to be something we are missing, just like we all missed when searching for the healing waters. Eventually we deciphered the signals, the pattern. The ship is full of people who figured it out, but not the dust. After all this time, the same people who found the waters can't find the dust.

Is the dust something that can even be found?

Does Dane actually know how to replenish it, and is lying about it? Or is it all real, and our time on the island is about to be infinite?

While I don't believe what Dane says about the Castaways anymore, I don't think he's lying about the dust. He can't be. But what I can't figure out is what he could possibly gain from keeping everyone here? He's the Guardian, the one that can bring us to and from Dawnlin, but why can none of us go back to him and ask to return? Does he really care about who comes and goes?

I scan the maps, trying to find patterns just as I did with the waters, but nothing stands out to me. All it is doing is making my head hurt and my frustration grow.

After I finish my food and still have come up with no new tactics, I finally give up and get into bed. A stack of books sits on my bedside table, and I grab one off the top. The island brought me some I haven't read before, and I hope they will provide a solid distraction from the continued laughter below.

I'm definitely not using them to stay awake until Weston returns.

Absolutely not.

CHAPTER THIRTY-THREE

Just as I turn the page to start a new chapter, a loud thud outside the room breaks my concentration. Jorn's boisterous laughter cuts through the quiet ship, followed by another thud, and I roll my eyes. The noise from the mess continued on late into the night, then gradually died down as I sat awake, reading. This might be the end of it, which can mean only one thing.

Weston is on his way back, and by the sounds out in the hallway, he either lost the game miserably, or he took heavily to the bottle.

Probably to make himself forget his mistake.

I stare hard at my page, but can't focus on the words. He's going to walk through the door any second, and I'm suddenly regretting being awake when he does. Although, the sheer amount of noise would have prevented me from sleeping even if I hadn't been reading.

I set my jaw and stare down at the page, trying to ignore the sinking feeling in my stomach, knowing I have to face him after everything that happened today.

The door slams into the wall as Weston stumbles to the ground, cursing under his breath. My spine straightens as I crane my neck, trying to see if he's alright, only to find him on the floor, on his hands and knees.

Laughing.

He shushes himself, then grabs hold of the doorjamb, trying to get to his feet again.

He must be beyond drunk.

My mood softens slightly, unable to be too mad or hurt when he's laughing at himself. Closing the book, I set it on the bed and watch as he rights his body, leaning his shoulder against the frame, until he looks up, his eyes falling on me.

"Shit," he mumbles under his breath. "I woke you."

"Being asleep would be a requirement for you to wake me. Everyone was doing a pretty good job of making sure that didn't happen."

"I'm sorry, princess," he slurs, glancing away.

He straightens and tries to step forward before swaying on his feet. He looks like he's about to fall flat on his face before he reaches out and grabs hold of the doorway again.

I stifle a laugh. Avoiding him is impossible, so I might as well get it over with.

I slide out of bed, feeling more exposed in Weston's shirt tonight than I ever have before. My bare feet pad across the wooden floor, and I watch as his gaze trails up my legs, stopping where the hem falls on my bare thighs. I doubt he even realizes he's staring, and I can't keep the heat from my face as his eyes darken the closer I get.

I've never dealt with anyone this drunk before, let alone someone of his size. Brynne has told me stories of having to manage off duty guards in the same state, but hearing a story isn't the same as trying to catch this large man if he falls.

"Come on, let's get you in bed," I say.

He shakes his head violently, squeezing his eyes shut and wobbling slightly.

"No. You're hurt. I would hurt you. I don't want to hurt you." He winces, then dares to look at me again.

"I'm not hurt anymore," I say, lifting my arm and moving it around. "See?" He watches me move without an ounce of pain, until his eyes fall to my thighs again, and I realize the flapping and waving only caused the shirt to hike higher up, exposing more skin.

"You were hurt. Bad," he mumbles, his voice so low I almost didn't hear him.

"I was, but I'm not anymore. Sig took care of me."

"It should have been me," he says, his words still slurring together.

"You weren't the one who jumped out of the lookout. It never would have been you," I say.

He heaves a sigh and shakes his head again. I wonder if he always feels he has to take the burden off everyone else. What made him feel so responsible?

"Alright, come on," I say, taking the last step toward him and reaching out to lift his arm. He jerks it away and turns his head in the opposite direction.

"No. I'll sleep in the tub," he says, and takes a step forward, before tumbling to his knees. I dart out in front of him, grabbing his shoulders and pushing them back to keep him from toppling over and slamming his face into the ground.

He falls forward, his hands wrapping around my waist, his fingers digging into my sides. I feel the flex of his fingers, before his hands fist in the fabric, and I realize the mistake I made, putting us in the same position we were in hours ago.

Except this time, he's on his knees.

And completely intoxicated.

He looks anywhere but my face, and I gulp down the lump forming in my throat. He won't kiss me again, not if he regretted it immediately last time.

"You're not sleeping in the tub," I say, my voice breathier than it should be. "Because if something happens, I can't lift you out of it."

"Jorn would help, just get Jorn," he says, his eyes still averted.

A laugh escapes me. "If you're any indicator, I don't think Jorn will be useful for anything tonight."

"Sig then."

I roll my eyes and groan. "Ugh, will you just do as you're told?"

A grin breaks out across his face, and he giggles like a little boy at some unknown joke. His chin lifts, and his eyes are full of laughter as they meet mine.

"Yes, princess," he grumbles, and a shiver runs up my spine.

Just get him into bed, Lennox.

Stepping to his side, I lift an arm so it is draped across my shoulders, and he pushes up to stand, wavering slightly once he's back on his feet. We take a step together, and I stagger under his weight. There's no way I'll be able to fully support him. He's more than double my size and towers over me, not to mention how heavy his limbs are because of the drink. We shuffle and stumble together across the room, just barely past the desk, when he clears his throat.

"I shouldn't have done that, princess. It won't happen again."

The low rumble in his chest would normally make my stomach flutter as I feel it where I'm pressed into his side, but the words filled with sincerity cause it to sink instead.

Even as I read, trying to drown my own thoughts away with someone else's words, I couldn't stop from replaying his kiss in my mind. The way he held me, the way he pulled me in tighter, his fingers twining in my hair, the scrape of his beard on my skin. When I kissed Dane, it was thrilling, exciting, and new. I enjoyed kissing him, and I wanted more.

But kissing Weston felt like I was on fire, and he was consuming me with every stroke of his tongue and press of his fingers. Every shared breath took mine away, and nothing else existed. Not the ship, not the crew, not the island, not even the immense pain I'd been suffering through all day.

I thought he felt it too, but I was right.

It was a mistake.

It's obvious now that every time we were close, there was something holding him back. But in that moment, he lost control. I could see the desire in his eyes, even now when he's too impaired to try to hide it, but desire wasn't enough to overcome whatever is holding him back after the unusual friendship we've developed.

I wasn't enough.

The last thing I want is for him to see any hurt in my eyes, to know that my fingers started tingling and my chest tightened the moment he said it will never happen again. I need him to think it meant just as little to me as it did to him.

A temporary lapse in judgment.

The result of being too close to someone for too long.

The result of sleeping in the same bed.

Just pent up tension and frustration that needed a release, and now we can move past it.

I must have stayed quiet for too long because he speaks again before I can think of what to say.

"I'll get in trouble," he mutters under his breath.

"In trouble?" I scoff. "By who? You're in charge around here."

He giggles softly, his shoulders shaking, and I can't help the smile that breaks across my face.

"I can think of a few people. You being one of them."

"It's alright, Captain. Chalk it up to a stressful day," I say, hoping to brush over the conversation and just focus on getting him safely across the room.

"So it's back to Captain?" He looks down at me, his eyes glassy and his face unreadable. "You called me Weston."

Calling him Weston was a slip of the tongue, mostly out of anger, and trying to get him to see the situation from my perspective. It wasn't intentional, but I can't say that it didn't feel good once I did, especially the moment I saw him realize it.

He leans into me, his weight pushing down on my shoulders as he brings his face closer to mine, his breath tickling my ear.

"I liked it."

My stomach drops again, but this time not in the bad way. I need more space between us, especially if his inhibitions are this low, and he can't control what comes out of his mouth.

"I shouldn't have done that. It won't happen again," I say, repeating his exact words back to him. I stare down at our feet and quickly add, "I was mad at you."

The last thing I need is him reading more into it, especially since I'm trying to convince him that the kiss was nothing. I don't want him to think I liked it, just like he liked when I said his name.

A grin breaks out across his face and his eyes sparkle. "You're always mad at me, princess."

"I am not *always* mad at you. I can't help it if you're an asshole a majority of the time."

He giggles again. "Only you think I'm an asshole."

"Hm, I wonder why that is?"

He nods exaggeratedly. "Point taken." He staggers again, falling onto me, and I struggle to push him upright. His arm has fallen down over my chest, and dangles as we walk. The pressure of his body leaning on mine pulls my shirt in all different directions, and I realize I probably should have put on pants before we did this.

"You are very drunk. Maybe I can handle drunk Captain."

"Don't get used to it, princess. It doesn't happen often." His smile softens for a second before he looks down at his feet.

So, it only happens when you have to wash away the mistake you made hours before.

We finally make it to his side of the bed, and I pull his arm away from my shoulders and try to stand him upright. He stumbles backwards, falling into the doors of the armoire, a fit of laughter taking over him.

"It's not funny," I say through my own giggles. "Can you hold yourself up? Lean against the furniture if you need to."

He leans back, stabilizing himself, his head lolling to the side as his eyes flutter closed. I take the chance to scan his vest, checking for any blades he may have tucked away, but it is empty. He still has his belt on, though his scabbard is empty. Thankfully, he removed any weapons before he started drinking because we could have been back in the infirmary with as many times as he's fallen tonight.

I hesitate for a moment, then get over it quickly. There's no way he will remember any of this tomorrow, and it needs to get done. I reach down and pull at the leather strap to undo his belt, and see his eyes stutter open out of the corner of my eye.

"Are you trying to undress me, princess?" he grumbles, and I squeeze my thighs together.

"No wearing outside clothes in your bed, remember? I'm just following orders, Captain," I say with a smirk, as I yank the belt off roughly and set it on the ground beside him.

"I think I'll make an exception." A muscle in his jaw ticks as he pushes off the armoire, swaying for a moment before catching his balance. "I can do it."

I take a half step back and try to catch my breath as my heart pounds in my ears. He looks down at the vest and reaches up, his thick fingers fumbling over the knots and only tightening and tangling them.

My shoulders heave with a sigh as I step closer again, reaching up to brush his hands away and take the laces in my own. I suck my lip between my teeth, ignoring the fire licking up my arms at the brush of our fingertips as I move him out of the way, and keep my eyes trained on the task.

Once all the knots he worsened are untangled, I push the vest over his broad shoulders, and it falls to the ground. Before I can step away, he reaches over his head and pulls his shirt off, dropping it to the floor beside him.

My breath stutters, and I try not to stare at the bare chest towering over me, the hard planes I was pressed against hours ago so close once again. It would barely take anything to lean forward and brush a kiss across his skin, and see if his breath stuttered like mine.

I take a swift step away and look off to the side, hoping my thoughts are not written all over my face. He sways and reaches out for my shoulders, steadying himself again, and I can feel his gaze searing into my face. I can't help but look up then, just as a pained look crosses his face and he pins his stare to the ground.

His voice lowers to a grumble. "I really don't want to ask for this, princess." He pauses, my mind wandering to all the possibilities of what his request could be.

"Will you help me with my boots? Please? If I try, I'll fall over. Or be sick. And I don't want to do either."

I chuckle at his vulnerability. I don't think Weston is used to asking for help from anyone. He's the captain, the strength for the crew. Asking for help probably doesn't occur often, especially in the state he's in.

"I should make you do it yourself as punishment," I say with a smirk. "That's what you get for drinking too much."

"It was necessary," he mumbles, and I feel a pang in my chest. My smile drops and I tilt my head so he can't see it before crouching down and pulling at the laces of his boots.

"You're not going to make some snide comment about me kneeling for you, are you?"

"I would never say something like that to you," he says, then chuckles. "Jorn might, but I'd kick his ass for it later."

"You didn't have a problem making a crude joke toward me before," I say.

It seems so long ago now, back when I wanted to hurt him in training, especially after making that comment in front of the crew about my dream. Not that anyone would know what he meant except for the two of us.

He winces, the drink making it so he can't hide it as well as he usually does.

"I shouldn't have said that. I was…distracted."

His voice seems sincere again, and I don't want to go further into it. Bringing it up already stirred up too many unwanted feelings that are just making our closeness worse.

I stand again and step out of his way. He keeps his pants on, sticking with his exception to the rule for tonight, and shuffles forward. He falls onto the bed, kicking his boots off behind him before spinning on his stomach toward his pillow. A deep sigh escapes him and his eyes flutter closed as his entire body relaxes, the tension in his bare shoulders loosening and the creases in his forehead disappearing.

"Thank you," he murmurs.

"Anytime, Captain," I mutter back, my feet stuck to this spot. He breathes heavily for a moment, and I tear my eyes away from him, bending to push his clothes out of the way so he doesn't trip if he gets up in the night. Just as I'm about to stand, he mumbles softly.

"You're going to ruin me."

My head whips toward him, but before I can respond, he's already deeply asleep and snoring softly. His arm dangles over the side of the bed, his demanding and crushing lips now soft and parted slightly.

It won't happen again.

I gulp down the disappointment and embarrassment and focus on finishing my task of making sure we still have a captain in the morning. Reaching down, I grab his arm to tuck it up under the pillow, and my eyes catch on the gold ring I saw before. After that night, my first attempt at escaping the ship, I never paid it any mind again, but now, after knowing his story, that he came to Dawnlin for a woman, I wonder if that is where this ring came from. It isn't a wedding ring, but maybe a promise ring?

But if he's promised to her, why is he kissing me?

His arm is dead weight as I lift, and something catches my eye.

I lean in, looking closely at his limp fingers, and notice the ring isn't the same size all the way around. The band changes shape as it disappears under his finger. I bite my lip, feeling like I shouldn't look, but my curiosity wins.

With a quick glance at his face to make sure he hasn't woken to my touch, I reach out and spin the ring, exposing the other side. The gold band expands into a wide, circular plane, and my eyes catch on the design pressed into it.

I almost drop his hand.

My breaths become shallow and ragged, and my head feels light and unsteady. Slowly, I set his hand beside his face, gentle enough that he doesn't stir. I back away quickly, unable to take my eyes off of the ring, even from far away. Throwing my hands to my head, I try to suck in deep breaths and calm the erratic beating of my heart and churning of my stomach.

I knew he was hiding something, but I didn't know what. My gut told me he had secrets, and I'd just discovered one. He's worn that ring facing in since I stepped foot on this ship so I wouldn't see it, wouldn't catch him in his lies.

My mind reels as I try to fit this new piece of information into the world around me, but I have no idea what it means.

I need answers now more than ever.

My feet have a mind of their own, and I pace the length of the room, glancing back every so often to make sure the noise hasn't woken him. I could wake him, demand he tell me what it means, and with the state he's in, I doubt he'd be able to effectively lie to me.

No. I'd corner him tomorrow. I'd get my answers. If he lies to me then, when he has the wherewithal to decide on his own, I'll know that this was all a game. I'd make my final decisions then.

He will have to explain, in detail, why he is wearing a ring with a seal stamped on it.

The seal of a kingdom.

The seal of *my* kingdom.

Weston is from Blackwood.

CHAPTER THIRTY-FOUR

ounding at the door makes me stir, and I squeeze my eyes shut, waiting for it to stop. I'm too tired to get up, because I couldn't fall asleep for what felt like hours after discovering Weston's ring. My eyelids feel like they are full of sand, and my vision blurs when I try to open them. The suns have barely begun to rise, and the room is still dim, so I shut them again and nestle back into the warm comfort of the bed.

Nuzzling back into the pillow, I shift my shoulder and press into something firm and warm. My eyes fly open and my body stiffens as I realize why I'm so warm and comfortable. Weston's body is wrapped around mine, and all of my senses heighten instantly. I don't move. If I do, I might wake him and I don't want him to know I found us curled up in each other like this.

His bare chest is flush against my back, pressing into me firmly, and the heat coming off of him sears me through the thin shirt. His arm is under my neck, his elbow bent so it folds over my chest, his hand clutching my opposite shoulder while the glint of that ring teases me in my peripheral vision. His breath tickles the hair on the back of my head, and I try not to squirm.

I must have moved though, because without warning, he pulls me in tighter, his arms constricting around me, and I swallow a gasp. The shirt has ridden up over my hips in sleep, and his other arm is draped over my hip, his hand splayed over my low abdomen. His skin sears mine, but I can barely feel it over the throbbing between my thighs as his leg presses, wedged between them.

His breaths are even with sleep, and I close my eyes, trying to slow mine to match. Heat pools between my thighs as he clutches me closer again, our aligned hips fitting more firmly together, as his hard length presses onto my backside.

How long have we been like this? The drink must have removed all his inhibitions, at least in his sleep, enough for him to migrate to my side, invading my space and forever altering what I'll think of whenever I get into this bed.

The pounding that woke me sounds again. Whoever was banging on the door clearly still needs the captain. Weston jolts behind me, inhaling quickly in my ear. I relax my face, trying hard to seem like I am still asleep despite the pounding in my chest and tingling over every inch of my body.

I know the second his mind clears because the heat disappears. Everywhere his body was pressed against mine is now cold and empty, and he slowly slides his arm out from under my neck. The bed jostles underneath me as he moves farther away, and I stay still, breathing steadily and focusing on keeping my face relaxed and neutral.

"Fuck," he curses softly behind me.

There's more pounding on the door, followed by Weston's footsteps crossing the room. The latch clicks as he opens it before murmuring, "I'll be right there."

He pads back over, and I listen to his every move, waiting for him to leave so I can relax. I'm not ready to confront him just yet, especially not after waking up to the press of his body on mine. I need to clear my head, to remember what I discovered, and the questions I want answered.

He leaves a few moments later and softly shuts the door behind him, just before the latch clicks, and I immediately roll to my back, chest heaving. My skin feels like it is on fire, and tingles everywhere he touched me, like it misses his contact.

He lost control again. This time, his subconscious mind took over and eliminated the space between us. I would be lying to myself if I said I didn't want to be close to him, too.

But after my discovery of his lies, after knowing he thinks it is all a mistake, I can't feel that way. I need to stay focused. I need answers.

Energy thrums through me, not just from what happened moments ago, but also from my discovery. The ring. Blackwood.

I will confront him, but first, I need to question someone I thought I trusted, someone who has been complicit in his lies this entire time.

Sig.

I dress quickly and push the door open, making sure he isn't in the hallway leading to Sig's room. The ship is quiet, the early morning rays just peeking in through the opening to the main deck. He's nowhere in sight, and I breathe a sigh of relief before striding swiftly down the hallway.

I burst through the door without knocking. Sig is sitting up in her bed, back against the wall, with Jorn's head propped up on her lap. She takes one look at me with whatever emotions are displayed on my face, and her expression falls.

"Shit. You need to leave."

Jorn looks confused as she pushes him up and rushes him out of the room. Tugging me inside, she closes the door firmly and leans her back against it.

"What did he do?"

I ignore her question. Now isn't the time to discuss how confusing Weston's actions have been compared to his words.

"What do you know, Sig?"

Her lips form a line. "I told you, I will tell you what I can. I've said that from the beginning."

"So you lied to me, too?"

She shakes her head. "No, Lennox, I haven't lied. Just tell me what happened."

"Where did he get that ring?"

Her mouth falls open slightly, eyes widening. I caught her off guard, because she clearly wasn't expecting the ring to be what I asked about. She hasn't had enough time to concoct a lie, so maybe I'll finally get some actual answers.

"He's always had that ring, as long as I've known him."

"Don't lie to me. Where did he get it from? He must have taken it from someone."

She takes a step toward me, her eyes pleading for me to believe her. "I'm not lying Lennox. I've never seen him take it off."

"I trusted you, Sig! And now I don't know what to believe!"

"I swear to you," she says, and raises a fist to her chest. "He's had it since the day we met, since the day he arrived on Dawnlin." She pauses and takes a deep breath. "I remember because that ring is what gave Dane his scar."

My stomach bottoms out and I gape at her.

"S-say that again?" My words stutter as disbelief courses through me. Surely I heard her wrong. Dane told me how he got that scar, the scar I wanted to run my fingers over, to brush my lips against. The scar that caught my eyes immediately back in Blackwood, part of what made him look so different from any of the men I'd ever seen before.

"Weston's ring cut Dane's lip open. That's how he got his scar."

"No, Dane told me how he got that scar. He said he tripped as a child and fell into a doorframe. His family didn't have money to take him to a healer."

She shakes her head. "That may have been what he told you, but I watched it happen, Lennox. I have no reason to lie about that, and you asked me how I knew he had it. Why would I bring it up if it wasn't true?"

My breaths become shallow as, once again, everything I thought I knew starts crumbling beneath me.

"I know you have training," Sig continues. "You're no novice to a fight. Throw the punch in your head. You'll know I'm telling you the truth."

I do as she asks, my mind's eye imagining Weston throwing a punch. The round, thick portion of his ring lining up right where Dane's scar cuts through his lip.

I sway on my feet, my eyes falling away from Sig as the reality of what she is telling me sinks in.

Dane lied.

On a night he said was all about earning my trust, he lied to my face.

Was anything he ever said true?

I know from living amongst the Castaways, from getting to know Weston, that what he's said about them hasn't been accurate, but I told myself there had to be a reason for such a mischaracterization.

"Why did Weston punch Dane? Why would he punch the Guardian?" I ask.

She pauses and I look up, searching her face.

"He wasn't the Guardian when it happened," she says. Her shoulders fall as she lets out a deep sigh. "Lennox, Dane killed the last Guardian."

A loud ringing fills my ears as I stare at Sig. This is it. The last sliver of hope I held that everything I had experienced with Dane was real and true. It is the final piece of the story that kept me from completely trusting Weston.

"No. Weston did," I say firmly, trying to keep my grasp on something Dane told me, something I knew to be true. But how did I know it was true? There was never any evidence, anything to convince me other than the word of the Guardian, the protector of Dawnlin. It was only ever a truth that was accepted among all the Voyagers, because the person we had to trust to bring us here was the one who said it.

"That's what Dane tells everyone," Sig says softly.

"Why would he tell everyone if it was a lie?"

"To hide what he did, to make sure everyone believes his illusion. But I saw it happen with my own eyes. I watched him stab the Guardian, the kind old man who had just brought me to Dawnlin hours before, and told me to wait for him as he left for another call."

My chest heaves with stuttered breaths, but I remain silent as she speaks, soaking in everything I've been wanting to know for months.

Her eyes squeeze shut before opening and landing on my face again, as if she's trying to convince herself that finally telling me what I need to know is the right thing, that she won't be in trouble for finally filling me in on the truth.

"The suns were descending in the sky, and I was worried I would be alone all night in this brand new place. I knew nothing about it other than it held the cure I sought. I sat at the plateau and waited for him to return until the air began to shimmer and the Guardian started to appear with a tall man standing beside him."

"Weston," I whisper, and Sig nods.

"They hadn't fully appeared yet before they were falling to the ground. Someone had catapulted through the glowing dust, taking them both down from behind."

I don't have to confirm it this time. I know that was Dane. Weston told me he came to Dawnlin the right way, for someone he cared about. Dane said he sought Dawnlin for his sister, but now I know that was a lie. It all was. I should have known the moment I found out he lied about who he was, when I laid eyes on him as the Guardian.

Sig continues.

"Everyone was stunned, the Guardian included. He confronted Dane, telling him his actions cheated the magic, and he needed to return immediately. Dane refused, only yelling he needed to be here. The Guardian reached into his pouch for more dust, and Dane pulled a knife, stabbing the poor man and killing him right in front of us."

A gasp rips from my lips as tears well in my eyes. I'm stunned, unable to move or do anything but listen as Sig keeps recounting her first experience in Dawnlin.

"Before I could do anything, even react, Weston punched him in the face and tackled him. Weston was already at a disadvantage, his sword useless when they were fighting on the ground, and Dane already had his knife. I watched Dane slice him open, heard Weston cry out as Dane rolled his body off him and watched as blood seeped through his clothes."

A sob wracks my body, and the tears that welled in my eyes stream down my face. I've seen that scar, seen how jagged and mangled it is. Weston hadn't lied to me. He told me Dane gave him that scar, and I assumed he did something to deserve it.

How wrong I had been.

Dane attacked Weston after committing a heinous act, all in the name of needing the magic of the island.

"Dane left Weston for dead, bleeding into the grass. He didn't even notice me standing there watching everything. He stole the pouch of dust off the Guardian's body, and ran, disappearing into the forest. I tied up Weston's injury and got us out of there as fast as I could, dragging him through the island until we found a cave that was hidden enough we couldn't be seen from the outside.

"We holed up there for weeks, and I was shocked when food magically appeared for us. It was rough for a while, but once he made it through, we were in this together. We got to know the island, mainly at night until the ship appeared. It was like Dawnlin knew where I was from, and the best way to hide us, just offshore.

"Eventually, we found the healing waters, and when we both weren't worthy, we had no way to get back. We've been watching and waiting ever since, trying to take innocent Voyagers out of Dane's clutches and find all of us a way home."

My legs threaten to give out underneath me, and I almost fall to the ground. My head spins and I stagger to the side, catching myself on the edge of her bed. I suck in deep breaths and try to blink away the dark spots that appear in my vision.

Lies.

Everything that I learned from Dane, all lies.

Dane killed the last Guardian, not Weston.

Dane didn't come to the island for genuine reasons, and snuck in after Weston called the Guardian.

Dane tried to kill Weston.

That last sliver of hope I held onto tightly, that everything I had experienced with Dane was real, splintered, cutting me deeply like a blade of truth.

Dane has been the one manipulating me all along, not Weston.

"If all of this is true, why didn't Weston just kill Dane? Why, after all this time, didn't he end him?"

Sig smiles softly. "We aren't like him, you know that by now. Weston won't kill him unless there's a reason. But…" she trails off, biting her lip nervously.

"What, Sig? Just tell me." I don't know if I can handle being shocked by anything more. I just need her to tell me everything, now, all at once.

"We think if someone kills the Guardian, they become the Guardian. Neither of us wanted to be tied to Dawnlin for eternity, so Dane lives."

"But now you're trapped here, anyway. You can't go back to him to go home, not after that."

She nods. "That's why we search every day for a way home, one without him."

My stomach rolls and I double over, bile burning the back of my throat as I heave and gag.

I thought I loved this man. I thought he was everything I ever wanted, and it turns out it was all a lie, concocted by a murderer to keep control of everyone on the island.

Sig's hand strokes circles on my back as my body heaves and sobs.

"I didn't know," I choke out.

"There's no way you could have."

I sit back on my heels and look at Sig, only to find sympathy written all over her face.

"It's Dane that wants the healing waters for himself, isn't it?" I murmur.

She nods, her eyes softening. "It's why Cap won't let any of us go back to him. Dane can't find out where the waters are hidden."

"How could I be so stupid?" I sob, running my fingers through my hair.

"You aren't stupid, Lennox. An evil person weaponizes love and affection. They use it to blind someone, and get them to believe it is all true, while tearing them down and making them dependent. Just because Dane did this to you doesn't mean it's your fault. It's hard to see it when you are immersed in it. Sometimes, we need someone to help us see through it, to show us that the reality we know isn't the only one."

Tears cascade down my cheeks as emotions crash through me. My shoulders shake and my face is swollen, but Sig stays beside me the entire time, letting me know I'm not alone.

"He let me hate him, all for what Dane did to him," I say, choking on the words.

"He tends to do that," Sig says with a soft smile. "He doesn't like to see other people suffer. He'd rather do that himself."

I scrub my hands over my face, trying to push away the pain that is overwhelming my body.

"You never answered my question," I say, once I'm finally able to catch my breath again. "Why does Weston have a ring with the Blackwood seal on it?"

"You'll have to ask him that."

I hold her gaze, trying to read what she isn't telling me, the part that she *can't* tell me.

Because he told her not to.

"You know who I am, don't you?"

"I—" she starts, then stops, her eyes widening.

I jump to my feet. "Don't lie to me, Sig! You know who I am, don't you? Does he know too?" I point behind me, toward the main deck.

"Lennox..." She pushes to her feet, her voice pleading, but I don't hear if she says anything more.

My head spins and rifles through every detail, every conversation, every word ever spoken between us.

The panic on his face when I almost died, his demands that I eat, his orders to confine me to the ship, to be in his presence, his constant protectiveness.

His regret after kissing me.

Princess.

It isn't just a stupid nickname he uses to irritate me.

Weston knows who I am. He forced Sig to keep it a secret.

I need to find out how.

Just when I think my world feels stable, something rips that feeling away from me. Everything has changed, and it all started with Mara attacking. I didn't expect the avalanche that would come after it and I feel like I'm drowning, and something tells me it isn't over.

I almost know everything I need to make my own choices, to see things in my own way, not just how others tell me. Dane took that ability away from me, just as my father has always done, but now I'm taking it back.

After all the chaos, the change, the feelings and emotions, there's one thing I know for certain.

I'm a Castaway now, and I need the truth from my captain.

CHAPTER THIRTY-FIVE

bang echoes through the hallway as Sig's door slams into the wall when I storm from the room. I fly up the steps to the main deck and spot Weston standing with his back to me, looking out over the side of the ship. He's not alone. Some of the crew have already started their daily tasks in the early hour of the morning.

Anger rises in me as my eyes fall on his back. Dane lied to me this entire time, but despite all the truth Weston has admitted, he's also lied about something that is too important for me to let go.

And after last night, after this morning?

After he keeps pushing me away, then drawing me closer?

Now, to find out that all of it has been laced with lies about what he knows?

I can't hold it in any longer.

Eirlik stands near the mainmast, and I stomp over to him, pulling his sword from his scabbard and marching straight at Weston.

"Oi!" Eirlik yells from behind me. "Captain! Incoming!"

He turns right as I level my sword at the center of his chest.

"You better start fucking explaining, Captain."

He is completely unfazed. The only acknowledgement is his eyes traveling up the blade of the sword, then landing on my scowl.

"I don't know what you're talking about, princess."

I swipe at him and he reacts, leaning back just out of reach before straightening again.

"Cap!" someone yells, and Weston reaches up, snatching a sword out of the air and holding it at the ready.

"I think you know exactly what I'm talking about," I say through clenched teeth.

"If you're going to point a sword at me this early in the morning, the least you can do is enlighten me, so I know what we're fighting about now."

He holds my gaze, and we stare each other down, waiting for the other to strike first. I could pick any number of things that have happened since yesterday, but there's only one thing that matters. He's told me to trust him, time and time again, and I do.

Did.

He needs to answer for the lies, for tricking me into believing that he was always telling the truth.

"You've been lying to me," I say, my voice hard and cold.

"I haven't lied to you."

"Lied to me, hid things from me. It's all the same!"

He shakes his head as we slowly circle each other. "It is not anywhere close to the same."

I narrow my eyes at him. "Where did you get that ring?"

A flash of surprise crosses his face and is gone the next instant, but I see his fingers flutter on the hilt of the sword out of the corner of my eye. He didn't know I discovered it. I use his surprise to my advantage and strike, our blades clanging as he matches every blow.

"The ring is mine," he says with a grunt as he pushes me back, blade to blade.

Another round of strikes, and I drive harder. My strength isn't what it was last time, and he isn't besting me as easily as before.

"Why do you have the seal of Blackwood on your finger, Weston?" I yell. I hear a quiet gasp somewhere on the deck, but ignore it.

My fury is bubbling over. All I want to do is wear him down and force him to tell me everything. My motions are out of my control, my body moving out of instinct and rage instead of calculation. My limbs shake, my mind races, and I struggle to put words together.

He steps backward, and I charge after him, swiping again out of anger, but missing as he steps away smoothly again.

"You're fighting with too much emotion," he says. "Focus." Our blades clash and he pushes me backward, allowing him time to recuperate. Leave it to him to still train me, even after attacking him on deck.

"I can't focus on anything other than how you hid everything from me." My voice wavers with fury and despair, as I try to fight back the tears I already spilled with Sig, but this time, they are filled with anger. "You let me believe everything Dane said when you knew he was lying. You let me hate everyone. Hate you! And then you hide from me that you're from my kingdom?"

The words slip, and I can't take them back. *My* kingdom. Not Blackwood, not home. Mine. His expression stays stoic as he watches me, without even a flicker of surprise.

"You wouldn't have believed me if I told you."

"Yes I would—"

"Don't lie to yourself, princess." Irritation coats his voice and his eyes narrow. He stalks toward me as he speaks, striking out and pushing me backward, our blades clashing as I block. "You wouldn't have believed a word I said. You didn't. You found every reason to believe someone who was manipulating you. The only way I could help you was to have you figure it out on your own. To show you all of this and lead you to the truth. Just telling you I wasn't the monster in his story would have done nothing."

I glare at him, my chest heaving as his words sink in. He's right. I didn't believe anything they told me. I was so convinced it was all mind games, part of a way to control me and turn me against people I cared about, that nothing they said would have changed my mind. It wasn't until after living with them for months, watching them care about me and trust me, and coming to trust them that I saw they weren't anything like Dane said.

But he still hasn't answered my question. He hasn't acknowledged the crucial piece of information he knew and that he hid it from me.

"You know who I am, don't you? You and Sig know."

He lowers his sword and stands up straight, his voice dropping low. "I do, princess."

My vision blackens around the edges as my anger hones in on him with the admission. Now it's my turn to stalk toward him. "*That's* why you treat me differently?" My hands collide with his chest as I push him with all my strength. He staggers back slightly, but stays silent. "*That's* why you are such an insufferable asshole?" I push him again. "*That's* why you're so overbearingly protective?" His face contorts with annoyance on the third push, and he shoots me a look, challenging me to do it again.

"You've been here longer than I've been alive," I yell. "I'm not your princess. I should mean nothing to you!"

"That's enough," he growls.

"No! It's not enough! Because you still aren't answering me!" I reach out one final time, but he swats my wrists away, his sword clattering to the deck.

A growl erupts from his throat and he stoops down, wrapping his arm around my thighs, and throws me over his shoulder. The hilt of the sword is ripped from my fingers before it clatters to the floor alongside his.

"Are you fucking kidding me, Weston? Put me down! Now!" I try to wiggle and roll out of his grasp, but he ignores me, his arm only clamping down harder as he walks toward the steps, taking them quickly down to the first deck.

"I order you to put me down!" I scream as I slam my fists into his back, trying to push away and break out of his grasp. If he wants to treat me like a princess, then I'll start acting like one.

He stomps down the hallway and I shriek when he tilts me backward as we pass through the doorway, so my head doesn't hit the wooden beam above. Slamming the door behind us, he crosses the room and I'm flying through the air, dropping right into his chair. Fire flares in his eyes as he grips the arms on either side of me, leaning forward so there's only a breath between us.

"There. Now you can scream at me all you want. You may be my princess, but this is still *my* ship."

I ignore him. He will not distract me from my anger by pulling rank.

"You've told me to trust you, but you've hidden everything from me! And now you're making this about you!"

"It's not about me. This has always been about you!" he yells and I shift back in the chair.

He stands, scrubbing his hands over his face, and I can see there's more he isn't saying. I don't care what Edmond has taught me about being diplomatic and not letting emotions get involved when you are negotiating. I'm furious with Weston. Furious about everything he's kept from me, and everything he let me believe.

"How did you figure out I was a princess?"

"I didn't have to figure it out," he snaps. "I knew from the moment I saw you who you were."

I rear back. How could he have known? I've never met one of the Castaways in my life, and no one on the island knows I'm a princess, not even Dane.

"How did you know? And why did you keep it from me?"

"What part of you weren't going to believe anything I said to you, don't you understand?"

"You could have tried," I snap back.

He turns his back to me and wrings his hands through his hair. "Fuck, Rem, she's as bad as you are."

My heart screeches to a halt in my chest.

Rem.

Does Weston know my father?

"What did you just say?"

He turns back around, his jaw working and the muscles in his cheeks fluttering. Hands held together at his waist, his fingers twist the ring around so the seal is now visible.

"You asked me where I got this," he says, the anger from moments ago gone and replaced with seriousness. "I didn't lie to you, princess. It is mine. I got it from the king…when he named me First Guard."

I suck in a breath, and his eyes roam my face, reading the shock there.

I stare right back in silence, trying to find the lie, but I can't see it. All words escape me as my eyes scan his. He's telling me the truth, finally.

But I can't believe it.

He breaks the silence first. "I turned it around so you wouldn't recognize it as the same one the current First Guard wears."

"We don't have a First Guard." My words come out in a whisper, the shock still making it hard to speak.

His gaze snaps to mine. "What do you mean you don't have one? Who has been protecting him? Traveling with him? Managing the guards for the kingdom?"

I shake my head. "We've never had one."

"Fuck, Remmington!" He paces the space in front of me, his chest heaving and jaw tight. "He never replaced me?"

"All I know is there is supposed to be one, but he's never chosen one. My guard wants it, badly, but he's never given it to her."

"So at least you're protected," he says, still pacing.

"It doesn't matter," I say, and he looks at me, confused. "We never leave. Coming here was the first time I've ever left the castle walls."

He stops pacing then, no doubt trying to equate the life in Blackwood he remembers to the one I'm describing.

"Why do you care, Weston?" I ask before he can respond. "You're here. You've never met me before. Why do you care?"

His throat bobs before he answers. "It's my duty to care. I'm the First Guard."

I shake my head. "You're not the First Guard here. You're the captain here."

"Where we are doesn't change who I am."

"I've had a guard for my whole life, and Brynne isn't half as protective as you've been."

His glare hardens, like I've said something that upsets him. I don't acknowledge it. Pushing up on the armrests, I stride toward him, not breaking eye contact as I crane my neck up and glare back.

"Don't lie to me, Weston," I mutter, and something inside him loosens. His eyes search mine, and I can see the moment he breaks, knowing he's about to tell me everything he's kept secret.

He heaves a sigh, but doesn't look away, his hands planted firmly on his hips.

"Remmington was my best friend. I couldn't let anything happen to his daughter."

My mouth goes dry.

Weston is my father's best friend and his guard.

I knew from the moment I saw you.

Not only has he known I am the princess of his kingdom, but he's known I'm Lennox Holt, the daughter of his friend.

My mind thinks back to what Stassia said, how stressed he was the day I showed up on the island. Everything is starting to make sense; why he followed me around the island, why he risked his life to save mine, why he wouldn't let me out of his sight.

It's everything a First Guard would do.

"I never lied to you, princess," he says, his voice low and soft. "I just wasn't ready to deal with everything you being here meant. An entire life has happened while I've been trapped here." He heaves a sigh and his arms drop to his sides. "I didn't want you to know who I was. I'm just Weston here, but I couldn't help but do everything I could to keep you safe."

"Stop calling me that," I say angrily as I swipe away tears that dared to fall. The twitch of his hand catches my eye, like he was stopping himself from reaching out toward me again.

Taking in deep, shuddering breaths, trying to still my anger and pounding heart, everything I just learned flies through my mind, until I snag on one detail.

"Who are you here for, Weston?"

His eyes soften. He knows I've figured it out.

A woman, a friend. Someone he would give his life to protect.

"I'm here for your mother."

I feel like I'm drowning, like a hole has opened up in the ship and the sea swallowed me into its depths.

He came here to save my mother. He lost years of his life, trapped in this place, all for the chance to heal her. Dane almost killed him and left him for dead. Any opportunity for a normal life was stolen from him the moment he couldn't return. The island deemed him unworthy, the same as me and everyone else on this ship, and now both of us have to deal with our failure and wondering if she wasn't ever meant to be saved.

My eyes snap to his as I remember one late night conversation, me asking about his scar, and him asking about...me. That's why he wanted to know how old I was. He was trying to find out how long he has been gone.

Twenty-one years.

"You sacrificed your entire life for your friend? For your queen?" I say, my eyebrows drawn in, giving away my sheer disbelief.

"It wasn't a sacrifice. It was my duty to protect them."

"It wasn't your duty to give up your life, Weston," I say harshly, my voice rising again.

"I didn't. The day I step foot back into Blackwood, it will be like no time has passed. I'm the same person standing in front of you right now that I was twenty-one years ago the day I called the Guardian. The only sacrifice I made was the life I had with them. I didn't sacrifice mine."

"But why you? Why did you choose to come here?"

He glances down at the ground between us, and doesn't look up again when he responds.

"I couldn't let him leave you alone," he grumbles.

My chest aches. Weston knew about me, knew I existed. That's why he knew who I was the second he saw me, because if he knew my father, he knew my mother too.

"My father was going to go."

He nods. "We discussed it. In the end, it made more sense for me to try. He couldn't leave the kingdom or you alone."

I scoff. "He doesn't give a shit about leaving me alone."

"I don't believe that."

"You may have been his friend, but you haven't been there. You don't know him anymore. We don't speak, he won't even look at me. I'm nothing to him."

His throat bobs and his brows draw in. "I wish things turned out differently for you. I'm sorry for whatever role I played in that."

There's no need for him to apologize, because he didn't play a role in that. Whether or not Weston ever made it back didn't force my father to treat me the way he did, or make decisions for my life the way he has. As far as I'm concerned, Weston wasn't part of my life at all until I learned who he was the day I stepped foot on Dawnlin.

"What if we can't ever get back?" I ask.

"We're not giving up hope. I won't ever stop trying."

Anger still courses through me, because I hate to admit it, but I trusted Weston, and he hid something this important from me. But even though I'm still angry with him, I can't help how my feelings have changed about the entire situation.

Everything he's done has been to protect me, to help me and my family. He says it is out of duty, but I can't help but feel there's more than he is willing to admit. The way he looks at me, the way he touches me, the way he *kissed* me, it doesn't feel like he's doing it solely because he swore an oath as the First Guard.

He says it is his duty to protect me, but what if it is his duty that is holding him back? What if that is why everything he's done in the past few days has been so confusing?

And how can I hate a man who has given up so much for me? Saving my mother would have changed my life, my childhood. If he had been worthy and returned home, everything would have been different. Even if he came home empty-handed, maybe he would have helped my father be a better man.

But Dane stopped him from coming home.

Dane is the one that hurt my family and hurt me, in more ways than one.

He is the one that is keeping everyone from their loved ones, refusing to give them the ability to say goodbye or move on with life.

It's Dane that needs to be stopped.

"Thank you for telling me," I say, my voice barely a whisper.

"I didn't want to keep it from you, princess. But I didn't see any other way."

"You were right," I say, the sound coming out garbled with the angry tears that are forming alongside the lump in my throat. "I wouldn't have believed you. I guess I get my stubbornness from him."

"That's not a bad thing."

I glare at him. "I don't want to be anything like him."

"He's not a bad man. He just may have gone about things in a bad way. You have to understand what he went through, too."

The anger bubbles up inside me again, too fast for me to control it.

"You have no idea what you're talking about. You talk about your life not being sacrificed here, how you'll walk back into Blackwood like no time has passed. That wasn't my life, Weston! My life was wasted away in a castle because I needed to be *protected*. He did that. He stole it from me, probably because he's so furious I stole her from him!"

He opens his mouth, but I cut him off before he can say anything else.

"Both of you, you're the fucking same. You won't let me do anything here, or you are furious if I do, because I need *protection*. I'm not fragile, Weston! He already took one life away from me. Don't take my life away here too!"

He looks like I've slapped him, but I don't regret what I said. He just wanted to be Weston here, so why can't he understand I want the same? To just be Lennox? Not the princess that needs protection, not the person who has others decide for her. I just want to forget it.

"Your duty is to my father, not to me," I say. "Here I'm just another one of the crew."

His jaw clenches and his body tenses. "If that's the way you want it, princess."

"It is," I say firmly.

My stomach sinks and my fingertips tingle, but I stand firm. I don't want him treating me differently and fawning over me, but somewhere deep down, I wonder if the friendship we've developed is even real, or if it's only been because of his duty. Has every part of our relationship stemmed from his duty, just like Brynne, and Tila, and Edmond? Has Sig's? Was everything I thought I had here not real at all and is about to slip through my fingers?

He nods and looks away, his eyes fixed on something across the room. He clears his throat before he speaks again.

"Now you understand why what happened last night can't happen again."

So he didn't forget, despite how drunk he was by the end of the night.

The kiss. The stares. The touches.

If I didn't think he regretted it before, he just confirmed it.

It was all a mistake.

"I agree," I say, and it feels like something inside me breaks.

Dane is a liar, and Weston is a guard.

Everything I thought I knew about them is wrong, and all the feelings and emotions that are very real to me are spiraling out of control. I need to get out of this room and away from him. I need to get my mind straight and figure out how I'm going to interact with everyone now that I don't know if it was really all a lie.

Wiping the tears from under my eyes, I set my jaw and look back at him.

"If that's all, I'd like to go complete my task for the day," I say, my voice hard and cold. I step around him, but he slides in front of me, blocking my path.

"One more thing," he says. He takes a small step forward, so we're toe to toe. "If you want to be treated like just another one of the crew—" I crane my neck back to keep my eyes locked on his, and he drops his voice lower. "Don't ever attack me on my deck in front of my crew again."

His jaw ticks and I clench my teeth together, and stare back with all the anger and frustration I can muster before answering.

"Understood, Captain."

CHAPTER THIRTY-SIX

Weston and I avoid each other like the moon and the suns, hovering in the same general vicinity but not interacting at all. He even started avoiding our room, coming in only when I was already asleep and leaving before I wake. The rumpled sheets on his side of the bed are the only indication he even came into the room at all.

I don't want to talk to him. I'm afraid of what I might say if I do. Even though I understand his motives, he still lied to me. His lie was different than Dane's and so much less severe, but that doesn't mean it didn't still cut me, especially after everything else that happened.

I push away thoughts of his lips crashing to mine, of him pulling me flush against him, of his skin hot on mine as he clutched me in his sleep, all things that blew apart whatever balancing act was going on between us. My chest aches when I think about what came next.

It will never happen again.

I don't know which feels worse, Dane's murder and betrayal, or Weston destroying the friendship that was slowly growing between us, making me question every interaction I've had with the crew I thought were my friends.

But beyond the hurt and anger, I know deep down I might actually miss him.

The part of me who is angry that my life was shut away in a castle, that I had to live under constant protection and could not decide for myself, rages at him for trying to do the same thing here, especially after getting a taste of freedom on the island. But the other part of me can't let go of the suspicion that there might be more to it than just his duty, no matter what he says.

I know a thing or two about duty and responsibility, but I don't want him to do it any longer. We aren't in Blackwood, and he isn't my guard. He has no responsibility for me more than that of the captain of this crew, especially now if he doesn't even want to be my friend.

The quiet, monotonous task of mopping the deck doesn't allow for any sort of distraction from all these warring thoughts and feelings. I huff a sigh and yank my shirt away from where it is stuck to my skin. The humidity accompanying the gloomy skies is much worse than a normal day, making everything still and sticky, and I'd do anything for a cool breeze off the water.

Dropping the mop into the sudsy bucket, I stride over to the mainmast, and slide my back down until I'm sitting, gazing out over the deck and everyone who is out this morning. Auralie and Fern sit off to the side mending a sail as Fin pulls the other side of it over stacks of crates and barrels, making his own castle. Veck carries crates down below, a large stack of them having appeared overnight full of supplies.

I raise a glass bottle I stored in the shade to my lips and savor the cool water as my only source of reprieve in this greenhouse. My shoulders sag with a moment of distraction and calm as I watch everyone around me work, but it only lasts a moment before Weston steps out from below deck, and strides over to where Veck is cataloging items in the crates.

My mood instantly turns sour and I'm ready to get moving again, so I don't have to look at him. I set my bottle back down in the shade and stand before I'm startled by a voice from up above.

"Break over already?"

Shading my eyes against the brightness reflecting off the cloud cover, I look up at the first rung to find Jorn, tying knots in a thick rope as he lounges against the beams.

"Hey Jorn," I say, my voice coming out more sullenly than I intend.

"What's got you down, Little Lennox?"

An unintentional laugh erupts at his nickname. I've never heard it before, but it's very fitting coming from him. His long, lanky limbs are perfect for climbing the mast, but make me look like a child in comparison.

"Nothing," I say, gesturing over my shoulder. "Just need to get back to work."

"Still mad at the captain, I take it." The lilt in his voice tells me Sig filled him in on what happened, especially with how little we've been near each other. How much he knows, though, is still a mystery, and I don't feel like explaining right now.

"I don't think I will ever *not* be mad at the captain," I say with a huff, fighting the urge to glance over my shoulder and sneak a glimpse of him.

"Because he's an asshole," Jorn says as he drops onto the deck beside me.

"Exactly. See, Jorn, you understand." I shoot him a sweet and knowing smile.

Jorn lets out a loud laugh, and I feel eyes on my back.

Don't look, Lennox. He doesn't deserve the satisfaction of knowing you feel him watching.

"An asshole he may be, but he's such a kind asshole." Jorn shoots me a dazzling smile and I can't help but return it. "You know, if it weren't for our lovely captain over there, I probably would have died twenty times already."

I quirk an eyebrow at him. "That sounds more like a you problem than anything he's done."

He shrugs. "Probably. But he still cares enough to save me over and over again."

I eye him warily. "Why don't you just stop doing stupid shit, then?" My mind drifts back to the Oasis, a situation that easily could have been avoided if Jorn hadn't been so competitive.

"That makes life less fun," he says with a grin. "Besides, isn't it nice knowing there's someone who cares?"

My stomach sinks. For twenty-one years, all I've ever truly wanted is to feel like someone cares more than just out of obligation. I thought I found that in Dane, but it turns out I can't trust anything he says. Just when I think Weston may be someone I can trust, who cares about me for me, not for me the princess, I find out he's just like everyone else in my life, following my father's orders and doing their duty to protect me. There may be some slight connection toward me like Edmond, Tila, and Brynne, but in the end, our relationship stems from duty.

Weston may not be my guard, but his position makes him the commander of them all. My protection falls under him, and while there's no one else around, no Brynne, no second guard, he views it as his personal responsibility.

He doesn't care, not like what Jorn is talking about, not like he cares about Jorn or Sig or anyone else on this ship.

Suddenly, I get an idea.

"Jorn?" I ask.

"Yes, Little Lennox?"

"Can you teach me to climb the mast?"

His grin grows impossibly wider as he rubs his hands together conspiratorially.

"You up for a little risk?" he says.

"No," I answer. "I'm up for a little fun."

And if there's some risk, I know it will piss Weston off. Even better.

"I like that answer," he says, and his eyes slide up and down me, assessing. "Do you have a belt?"

Glancing down at my pants, I shake my head. I've always carried my dagger in my waistband, and preferred my bow over carrying a sword, so the island never gave me one. We don't need weapons to climb, so I don't know what Jorn wants it for, but I know exactly where I can look.

"Give me two minutes," I say and turn on my heel, heading straight for the stairs. I trudge past Weston and Veck, keeping my gaze forward as I disappear into the darkness below and head to our room.

The hinges of the trunk at the foot of the bed squeak as I lift the lid, the scent of leather mixed with Weston overwhelming my senses. Weston's things are piled inside of it, and I start digging around, searching for something I hope is hiding. Shifting the items aside, I feel around until my fingers brush a thick, familiar fabric. I pull it out from under the collection of his things to find a cloak, almost exactly the same as mine from home, the one that is still sitting in my bunk back at camp.

I push away the other items, trying to reach where the cloak was hidden at the bottom. My breath hitches when I see it, the clothing that is so familiar, yet feels like I haven't seen it in a lifetime.

His guard's uniform.

It's exactly like the one Brynne still wears beneath her armor, and something in me settles, knowing he wasn't lying about this too. The proof is right here beneath my fingertips; another connection he has to Blackwood. I shift it to the side, and my eyes fall on a dark stain, before they start to well with tears.

Pulling the thick shirt out from under the pile of clothing, I see the slash through the front, the stain from Weston's blood darkening it. Sig didn't lie either, the evidence of Dane's violence is right here beneath my fingers. Weston almost died, and the reality of what that would have meant for everyone in the crew is something I don't want to consider.

Blinking away the moisture in my eyes, I focus back on the trunk. I feel around, but there is only the uniform, no armor that would have protected him against such a vicious attack, and now I understand why Dane was able to injure him so badly. I push the uniform to the side, hoping what I'm looking for is beneath it.

It has to be in here.

When my fingers brush the worn leather, the corners of my lips lift in a smirk. I pull Weston's guard belt out of the trunk and wrap it around my hips, cinching it tightly. It's exactly like the ones I've trained with for years, and it feels comfortable and reassuring.

I also know it will irritate him when he sees me wearing it, and I can't wait to see the look on his face when he notices. I want him to know I found it and took it, claiming something that signifies what he's been hiding from me for so long as mine.

I slam the trunk closed and head back to the deck, walking straight to Jorn, waiting for me at the mast.

"Perfect," he says as I approach. A crate slams into the deck behind me, vibrating the boards under my feet. I can't keep the smirk off my lips, knowing Weston must have already noticed, and he feels some sort of way about it. Jorn looks over my shoulder, confused, but shakes his head quickly and brings his attention back to me.

"Why do I need a belt to climb the mast?" I ask.

He holds up the end of a rope in front of me. "Because, even though it's fun to do risky things, I still don't want you to fall and break your neck. Captain probably wouldn't be too happy with me if that happened."

"Don't worry about him," I say firmly. "I'd convince him to leave you alone."

More like order him.

"Can't convince him if you're dead," Jorn jokes with a wink.

I roll my eyes but can't hide the smile he brings out. During my time here, I've grown to really like Jorn. His lighthearted nature, his outlook on life, even the never-ending life on Dawnlin, is so refreshing, and I wish I was more like him. I don't want to think about how hurt I would be if the friendship between Jorn and I wasn't real, because I don't know how much Sig has told him.

Jorn reaches out and grabs my belt, looping the rope through it, then tying it off in an intricate knot, his fingers flowing like it is second nature.

"You're on one end, and I'll be on the other. That way, if you fall or slip, my weight will support you." He ties the other end of the rope around his waist and belt in a similar fashion.

"But what if you fall?" I ask, looking him up and down. "I have a feeling I will not be able to support you."

He shoots me a look, and I laugh. "Alright, alright, you aren't going to fall."

"No, I will not." He looks around us, eyes scanning the nearby deck before he reaches up to scratch his chin. "You, uh, might struggle to reach the first beam to get up. Normally I would say just use a crate or barrel, but I take it you don't want to go over and ask Captain for one."

"I applaud you on your observation skills."

He laughs at my poor attempt at humor, but then his cheeks tinge with pink, and his enormous grin turns sheepish.

"I can lift you up, but only if you're alright with it."

"As long as you don't drop me," I say and turn to face the mast.

"You're safe with me, Little Lennox." He looks over my head again, and I know exactly where he's looking, rather, at who. He gives me instruction on how to place my feet when he lifts, so I can get the feel for climbing up the pole. I listen carefully, visualizing the moves he tells me before I'm ready to go.

He comes around behind me, standing close and places his hands on my hips.

"Alright Little Lennox, up you go."

Jorn hoists me up over his head, and I grab onto the mast, following his exact instructions to clamber to the crossbeam. Once I reach a certain height, his hands clamp onto my thighs, just under my backside, and push me up farther, enough that I can wrap my arms around the beam and swing a leg over.

Jorn's hands on me do not have the same effect as Weston's. There's no tingling of my skin or pounding of my heart, no desire to get closer or a feeling of loss when he's no longer touching me. I don't want to think about what that means. It's more important that I focus on not falling to my death.

Once I'm sitting on the crossbeam, I lean over slightly to peer down at Jorn, who meets me with a huge smile and two thumbs up. Returning his smile, I sit up straight, gripping the wood underneath me, and look out over the deck. The world looks so different from here, and I soak in this new perspective. Despite being confined to the ship, being up on the mast like this makes me feel a little more free.

My gaze roams over the waves rolling into the cove, and the empty beach, before coming back to the ship. Weston's eyes find mine, and I look away quickly, but not before I notice the scowl on his face and the tension in his crossed arms.

Take that, Captain.

Jorn pulls himself up onto the crossbeam, standing casually next to me as if he was born to climb.

"Ready?" he says, and I nod enthusiastically.

We spend the next hour on the mast, Jorn giving me careful instruction and demonstrating every move for me before I do it. He is patient and encouraging, and I can tell that this is something he truly loves and takes pride in.

Weston and his confusing actions couldn't be farther from my mind as Jorn and I climb. Focusing on staying stable and keeping my balance despite my shaking limbs proves to be just the distraction I need. It isn't until we are underneath the crow's nest that I look down and remember just how high up we are.

My fingers grip the ropes tighter as a wave of unease washes over me, but as I look down and see what I just accomplished, it isn't just nerves I feel.

It's satisfaction. Thrill.

I'm proud I did something that terrified me, that I'd never thought I could do. I'm glad I took a risk and proved to myself that I am capable.

I'm also proud that I probably will be returning to an angry captain, who I know is down there worried about my every move with his over protective nature, knowing there's not a thing he can do about it except watch and wait.

Jorn reaches down and grasps my forearm to help me into the crow's nest. I'm speechless as I look out across the island. I thought the view from the platform when we landed was amazing, but this takes my breath away. We stand in silence together, looking out over the island, and I can see why Jorn finds happiness up here.

While being confined to the ship can feel a little like being confined to the castle in Blackwood, looking out over the island like this feels like the world is open to me, that I'm not trapped or hidden away. It's amazing, and I'm so grateful he taught me how to climb it safely.

The helio is perched on the back of the platform, facing the island. Jorn gives me a quick rundown of how it works. I can see how something like this would be useful if you lived in a kingdom that ever saw the sun.

We sit down, feet hanging over the edge, and just talk. Jorn talks about home, and his twin brother, the person he came here for. He entertains me for a while with stories from over the years, including ones he says should make Weston seem like less of an asshole. I find myself laughing at their interactions, the exasperated way he describes Weston scolding him after he does something stupid. Weston seems like he's the same with me as with all of them, but maybe Jorn is right. Maybe I just interpret things differently because of my history and my position.

My heart swells the longer I'm up here with him, because yet again, the Castaways have proven that everything Dane told me, everything he is convincing all the Voyagers of, is all lies. Everyone on this ship used to be a Voyager, and now they are all just looking for a way home after dealing with the same failure and loss I have accepted. There are no ulterior motives, no secret plans, just a group of people who are making the best out of the eternal life they've been handed.

Silence falls between us as we gaze out over the land, the thick grey clouds brightening as midday approaches. I'm so glad I came up with Jorn today. After the morning we've spent together, my doubts and worries that his friendship wasn't real disappears.

I sit and watch as the waves beat on the shore with a soft smile on my face, my thoughts reeling as I process everything that has happened since I stepped foot on this ship. The moment Weston carried me onto this beach, how full of hatred I was, and how badly I wanted to escape these people as quickly as I could.

Now, everything has changed.

I can't fathom feeling like I want to escape again, not to go back to a place full of lies and treachery. The only way I want to leave is if we all get to go home, every last one of us.

Sig's plan comes barreling back into my mind. She wanted to send me back, to get close enough to Dane to take the dust and get at least some of us home.

Could I do it? Could I follow through with her plan and actually take the dust? Even if I did, who would we choose to send back? Or would taking the dust be futile, since the Guardian is the one who uses it?

Questions swim through my head as my vision blurs, my focus no longer on the views before me. I've gotten so close to them now, learned so much about why they are here and how long they've been holding onto hope for a way home. I owe it to them to try, because Sig is right; I'm the only one who can get close enough to Dane to do it.

I don't know how I would manage it, or how I'd convince Weston to let me go, but Sig spoke the truth. They've been searching for years, and time is running out. I'm the best shot they have, and I just need to figure out how to make that happen.

"Here we go!"

Jorn's excitement breaks my trance and I look over to find him jumping up onto his feet.

"What? What happened?" I ask, following suit.

He points out in the distance and I follow the direction.

"See that light right there? The purple color above the trees?"

"Yes," I say, squinting to make it out.

"That's our signal," he says with a smile.

"What does purple mean?"

"It means we have to get ready." He lowers himself down to the beam underneath the crow's nest.

"Ready for what?" I say as I peer down through the hole in the platform.

"Get ready to go to the beach, Little Lennox." He grins up at me, reaching out to take my hand. "Someone found the waters."

CHAPTER THIRTY-SEVEN

My boots slam into the deck as I jump down from the final crossbeam, Jorn hopping down more gracefully a second after. The high of being at the top of the ship mixed with the excitement of what is coming with a new Voyager joining the crew has me grinning, forgetting all about the grumpy captain I know I'll have to calm down now that I'm back on solid ground.

"Captain!" Jorn yells before turning toward me and reaching for my belt. He steps closer, invading my space and making this feel way more intimate than it should as he grabs hold of the rope that kept me safe during our lesson. I start to step back when his grip tightens, holding me in place, then sends me a wink before looking back down at his task.

Angry footsteps stomp across the deck us, and I hear Jorn snicker under his breath as his fingers fly over the knot, loosening the loops.

Is he taunting Weston? Does Jorn know something more that I don't?

If looks could kill, Weston's face would strike someone dead, but it isn't me that has to worry since all the fury is directed right at Jorn.

"What?" Weston snaps. He stops a few paces away from us and crosses his arms over his chest, his glare falling to Jorn's hands at my hips as he finishes untying the rope.

Jorn chuckles softly, so only I can hear it.

"Little Lennox has my stamp of approval for climbing the mast." His focus remains on his task until the knot falls away, and he pulls the rope out from my belt. He winks at me again and I can feel tension seeping off of Weston's body. "She'll still need a couple more times with my supervision, of course." He reaches out and musses my hair, the gesture completely platonic, but Weston's jaw looks like it might crack if he clenches it any tighter.

"Is that all?" Weston growls, his anger not seeming to affect Jorn one bit.

"Yes," Jorn says as he wraps the rope around his hand and elbow into a ring of loops. Weston turns to walk away just before Jorn speaks again. "Oh, and we got a signal."

Weston turns back to us, rolling his eyes. "Why didn't you just say so?"

"Where's the fun in that?" Jorn says, his eyes sparkling.

"Go get Sig," Weston commands. "Tell her to get the collection crew ready." He turns away again, stomping back toward the entrance below deck without even a glance at me.

I guess I escaped the wrath of the captain.

"What's the collection crew?" I ask Jorn once we are alone.

"The aggressors," he says. He starts off toward the stairs and I follow. "It's pretty much the oldest and strongest crew. We never know if the greenhorn is going to put up a fight."

We descend the steps to the second deck, and Jorn calls out, "Sig! Collection crew!"

"Really? Already?" Stassia says as she sits up in one of the chairs in the lounge. "How are there so many coming so close together?"

I shrug. "I didn't tell anyone my methods. Maybe it's the island?"

"Could be," she says. "Maybe it wants things to change around here."

I feel a small twinkle of hope within me as my mind drifts back to my thoughts in the crow's nest. Maybe the island does want things to change. Now that I know Dane has been lying, I agree with it, and something more needs to be done.

I need to talk to Sig, but now, with all the commotion and excitement, it isn't the right time. We need to come up with a way to convince Weston to let me go back, and that is going to take some planning time that we don't have.

"You're coming, right?" Stassia asks. She lounges back down, not looking at all like she's about to leave to fetch a new Voyager.

"Yes, she's coming," Sig says as she strolls down the stairs toward the mess. "Collection crew! Get prepped!" she yells into the room, followed by various forms of acknowledgment.

"I'm not allowed to leave the ship, remember?" I say. I haven't left since Weston forbade it, after I returned covered in blood from Mara's knife.

"I'll handle Cap. If he doesn't agree, I will convince him." Sig plops down into a chair next to Stassia and I take one as well. "If the Voyager is hostile, you might be the best person to get through to them. Having you there will be more helpful than hurtful."

"Unless it's Mara," I say with a wince. My arm is fully healed, thanks to the magical salve, but the memory is still too fresh. I don't know what it would be like if she steps out of that portal. The hatred inside her is already too fierce, so she might take longer to break than I did. Part of me hopes it isn't her, so we don't have to deal with that while also convincing Weston to send me back for the dust.

"That would be unfortunate," Sig says.

"Don't we need to get to the beach?" I ask, looking around at everyone and their lack of movement. "Why aren't we getting ready?"

"Oh, we have time," Stassia says.

"The mountain takes all day. No one comes out before nightfall, so we have time to get into position," Sig says. "You can do whatever you need to do, just like before a shift, but make sure you're ready. We don't know what to expect when we get down there."

I finish the rest of my chore that I abandoned to climb with Jorn just before Stassia comes to find me to prepare for tonight. The mess is full, commotion and laughter ringing through the space while we eat when Sig drops into the chair across from me.

"Cap's all taken care of. You're clear to come tonight," she says and takes a bite of her food.

"What'd you have to trade to make that happen?" I ask.

After the way he glared at Jorn and me today, and as angry as he was when he took away my shift, I figured he wouldn't agree to let me come, no matter what Sig tried.

She shrugs. "Nothing. He didn't put up a fight at all. Just agreed."

"Are you still not talking?" Stassia asks.

"Nope," I say and stab a roasted vegetable before popping it into my mouth.

"Are you ever going to tell us what happened?" she asks. Sig looks down at the table, just as Auralie walks up with her plate and sits down in the last empty seat.

"What happened with what?" Auralie asks innocently, glancing between us.

"Why Weston and I aren't speaking," I answer.

"Oh, *Weston*. It's *Weston* now?" Stassia teases.

I roll my eyes at her and take a bite of another vegetable. I'm not sure it really matters if I tell them or not. None of it is a lie, and he didn't say any of it needed to be kept between us. What do I have to hide?

"He kissed me, then told me it will never happen again, all before I found out he's been hiding the truth from me about who he is, and that's why he's been acting the way he has." The words string together as I try to get everything out before my courage disappears. It seems to have the expected effect, because Stassia audibly gasps and Auralie stares blankly. Even Sig looked up when I mentioned the kiss, a slight look of shock on her face.

I guess Sig didn't know everything.

Silence falls over our table, and I look down at my plate, continuing to eat as they digest my statement.

"What is wrong with him?" Stassia finally says, and I can't stop the giggle that erupts. It feels good to finally talk about it, and have someone who understands my feelings.

"A lot of things, it would seem," I say.

"He needs to figure out what's going on in that beautiful head of his, because he is not thinking clearly," she says.

"It's fine," I say, then blow out a sigh. "I thought we were starting to become friends, but I don't think friends keep something like that from each other."

"I don't blame you," Auralie says.

My gaze falls to Sig. "I'm not talking about you. I know he ordered you not to say anything."

Her face softens and my chest squeezes. Has Sig been worried that I'm upset with her, too? If anything, Sig has helped me get through this, making me feel like I am not alone, and giving me perspective on life. I don't know how I'm going to return to the real world without her.

"I'm too mad at him to even ask how the kiss was," Stassia says. My cheeks heat and I clear my throat, hoping no one else sees how just the thought of it has me rattled.

I haven't been able to stop thinking about that kiss since it happened, no matter how mad at him I've been. If Stassia got wind of that, or the way he held me in bed the morning after, she'd never let me hear the end of it.

That kiss all but erased every single one of Dane's, and after I found out about his deception the next morning, it was as if Dane didn't exist anymore. If anyone made a mistake, it's me.

I know how Weston feels, but that doesn't stop my stomach from tumbling every time I find myself thinking about it, knowing that deep down I want it to happen again.

"Leave her alone, Stass," Auralie whispers. "Not everyone is as open as you."

"I'm alright," I say. "It doesn't matter how it was, his feelings about it are clear."

Stassia and Sig exchange a look, but no one says another word. We finish our meals quickly and stop at the armory before meeting everyone on deck. The suns have set, the cloud cover from the day casting a deeper darkness over the island, but it doesn't cause any hesitation. Excitement still buzzes amongst the crew as we wait for the next direction.

Weston is already there, standing in front of the gangway, weapons strapped to him just like for his shifts. His eyes scan the gathering group until they fall on mine, but I look away quickly. He may have agreed to let me come tonight, but that doesn't change anything between us.

"Listen up everyone!" he calls out, and the voices quiet as all eyes look toward him. "We all know how this goes. Everyone stay alert and look after each other. Pay attention to your surroundings, and move with a purpose. If things go badly, let me handle it, understood?"

A chorus of ayes sound around me and the group pushes forward, heading down the gangway toward the portal. Weston and Sig stand on either side of the opening in the deck as we all bound down it, waiting to bring up the rear.

I feel Weston fall into step behind me, aware of his presence the same way I am aware of Brynne's back home. It feels so out of place here, like it's bringing me back to the person I was, a person I may need to return to, but not the person I am here and now.

"You aren't my guard, you can stop following so closely," I seethe, refusing to address him directly. These are the first words we've spoken to each other in over a week, and I am mad at myself that I broke the silence first.

"You should be used to it by now, princess. You've had a guard at your back since you were a child."

Now that the truth is out between us, he's not holding back from talking about it.

"I have, but it wasn't you."

"So pretend it's not."

Sig rushes past me, her sure footsteps helping her catch up with the end of the group. We'd fallen behind in part because of my short strides, but also my distraction at arguing with Weston.

I let out a harsh sigh and try to speed up my steps, doing anything to put distance between us, but he keeps up easily.

"I don't need you following me," I grind out.

"The last time you were out on the island, you came back to my ship covered in blood. Forgive me for trying to protect you."

As if the island is taking his side, my boot slips on the slick rock beneath me and I stumble. I throw my arms out in front of me, ready to hit the jagged ground, but I'm yanked backward, his hands grabbing firmly to the belt I still wear on either side of my hips. My back collides with his front as he steadies me, and I try to suppress the shiver that runs up my spine when I feel his breath on my ear.

"You stole my belt, princess."

He did notice.

I lean into his chest for a second longer than I should, before snapping out of the trance that the feel of his voice rumbling against my back put me in. I'm angry at him, and he won't distract me from that anger. I push his hands off me and trudge forward, trying to shake off how unsteady I feel.

"It's mine now. It was in my room," I call back at him, keeping my eyes trained on the ground so I don't fall again and give him another reason to touch me.

"I'm pretty sure it was in *my* room," he says, his voice right behind me once again.

I turn on him quickly, taking him off guard and causing him to stop abruptly so he doesn't plow me over.

"If you want it back, then come take it." I cross my arms in a challenge, waiting for his next move. His eyes darken as he stares me down, but doesn't move a muscle. "That's what I thought," I say, and turn back around, moving quickly to try to catch up to everyone.

"Keep it, princess," he says from farther behind, "it looks better on you, anyway."

I stop in my tracks, just as my boots sink in to the sand. Whirring around, I pin him with a glare. "What did you say?"

His last words were murmured, but I swear I heard him correctly. I'm not going to let him get away with saying things like that, not after how confused he's made me already.

"I said you can hold more weapons that way."

I glare harder, knowing he's lying, and he matches it. "Fuck off, Weston." I bound across the beach toward the portal where everyone else has already disappeared inside.

"Captain," he says as he steps through it behind me.

Tension is thick between us once we are inside the tunnel, and I can tell he hasn't finished talking yet.

"Say what you need to say, *Captain*, then leave me alone."

"I don't understand why you're so against me doing my job."

"Because it's not your job. It's Brynne's job. You have no responsibility over me. Plus, I don't need it. Not here. I'm not a princess here."

"You're always a princess. Doesn't matter where you are."

"Not to anyone here but you."

He scoffs. "I'm not allowed to keep you safe just because you don't want to be a princess."

"No, I don't want you to treat me differently than everyone else just because I'm a princess. It's not the same." I speed up my steps, trying to catch the group, not wanting to be alone with him for the first time in so long.

"So, it's fine for Jorn to touch you and keep you safe, just not me."

His words stop me in my tracks. I spin on my heel and stare up at him, his face drawn and unreadable.

"Are you *jealous?*"

He crosses his arms and glares at me. "No."

The twinge of the muscle in his cheek tells me I'm right, even if he won't admit it. He's jealous I let Jorn touch me and help me, and do things to keep me safe. Is that why Jorn did what he did earlier? Was he *trying* to make Weston jealous?

I take a step closer; this time I'm the one closing the gap between us.

"I told you to stop lying to me."

"I'm not jealous."

"You could have fooled me."

We're almost chest to chest, so close I have to crane my neck up to keep glaring at him.

"I'm not trying to fool you, princess."

"Then what are you trying to do, Weston? You're the one who lied and didn't tell me who you were. You're the one who said that kissing me was a mistake, and now you're mad at me for having someone else help me? For making friends with people who want to be around me?"

His jaw clenches harder. "It's my responsibility—"

"Oh, fuck your responsibility. What is the point of going through years' worth of training if I'm just going to have you hovering over me for the rest of my life?"

"You're my princess."

"I'm not *your* anything. You made that blatantly clear."

Fire burns in his eyes, but he says nothing.

"Do you want me to act like a princess and command you? Is that what you want? Fine. I command you to leave me alone, and let me take care of myself."

He leans closer, hovering over me so there's only a breath between us. Our glares fight to overtake each other.

"No."

I rear back in shock. "No?"

"Like you so graciously reminded me, my duty is to your father, and he commanded me to keep you safe." He reaches out, catching my chin between his thumb and finger and lifting it so I can't look away. My lips part as he leans in closer, our argument all but forgotten when his eyes flicker to my lips, then back up. His eyes are a deep blue in the dim light of the tunnel, and my stomach flips as I stare into them.

"You can hate me all you want, princess, but I don't have to answer to you. You can't tell me not to protect you."

His fingers release me and he straightens, brushing past as he strides down the hallway.

"You don't know where you're going, so I suggest you keep up," he yells over his shoulder.

Anger courses through me, along with something else entirely. Desire, burning and licking through my veins. I wanted Weston to kiss me, to close the distance and press his lips to mine, completely defying me and my order.

Jorn is right, it feels good to have someone care about you, but I don't want them to only care out of duty and obligation. Out of responsibility. Weston made it clear that is the only way he cares, because of the oath he gave to my father. Whatever attraction is between us is only that. Attraction. It doesn't override his responsibilities.

I misread the situation, *again*.

I hurry through the tunnel, only to find him waiting for me around a bend just ahead. Even though he seems angry, he doesn't want me to get lost. I swallow the lump in my throat, and keep my gaze fixed on the path ahead of us, blindly following his movements and turns.

We walk in silence until we reach the portal that leads out onto the beach, letting us out among the large boulders and rock pillars that jut out of the cliff wall. So many perfect hiding spots for the Castaways sit in this space, and I can't believe none of us had noticed them before.

Weston stops between two boulders and reaches into his pocket, pulling out a large square of fabric and holding it out toward me.

"What's this for?" I whisper, feeling like anything louder than that will disturb our hiding place. The beach is completely empty and dark with the lack of moonlight, but I know the Castaways are hidden all around us.

"To cover your face. If you want to," he adds on quickly. I peer up at him, but the shadows cast over his face make him hard to read.

Did I actually get through to him, despite his refusal to bow to my command? Is he giving me a choice instead of just being overbearingly protective?

"They all know who I am. It's not like I need to hide."

"They do, but we don't know who is going to come through that portal. I don't need someone attacking you again the moment they see you."

I know he's talking about Mara, and the last thing I want right now is for her to come after me in front of him. It would only prove him right, and make him even more unbearable.

"Fine," I grumble. Giving him a little concession after he gave me one, won't hurt. In all reality, I may be around Weston for the rest of my life if we can't figure out how to get back home, and even if it isn't forever, who knows how long it actually could be? I may be mad at him now, but I can't stay that way forever. Neither can he.

I reach for the cloth, but before I can, his hands fall on my shoulders, spinning me around so my back is to him. Both arms reach over as he drapes the scarf across my chest, and my heart starts pounding in my ears. This feels so intimate, and after pressing my body into his chest back on the beach, I can't help but feel the temptation to do it again.

His fingertips brush the back of my neck as he pushes my hair out of the way, and my breath hitches. I stare straight ahead, trying not to move, so he doesn't touch me again and I don't do something stupid. He ties a knot in the back, leaving the kerchief hanging over my neck, ready to pull up to my face the moment I need to.

"Thanks," I mumble, and he strides away, settling down between two boulders giving him a clear view of the portal, without a word or glance back toward me. I look around quickly, finding Stassia and Sig tucked away in a corner, and sink down to join them.

Stassia quirks an eyebrow, making it clear she watched that entire interaction.

"Talking again?" she asks in a whisper.

"It's nothing," I murmur and adjust my body in the space, sinking down so I'm comfortable for however long this will take.

"Doesn't look like it's nothing," she says. "Especially not for him." She juts her head forward, and I follow her gaze toward where Weston perched, only to be met with teal eyes looking back at me. He breaks away first, looking back toward the beach and the portal.

"Nothing can happen, Stass. He's made that very clear. Besides, a princess can't be involved with her guard."

Stassia doesn't balk at my princess comment. She just brushes it aside with a shake of her head. "This is Dawnlin, Lennox. Nobody is anybody here. We're all just trying to stay alive, and live the best life we can."

"He doesn't agree with that. He only cares about his oath."

Sig is quiet on the other side, but I can tell she's listening. Stassia says nothing for a while, and just when I think she's dropped it, she whispers again.

"I've been around for a while, Sig even longer, and I'm sure she'll agree. Captain hasn't ever so much as glanced at any woman that's stepped onto his ship. Until you. Something tells me that even though he's saying one thing, maybe deep down he feels something else. Maybe he keeps saying it because he's trying to convince himself of something that doesn't feel right."

Clamping my lips shut, I turn my focus back to the beach and let her words sink in. Why does it feel like everyone in the crew seems to see something more? First Sig, then Jorn, and now Stass. All of them have done or said things that make me believe Weston does care, and so does he.

He acts one way, but says another, and I'm so confused. I don't know whether to believe his words or his actions, and don't understand why they don't match. All I can think right now is maybe I don't want to be mad anymore, and maybe he doesn't either, but both of us are too stubborn to give in.

CHAPTER THIRTY-EIGHT

Time passes slowly as we sit in hiding, waiting for the Voyager to walk through the side of the cliff. My legs are stiff and I'm eager to get out of this place, not only to work the tension from my limbs, but also to end all the uninterrupted thinking.

Stewing in my thoughts hasn't helped at all, and I feel even more confused than before.

Movement catches my eye, and I peer over the boulders toward the portal where a tall, shadowy figure appears. It can't be Mara, and I'm almost relieved until my heart stutters.

Did Dane find the waters?

Weston stands silently from his position and strides across the beach, sword drawn as he slowly creeps toward the open sand. My breath catches in my throat and panic rises in my chest. What if that is Dane? Weston is going out to confront him, alone. What if Dane hurts him again?

My muscles seize as I hold myself back from storming out behind him, and instead I watch with bated breath as he slinks into position behind the Voyager.

Is this how Weston feels whenever I put myself at risk?

Sig and Stass both pull their scarves over their faces, and I follow suit. They slide out silently from behind the boulder, their movements small so as not to draw attention, but mine are not the same. I can't pay attention to what I am doing. I can only watch Weston.

The figure takes slow steps down the beach, his shoulders slumped and head hung as he kicks the sand. My panic calms slightly when I watch his mannerisms. I know how Dane moves and the way he walks. This person can't be Dane, which means it has to be someone else.

He must have been unworthy, too.

The rest of the Castaways are moving, creeping across the sand and slowly surrounding Weston and the figure from behind.

Weston levels his sword at the man's back, and his voice rings out over the quiet beach.

"Stop where you are."

The figure freezes in front of him before turning around quickly, his eyes drawn right to Weston's blade. Everyone moves quickly after that, encircling the pair, just as they did with me, cutting off all pathways to escape. If he tries, he's going to have to go through one of us.

I fall in next to Sig, not knowing if there's something I should be doing. I was too focused on Weston holding me captive with my dagger to know what the rest of the crew did.

The Voyager looks up at Weston, and his eyes widen with fear.

Taril.

The last time I saw him, he was showing me to the cabin at camp, helping me prepare for the night that would change everything, the night they took Fin.

"I'm not going to hurt you," Weston says, but Taril doesn't hear it. He's too focused on everything else, frantically looking around at all of us, masked and surrounding him.

"You're going to come with us now," Weston says, and that catches Taril's attention.

Taril's gaze shifts back to Weston, then beyond again, moving from person to person. It's easy to see the thoughts run through his head, assessing the threat and trying to decide what to do. The fingers on his hand twitch, as if he's thinking about grabbing his blade and striking at Weston.

Instinct takes over, and I can't stop myself. I can't just stand here and watch Weston get attacked. He told us to let him handle whatever goes poorly, but all I can think about is Dane slicing him open and how, even through all the anger, I don't want to watch him be hurt again. Especially if there's something I can do about it.

"Taril, don't!" I call out, charging forward from my spot in the circle and holding my hands out, my arms held up, showing him I'm not trying to attack him.

Taril pulls his gaze away from Weston and it falls on me, right as I pull the scarf down under my chin.

"Lennox?" he says, his eyes widening.

"It's alright, Taril. Just listen to him. He's telling the truth. We won't hurt you."

Weston's eyes sear the side of my face as I stand next to him, but I refuse to look over, keeping my focus on Taril.

"Are you trying to trick me?" Taril asks, directing his question at me.

I understand how this would be his first reaction after everything Dane has said. It was mine too, except mine was already coated with anger because of everything that happened with Fin leading up to it, and having already met Weston.

"No," I say, shaking my head. "I promise it will be fine. No one is trying to trick anyone here."

He quirks his head, then thinks for a moment before slowly raising his hands in surrender. Weston nods at the group across the beach and shifts to the side, stepping between Taril and me, his broad body shielding me from the potential of him lashing out. Jorn steps forward this time, and goes through the same process Sig did, pulling all the weapons off Taril and tying his hands together.

Just before he reaches around to tie the blindfold over him, Jorn pulls down his scarf to reveal a huge smile.

"Jorn," Taril breathes.

"You finally made it, brother," Jorn says happily, clapping Taril on the shoulder. Taril visibly relaxes and lets Jorn tie the blindfold and lead him back to the portal without a fuss. The tension on the beach eases as everyone quietly follows to the safety of the tunnel.

Weston's hand falls on the small of my back, the heat from his hand warming me through the shirt as he gently nudges me forward.

"You shouldn't have done that," he mumbles, scanning the ledge of the cliff as we walk across the beach.

"So it's fine for you to not want me to get hurt, but I can't do the same for you?"

He doesn't respond, but I see his jaw clench as he continues to look anywhere else but at me.

"Besides," I continue, "you were right there if anything happened. I knew Taril wouldn't hurt me. But you? He probably would have tried to hurt you."

His hand flexes on my back and I watch the uneven sand under my feet, changing the subject quickly.

"That went quite a bit differently than when you took me. You were a lot less threatening."

"He hadn't already tried to stab me." I can hear the smile in his voice and feel my lips turn up.

"That is true," I say as I step up into the open side of the mountain. Weston reaches back and closes the stone door behind us, sealing off the outside world and casting us back into silence.

"Stassia said something earlier, and I can't get it out of my head," I say.

He stays quiet, waiting for me to continue.

"Don't you think it's odd that three of us have found the entrance so close together? Isn't it normally a long time between collections?"

He rubs his hand over his jaw. "I had the thought."

"So what does it mean? Is it just a coincidence?"

Weston lets out a slow breath. "That's the only thing it could be. Everyone finds the waters on their own, with their own methods. Dawnlin doesn't give us clues. It tries to keep us away. It wouldn't make sense for it to be changing now."

"But what if it's a sign? What if the island wants things to change?"

He glances down quickly before staring back down the tunnel.

"If the island wanted things to change, it would give us a way home. It hasn't."

"But didn't Sig say that I could help with that? Maybe bringing more of us here is the sign—"

"No."

"But it makes sense!"

"No, it doesn't. It's just a coincidence."

He starts down the tunnel and I trail after him. His entire demeanor has shifted, and I know, no matter what I try, I won't get any farther tonight. Once he closes himself off, he's difficult to get back open again.

After the worry of watching him put himself in danger, and watching Taril think about harming him, it's like my anger has disappeared and it feels like his has too. Now that the tension is broken, I just want to talk to him again, back to how it was before I found out about the lies.

"How long are you going to keep him in the brig?" I ask as I fall into stride next to him.

"As long as it takes. Dane is convincing, and I need to make sure he isn't going to hurt anyone."

"You let me out before that. I tried to jump off the ship."

He smirks at the memory, the fire from the torches dancing in his eyes.

"I did what I had to. You probably would have only hurt me, and I wasn't worried about winning yet another spar against you."

I shoot him a glare, and he laughs, the sound echoing in the tunnel and sending a shiver down my spine.

"He knows Jorn, so it will probably be quick. Hopefully *he* doesn't starve himself."

I roll my eyes. "You know I've had hostility training. You can't blame me for trying to protect myself."

"I can blame you if I have to watch it harm you."

"Is that why you sat outside the door? Because I wasn't eating?"

My mind flashes back to hearing him argue with Sig. Gods, it feels like a lifetime ago now.

He doesn't answer right away, and when he does, his voice drops even lower than before. "I had to make sure you stayed alive. I knew what you were doing, but I did everything I could to get you to stop."

"You sent Fin in."

He nods slowly. "I knew you wouldn't listen to me, but I hoped you'd listen to him."

"You were right."

"I usually am, princess." His lips break into a sly grin, and I feel the urge to shove him with my shoulder, but I don't. I keep my distance, knowing that every time he touches me, feelings I try to suppress come flooding back, and all I can think about is wanting his hands on me again.

The portal comes into sight, and I can see the rest of the crew crossing the beach onto the reef in the distance when Weston turns and stops in front of me. I stop abruptly and look up at him, but he stares at the ground, his brow furrowed.

"I don't know who you've dealt with back home, what your relationships are like with your handmaids, and guards, and everyone else," he says. "But I'm not like most of them. Remmington and Lyla were my friends. I cared about them. I'm not just someone who tried to climb the ranks and get to the top."

He pauses, as if he's trying to find the courage to say whatever he is thinking, and I seal my lips shut so I don't interrupt.

Is he actually going to be honest and tell me how he feels?

"Keeping you safe is my job. I may have sworn an oath to the crown…" His teal eyes meet mine, shining with an intensity that makes my chest tighten. His arm extends slightly and I jolt at the whisper of a touch as the pads of his fingertips brush against mine. Fire burns low in my abdomen and I swallow hard, my eyes not leaving his. His voice is gruff as his molten eyes caress my face.

"But I do actually care. Even if I'm not supposed to."

He holds my stare as he slowly steps backwards through the portal, before turning his back to me and striding toward the beach.

"Hurry up, princess," he calls over his shoulder, but I just stare at his back, stunned.

Did I jump to conclusions because of my insecurities? Is it fair that I pegged Weston's motives as solely from his duty and nothing more?

Yes, he treats me differently than the rest of the crew, but he does whatever he needs to do to save them. Jorn proved that. Weston saved his life numerous times.

Is being overbearingly protective how he shows he cares? Is that why he agreed to be my father's First Guard to begin with, because of his love for his childhood best friend?

Maybe I don't understand Weston as much as I thought I did. This caring man is hidden under a rough and protective exterior. He took on the responsibility for everyone in this crew, despite having no relationship with any of them before. He has been in this role for over twenty years, stuck here, fighting for a way home.

He wouldn't be doing all of that if he didn't care deeply, even if he has a terrible way of showing it.

This is why everyone says I'm the only one who thinks he's an asshole.

I step through the portal and trudge after him, no closer to figuring out how I feel about any of this. Maybe I misjudged him, and maybe if I accept how he is, we can go back to being friends.

Because I won't be able to handle an eternity without friendship if this ship becomes my permanent home.

CHAPTER THIRTY-NINE

"He's almost ready to come out."

Sig and I spend the next afternoon on deck, watching Fin and Jorn play on the mast. She offered to practice disarming with the dagger, since I haven't really practiced any more after Weston taught me.

"Really? It's barely been a day," I say, as I grab her wrist and wrench it down. My movements are more fluid, and I fumble with the blade less often than when we started. Sig's hands are almost the same size as mine, though, and I worry about being able to do it in an actual fight on someone larger than me.

Like Weston.

Sig holds her hand out for the dagger, and I place it on her palm. "He hasn't given us any trouble. It seems like he understands everything, especially after Jorn talked to him."

"They knew each other from before?"

She nods. "I think it goes back farther than on Dawnlin. Jorn hasn't really said, but they are from the same kingdom."

It took me by surprise when Jorn greeted Taril so comfortably, like he had been waiting for his arrival. None of the Castaways really talk about the Voyagers that are back at camp, so it is hard to know who was around at the same time.

"Are they actually brothers?" I ask, remembering what Jorn said to Taril down on the beach.

"No," Sig says. "But maybe friends. I was waiting for him to tell me. Now that Taril is here, I'm sure he will."

I flip the dagger at her, that attempt the smoothest so far, and she gives me a nod of approval.

"Do you think I could talk to him? Before he comes out?" I ask.

There's a lot I want to know from Taril, especially with what we've seen of the Voyagers since I left. After everything I've learned about Dane, I still feel like I need closure. I don't know if Taril can give that to me, but I hope I can get something.

I'm also worried. I know what I thought when I was captured and brought here, and I know what my plans were. Now that I know these people and care about them, I don't want anyone to hurt them. I need to know for myself that he isn't plotting anything harmful.

"It's not me you have to ask," she says, tilting her head toward the quarterdeck, where Weston sits with a group of the crew who already finished their tasks for the day.

I slide my dagger into the sheathe at my back and she plops down on the floor, leaning against the wooden pillar. I climb the wooden stairs up to the quarterdeck and feel Weston's focus catch on me the second I am in view. He watches as I take a step toward the rail and gesture over my shoulder, away from the group.

"Captain? Can I talk to you?" His brows draw together as he pushes to stand and leads me to the opposite side of the quarterdeck, near the other set of stairs.

"What do you need, princess?"

My stomach tumbles at his tone, not at all annoyed or bothered that I interrupted him, but helpful and sincere. We haven't talked since last night, since his admission in the portal, and it feels different now that I've decided to give him some grace. I want to be friends again, and I am nervous that he doesn't feel the same way.

"I wanted permission to talk to Taril," I say.

He crosses his arms and leans back on the rail, quirking his head to the side. I try to stay focused on his face, but the rippling muscles in his forearms beg for attention.

"You're asking permission? That does not seem like you, princess."

"Would you rather me just go down to the brig and talk to him without you knowing?"

Trying to accept his protective nature is going to take getting used to, but just because I'm trying doesn't mean I can't have a little fun with him about it.

His eyes narrow slightly. "Why do you need to talk to him now, and not when he comes out?"

"I just," I pause, trying to make sure I find the right words that won't make him jump to his favorite word, 'no.' "I want to make sure he's alright, but coming around this quickly is suspicious. I want to make sure he isn't faking it. I'm intimately familiar with the poison Dane spewed, and how it can affect someone when they come here."

He stares, his eyes boring into mine, and I don't know which part of what I said caused him to react. I shift on my feet, waiting for an answer.

"Are you telling me you were faking your behavior?" His jaw is tight, the earnestness from a few moments ago gone.

Oh no.

We'd never talked about anything from before, and I just slowly changed after spending time with the Castaways, but now that I just admitted to him what I had been doing, I'm worried this will start yet another argument.

"Maybe," I mumble, and look away.

"Are you faking now?"

"No," I say firmly, with a shake of my head. I meet his stare again, hoping he can see that I'm telling the truth.

"What made you change your mind?" His face remains stoic, but his forearms ripple again, like he's clenching his fists where I can't see.

"Honestly?"

"Always, princess."

"You."

Surprise flickers over his face, and is gone in the next second, his emotionless mask back in place.

"Me?"

"And the truth. You, and the truth."

"Why me?"

A sigh heaves from my chest, and I cross my arms now, trying to hide myself and rein in the vulnerability I'm feeling take over.

"You're really going to make me say it?"

"You're not just going to admit that you were pretending with all of us and get away with it. Tell me." The subtle command in his voice makes me bite my tongue and push away thoughts of him using that tone for other reasons.

"Fine," I huff, and the words come tumbling out, fast enough that I can't stop them and hopefully intelligible enough that I won't have to repeat them. "I saw you weren't at all how Dane described. You care about everyone around you, and while you piss me off to no end with your overprotective First Guard bullshit" —He cracks a close-lipped smile at that but doesn't break eye contact—"In a way I think that is how you show you care and I was just not willing to accept it because I was trying to break out of the overbearing wrath of my father. I didn't need it from you too."

"I'm sorry I made you feel that way. I don't know what Rem did or how he made you feel, but I wasn't trying to do that to you again."

My jaw falls open. "Did you just *apologize?*"

"Don't get used to it," he says with a grin. "I'm usually right, remember?"

I roll my eyes and he laughs. Not a quiet one, an actual Weston laugh that I've only heard him give to other people, or when he was drunk.

"Thank you for the apology," I say.

"I will do my best not to be overbearing, but I can't just stop, princess."

"Can you stop calling me princess?"

"No," he says and steps away from the rail, closing the distance between us. My body stiffens as he leans closer, and his voice lowers to a rumble.

"I think you like it. Princess."

My knees threaten to buckle and my abdomen tumbles. I need to take a step back, to get farther away from him so I can think straight again, but I don't. And neither does he.

"Do you think he will hurt you?"

My brain stutters as I try to figure out what he is asking.

"Who will hurt me?"

He smirks, as if he can tell he flustered me. "Taril."

"Oh, uh, no. I don't think Taril will hurt me."

"Are you going to jump off my ship again?"

"Technically, I never actually jumped off."

He levels a look at me. "If he says something that you like or don't like, are you going to try to leave?"

Straightening my shoulders, I look him in the eye and feel the truth in my entire body as I speak it. "No, I'm not going to leave."

He nods in acceptance. "Then yes, you can go talk to him."

My body feels lighter with his permission. I didn't realize how much him trusting me to take care of myself would affect me, but it does, enough that the desire to tease him comes back again. Stepping away abruptly, leaving him waiting for a response, I stride toward the set of stairs nearest us.

"You can stand outside the door if it makes you feel better," I call over my shoulder.

He chuckles, and I feel a sense of satisfaction wash over me.

"Don't tempt me, princess."

CHAPTER FORTY

aril sits on the cot, a plate of food in front of him, when I open the door to his room in the brig. He looks up at me with a small smile and a weak wave, and I return both. "Do you mind if I come in?" I ask, waiting in the doorway for his answer.

"Sure," he says, and dusts his hands off over the plate before sliding it to the side. Before I step through the doorway, I spot the chair Weston slept in all that time ago. I drag it into the room and close the door behind me.

If he comes down and waits outside the door, he won't have anywhere to sit.

I plop into the chair and cross my ankles in front of me.

"How are you doing?"

If I look as uncomfortable as I feel, he doesn't seem to notice. Sig said Taril has caused no problems, but I know how it feels to be captured, the things that Dane has said recently, and I know it is possible he isn't taking it well. The abrupt change from being a Voyager for so long, accompanied by being unworthy of the waters, isn't an easy combination to handle, especially alone.

"I'm alright. Honestly, this is better than I ever imagined, even being locked down here. I was half expecting to be beaten within a thread of my life."

I shake my head. "It's not like that here. It isn't the picture Dane painted for all of us."

His brows raise. "So none of what Dane said is true?"

"No, it isn't."

His shoulders sink. "Wow. I don't know, I just...started to have doubts."

Taril was doubting Dane? How did no one notice? I think back to my very few interactions with him, and I never picked up on anything.

Probably because you were with *Dane.*

Taril never would have wanted me to know if he was doubting him, especially if it looked like he would try to leave the Voyagers. But did it happen before or after I left?

"That's part of why I came down," I say. "I know you don't know me very well, but despite how close I was with Dane before, I wanted to make sure you knew that none of it was true. It isn't at all what he told us, and I know that now."

He nods slowly, picking at the fabric of the blanket. "I assumed as much when no one hurt me, and they fed me. Jorn stopped by earlier and talked to me, and that helped piece some things together."

"Sig said you know him from before."

"I do. We were friends growing up. We didn't find Dawnlin together, but we were both at camp for a while before he disappeared." He shakes his head before looking up and meeting my gaze. "I didn't think Jorn would ever do what Dane said Weston and the Castaways were doing. It never made sense to me. But I didn't argue. I just kept trying to find the waters."

I lean back in the chair and my shoulders relax. "You're taking this all really well. It was not the same for me."

"Really? How did it go for you?" he asks.

"They didn't hurt me," I say. "It wasn't anything like that. Let's just say Weston and I had history, so I didn't believe anything anyone said."

His head tilts to the side and his eyebrows knit together. "You had history?"

I nod. There's no point in keeping anything from him now. He's one of us, and I'm sure he will find out eventually. He's had doubts about Dane for who knows how long, and he isn't hostile, and I honestly don't care if it ever gets back to Dane that I kept that secret from him.

I'm glad I did.

"I met Weston before I found the waters. Twice," I wince.

"But you didn't tell Dane."

"No, I didn't."

"Why?"

"I can't really explain it. Something deep down told me not to. Sometimes I think maybe it was the magic, or maybe I just sensed something was off. I kept it a secret, but that didn't mean I trusted him when I got here. I actually fought him every chance I could."

Thinking back on it now, I see how I played right into Dane's lies, and interpreted everything Weston and the Castaways did in a negative light. I can see how he tried to protect me and take care of me, even though I fought him with everything I had.

And even after I did all of that, even after I treated him so badly, even after I physically hurt him, he still kept coming back, kept breaking through my tough exterior and defiance to show me I could trust him.

"Seems like everyone has secrets."

I nod slowly and swallow the lump forming in my throat. "How are things back at camp?"

"Honestly? Really odd. Everything just feels…uneasy. It's the worst that it's been since I came to Dawnlin."

"What do you mean?"

"There's never been fights or any turmoil between us, but Mara has been on a tirade since she says she saw you. Did she really see you? I didn't know if I could believe her or not."

"She did," I say. "It wasn't on purpose. Roley was in trouble, and I was trying to help, but she attacked me when she did."

"Ever since that day, she's been searching for you now more than the waters. She keeps telling everyone you're a traitor, and trying to convince them you're as evil as Weston. I didn't know you that well, but again, I had my doubts."

My stomach sinks. Mara was my friend. *Is* my friend. How could she turn on me so easily? If she ever found the waters and we had to take her back to the brig, she would take even more time to acclimate than I did. I shudder at the thought of what she would try to do to Weston on the beach if that day does come.

"Do people believe her?" I ask.

"Dane shuts her down quickly, so no one really responds to her. He keeps reminding her we don't harm our own. He was pissed she hurt you."

I expect to feel something, some warmth and happiness at hearing anything confirming Dane's affection toward me, like I felt when I knew he was still searching for me, but I don't. He's caused too much harm to people I care for, lied about too many things from the moment I laid eyes on him, and all of that overshadows any feelings I may have had for him.

"How has Dane been with all of this?" I ask.

"Not good," he says. "He's…different. It's like something flipped inside of him when you left. I don't know how to explain it, but camp hasn't been the same."

Has Dane really been that affected by my absence? We were friends, and he made me feel desired and excited to live, something I'd never felt back in Blackwood before. But anything between us always had a time limit, and he knew that. We discussed it on the cliffs when he brought me to see my first sunrise.

He has no way of knowing that when the island denied me the healing waters, I wanted to stay, to abandon my duty and my kingdom, and live with everyone here. But now? After everything I've learned, after all the deceit and most importantly realizing what I would give up, I don't want that anymore.

Dane knows none of it. My disappearance to the Castaways is the same as if I had just gone back to Blackwood, with or without the waters in hand.

So why is he reacting so oddly?

"I'm sorry. I can imagine all of that has made it difficult to search every day."

"I've just kept to myself. It's kind of my way, anyway," Taril says and leans back against the wall. "How are things here?"

I let out a breath. "They're actually great," I say. "I'm sure Jorn already told you."

"Do you trust him?"

Weston. That's the question, isn't it? Do I trust Weston?

"I do," I say, admitting it to myself just as much as I am admitting it to him.

"More than Dane?"

I nod. "I don't trust Dane."

"So you never tried to come back?"

To him.

Taril's unspoken words echo in my head.

"I did at first," I say. "That's part of the reason I came in to see you. I wanted to make sure you weren't trying to do the same."

He shakes his head. "There's nothing for me at camp anymore. I found the healing waters, and didn't get them. What's there to go back to?"

His eyes glimmer, and I feel a sense of understanding from him. He knows how things were back at camp before I was taken, and now, sitting here in front of him, telling him I am no longer a Voyager, and I don't trust Dane, he knows what I'm saying. No matter what happened between Dane and me before, it wasn't enough to overcome the lies and manipulations he had me under.

I give him a small smile. "I understand. How is Roley? I didn't really get to check on him after Mara attacked me."

"He's been quiet. Hasn't really talked much, especially with everything Mara is saying. I don't think he agrees with her, so he's just keeping to himself."

"He's a kid," I say. "I can't imagine how he's feeling with all this change."

I watch the way Fin became one of the crew here so quickly, his resilience and childhood innocence keeping him from truly being able to carry any anger or resentment toward anyone. I hope Roley still has enough of that to be able to stay strong and make it through everything going on back at camp.

"When do you think they're going to let me out?" Taril asks, his face turning hopeful.

"I don't know. That's up to Weston, but probably soon." I stand and drag my chair to the door, opening it and sliding it on the other side. Before I step through, I stop and turn back to him.

"Hey Taril?" He looks at me, waiting for my question. "After all this time, how did you find the waters?"

He thinks for a minute. "I already told you I started to question things, especially with how Mara and Dane have been acting. I honestly thought about you a lot, Lennox. You were basically the newest Voyager, and you disappeared so quickly. Finally, I just got frustrated and started looking out for myself, and making up my mind about everything that was going on."

I listen, seeing myself in a lot of his story, but what he says next is what sets my mind off into a spiral.

"Then one day I decided not to trust Dane anymore, and I asked the island for a map."

"So did I," I say, unable to keep myself from smiling.

"Looks like we really do all have secrets."

"We do," I say. "But they helped get us here, so I don't consider it a bad thing."

"Thanks for coming to see me, Lennox," he says with a small smile.

"Of course. Hopefully, I'll see you out there soon." I jerk my head toward the deck, just before closing the door.

I turn quickly, expecting to find Weston standing in the room, waiting for me, but it is empty.

He kept his word. Even after my teasing, he still didn't hover. He trusted me and believed I could handle myself. My chest tightens, but the feeling quickly turns heavy as I think about everything I just learned from Taril.

Something more is going on with Dane.

Could it have to do with the dust? Is he becoming more erratic because it is dwindling further, and he still doesn't have any answers? Unless he's told more of the Voyagers, Weston, Sig, and I are the only ones who know it is almost gone and that he doesn't know how to replenish it.

The news of Dane's odd behavior only makes me firmly believe what we already knew. Sig is right; I am the only one who can get close enough to Dane. I thought I wanted to be sent back so I could get away, to return to my life as a Voyager, but now I know what I need to do.

I need to go back, and I need to take the dust, not just for me, but for as many of us here who want to return. Without it, no one even has a chance. My crew doesn't deserve to be held hostage on the island by Dane, no matter what his reasons.

I don't care if I have to put myself at risk to try to get it back, to give some of us the chance to return.

I'm the only one who can, and I'm running out of time.

I need to talk to Sig.

CHAPTER FORTY-ONE

eston lets Taril out of the brig the next morning, and Sig starts him on his tour of the ship, just like she did with me. Except Taril doesn't try to escape.

Turns out, he actually knows more of the crew than just Jorn. Fern gives him an enormous hug as soon as he comes on deck, and Eirlik claps him on the shoulder with a wide smile, and you can't help but feel a sense of contentment watching the reunions.

I'm halfway through my chore as Sig points out the areas of the deck when the mop lifts out of my hands.

"This isn't yours anymore," Weston says, and drops it in the bucket next to me.

"Thank the gods," I say, extending my arms over my head and bending side to side. Despite doing this chore for months now and building my strength every day, it still is tough work and I'll be glad to be rid of it. I bend at my hips, dangling my arms to the ground, feeling my low back pull. I groan quietly with the stretch and hold it for a few seconds more before straightening and turning toward him.

Weston clears his throat, his eyes averting quickly as if I caught him watching, and I roll my lips in, trying to hide a smile.

I gesture toward the bucket, ignoring the tension now settling between us. "Is this the chore you use to break all the newest Castaways?"

"More or less," he says. He glances toward the opposite side of the deck, where Sig is still showing Taril around.

"Should I go hide the mop?" I ask, reaching out for the handle.

"No, princess, that was just for you."

I can hear the smile in his voice, and my mouth falls open.

"What do you mean, it was just for me?"

His lips turn up in a smirk. "You had to learn I was in charge somehow. Plus, I had to tire you out so you wouldn't try to escape." He glances down at me, his smile widening. "That didn't work as well as I planned."

Pain erupts on my tongue as I bite down hard, trying not to give away any indication on my face that I'm remembering what happened that night, and just how he stopped me from escaping.

I was right though, he *was* trying to exhaust me.

I cross my arms over my chest and look out over the deck, watching everyone who is out today, just as he is.

"You're an asshole." There's no malice in my tone, because I know I don't believe it anymore.

He chuckles softly. "I never said I wasn't, princess."

"I told you to stop calling me that," I say, glaring up at him.

His gaze meets mine, his eyes glimmering as his lips twitch, trying to stifle more of a smile. "And I said no."

"Ugh," I grunt and turn away again. "You're lucky we aren't in Blackwood. You wouldn't be able to tell me no then."

The smile falters, and I catch his throat bobbing from the corner of my eye.

"You're right. I guess I am lucky we aren't."

My fingertips tingle as the energy between us changes. What was meant to be playful and teasing, turned tense and uneasy in an instant. Did I upset him with something I said? I need to change the subject quickly, if only to help ease my discomfort from feeling like I hurt him.

"So, what's my new task? I assume Taril is going to finish the rest of it this morning."

"I haven't figured that out yet," he says. A bird call rings out across the deck, and I look toward the mast to find Fin, hanging upside down by his knees off the cross beam; his hands curve around his mouth as the sound erupts again.

"It might include wrangling that monster because I am exhausted." He runs a hand through his hair, and I try not to track the way his muscles flex through his sleeves. "I can only play so much hide and seek."

I laugh and watch as Fin swings back and forth, changing the sounds he makes every few seconds.

"Do you ever wish you could have a family?" My gaze stays locked on Fin, and it only takes a moment to realize that I voiced the thought out loud. I clamp my lips shut, trying not to look over at him.

"I have a family," he says, and nods toward everyone out on deck. "It's more than any family I would have had back in Blackwood." He raises his right hand and flashes me the ring on his finger, and the significance of it settles over me.

While it's not expressly forbidden in our laws, most of the higher-ranking guards never marry or have families. Their commitment to their position and protecting the king and queen, and in my case, the princess, takes up most of their time and focus.

Weston has never taken the ring off, and still, after all this time, holds true to his oath as First Guard. Maybe he's had no intention of taking a wife or having children. My throat tightens, and I keep my eyes trained on Fin. The thought of Weston never being a father after he clearly cares deeply for those around him is hard to swallow, especially knowing the reason he is doing it, to protect the king.

To protect me.

I need to change the subject, to rid my mind of the thought of Weston being with someone else, having a family with someone, or never at all. I don't want to think too deeply about the way all the things those thoughts are making me feel.

I nod toward Fin. "It was easier when he had an entire island to run around on. I'm sure being only on the ship is hard for him."

He strokes his jaw for a moment. "Maybe I'll take him to the Oasis more often so he can at least run around."

"I thought wrangling the monster was going to be my job?" I joke.

"There's no way I'm sending you off to the island, alone. Nice try, princess."

I roll my eyes, but I doubt he saw. "I told you, I'm not going anywhere."

Just when I think he's about to say something, Fin calls out, "Mister Weston! Look at me!"

Without another word, Weston crosses the deck to Fin, and catches him as he flops off the beam, flipping Fin over his shoulder. Fin sticks his arms and legs out to the sides and shouts of excitement and encouragement erupt from his little body as Weston spins him in a circle.

Weston may be exhausted, but Fin would never know it by the way he smiles and laughs as they play together. I watch for a few moments before Sig and Taril step up beside me, pulling my attention away and back to what I actually need to accomplish today.

"It's all yours," I tell Taril, gesturing to the mop handle. Sig starts to walk away but I call out before she can make it too far. "Hey Sig, can I talk to you? Alone?"

She raises an eyebrow and looks between me and Taril. "Meet me in my room once you're done," she says, then turns and heads down the stairs.

I give Taril a quick explanation of the chore and point out what I had already finished this morning, then head straight to Sig's room. The first deck is quiet, so I quickly open the door, sliding inside and closing it behind me. I lean against it, my shoulders stiff as I try to muster the courage to tell her what has been running through my mind since I spoke to Taril yesterday.

She takes one look at me and her eyes narrow. "What's going on?" she asks.

"I need to go back to the Voyagers," I blurt, keeping my voice low in case anyone walks by her room at this exact moment.

"Say that again?" she says, taking a few steps closer to me.

"Whatever you're thinking, it's not that." I let out a breath and start again, trying to keep up the confidence that is wavering now that I'm actually voicing the thoughts. "I need to go back to the Voyagers. You were right before. I'm the only way to get close to Dane."

She quirks her head. "This isn't some twisted way to get back to him for good, is it?"

"Honestly? It was. But it's not anymore." She shoots me a look, but all I feel is relief. Now both Sig and Weston know what I had planned, but they also know that I no longer feel that way. Camp isn't my home anymore. This ship is, at least while I'm in Dawnlin, but more than that, it is the people that I care about who have been harmed and wronged. I won't leave them, and I will do everything to help every Voyager who walks through that portal.

My shoulders slowly rise under her hard stare, all the explanation tumbles from my mouth. "I may have overheard you trying to convince Weston of your plan to send me back, and I thought I could use that to get back to them. I told you about the dust because I wanted you to send me back faster, and I just wouldn't return."

She crosses her arms, obvious annoyance written across her face.

"I know, I know." I sigh. "But that was before, and now I know the truth. I don't want to go back. Not for good, anyway. Only long enough to get the dust from Dane."

"If you're fucking lying to me, I'll come after you myself before he even can," she says, her eyes narrowing, and I know exactly who she is referring to.

I roll my eyes. "Sig, do you think I would tell you if I was going to stab you in the back? I've had enough of that from Mara."

She huffs a laugh. "What made you bring this up again? Why now?"

"Taril said something yesterday that got me thinking. He told me that since I left, Dane has been…different. Erratic. Emotional. We've already seen it both times we ran into him on the island. That isn't at all how he was with me, and it makes me think there's something more going on. I'm worried the dust is almost gone, and if we don't get it now, we'll lose the chance for any of us to get back."

Her eyes glaze over as her focus drifts away from me.

"I need your help, Sig."

She snaps out of her daze and her eyes meet mine. "What should we do?"

Pushing off the door, I cross the room toward her. Now that we're actually thinking about this, I really don't want anyone to overhear. "You need to convince Weston to let me go back," I whisper.

She shakes her head. "He won't listen to me. I've tried."

Sig is the only one that can challenge Weston, who pushes back against him and who he actually listens to. After hearing about how they met, how they were thrust into a friendship based on survival, it makes sense why she is the one who can do that. But if he won't listen to her on this, will he listen to anyone? To me?

"Did you ever have any other plans?"

Edmond always taught me to exhaust all options when strategizing an attack, and despite this being the easiest and most direct way of getting that pouch from Dane, I still want to know if they have ever tried anything else.

"Everything we've come up with has always seemed too risky. Sneaking into camp has never been a possibility. Capturing Dane hasn't either. The problem is, he never takes it off. So someone literally has to get close to him, and we can't."

"But I can."

The pit in my stomach feels like it is going to swallow me whole. I am the only one who can get *that* close to Dane, close enough to touch him. I'm the only one who can get him to let his guard down enough so I can take it, hopefully, without him noticing. I'm the only one who he's trusted with the knowledge of replenishing it, the only one who could bring up the dust without seeming suspicious. But I'm here, and I can't do any of that from this ship.

Her face is somber. She knows it is the truth, and that the fate of every one of us trapped on Dawnlin lies in my hands.

"We have to convince him to let me try," I say.

"Maybe you can. He won't talk to me about it anymore. He says he just wants to keep looking."

I nod. "I'll work on it."

I don't know how I'll convince him, but I won't be able to live with myself for eternity if I don't at least try, because unfortunately, if I don't soon, I risk losing my chance. If Weston can keep holding on to hope of finding the dust, I can hold on to hope that he will listen to me.

"Good. The faster you can, the better," she says.

"What are we going to do when we get it? How are we going to decide who gets to go back and who doesn't?"

She shakes her head. "We'll worry about that when we have to. Right now, we just need to focus on getting that pouch."

My stomach somersaults as I think of everyone on this ship who deserves the ability to return home. All of them should be able to see their families again, and hopefully the person they came here to save. Trying to decide who to send back will be one of the hardest things I'll ever have to do.

Bile sears the back of my throat and nausea overtakes me as I realize exactly what would happen.

Weston would send me home.

My body feels numb just thinking about it. He knows who I am, knows what I left behind in Blackwood, and that the fate of my kingdom, the kingdom he swore an oath to, lies with me. The First Guard would never let the leader be removed, which means if I am successful, if I bring that dust back with me, he won't hesitate to send me back.

And he would stay.

He would never choose to return to our world over giving someone else in his crew the opportunity. He would never leave knowing there were people here that still needed protection, even if it meant breaking his oath and not being there to protect the king. He'd sacrifice the life he envisioned to make sure someone else had a chance at theirs.

And I would never see him again.

Or Sig, or Stassia. Jorn and Auralie.

Fin.

My breaths grow shallow and tears prick at my eyes. I can't get emotional about this. Both Brynne and Weston constantly remind me I fight with too much emotion, and stealing the dust might be the biggest fight I'll ever be part of. I have no choice; I have to win.

"We have a problem though," I say, thinking back to what Taril told me yesterday.

Sig waits quietly for my answer.

"Mara. She's trying to convince them all that I'm a traitor. Taril said Dane doesn't believe it, but I'm going to have to deal with her. There's no way she will believe anything I say."

The spark of an idea glitters in her eye. "What if we make it look like you escaped?"

"How would we do that?" I ask, my brows narrowing at her. "She saw me protect you and run away. She's going to see right through it."

Sig steps closer, excitement rising in her voice. "You could convince them it was all a ploy, that you were trying to make us believe you were on our side so you could escape. You can do to them what you tried to do to us."

"That could work," I say slowly, thinking through the plan. "If we make it look like I escaped, I could use that to convince Mara that it was all an act. I could pretend that I was discovered and imprisoned again, but finally got away. That way, they really wouldn't have any reason not to believe me."

"For this to work, you would have to get close to Dane again." She meets my eyes, imploring, trying to read my emotions. "Are you alright with that?"

I know what she means by close, and it isn't just in proximity of camp. *Close.*

My stomach churns just thinking about having to pretend with Dane, having to act like I know nothing of the lies he's spewed, the manipulation and coercion. The thought of kissing him, touching him, and having him touch me makes my skin crawl, especially since I haven't been able to stop thinking about another man's lips and touch instead.

"I can handle it." I don't need to say anything more. Sig knows I will do what needs to be done, despite my feelings for Weston, feelings I know I haven't been able to hide from Sig. She sees right through me, and I know that's why she asked.

"This could work, Lennox." I see a sparkle in her eye, and I recognize it immediately.

Hope.

Weston keeps saying he won't give up hope that we will find the dust, or how it is replenished, but what if *this* is the hope we need to have? What if we have to take action, and the island has been making moves, pushing us in certain directions to allow it to happen?

"I think it could," I say. "I just have to get Weston to believe in me."

And let me out of his sight, which has proven to be the most difficult task of all.

CHAPTER FORTY-TWO

"Lennox! Come with me!"

Fin's voice carries across the room, pulling my focus from the book I'm reading. I look up to find him dragging Weston by the hand up the stairs to the first deck. He extends his other hand out toward me, flapping it up and down.

"Come on!" he calls out, then flashes me with a toothy grin.

I close the book and set it on the chair, only for Stass to snatch it out from behind me and flip it open to the first page.

"I want that back," I say, before striding across the room toward the stairs.

"Mmhm," she murmurs, her eyes not leaving the page to even acknowledge me.

Fin's smile gets wider with every step until I'm next to him, wrapping my hand around his tiny fingers.

"Where are we going?"

"To my bed! Will you help tell my story tonight?" he says, his eyes wide and pleading as he looks up at me.

I glance up at Weston, catching the slight pink tinge to his cheeks.

He's been telling Fin stories every night?

My mouth falls open slightly in disbelief. How can this man who cares so deeply about the people around him not want a family? Is his decades old friendship with my father worth the sacrifice of something he so clearly enjoys and desires?

"Of course," I say, turning back to Fin. "But I've never told a bedtime story before, so you might need to help me."

"Mister Weston can help you. He's really good at them," Fin says and yanks us both up the steps behind him.

Fin releases our hands just as we reach the door to the crew's quarters and races inside, disappearing around the corner. Weston shifts in the doorway, turning sideways, trying to keep his bulky body out of the way. He gestures for me to enter, so I stride past him, my shoulder brushing his chest as I squeeze past in the narrow doorway.

I ignore the heat and tingles spreading over every point of contact and walk straight into the room, scanning the space for Fin, spotting him just as he jumps onto a bed that is tucked away into the corner of the room. He flips his body around on the bed and slides under the blankets, pulling them to his chin and waiting for us.

I'm too aware of how close Weston walks at my back, close enough that if my steps were to stutter at all, he would bump into me.

Don't do it, Lennox.

We reach his corner, and I sit down on the side of the bed, Weston kneeling beside my knees, facing Fin. It's obvious this is a nightly occurrence with how comfortable both of them look at being near each other. My chest aches as I watch them silently, thankful Fin has someone that cares about him as much as I do.

"Any requests tonight?" Weston asks, as he leans his elbows on the edge of the bed, clasping his hands in front of him. Fin's face lights up.

"I want Lennox to tell it!" he cries, looking past Weston to me expectantly.

The room is empty, the rest of the crew not yet turned in for the night, so I don't have to worry about anyone listening to me stumble through trying to tell a story. I'd heard plenty over the years from Edmond, but in this moment, my mind is blank of every single one, except for the one that brought me here. I need to make up one of my own and hope it is enough to ease him to sleep.

"Once upon a time," I start, then pause to think.

Fin doesn't know who I am; I've kept it a secret, so to him, I'm just Lennox, the girl who came to Dawnlin right before him, and taught him to shoot a bow. I know he would be my selection of who among us should be sent home when we get the dust, and I don't want him to leave without knowing me, the true me, even if he doesn't realize it.

Maybe someday he will piece it together.

"Once upon a time," I say again, "there was a princess who lived in a big, stone castle." Fin's smile widens at the mention of a princess and castle, so I keep going.

"She never left the castle. She only knew everyone who worked there, so she didn't have any friends to play with."

"Poor princess," Fin says, a frown forming on his lips.

Weston's head sinks slightly, his chin dipping to his chest, and I wonder if he realizes I'm talking about myself.

"She may not have had any other children to play with, but she had lots of books to read. She would read about different worlds, with princes and dragons and giants. Every day, it was like she lived in another place, even though she never left the castle.

"Her favorite parts of the books were when the princess could go to a grand ball, with lots of food and music and pretty dresses, and dance with princes. She wished she could go to a ball of her own and waited a long time until one was planned to celebrate her birthday. She was so excited to meet new friends and dance and sing. She dressed up in a brand new big gown and got ready for the party, but when she opened the doors to the ballroom, no one had come."

Weston lets out a breath through his nose and shakes his head slightly. The knuckles on his outstretched hands are white, and I pull my eyes away from them and look back at Fin.

He understands.

"Oh no," Fin says, his eyebrows crunched together and forehead creased.

"She was very sad, and just wanted to leave and escape to one of the worlds she read about in her books, but—"

"But just when she was about to run away," Weston cuts in, taking over the story. I clamp my mouth shut, waiting to see where he is going with it. "One of the castle guards saw how sad she was and asked her to dance. The music played and even though no one else was there, she still had a great time at the ball. After that night, the princess and the guard became friends, and went off on all kinds of adventures, just like in the books she had read."

"Where did they go?" Fin asks. "Did they see a dragon?"

"That can be another story for another night," Weston says, reaching out to ruffle Fin's hair.

He rolls to his side and curls into a ball, his eyes softly falling closed. "I'm glad the princess made a friend," he says with a wide yawn.

Tears fill my eyes and I turn away before anyone can see them threatening to fall.

"Goodnight, Lennox. Goodnight, mister Weston," Fin murmurs.

Clearing my throat, I reach over and squeeze his leg before whispering back, "Goodnight, Fin."

The room dims around us as I stand and walk toward the door, trying to swipe at my eyes discreetly. Weston follows wordlessly behind, his presence at my back just as close as it was before.

Once we are in the hallway, my head falls back with a sniffle, and I blink away the remaining tears, trying to compose myself. I don't want him to see me cry, knowing that it was his fantastical story about showing me kindness that did it.

"You and I are on tonight," Weston says behind me.

I clear my throat and turn around. "Doesn't Jorn normally go with you?" My voice wavers despite trying to pull back all the emotion.

His eyes are softer than normal as they trail over my face, looking for any evidence of tears that had fallen. I don't want to admit how much a simple story broke me, causing all the loneliness I felt that night to rush back, the stark contrast to how many people I have who care about me now.

"He asked to stay back with Taril. I can get someone else if you don't want to."

"Are you telling me I'm allowed to go back out?"

The night he kissed me, he forbade me from going out on my shift. Besides the permission he gave Sig that I could join the collection crew, he hadn't revoked the order, and I need to hear him say it.

"Yes, you can go back out," he says.

"Not just with you?" I quirk an eyebrow, challenging him to say no.

"Yes, princess."

I nod. "Alright, then I'll go."

Sig and I agreed I needed to talk to Weston as soon as possible, and the perfect opportunity just fell into my lap. No matter what that story made me feel, and how much I want to go curl up in bed and cry myself to sleep, I am not going to pass it up.

"Meet me on deck in a few minutes."

I step back against the wall, letting him pass me, feeling the heat coming off him as he gets close, before he disappears down the steps. The creak of hinges startles me, and I look across the hall to find Sig peeking through a crack in her doorway.

I point in the direction Weston just disappeared. "Were you behind this?"

"Maybe," she whispers. "I figured it would be a good time. We need to act fast."

"I agree," I say, and sigh. "Wish me luck. I'll find you in the morning."

I grab my bow from the armory and my dagger from the bedside table before heading up to the deck. Weston isn't here yet, so I tilt my head back to stare up at the sky, at the same stars that amazed and excited me when I got here, but now I can't help but want to go back home where I won't see them again.

As long as I'm not alone.

So much has changed since I stepped foot onto this island and took in the sky for the first time. I soak it up now, knowing that there is a possibility my time with it will end. Closing my eyes, I listen to the waves roll into the cove, and the breeze ruffles the sails. I breathe in the salt and water, and the fragrance of the beach, trying to commit every piece to memory for the day that comes when it is all gone.

I want to see more of our world; being on the island has taught me that. When the day comes, if it ever does, that I make the decisions, no one will be able to stop me.

"Ready?" Weston's voice breaks my train of thought, and I open my eyes to find him watching me, his expression unreadable.

"Yes," I say. "Let's go."

CHAPTER FORTY-THREE

Weston doesn't say a word as we trudge through the tunnels, his stoic mask firmly in place as he stares ahead, keeping pace with my short strides. His quiet and borderline monosyllabic nature isn't new to me, but this feels different.

Had the story affected him as much as it did me?

Is he worried about the dust?

Is there something else going on?

My thoughts are consumed by wondering what could be making him even more irritable than usual, and this is not where my focus should be on this shift. I have to find the right time to ask him to send me back, but with the shift in his mood, I'm worried this chance Sig dropped into my lap will be wasted. Changing his mood may be the only hope for a different outcome, so I need to ease the tension.

"Where are we searching tonight?" I ask.

We take a few more steps before he answers, as if he had to convince himself to respond, and when he does, his voice is a low grumble, his words short.

"Where do you want to search, princess?"

Ignoring it and the way it makes me bristle, I continue on. "You mean there's no plan tonight?"

"We can make whatever plan you want."

I can feel my irritation rising, but I stomp it down. It won't get me anywhere if we start bickering again.

"Have you searched a lot around the mountain? That is where the cure is, so it could make sense that the dust is there too."

"We can look."

"With all the activity there recently, maybe the island will show us something."

"Maybe."

"Are you alright?" I say, stopping in front of him and spinning so I'm blocking his way. I cross my arms over my chest, unable to hold in my rising irritation any longer. "You seem like you're pissed at me, and I don't know why."

"I'm fine, princess."

"Did I do something?" I ask, a twinge of nerves settling in my stomach. I don't know if he'll tell me, but I need to at least pose the question. If it was something I said, I want to clear it up before I bring up what I really need to talk about tonight.

"No." He stares down the tunnel over my head, refusing to look down at me, making me feel like his words and his behaviors are not aligning.

"Fine," I say, turning on my heel and storming through the tunnel. If he doesn't want to talk to me, then I won't talk. We can search in silence and I'll just blindside him with my question instead. Maybe the element of surprise will help catch him off guard enough to say yes.

Bounding ahead, I lead the way through the tunnels, the pathway there more familiar with the number of times we've gone back and forth through it, but this time we're not going to the lookout. A small tunnel branches off the main, and I take it, climbing the steps at the end until my head almost hits the top of the tunnel. I push slowly, lifting a trap door above me, and peer out, scanning the surrounding area for any movement or signs of Voyagers. Once it feels safe enough to leave, I prop the trapdoor open and climb the rest of the steps, Weston close behind me.

He lowers the door with a thud, and I don't bother with any more niceties.

"Are there more caves?" I ask pointedly.

"More caves?"

"Yes, like where we met. Are there more of them?"

"Yes."

Huffing loudly, I start toward the stone bridge. The only cave I know exists is where I met Weston, but knowing that one is hidden behind the falls of the lagoon, I assume there are others tucked away in the same area. Our cave was empty, and led nowhere, not counting when the island opened up and let Weston leave through the solid rock, but that doesn't mean there isn't a clue in another.

"This way."

Weston steps in front of me, and my breath hitches as he reaches back, lacing his fingers through mine. His thumb presses tightly to the back of my hand as he guides me through the landscape, and all my irritation melts away with the contact. Flames lace up my arm and my heart pounds erratically in my ears as I trail behind him, trying to calm the frantic thoughts in my head.

I never knew holding someone's hand could feel this chaotic, this protective.

This possessive.

Moments ago, he couldn't even meet my eye, and now he's pulling me behind him, leading me through the jungle, his firm grip clutching me as if he doesn't want to let go. No other guard would have dared to touch me this way, not even Brynne, but he didn't hesitate.

The mist from the falls quickly dampens our clothes, and my hair sticks to my neck as we cross the bridge to the same side as the lookout. Following the curve of the lagoon, we walk along the edge, the nearby trees giving us some cover in case anyone is prowling the area at night, or might come around the bend of the main path.

Weston's grip on my hand doesn't loosen as we approach the edge, the dark water below making the lagoon seem like an endless abyss, and my stomach flips at the mental image of falling in again, even though I know how to swim.

He releases my hand and the absence of his is too apparent as I watch him lower himself over the edge until he's standing, his chest even with the ground. Arms raised, he beckons me forward without a word, so I take the last few steps and plop onto the ground, scooting myself through the grass and reeds and letting my feet dangle over the side.

I don't know how far down the ledge he's standing on is, but I know I'm not as tall as Weston, so it is a farther drop for me. I slowly slide over the end, pointing my toes and trying to feel for the perch, when his hands wrap around my ribcage, lowering me in front of him.

My eyes don't stray from the laces on his vest as he cages me against the sheer rock face, and I don't know if the fluttering in my low abdomen is from fear of falling, or fear of his proximity. Before I can decipher which, he breaks the silence.

"There's an entrance just that way. You go first, I'll be right behind you," he murmurs, and I nod in acknowledgement.

He pushes off the wall, giving me enough space so I can spin around and scale the ledge, moving in the direction he indicated. Before I can step out of his reach, his hand presses into my low back, supporting me and sending shivers up my spine.

Heaving a breath, I focus on my steps and my grip on the rock, not on the heat from his hand, burning me through my shirt. The entrance to the cave is dark, and I step inside with a sigh of relief that doubles once I hear his footsteps on the stone behind me.

"Are they connected at all?" I squint into the darkness, trying to make out the shape of the space, but I can barely see a few paces in front of me.

"Some of them are, but they don't go all the way around. The one I brought you to before isn't."

"You did that on purpose, didn't you?" I ask, glancing over my shoulder. The moonlight illuminates the entrance, casting him in complete shadow, so I can't see his expression.

"I've gone this long without being found. That wasn't going to change."

"But you got out, even though there wasn't a way."

His dark figure shrugs slightly. "I know the island. You didn't."

I look forward again, facing the darkness before us. "I'm still not going to know the island if we can't see where we are going," I mutter, and the moment the last word leaves my lips, a torch appears on the wall, casting the cave in a dim glow.

"Thank you," I whisper to whatever powers are watching.

Weston lifts the torch off the wall, and walks toward the back of the cave, where a jagged tunnel cuts into the rock. We wordlessly trudge through the cave, following the tunnel as it carves through the land. The tension from before is back along with Weston's scowl, so I focus on the task, scanning the surfaces for carvings, trying to find doors or levers. The island doesn't change, does nothing to alter our course, which I take as a sign. Maybe we are on the right track.

Hours pass and we emerge into a large shallow cave, the round opening in the cliff face pointed directly at the mountain across the lagoon. I walk over toward the edge and peer out, getting caught up in the view of the moonlit falls cascading down into the dark water.

"Was what you said true?"

I pull my eyes away and turn back to the cave to find Weston standing in the middle of the space, watching me.

"What did I say?" I ask.

Is he finally going to bring up what is bothering him? He said I did nothing before, but was he lying? Again?

"Was no one there? For your ceremony."

Oh.

It was the story that bothered him, but not the story specifically, what inspired the story. He's been quiet since we left the ship, and I wonder if he has been brooding about it since I uttered the words.

I look down at my boots and nudge a pebble around on the ground.

"It may have been a story, but I wasn't making it up," I say. Admitting this feels harder than it should, especially after deciding to tell Fin because I wanted him to know about me, about how I got here. Weston knowing feels infinitely different, more vulnerable and raw.

"He invited no one?"

He mentions my father so casually, and it is still hard for me to connect them together, even though it feels like a past life. I curse the tears that well, blurring my vision as I look up at him, his teal eyes burning into mine.

"He didn't let them in."

The muscles in his jaw ripple, clenching harder than I've seen before, and the intensity of his gaze only deepening.

"I wasn't lying when I said I was alone," I say, trying to smile through the pain and loneliness that comes rushing back once again. I don't know if my time in Dawnlin will ever fully erase it, especially since I need to go back, and nothing there will have changed. I'll just know everything and everyone I'm missing until I am the one who can make the decisions.

He turns away suddenly, walking to the wall and reaching up to wedge the torch into it. Striding over to me, he stops just a pace away and dips into a deep bow.

"What are you doing?" I mutter, watching him rise back up again before extending his hand forward.

"May I have this dance?"

My stomach flips as I stare at his outstretched hand, waiting for mine to take it, and I shake my head rapidly.

"You don't have to do this. Really, I'm fine." I try to step past him, to get out of his proximity and back to our task, but he steps in front of me, blocking my exit and closing the space between us. His fingers brush the underside of my chin and gently lift until I have no choice but to meet his gaze.

"Princess," he murmurs. My chin quivers and the tears finally fall down my cheeks as I blink up at him. His eyes flicker between mine, looking past all the hurt and loneliness, searching for something. "Dance with me."

Hand shaking, I place it in his, and he grips it firmly. Dance customs from every kingdom were drilled into me since I was a child. I knew the steps, the formalities, but all the lessons fall away the moment he reaches out with his other hand. He slides his fingertips down the back of my arm and across my palm, my skin tingling in their wake, as he slowly lifts my hand and sets it to rest on his chest.

I can't breathe.

Gone is the smirking, overbearing asshole captain who tested me and pushed me as often as he could. In his place is Weston, the man who saved my life, who made sure I survived, who taught me to swim and disarm an opponent, so I felt safe. The man who let me hate him, just so I didn't hate myself. The man who is so clearly upset that no one showed up for me, and even though he has absolutely no responsibility for my emotional state, he is shouldering that hurt, anyway.

When he wraps his hand around my waist and takes the first step, my instincts take over. With every step he leads, I follow as we turn around the cave in a simple waltz, the only music the gentle lapping of the lagoon and distant roar of the falls.

I can't look at him. I don't want him to see how much this means to me. He can't see everything I've been trying to hide since the moment he kissed me, since I found out about all of Dane's lies, since he said it would never happen again. I don't want him to see how I've fallen for him, and how much it hurts, feeling like nothing will ever come of it.

The princess and the First Guard.

Some would say, maybe in another life, but we *are* in another life, and he still won't allow himself to feel what deep down I think he feels. I don't want him to see the devastation building inside, knowing he is just another thing my duty has taken from me.

Instead, I close my eyes and try to hold on to this moment for a little longer.

He must notice, because without warning he spins me multiple times, the rapid, continual spins that force me to open my eyes and focus back on him so I don't fall over. On the last turn, he pulls me toward him, our chests colliding as he holds me tightly.

Our steps transform into a sway, completely abandoning the formality of the waltz. My chest heaves against his, growing more rapid with every movement as his arm relaxes, tucking closer into our sides, and his chin settles into my hair. Flames light inside me, the heat consuming me from the inside out as I melt into him, resting my cheek against his chest and feeling the pounding of his heart beneath.

Nothing else exists outside of this cave, not the threat of the Voyagers, not Dane, not the worry that we'll be trapped here. I just want to forget it all, and live in this moment for as long as we can.

Time passes, slowly, quickly, I'm not sure.

"What are you thinking?" Weston says, finally breaking the silence. His voice rumbles through his chest, low and deep, like he's trying to keep others from hearing, despite being completely alone together.

I can't tell him my real thoughts, the ones I am holding captive deep inside, but I know what I need to do.

I swallow the lump forming in my throat and fight the sinking feeling in my stomach. This is it, this is the time. I can't back down now.

"I need to tell you something," I say, lifting my head from his chest and taking a small step back. I can't be this close to him as I try to gather my courage and calm my pounding heart.

"Yes, princess?" His gaze drops to my lips, and I catch the corner of my bottom lip between my teeth. Eyes darkening, they stay trained on my mouth as his hand tightens, the pressure pulling me infinitesimally closer.

I inhale quickly and unleash the words in a rush of breath before I can change my mind.

"I need to go back to the Voyagers."

We stop moving instantly, and his eyes snap to mine. All the molten warmth found there a moment ago has disappeared.

"Let me explain before you say anything, please?"

His muscles stiffen under my touch, and I know I'm losing my chance, so I let the words spill out, trying to at least get him to hear them before he completely shuts down and denies everything Sig and I are hoping for.

"I know you said no to Sig before, but I really want you to rethink this. The dust is running out. I know we keep looking for it, but you've been looking for twenty years and haven't found it. The only chance any of us have at getting home is getting that pouch from Dane."

His face draws tighter and fury flashes in his eyes at the mention of Dane.

Shit.

"I know you don't trust him," I splutter, "and now I don't either. But that is all the more reason for me to go back and try to take it from him. We can't let him strand us here. You know I'm the only one who can get close enough to him to take it."

"No," he growls, his hands dropping away from my body as he steps backward.

"Weston, please," I beg, my skin suddenly feeling cold in every place we were pressed together.

"No," he says again, his voice harsher than before. He doesn't even acknowledge that I called him by his name, unlike the last time it happened.

"Taril said things were different at camp, that Dane was behaving oddly."

"You told me nothing Taril could say would make you want to go back," he says, and a chill slides up my spine.

He's right, I said that, and I had no intention of going back when I made that statement. But now, after hearing from Taril and talking to Sig, I just don't think we have a choice.

"I know what I said, but I think something is going on. I need to go back now. If I don't try, we're going to be trapped here."

"I've been trapped here for twenty years, princess. I've made my peace with it." His voice rises and his lips turn down in a scowl.

"That's bullshit, and you know it," I say, my voice rising to match his. "If you had, you wouldn't keep searching. You wouldn't keep holding onto hope. You're still trying to get home. Let me help!"

"You're not going back." He brushes past me, crossing the cave toward the torch, but I'm not letting him shut this down that easily. I follow right behind him, refusing to back down.

"Why? Give me a good reason."

"Because I said so."

Reaching out, I grab hold of his vest, yanking him to a halt. He turns and faces me with an aggravated sigh, planting his hands on his hips as he glares down at me.

"That isn't even close to a reason, Weston! I don't understand what more I need to do for you to believe in me."

"Believing in you isn't the issue," he huffs and turns back toward the wall again.

"Then let me go back," I say, yanking on the leather again. I need him to listen to me, not to just brush me off with an already made up mind.

"No."

"Why. Not!" I yell.

"You just need to trust me!" he roars, whirring around and towering over me. I stagger backward at his anger, as his yell bounces off the walls of the cave, but it isn't just his outburst that startled me. There's something more, something I feel like I still don't know.

Something he's still hiding from me.

"I do trust you," I say, my voice dropping, but my anger still makes the sound tremble. "But now I think there's something you aren't telling me."

He stays silent and runs his hand through his hair, his gaze fixated on the ground beyond me.

"What aren't you telling me, Weston?"

"Just drop it, princess."

"How am I supposed to trust you when I feel like you're hiding something more from me?"

Closing the distance, his hands find my face, palms cradling my jaw as his fingers dig into my hair. My mind flashes to the last time he held me like this, and my lips part, expecting his face to drop to mine, taking my breath away.

But he doesn't move. He holds me in place, an internal war raging behind those teal eyes.

"You're not going back," he murmurs, more calmly but just as directly. His thumb strokes my cheek as his eyes dart between mine, pleading. The anger is gone, and my knees weaken when I realize it's been replaced with something that looks a lot like fear.

Why is Weston afraid of me going back?

"I just need you to trust me...Please," he begs, bringing me back to the last time we stood in a cave, and he was pleading with me.

I trusted him then, and look at everything that happened, everything that changed. Why would this be any different? Whatever he isn't telling me, maybe he has good enough reason.

"Alright," I breathe, and relief flashes in his eyes. His thumb continues to slide over my skin, and I silently beg him to lean in, craving the feel of his lips on mine, even if it is only the merest of brushes. I'd take anything after tonight. With one final stroke, his hands fall away from my face, and he steps back, snapping the taut cord and bringing me back to the reality that he won't kiss me again.

I clear my throat and avert my eyes. He may have told me no, but this conversation isn't over. He can't decide to take this hope away from me, away from everyone else in the crew, and keep everything a secret.

"If you're going to make this choice for everyone," I say, glancing back up at him, "they deserve to know."

His head hangs slightly as my words sink in.

"I know," he mumbles.

"It can only come from you. They trust you."

He lets out a deep sigh and meets my gaze. "I know. I will tell them."

"Soon."

He nods and looks away. "I will tell them soon."

The sky is just beginning to lighten when Weston and I step back onto the deck. Neither of us speak a word to each other after he agrees to tell the crew. Instead, we search the rest of the night in silence, giving my mind plenty of time to race through all the thoughts and possibilities for the future, and what it means to give up now.

Weston heads toward the armory to unload his weapons and holds a hand out to me at the bottom of the steps. Pulling my bow and quiver off my shoulder, I hand them to him and he takes them wordlessly, disappearing down the hallway.

Footsteps approach from behind, and I glance over my shoulder to find Sig cautiously descending the steps. She catches my eye and I tilt my head toward the showers, the first place I normally go after a night of searching.

Weston shouldn't suspect anything.

She follows behind, and we slip into the room, Sig closing the door firmly behind us. It's empty, still too early for most of the crew to be up and moving yet, except for whoever is at the lookout today.

I step inside the stall and the water starts; the sound providing a decent cover for our whispers.

"What did he say?" Sig says, her expression hopeful. I level a look at her and watch as her face falls when she realizes she already knows my answer.

"He said no."

Her jaw works, her gaze falling to the floor as she nods and clears her throat, trying to hide the emotion clearly welling up inside her.

"I know you tried. It's not your fault."

"No, Sig, you don't understand. I'm still going."

Her head snaps up, the hope returning to her face. "What?"

Weston told me to trust him, begged me to, and I do, but I can't live with myself if I give up and don't try. This may be the only way I can truly help the Castaways, and I'm the only one who can do it.

There is no other choice, but he doesn't have to know.

"He may have said no, but this is our only chance. I think our plan will work. Now we just need to figure out how to sneak me off the ship."

"Are you sure? This isn't a game. He will figure it out, and when he does—"

I shake my head. "I will deal with him when that happens. The bigger issue is you. He will be *furious* with you."

"I've had twenty years of dealing with that man's emotions. I can handle his mood."

Taking a step closer, I grip her arms tightly and drop my voice even lower. "He can't follow me, Sig. You can't let him. It will ruin my chances if he tries to come after me."

She lets out a huff. "I may need to enlist some help on that."

"Do whatever you need to do. Just wait until after I'm gone, so no one gives it away."

I'm sure Jorn would help with whatever Sig needed. They might be the only ones who can actually get through to Weston and convince him to let me do what needs to be done.

"Agreed," she says with a nod. "When are we doing this?"

"I don't know. We need the right opportunity, but we need to be ready."

She clasps my shoulders, drawing us closer. The earnest confidence in her face fills me with warmth and anticipation.

"You can do this, Lennox. I know you can."

"Thanks, Sig. No matter what happens, I'm really glad I met you."

"You're not getting rid of me that easily," she says, shoving me off so I almost stumble back into the stream of water. "We're still trapped here, remember?"

I chuckle. "Hopefully not for long."

We figure out more details in the next few minutes before deciding to separate. Time is ticking, and the longer we talk about it, the more risk we have of anyone walking in and overhearing us.

Once she leaves, I strip down and stand under the warm flow of water, letting it ease the tension in my neck and back, even if only slightly. Now that I'm alone, I can sit with my thoughts and our plans.

Weston's expression when I said I needed to go back to the Voyagers replays in my mind, over and over again. The shock, the hurt, the anger. Tenderness wasn't something he often shows to people, but he showed it to me tonight. He cared about my past and wanted to do anything he could to right it. I think he feels some responsibility for it, because maybe if he'd been there, my father would have been different.

But if he'd been there, there would be no Weston, not the way there is here.

Even though he still pushes me away.

The way he held me, the way he looked at me, was only what I've ever read about in books, the way I've always wanted a man to look at me, and be unafraid to touch me. He could have kissed me, and now, I don't know if he even wants to talk to me.

But more than that, I need to mentally prepare myself for what is about to come. After telling him I trusted him, disappearing and going back to the Voyagers, back to Dane, will hurt Weston. I don't want to hurt him, not after everything he's done to keep me from being hurt, but it is the sacrifice I have to make.

I'm doing this *for* him, for everyone here who deserves the chance to get home. Dane can't keep holding us here against our will, and he can't find out about the location of the waters.

So, I have to try, not just for me, but for every single Castaway that had their hope and life taken away.

I close my eyes and let the water fall, remembering all of my training, both physical and mental. I can do this. I can convince Dane that I'm back, that the Castaways kept me hostage, and that I wanted to return to them. If I can convince Dane, Mara will have no choice but to follow, and if she doesn't, at least Weston taught me how to disarm someone if she tries to stab me in my sleep.

Now I just need to find the strength to walk back into camp, to be with Dane the way I was before, and most importantly, figure out how to leave Weston behind.

CHAPTER FORTY-FOUR

Dawnlin always seems to know when things are happening, and tonight is no different. Energy hums through the ship, and the crew feels more alert. Once the suns begin descending in the sky, Weston cancels the shifts for the night and tells everyone to meet him on deck after dinner. The mess is charged and full of whispers, as everyone eats and speculates what could have caused him to cancel a shift, because apparently it takes something big and usually dangerous for him to do so.

It's been over a week since Sig and I started making our plans, and we have been slowly taking steps to ensure we are ready when the right moment comes. During my shift this week, I smuggled my old set of clothes out and hid them in the tunnels, so there's one less thing to worry about when the plan is put into action.

And by the way everything feels, something is telling me tonight might be the night.

Sig and I stand on deck behind the rest of the crew, waiting as Weston scans the group, waiting to make sure everyone is accounted for. Auralie and Stassia come up alongside us and Fin weaves through everyone's legs, talking and laughing as he goes.

Weston waits at the top of the stairs to the quarterdeck, arms crossed and face drawn. His eyes find mine through the crowd, and I know exactly what is happening. He's about to tell everyone about the dust. I give him a small nod, and he breaks contact, his gaze dropping to his boots, before clearing his throat and looking up to address the Castaways.

Silence falls, and all eyes are trained on him, the hum of energy still constant.

Small arms wrap around one of my legs as Fin squeezes in close, and I set my hand on his shoulder.

"I have some news I need to tell you all," Weston starts. His throat bobs, and I know he's trying to find the courage to break everyone's hearts, to tear away their futures. "I found out some more information recently, and it is important you are all aware. We all know the dust is the only way to get on and off Dawnlin, and the Guardian controls the dust. You've all met Dane. He brought every single one of you here, but he can't bring you back. That's why you're here, with us. We've been searching for a way home for years. We've tried to find dust ourselves, and we still search, but we haven't been successful."

I sneak a glance around, looking at the faces of the Castaways around me, expressions all ranging from confusion to hope.

"I found out recently that the dust is almost gone, and Dane doesn't know how to replenish it."

Weston's jaw tenses as he waits for the words to settle. A few gasps sound from the crowd, and I look over to find Auralie, hand over her mouth as tears cascade down her face. Stassia is stoic for the first time since I've known her, the joy she normally wears completely leached from her body.

The moment I learned we might be trapped on the island forever, I felt hopeless and scared, but I had only just arrived in Dawnlin. A storm of emotions must be going through each of them as they realize what Weston is telling them, and my heart breaks as I look out over the faces of my friends, the faces that have become my family, and possibly the only family I will ever have.

"It is possible that very soon, no one will be able to come to Dawnlin," he pauses, and I can see a flash of pain on his face. "Or leave."

Sig shifts uncomfortably next to me, but I keep my focus trained on Weston.

"I still have hope, and I don't intend to stop searching. I understand if any of you do not want to continue, and I won't fault you for it. I don't know what this means for Dawnlin, and how things will change once we are all trapped here, us and them. But I will be here for each of you for as long as I live."

My chest aches as I watch Weston stay strong for his crew, knowing he isn't lying or exaggerating in his last promise. He has already taken on the burden of leading and protecting everyone here from Dane, and he will continue to do so. Even though he told them all today that the situation has changed, he only did so at my urging. He doesn't want to give up, doesn't want to stop, and I know he will live the rest of his life searching for a way home.

Motion catches my eye and I watch Jorn jog up the steps and wrap his arms around Weston, clapping him on the back.

"We love you, Cap," Jorn yells, releasing him to a chorus of agreements from everyone around me.

Weston scratches the back of his head, his eyes downcast, and nods to everyone.

"Alright, that's enough," he says. "I canceled shifts tonight because I know this is a lot to accept, and I wanted us all to be together as a crew and enjoy the evening." His eyes find mine again for a second before looking away. "I'll be here if anyone needs to talk."

Murmurs start as everyone disperses, and the energy is a conglomeration of every type of reaction to this hopeless news. Some are clearly upset, while others seem to be taking everything in the most positive light possible. A few of the guys approach Weston, talking to him and clapping his shoulder just as Jorn had, and I smile, knowing as hard as that was for him, no one seems to blame him. They know how much he has supported them over the years, and now they are doing the same for him.

"What does he mean, Lennox?" Fin asks, gazing up at me as he squeezes my leg a little tighter. I peel his arms off of me and sink down to his level.

"It means we might not be able to go back to our world," I say calmly.

His eyebrows meet in the middle, and his lip starts to quiver. "So I won't see my family anymore?"

I shake my head. "No, Fin, none of us will."

"Will you still be here with me? And mister Weston?"

I rub my hand over his hair. "Yes, we will all be here with you. We're not leaving you."

If there is any reassurance I can give Fin, any light in this awful circumstance, it is this. He will not be alone, not as long as this crew exists. He may not ever see his family again, and he may be a little boy forever, but every person here loves him, and would do anything for him.

"What about Roley?" he asks, tears misting his eyes.

"I hope we can see Roley again soon," I say.

He leaps forward, wrapping his arms around my neck and squeezing me tightly. "Lennox, I'm sad."

"Me too, Fin. I think we're all a little sad." I pull him off of me and hold him at arm's length. "But let's try to have a little fun tonight, alright? I'm sure Weston will let you stay up late with everyone."

"Yeah?" His eyes widen and eyebrows rise, the distraction easily working on his childish innocence.

"Yeah," I say. "He might want you to go play some games with him." I nod in his direction, and Fin's face lights up.

"Hooray!" he cheers, and speeds off toward Weston, tackling his legs and swinging back and forth.

Standing again, I turn toward the girls, and the happiness Fin brought me for a moment sinks away again. Stassia stands with her arms wrapped around Auralie's shoulders as Auralie sobs into her chest. Tears prick my eyes, and I have to look away. I may have known this was coming; I was the one that brought them the information, but despite being one of the newest ones on the island, it is still difficult for me, too.

Especially after everything Sig and I talked about weeks ago.

Fingers wrap around my elbow, and I startle as they pull me away. Glancing over my shoulder, I find Sig, and follow as she leads me toward the side railing, far enough away from the group to be just beyond the risk of overhearing.

"I think this is it," she murmurs as she looks out over the deck. "This is the most unsuspecting time, and everyone will be distracted." She glances back at Weston, who has a group forming around him, and I look over the crew too. People are moving crates and bringing up chairs from below. Someone is setting up a large low barrel in the middle of the deck and organizing the seats around it.

"I think you're right," I say. Everyone will be too focused on processing the news and enjoying the evening to be paying attention to my whereabouts, especially if someone brings out the bottles.

"Just act normal," she says. "I'll be around."

She disappears into the bustling deck, the area now transformed around me. A robust fire is burning in the barrel, and soft music floats through the air as Eirlik strums an instrument. It's peaceful, a stark contrast to the intensity on deck just minutes before.

Auralie rests her head on Stass' shoulder as they sit in front of the fire on a large crate. I head over toward them, noticing that Auralie's sobs have reduced to sniffles as she stares into the fire, but Stassia has the same stoic expression as before.

"Mind if I sit?" I ask.

Stassia lifts her other arm and holds it out, giving me space to slide in next to her. She drapes her arm across my shoulders and I sidle up to her, watching the flames dance in front of us, just as they are.

"How are you doing?" Stass asks me softly.

"I'm alright," I say. My heart aches as I watch Stassia and Auralie take this news so badly, and I can't keep hiding from them. From the moment I met them, they've been nothing but honest with and accepting of me, and I need to do the same. I need to make sure that they know I care about each of them before heading into this eternal unknown. "I was actually the one who told him about the dust."

"You knew?" she asks, looking over at me, obvious shock on her face.

"I did," I say, sinking into her side a little lower. "I'm sorry. I couldn't say anything."

She nods slightly and turns to stare back into the fire, the stoic mask returning. "Makes sense why you are so calm."

"Dane and I were going to try to figure out how to replenish it, but then I came here. I never got the chance to figure it out."

"It's alright," she says, and Auralie sniffles a little louder. "It isn't your responsibility. I guess this was just the way it was supposed to be for us. At least we all like each other." Her lips turn up slightly, but the smile doesn't reach her eyes.

"I'm glad to have you both in my life," I say, wrapping an arm around Stassia's back and squeezing her in a quick embrace.

My eye catches on Sig, emerging onto the deck from below, with two bottles in each hand. She crosses the deck, walking straight toward us and stops in front of the crate, wordlessly handing one to each of us before plopping down on the edge of the crate next to me.

Stassia immediately tips the bottle back, taking a few hefty gulps, while Auralie takes a small sip. I lift mine to my lips, ready to tilt it back, when I hear Sig mumble next to me.

"Yours isn't wine," she says, then takes a swig from her bottle.

I press the bottle to my lips and take a drink. The sweet flavor of fruits flows over my tongue, but there's no bitterness that follows. I tilt the mouth of the bottle slightly toward Sig, acknowledging this element of the plan.

Having the bottle in my hand will make it look like I'm participating in the activities, enjoying the night just like the rest of the crew, but the juice instead of wine will keep my wits about me, keeping me able to enact the second part of the plan.

Now that drinks have made it onto deck, the liveliness picks up. Eirlik's music shifts to something more upbeat, and someone has joined in with him, using a crate like a drum. Peals of laughter rise into the night, and some of the crew even start to dance.

Jorn's voice rings out over the music, calling people over to a space he has cleared on the floor, I assume to play the game he and Weston played after he kissed me.

"Little Lennox! Are you in?" he calls out to me, and I see the same items in the middle of the forming circle he had on the night Weston got drunk. Which means one thing: there are going to be a lot of very unobservant Castaways in a while, Jorn included.

Stassia lifts her arm off my shoulders and shoos me with her hand. "Go, I'll probably come join in a bit."

Sig nods as well, so I walk over to the circle and stop just outside of it.

"I don't know how to play," I say, eyeing the pieces resting on the floor.

Jorn pats the boards next to him. "I'll teach you. Either you'll be really good, or you'll be wrecked by the end of the night."

I sit down next to him and cross my legs under me as he goes through the rules, making sure everyone has a drink before passing the dice off so we can start. It seems simple, a game of chance and bluffing, but as more drinks are consumed, one of those things will get more and more difficult.

The nature of the game means that I am going to have to act like I am drinking as much as the rest of them, or it will be obvious that something is different about my bottle. I can't risk them finding out and trying to switch it out, or even worse, suspecting something more is going on.

I need to start my act now. I have to pretend, and get worse the longer time goes on.

In a way, this might be helpful. No one will suspect I have any plans of leaving if they think I am drunk. I won't stand out, I won't call attention, besides whatever I do to convince everyone with my behavior.

I pay attention to every time the bottle comes to my lips and slowly loosen up, but even without the wine, I feel myself lightening. The game is actually fun, and everyone's laughter is contagious. I can't help but enjoy myself, forgetting for a while that I'm about to leave these people. I have every intention of coming back, as long as everything goes according to plan, but I still feel a twinge of sadness at the thought of leaving my friends.

I lose a round, Veck easily calling my bluff, and raise my bottle to my lips only to tilt it back and find it empty. My face heats, and I feel eyes on me, but I know it's not the stare of the others playing the game. I know Weston is watching.

Be convincing, Lennox.

"Sig!" I shriek with a giggle. I look around for her, exaggerating my movements and waving my bottle in the air. "Sig! I need more!"

"Here, you can have some of mine," Jorn offers, extending his bottle to me.

I scrunch my nose and stick out my tongue, pushing his bottle back into his chest. "I'll have my own, thank you."

"Whatever you say, Little Lennox," he says and tips the bottle back, taking a large gulp. The side of my face burns as I look through the crowd for Sig, spotting her as she stops behind Jorn. She raises an eyebrow and hands me a fresh bottle, taking my empty one out of my hands.

"Thank you," I say, drawing out the sound before taking my round losing drink. I turn back to the game and hazard a glance up, my eyes colliding with the molten teal ones I know have been watching me since the moment I sat next to Jorn.

The wine may not be real, but the energy buzzing through my body definitely is the same. Everything is going to change after tonight, and I don't know how Weston will react. I don't know if he'll ever look at me with the same intensity ever again after I betray him and go back to Dane. I don't know if he will ever believe I trust him again, or trust me the same way, but tonight, I'm going to use the situation to my advantage, and finally say what I've been wanting to say for a while. Even if he only thinks my lips loosened because of the wine, I'll know they hadn't.

I'll know my words are real.

I just need him to hear them.

CHAPTER
FORTY-FIVE

Leaning against the rail with his ankles crossed out in front of him, Weston stands alone, a bottle dangling from his hands in his lap, watching the game. Specifically, watching me. My eyes snag on his and I look away quickly. My cheeks already hurt from smiling and laughing as we play, but I can't hide it when I catch him looking. I lift the bottle to my lips again, trying to hide the smile and focus back on the next few rounds.

Hopefully, my ruse is working.

Eventually, Stassia nudges my shoulder, trying to squeeze her way into the circle.

"I'm in! Move over!" Her mood seems to be considerably improved, her joy having returned and I shoot her a smile.

"Take my spot Stass," I say. "I need a break."

A chorus of boos led by Jorn sounds around me as I withdraw myself from the circle. Stass slides in behind me, and I fake a stumble into her back as I try to step away. The group laughs, and I join in, faking another wobble before righting myself and making my way across the deck.

Right toward Weston.

He's motionless as he watches me the entire way, except for his eyes, tracking my every movement as I stumble my way up beside him.

"You didn't want to play?" I ask, pointing my thumb over my shoulder back at the circle just as a burst of laughter rises into the night.

"I was enjoying watching." My cheeks heat, and I can't blame it on the wine.

"But you're over here by yourself," I say, leaning my hip onto the rail.

"Not anymore."

I take a swig of the juice as a distraction from the flame that flickers in my belly at his words.

He tracks the bottle as I lower it, and I raise my eyebrow. "What? Are you going to tell me to slow down?"

Making sure the rest of the crew saw me partaking in the fun was important, but not as important as Weston. Knowing Sig and I are moving forward with our plans for the night puts me more on edge, and makes me worried he might suspect something is going on, when he otherwise wouldn't. I need to be sure. I need to convince him there is no reason to worry, no reason to try to keep track of my whereabouts.

"No, princess," he says and takes a drink from his own bottle. He swallows and clears his throat. "But if you decide you want to go for a swim after two bottles, then I'll have no choice but to stop you."

"You can try," I say, narrowing my eyes in a challenge.

He smiles, one of his rare full smiles that makes my insides melt. He looks down at his feet like he's trying to hide it. "Why do you keep putting yourself in danger?"

A thrill courses through my body like a shiver, and I think back to how loose his lips were after he played the game, how he said things I'm sure he wouldn't otherwise say. Tonight feels like the right time with a good excuse to say them, especially knowing that everything could be different in a matter of hours.

I can't deny my feelings for him, and how he makes me feel about myself. Behind the tough exterior and the constant denials, I think he feels it too, more than just this physical attraction that keeps drawing us together.

But there's something stopping him, and it isn't Dane.

Is it my title? Or his? Is it my father?

He refuses to accept that we are not in Blackwood, and it is likely we never will be. The expectations and restrictions don't exist here.

I can't keep pushing down the pull I feel toward him any longer. From the moment I opened my eyes and found him hovering over me, begging me to breathe, I've felt it. There's always been something in the way, but tonight, I want to break down all those barriers, before I put up another one, one he may never get past.

Before I leave and possibly destroy it all.

"Maybe I changed my mind," I say, my eyes staying fixed on his face. "Maybe I like being rescued."

He tries to fight it, but loses, and drags his gaze up, teal eyes meeting mine.

"I don't want to have to, but I will always rescue you, princess," he grumbles, and a muscle twitches in his cheek. "Please don't make me have to."

Clearing my throat, I turn my head, dropping my chin to my shoulder and gaze out over the water. I can't handle the emotion behind his words, behind his stare, not tonight of all nights. Not when I know I'm going to do exactly what he doesn't want me to, and told Sig not to let him rescue me.

A sharp pain slices through my tongue as I bite into it, trying not to respond to the conversation I had started. I tap my hand on the wooden rail, trying to find a way out of this corner I've backed myself into.

"You did great earlier, with what you said. I think the entire crew appreciated you being honest with them."

"Thank you," he murmurs. The glint of the fire on the glass bottle catches my eye as he raises it to his lips.

"What were they saying? The ones who came up to you after?" I ask. I set my bottle down on the rail and face him again.

Jorn had been so understanding and supportive, probably knowing it was extremely hard for Weston to get up and address his crew about something he considers a failure. Others might not have been so understanding though, and I worry that even though everyone seems to be moving forward now, they gave him grief in the moment.

"They weren't upset with me, if that is what you are worried about."

"Good," I breathe.

"They more want to talk about what comes next and how we're going to exist here forever with the Voyagers still on the island. I don't think anyone wants to stay on this ship forever."

"Are you thinking about some kind of truce?"

He shrugs. "If there's no way to leave, then we have to figure something out. At that point, finding the waters means nothing, and it wouldn't matter if Dane knows where they are because he can't leave either. We'd need to find a way to coexist."

He is right. We can't stay in hiding forever, especially if there is no way to get off the island with or without the waters. We would need to make contact with them and work out some sort of life together.

Only if my plan fails.

"I can't imagine how different that would be, all of us together on the island."

He takes another sip from the bottle with a slow nod. "It would be."

"Are you worried about Dane?" I ask.

Worry etches across his forehead, and every hint of his smile from moments ago is gone. The thoughtful, serious captain is back, and I can't help but remember how I still feel like there is something he isn't telling me.

"Are you?" His eyebrows draw together as he tries to read my face.

"No."

The tension in his shoulders drops and his forehead relaxes.

"I realize how much he lied to me, and how quickly I believed everything he said because I was starving for friendship." I gulp down the lump in my throat, the realization of how badly Dane hurt me finally hitting. I hadn't planned to admit this all to Weston tonight, but if this is what he needs, this reassurance that I don't have any feelings for Dane any longer, and that they were all based on a lie, then I'll give it to him.

"He used that against me. He exploited my one true weakness, and the worst part is, I don't know why. Why me?"

His throat bobs and I think he wants to say something, but I don't let him. I want to get this out, so he has no more reasons to hold back.

"In the end, it doesn't matter why, it just matters that it happened, and it's over. I'm not the same person I was when I met Dane, and I never will be again. I don't want him to affect my relationships anymore. He may control the island, but he doesn't control me."

"I'm glad to hear that, princess."

His eyes soften, and I step in front of him before I lose my nerve. A look of confusion comes over his face as he uncrosses his ankles, shifting to stand, but he freezes and watches as I close the space between us, stepping between his knees. I grab the bottle out of his hands and lift it to my lips, taking a quick pull. The burn of the drink heats me from the inside out, but I need the bit of courage that my bottle won't give me.

Reaching over and leaning into him, I set it on the rail, hoping that will be enough to let me say what I want to say. My breath catches as I feel his hands wrap around my waist, his fingertips pressing into my sides.

"What are you doing?" he says softly, and the entire ship drops away. It's only me and him, standing under the stars.

My heart pounds in my ears as I step closer, leaving only a breath between us, and reach out to grasp the bottom of his vest. The feel of the leather on my hands and the brush of the linen shirt on the backs of my fingers grounds me. I don't trust myself touching him, but my fingers itch to slide under his vest and run over his firm chest. If I do, I don't think I could stop there.

Gulping, I push the thought of his round, firm muscles out of my mind.

"Giving you your truth," I say. I try to keep my voice giddy and bubbly but don't feel convincing, not after how erratic being this close to him is making me feel.

We may never be this close ever again, not after tonight.

I hope he forgives me.

"I didn't win the bet," he says. His voice is low, and his chin is tucked to his chest as he watches me.

I lean closer, my chest brushing against him, and I feel his stomach tighten.

"We could make another one," I whisper playfully.

I can blame the wine if I need to.

The corner of his lips twitches as he slides his hands down my sides before settling on my hips, his thumbs pressing into my hipbones and sending off flutters between my thighs. His eyes are dark, his pupils wide as he takes me in, and the way he's looking at me makes me think he's also forgotten we're standing in the middle of the deck, surrounded by the crew.

"What do you want to bet?" he murmurs.

Fuck.

I hadn't thought this through, hadn't come up with an idea because I wasn't expecting him to keep me from telling him. My mind is blank of anything that would be worthwhile, because I am too focused on the feeling of him holding me, of pressing into him, and on doing whatever I can to stay right here for as long as possible.

"I bet…" I break my gaze away from him and look around, trying to come up with something, when I spot the bottles I abandoned on the rail, and an idea sparks. He won't be as drunk as last time, but if I can at least loosen him a bit, I'll have a better chance of slipping out of the room unnoticed. He might also forget all of his hesitations and stop fighting whatever internal war he is waging.

Releasing his vest, I reach out and grab both our bottles, holding them out beside us.

"I bet I can drink this," I raise my bottle a little higher, "faster than you can drink yours."

He quirks his head to the side, his eyes glimmering in the moonlight. "You really think you can win that game?"

"Yes, I do."

He chuckles softly and I feel a slight flutter of his fingers on my sides. "If I win, I get my truth."

I nod exaggeratedly.

His eyes narrow playfully. "And if you win?"

I bite my lip, pretending to think for a moment. I know what I want. I haven't been able to stop thinking about it since the first time it happened, especially whenever he touches me, and we're way past the simple brush of a hand right now.

I push his bottle to the middle of his chest with a dull thud. One hand releases my hip as he plucks it from my grip, while the other smoothes over my back, pressing into me and pushing me more firmly against him.

"If I win," I say, looking him straight in the eye, hoping he doesn't see any sliver of hesitation, only the desire I've been trying to hide. "I want you to kiss me."

His eyes darken, his jaw clenching and unclenching as he holds my gaze. My stomach bottoms out and I have to squeeze my thighs together to keep from squirming under the intensity.

"How do you know I won't let you win?" he murmurs.

My lips tip up in a deep smirk, and his eyes drop to them. I lift onto my toes, my breasts sliding against his chest as I inch closer to his face. His chest stills, like he's holding his breath, like he thinks I'm the one who is going to kiss him this time.

"You're too competitive to let me win," I taunt.

Challenge dances in his eyes as he lifts the bottle to his lips, holding it there, silently agreeing to the terms of the bet. My tongue darts out, wetting my lips before I follow suit, pressing them to the mouth of the bottle. We tip them back at the same time, each taking slow, measured gulps, refusing to be the first to break eye contact.

He doesn't know I am just drinking juice, and I can tell the burn is getting to him, but he doesn't want to let me win. Whatever is stopping him is stronger than his feelings, because it would be so easy for him to stop, to pull my face to his, and give me what I want.

But I also want him to win. I want him to kiss me and to know I want him to, but I don't want to leave tonight without saying what I need to say. If he won't let me tell him without winning this game, then I need to make sure I lose. After all the grief I caused him when I first came here, all the doubt and fights and wounds, I need him to know that it all changed.

I pretend to choke on the drink, but instead inhale the liquid, sending me off into a coughing fit. He lowers his bottle, and what looks like regret flashes in his eyes. The hand on my low back moves higher, gently stroking circles as I heave coughs into my arm. He reaches to the side and sets his bottle down, before his hand finds my hip again.

"You won," I choke out, involuntary tears welling in my eyes. The coughs subside and I can finally take a deep breath, Weston's scent and that of the sea filling my lungs.

He shakes his head and gestures toward the still very full bottle next to him.

"I think we both lost."

Shit.

That hadn't gone as well as I planned, and I need a new tactic.

"So, does that mean we both win?" I say, raising an eyebrow.

"Whatever you say, princess."

"Well then." I set my bottle on the rail next to his and rest both my hands on his arms, feeling the swell of his firm muscles under my palms. I hold his gaze, hoping he can feel the sincerity I'm pouring into my truths.

"Despite all the things I said and did before, I really do think you're a great captain, and Blackwood is lucky to have you as the First Guard."

Something between us shatters the moment the words leave my lips.

I can feel it in my chest as I watch his body stiffen. My truths were from my heart, because I wanted to leave making sure he knew that even after everything that happened before, and how our friendship started, I appreciate him.

It doesn't feel like my words had that effect at all.

Weston stands, pulling his gaze away from me as he looks out over the deck. His hands tense, his arms extending and lifting me away from him, a void of space now between us. His hands fall away and I feel the loss of heat and pressure, missing it instantly.

I fix my face into a mask of neutrality, trying to hide the confusion and hurt at the rapid change of pace.

What did I do?

The little bubble we were lost in bursts, and the noise and laughter returns, forcing me to remember where we are. I watch as his jaw works, and fight the urge to look over my shoulder to see what he could be looking at as he ignores me standing in front of him.

He clears his throat, but still won't look at me. "Have fun tonight. Looks like there's still some room in the game."

A chasm splits my chest in two as I watch him disregard the truths I told him, the ones he wanted to know from our last bet. I clench my jaw, and inhale through my nose, trying to slow the heaving breaths and wavering chin I feel coming on quickly. I've been trained for this, how to take unwanted news regally. I've lived my entire life not showing emotion to my father every time he's upset me like this, disregarding me and brushing me aside.

If I could do it then, I could do it now.

Weston steps around me before pausing, and I catch a twitch of his fingers, like he's trying to stop himself from reaching out.

"Let me know if you decide to jump off my ship and go for a swim."

He leans to the side and presses a firm kiss to the top of my head, a few heartbeats passing before his lips leave my hair, and he walks away without even a backward glance.

Painful tears prick my eyes, and my chest heaves with the breaths I didn't want him to see. The kiss feels like a slap, and watching his back as he walks away feels like a door firmly closing on any possibility with him, especially in the wake of tonight.

It's over. This was my last chance.

My chest feels like it is caving in, my stomach sinking as I fall in on myself. Folding my arms over my abdomen, I watch the rest of the crew out on the deck enjoying themselves. I spot Fin curled up and asleep on a large cushion, a blanket draped over him, the excitement obviously too much.

I fight back tears as I watch everyone I have grown so fond of, knowing that I am about to walk away from them, even if my entire goal is to help. They might not see it that way. They might not think I'll come back, and maybe they'll believe that my entire time here was a lie, despite it starting out that way.

No one has ever left and gone back to the Voyagers.

I will be the first.

But I will return, dust in hand. There's no other option.

I didn't want to leave like this, not feeling hopeless and worried, not leaving Weston with any question that I wouldn't return. After the way everything unfolded, the feelings of rejection coursing through me, I can't help but wonder if I made a huge mistake.

CHAPTER FORTY-SIX

L ying in bed, pretending to be asleep feels too familiar, like I'm reliving the night from months ago, waiting for Weston to fall asleep before I try to escape. So much has changed since that night. I'm not the same person, and I'm not doing this for the same reasons.

After watching him walk away from me on deck, I spent the rest of the evening on the cushion next to a sleeping Fin, watching the fire as Auralie and I talked, occasionally joined by various members of the crew. Sig hovered in my periphery, faking the same joviality I had been with Weston. I know because every so often we would make eye contact, and I knew the plan was still underway.

We were still leaving tonight.

Weston watched me all night; I could feel his eyes on me, but I refused to look. He had been the one to kiss me, but clearly, whatever was between us wasn't enough to overcome whatever was holding him back. It didn't matter how his actions and touches told me one thing, but his words said another. I wasn't going to let him see the hurt in my eyes, so I focused on the flames and the rest of the crew's happiness.

My shoulders tensed when I felt him approach at one point, but he only leaned down to pick up Fin, bringing him below deck to bed. Keeping my shoulder angled away, ignoring him, I used it as an opportunity to head to bed, disappearing from the deck before he returned.

Hours pass before he finally comes to the room, not anywhere close to drunk like before, and I worry about the possibility of getting caught. I listen and wait until the breaths I have become so familiar with even out, and I know he is asleep. When I think it has been long enough, I roll gently to my back and look over at him, watching his back rise and fall in measured breaths.

Sliding to the edge of the bed, I gently press my feet into the floor, doing everything possible not to make a sound. Dressing quickly, I grab my dagger and walk toward the door, slowly pressing each step into the ground intentionally, trying not to make any of the boards creak under my weight.

When I make it just past the desk, the rustling of the sheets makes my body freeze. I close my eyes and bite my lip, breathing deeply to stay as still as possible, and praying to the gods he didn't wake.

"Please don't leave."

Fuck.

My spine stiffens and my skin breaks out in a sweat as excuses for why I'm dressed and armed race through my mind.

Spinning around, my mouth falling open to rush out an explanation, I'm ready to face his wrath, but he's not standing, glaring at me. My eyes fall to the bed, on his muscular back, still laying face down.

I wait for a moment, confused and waiting to see if he will speak again, but there's only silence and the quiet sound of his breaths. Taking each step just as carefully as before, I slowly creep around the desk toward his side of the bed, peering through the darkness to get a glimpse of his face, but it's hidden behind his broad shoulder.

I tiptoe closer until I can see his eyes clenched shut with a grimace on his face.

He's dreaming. In all the nights I've slept beside him, he's never spoken in his sleep, never had a nightmare like I had back at camp and in the brig. He's never woken me with any sleep disturbances, so why tonight?

My mind screams at me to walk away, to get out while I can because he could wake at any moment.

But I can't.

I can't leave him in pain like this, knowing exactly what it is like to be trapped in a world inside of your mind, where your deepest fears are coming true.

I'll take the risk.

Inching closer, I reach out my hand and set it on his forehead, pressing gently into the furrow lines, only for his eyes to clench tighter. Stroking back through his hair, my fingertips lightly graze his scalp, back and forth until I watch his face relax. His quick breaths elongate again, and the tension falls out of his shoulders. My chest aches as I watch him sleep, continuing to stroke his hair and memorizing the details of his face.

"Please don't hate me," I whisper unintentionally, then hold my breath, silently cursing myself for speaking. But he doesn't stir. His body is already back into the relaxed state it was in before, and I know I can make it out without him noticing.

Reluctantly, I pull my hand away and make it across the room to the door. Sig should be ready and waiting, knowing she can't come to get me and possibly tip off Weston if he was still awake.

I reach for the handle, ready to get off this ship and set this all in motion, but stop short.

Shit.

I've spent months not worrying about getting out of this room, with Weston leaving the door cracked for me so I could do my chores after I woke. When making the plan with Sig, I'd forgotten one very important detail.

I can't get out.

"Fuck, fuck, fuck, fuck," I whisper to myself, my hands wringing in my hair as I try to figure out what to do. This is our chance, the night this plan needs to take place, and I can't get out of this room. I have no way of signaling Sig, no way of crawling out a window, or getting anywhere without waking Weston.

Heart racing, I shake out my hands, trying to do anything with the nervous energy that is telling me to pace, because I can't risk the sound of my boots on the wood. My answer is to sit and wait for Sig to come get me if she gets curious about what is taking me so long, even though that is the exact opposite of the plan.

My only other option is to try.

I haven't actually tried getting out since those first few days, and I assume nothing has changed. I need to try anyway.

My fingers wrap around the handle, and I hold my breath, wincing slightly as I turn the knob and pull. I expect the resistance of the magic, keeping the door shut just like it had before, refusing to let me leave.

But it opens.

I slam my other hand over my mouth, stifling the gasp that threatens to escape as I watch the door soundlessly swing into the room.

A swell of excitement explodes inside me, not only because this perfect opportunity for our plan isn't wasted, but because this is the confirmation I needed. I've been worried that maybe this wasn't the right decision, and that I should accept the fate handed to all of us.

But the island doesn't want me to.

It is letting me out, letting me return to the Voyagers.

Dawnlin wants me to leave.

CHAPTER
FORTY-SEVEN

The irony of what I'm about to do isn't lost on me as I swing my legs over the rail. I plant my feet on the other side, prepared to jump off the side of the ship, exactly as Weston told me not to. Sig is below deck, doing one last check to make sure we won't be caught before she pops through the opening and nods.

We can't use the gangway. The noise might wake Weston, and I know he would do everything he could to stop me, nothing short of throwing me back into the brig. There's only one other way off the ship.

"We're clear. We need to move now," she whispers and throws her legs over the side as well.

I stare down at the dark water below, watching the waves churn next to the ship as I prepare to throw myself into them. Sig instructed me on the proper form to make as little sound and splash as possible, just another element to keep us from being discovered.

"Are you ready?" she asks, her voice strong and confident.

She grew up in the water. I'm sure jumping off the side of a ship doesn't phase her, but to me, it isn't easy. Jumping off the cliff was a sheer act of survival, and the blood pounding through my veins and stifling all my fears as I ran to get away from Mara didn't give me a chance to think about what I was doing.

I don't have that now.

"I'm good." I nod, keeping my eyes fixed on the surface.

"Let's go," she says before she steps off the side of the ship and falls, slicing through the surface with barely any noise.

I suck in a deep breath and squeeze my eyes shut before stepping off behind her. Wind whips my hair and I wrap my arms around myself, pointing my toes, trying to remember all the instructions Sig gave me before I crash through the surface. The temperature of the cool water shocks my eyes open, and I immediately begin kicking, keeping my gaze up to the surface until my head breaks through with a gasp.

We paddle to the side of the ship, bobbing there for just a moment to listen for any sign we were heard, but the night is still.

The first step, getting off the ship, is complete, and I can't believe we actually made it with no obstacles. Sig takes off toward the beach, her strokes fluid and graceful. I follow behind, much less graceful and a lot slower, but I keep my focus on my breaths and the form Weston taught me, not letting the land out of my sight.

It feels like no time has passed before the waves are crashing over me as I crawl up onto the beach, my clothes and the sand sticking to me. Sig is already on her feet and watching the ship to make sure we still haven't been detected.

"Hurry," she hisses, and I scramble to my feet, stumbling through the sand toward the portal. We both barge through it, and as soon as we are under the cover of the magic, I let out a breath.

"Holy shit. We made it," I pant.

"Don't get too excited, we aren't done yet," she says. "Take your clothes off."

She disappears around a bend in the tunnel as I rip my shirt over my head and lean down to unlace my boots. When she reappears, she has my dry set of clothes from camp, the ones we stashed away during our last shift. I didn't want to risk anyone noticing the differences in my Castaway clothing, and trying to figure out where on the island we could be because of it.

After pulling the final lace, I kick off the boots and shimmy out of my soaking pants. She holds the dry clothes out to me and I quickly pull them on. They're filthy and torn, just as we had discussed, to keep up the act we agreed upon.

"Recite the plan," she says as I slide one leg into my pants.

"Take the tunnels to the far side of the island, in case anyone is out and spots me. Go back to camp and find Dane. Tell him I was taken when I was searching and held captive for a long time until I convinced them I was on their side. I fought Weston's coercion, but made everyone believe I fell for it. That's why Mara thought I was protecting you, to keep up my cover until I could try to escape. When I tried, they caught me and held me captive again. I broke out and came straight home."

"Good. What if he asks you where we're hidden?" Sig says. She stands watching me transform back into the old Lennox, at least on the outside. Her body is as tense as I feel, and I know she agrees everything is riding on this plan.

"I say you forced me to drink a potion from the island that won't let me give it up, no matter how hard I try."

"Right. And how do you handle Mara?"

"Lie like my life depends on it, and try to convince her my story is true."

She nods. "What if she attacks you?"

"Defend myself, but don't draw attention. Make sure Dane believes she's wrong."

"Good. Then what?"

"Stay for two days. Try to find out if Dane has learned anything about how to replenish the dust. On the second night, get him to the Voyager safe house on the beach, around the bend from the cove. I'll wait until he's asleep and then take the dust off him. You'll be waiting in the rocks there, and we'll go back to the ship."

"Yes. I will be there if anything goes wrong." She tosses my shirt at me, and I pull it over my head.

"You can't let Weston ruin this, Sig. He can't risk being discovered. He can't come into camp, he can't follow me around if I leave. Tell him he needs to trust me."

She nods, her face drawn. "I will do my best."

"Jorn will help you. Taril and Stass and Auralie too, especially if you tell them what I'm doing. They want it just as bad as we do."

"I'll tell them if I need to, but I hope he just accepts it and lets you do what needs to be done."

I let out a sharp breath. "Alright." I squeeze out my hair, hoping that the waves will be dry by the time I'm back at camp, erasing yet another clue that we're hidden near the water.

"Lennox?"

I meet her gaze, only to find concern there. Worry. "What's wrong?"

"You remember you have to get close to Dane, right?"

My breath hitches and my mind instantly pictures how we were before I left. His hands cupping my face, my thigh, his lips pressing into mine. Thoughts that before would have made me feel excited and warm, now only make a chill run down my spine and a pit form in my stomach.

I've been preparing myself to be back with Dane ever since Sig and I made this plan, but I know with every touch I'm going to be picturing someone else's hands and lips.

Pretending it is him.

"I know."

"You don't have to do anything you don't want to do," Sig says.

"I'll do what I need to do."

The feelings I had when Dane touched me aren't even close to what happens to my mind and my body when Weston is near, but I have to fake it. I can't let him suspect anything is different between us, or he might realize there is more going on.

She nods as I lean over to tie up my laces and grab my dagger off the ground. I can't keep it where I normally do, because Dane can't know I have it. If he's going to believe I escaped from captivity, he would question why they let me have it if he found it. There's no way I'm walking back into camp without it, and Weston would be furious with me if he found out I wasn't armed, so I slide it into my boot instead.

Sig pulls her own blade off her belt and holds it at me, poised to strike.

"Practice. In case Mara comes at you," she says.

I wrench her wrist and disarm her easily, flipping the blade in my hands just as Weston does. We practice a few more times before she is satisfied and shoves it back in the sheath.

"Time to make this look convincing," I say as I search my clothes for the tears Sig ripped into them. I rub each patch of skin beneath the tears against the jagged rock on the wall of the tunnel, wincing as I scrape my skin open and let the blood soak into the fabric. The stings will be short-lived, because I know Dane will make sure every single one is covered with salve as soon as possible.

I step away from the wall and assess myself, satisfied with our work.

"Hey, Lennox," Sig says.

"Yes?" I say, looking up at her, but my face is met with her fist, crashing into it and sending me staggering backwards.

"What the FUCK, Sig?" I scream, clutching my face as I glare at her.

She shakes out her hand with a grimace. "Fuck, he's going to kill me when he hears about that. Trust me, it would have hurt more if you were expecting it." She takes a step and waves me over to her. "Come here, let me see."

My eyes are tearing as I stop in front of her, and she turns me around, so the torchlight falls across my face. She moves my chin around in different directions, nodding at her accomplishment.

"It's bruising already. That will definitely look convincing."

"If I didn't have somewhere to be right now, I'd punch you back," I grumble.

"Save it. You can hit me later," she says with a grin.

"I'm not going to ask where a princess learned to throw a punch like that."

"Probably the same place you did," she laughs. "Come on, we need to move. We've already been here too long."

We jog through the tunnels, passing under the river to the far side of the island until we reach a gentle slope that will open up right near the plateau where we arrived in Dawnlin.

"You should go back. I can make it from here," I say.

I can feel my emotions rising as tears threaten to fall, and I don't want to look at Sig. Even though I chose this, I planned this, it still feels terrible going back to camp and back to someone who lied to me like Dane did.

"Lennox, wait," she says and grabs my elbow, turning me to face her. She sees the tears in my eyes and her face softens. She places a hand on each of my shoulders and lowers down to my level until her face is all I can focus on.

"You can do this. You are strong and fearless. You are a great leader, and you are going to get back to your kingdom." My chin wobbles as her words sink in, her sincerity wrapping me in a hug that I didn't know I needed. "Don't let him change you. You know who you are. You know who we are. Come back to us."

I can't stop the sob that escapes and the tears that fall as I throw my arms around her, squeezing tight and nodding into her shoulder.

"I will. I promise," I choke out.

I pull away and take a step backward, sucking in a deep breath before I turn my back on her.

"Oh, and remember, Lennox, whatever happens, don't kill Dane."

I let her words fuel me, and push me through the portal at the top of the slope, reminding me of the entire reason we are doing this. Dane controls the island, and he has lied and manipulated each one of us to get the healing waters. He cheated the magic, then took it over, holding the island and everyone on it hostage, all to get what he wanted.

I can hate him, but I can't kill him, and I have to pretend that I'm still in love with him.

The night is dark and still, the moon barely a sliver in the sky. I glance around, making sure there is no one within sight before I drop to my knees. Digging my hands into the moist soil, I scrub the dirt onto my skin, dirtying myself and my clothes even more, shoving it under my nails so it looks like I went through hell to get back.

I let myself feel all the emotions from a moment ago and will the tears to keep falling. I need them, if not for the reason the Voyagers think.

Then I take off, tearing down the path and through the trees, running as fast as my legs will carry me, straight to camp. I need to be breathless and panicked. I need to be hysterical.

I need to be convincing.

I reach the trees, letting the branches and leaves whip at my face and push through the vines. The magic of the portal surrounds me as I push into the darkness, breaking through the other side to the same familiar clearing I considered home not that long ago.

My knees hit the grass, followed by my palms, and I grip onto the earth, mustering all the emotion that I can until my shoulders are heaving with sobs. Sucking in the deepest breath, I will all of my fears and fury and hope into my throat, as a scream erupts that even I barely recognize, but I hope they do. I hope he does, because it all starts now.

"Dane!"

CHAPTER FORTY-EIGHT

My voice is hoarse as I repeatedly scream Dane's name, sobbing on the ground in the clearing until I hear noises come from above. One hand after the other, I crawl through the grass, tension pulling at my shoulders as tears continue to stream down my cheeks and fall to the ground.

Multiple sets of footsteps pound on the boards above, but I can't tell from where. Camp has been tainted, and the surrounding trees, the lit torches and rope bridges, feel so familiar, yet not. It makes it easy to focus on my goal, not feeling any sentiment toward this place any longer.

"Lennox?"

Dane's voice bellows through the clearing as heavy footsteps thunder across the planks, heading toward the platform. I hear the clink of the latch through my sobs, followed by the thud as it hits the ground.

"Lennox!" he calls again, and I look up to find him running through the clearing, straight to me.

More sets of footsteps echo around camp, torches lighting everywhere as Voyagers wake to the commotion.

I brace myself as Dane reaches me, falling to his knees and scooping me into his arms.

"You're here. You're back," he says, squeezing me to his chest.

My hands fist in his shirt, and I fold my arms against myself, letting them act as a barrier, just a small amount of space between us that would never be noticed, but helps me catch my breath as I acclimate to his presence again.

The sobs don't stop, they only come harder as the reality of what I've done truly hits me. A sharp pain shoots through my chest as I think about the morning, and see Weston waking to find me gone. It makes it easier to cry.

Voyagers gather around us, some in the clearing, and some leaning against the ropes and rails up above, each of them taking in the scene.

Dane pulls back and his hands move to my face. I try not to flinch when his skin brushes mine, and if I did, I can easily blame it on the pain from Sig's punch.

"Are you alright? Gods, what did they do to you?" He examines my cheek, his brows furrowed as he looks me over.

I ignore his question, instead focusing on staying as distraught as I can.

"I tried to come back," I cry. "I tried, Dane."

"Shh," he coos. "You made it. You're safe."

He leans forward and plants a firm kiss on my lips. I feel nothing.

Not a spark, not a flutter.

Nothing.

This was not the kiss I wanted tonight, but it's the one I have to endure. Weston's denial mere hours ago made me feel infinitely more than the press of Dane's lips, and the only way I can stomach it is by pretending they are Weston's.

He can't know that anything has changed.

He pulls back, and movement catches the corner of my eye. I look past Dane's shoulder and see someone barreling toward us.

"You!"

Mara charges at us and I stagger to my feet, trying to stay out of her reach. I can't see if she's armed, but I don't have time to look before Dane is stepping in front of me, holding his arms out toward her.

"Mara, stop!"

She slams into him, trying to push past him and get to me. Taking a few quick steps back, I watch as he wrangles her into a hold, fighting against her lashes and wrenching of limbs.

"She's a fucking traitor, Dane! I saw it with my own eyes!" Mara screams. Her face exudes hatred, and something in my chest cracks. This isn't the Mara I knew, and I don't know if I'll ever know her again.

"I'm not!" I cry, shaking my head, trying to fill my eyes with fear, which isn't difficult after seeing how aggressively she's trying to attack me.

"How can you let her back here? She needs to be thrown into the cage and questioned! She has information!"

"Mara!" Dane yells, and her attention snaps to him. The last time I heard his voice that authoritative and angry was when they locked me in the cage on my first day here. It's clear his influence over the Voyagers hasn't changed since I've been gone.

"She's not a traitor! She came back. Look what they did to her!" He throws his arm out toward me and her gaze follows, eyes trailing over my ripped and soiled clothes, blood soaked and scraped skin, and ending on my bruised face.

Mara says nothing; she only glares at me, her jaw clenching tightly.

She promised me long ago that if I ever turned on them, she would end me, and now, after seeing how easily her feelings toward me can change and remembering the knives she threw at my back, I know she was being honest.

"I had to, Mara. That was the only way they would let me out. I had to pretend I was one of them," I say, pleading with her.

"Liar!" she spits at me. I feel everyone around us watching the even bigger spectacle Mara has made my return into, and realize that everyone is awake now, watching everything unfold.

A small cry breaks out across the clearing, and I look past Dane and Mara to find Roley running straight toward me.

"Lennox!"

My knees barely hit the ground before he's crashing into me, wrapping his arms around my neck.

"You're okay!" he squeaks, and I hold him tight.

"So are you!" I cry. "I was so worried."

I truly was worried. Taril told me Roley survived the incident, and had been quiet since then, but I needed to see for myself.

He pushes off me, his eyes snagging on my injured cheek before meeting mine. "You saved me."

"Of course I did, Roley. I wasn't going to let anything hurt you." I hug him again tightly, then get back to my feet.

"You're not one of us anymore," Mara spits at me.

"You don't get to decide that, Mara, I do!" Dane yells, his face twisting into fury as he shoves it in hers. "Say one more word against her, and I will bring you back home immediately."

Mara's face drops, eyes widening as she stares at him in complete disbelief.

Hope swells in my chest. If Dane is threatening to bring Mara home, he must not be worried about using the last of the dust. Maybe he found a way to replenish it.

If this works, I can help everyone get home.

"Go back to bed, everyone. Now!" Dane yells, and the Voyagers meander back to their beds. Mara gives me one last look of disgust before turning on her heel and walking to the ladder, followed by everyone else who made it down to the clearing.

"Goodnight, Lennox," Roley says with a small wave. "I'm glad you're home."

My chest squeezes as guilt courses through me.

This place isn't my home anymore.

Roley sprints to the ladder and climbs up, waving as he runs through the pathways back toward the bunks.

"Come on," Dane says, his hand wrapping around mine. I take a deep breath, trying to hide the revulsion I feel, and squashing the reaction to pull my hand away. "We need to talk."

He leads me to the platform, and we wordlessly weave through camp to the infirmary. The door barely shuts behind us before Dane is pulling me farther into the room and wrapping me in his arms.

"Gods, I missed you. I can't even tell you how relieved I am. I searched for you every day."

The pressure of his body is stifling, but I fight it and hug him back. "You did?" I say.

He leans back quickly, his gaze imploring. "Of course I did. I could barely rest knowing that he had you."

I gulp as a tear slides down my cheek. Dane had been searching. I'd seen it myself, but the feelings his words brought up then, are entirely different from the ones now. He needed to find me, at all costs. He couldn't let Weston convince me. Back then, both times I saw him on the island, he sounded desperate, crazed. It lines up with what Taril told me had changed at camp.

He swipes it away with the back of his fingers and I try not to flinch.

"Hey, it's alright. Let's get you fixed up."

He looks over my scrapes, applying the salve heavily and making sure each one is cleaned and covered. When he gets to the bruise on my cheek, I stop him.

"I can do it," I say, reaching to take the salve from him. I need a break from his hands on me already, and I've only just gotten back to camp.

I cringe inwardly, anticipating the next two days.

He watches me massage the salve into my skin, but stays silent. The look on his face tells me there's a lot he wants to say, but he's holding back, taking it slow.

"I don't want to pry," he says warily. "I know you just got back, but we need to talk about what happened."

I finish rubbing the salve into my face and wipe my hands on my pants, dropping my chin so I don't have to meet his eyes.

"I know," I say. This is it, everything Sig and I planned for and rehearsed. I need to tell the truth where I can, so he doesn't catch inconsistencies, but I need to protect everyone back home.

"Let's start with what happened?"

I heave a deep sigh. "Honestly, I don't know. I felt a blade at my throat and I froze. People appeared around me and took my weapons. I didn't recognize anyone, and I got scared. I just listened and did what they said so they wouldn't hurt me."

"Did they come into camp?"

"No," I say with a firm shake of my head. "It's my fault. I know I was supposed to stay at camp that day, and I left. I thought staying put would help me deal with losing Fin, but it didn't. I started getting so anxious and worried, and I just needed to get out."

"Where were you when they took you?" His voice remains calm, and he hasn't given me any indication that he doesn't believe me. A bolt of confidence shoots through me, and I keep going, especially knowing the questions are only going to get harder.

"I was near the marshes, just below the plateau."

Lie.

He takes it, without question, moving on to the next.

"Where did they take you? Where is their camp?"

This is the part I'm most worried about, the part I really need to sell.

I start to move my lips, soundlessly choking on my own words, and feigning frustration with each new attempt to speak.

"Ugh!" I groan and shake my head. "They forced a potion down my throat as soon as I was at their camp. I can't tell or show anyone where they are, no matter how hard I try. I think it's what has been protecting them."

He grumbles, his face drawing in anger as he crosses his arms and runs his fingers over his lips. "I'm sorry they did that to you, but it's not your fault."

"I'm so sorry, Dane. I just want this nightmare to be over."

"It is," he says, softening again. "It is. It's over. I got you back now."

A chill runs up my spine. Has he always sounded this possessive? Like I was an object he controlled or owned? How didn't I notice it before?

He pauses and collects his words before starting again. "I know her side, but I need to know yours. What happened with Mara?"

"I told her the truth in the clearing. I even tried when she was attacking me out on the cliffs, but she wouldn't stop to listen to me. There was no other choice. I had to fake being on their side. You warned me about Weston's manipulation since the day you brought me here, so I tried to fight it. I tried to spin it back on them, making them believe I was on their side so they would trust me. It worked for a while, but when I saved Roley, they started to question me. I knew I had to try to leave then. I couldn't stay longer. Weston caught me and locked me up."

"How did you escape?"

"Attacked the Castaway that was guarding my cage when I said I needed to use the bathroom. We got into a fight, that's why I look like this. I got away, but they will know I'm gone soon."

His spine stiffens. "Everyone needs to be alert. They might come looking for you."

"Please don't let him take me again," I plead, my voice laced with fear.

"Trust me, I won't. You aren't leaving my side."

I shake my head. "I'm going to have to. I have to keep looking for the cure."

"Don't worry about that right now. We will figure that out when you're ready to look again."

I nod and sniffle. He hasn't questioned any part of my story, and I can't decide if that is a good thing, or a bad thing. Does he believe me implicitly, or is there something more that he knows? I thought I could trust him, thought we spent all that time building it between us, just to end up questioning every word he says and every thought he has.

"What about Fin?" he asks.

My face falls again. "He's too far gone, Dane. I tried so hard, but Weston's tricks worked on him too easily. He's just a child. I wanted to bring him with me when I left, but I couldn't. I just needed to get out."

"And Taril?"

Shit.

Sig and I hadn't prepared for how to deal with Taril being taken. I decide quickly to go with complete ignorance.

I snap my eyes to his, widening them in shock. "They took Taril?"

He narrows his gaze. "You didn't see him?"

"No," I say. "They had me locked in a room for days, or weeks. I don't even know how long. I never saw him."

"Shit," he says, and lets out a deep breath. "I think that's enough for tonight. There's nothing we can do right now, anyway."

I give him a small smile, grateful to be out of his scrutiny for now.

"I'm just glad you're back. I'm sure you are exhausted. Do you want to go lay down?"

I nod and slide off the table. He grabs my hand and guides me down until my feet plant onto the floor. Before we make it to the door, I stop, turning back toward him.

"Wait, Dane?"

"Hmm?"

"Did you mean what you said to Mara? That you would bring her home?"

His face hardens.

"I will not let her treat you like that. You are not responsible for what he did to you."

What he did to me.

Weston did nothing to me but protect me. He frustrated me, and challenged me, and hid things from me, but he also made me love him.

Dane's right, no one is responsible for that except Weston.

"Thank you," I say, gazing up at him, hoping my expression looks loving.

"Of course," he says and leans forward, brushing my lips with a quick kiss.

"Does that mean you figured out how to replenish the dust?" I ask quietly.

His face draws in again. "No. I haven't. I was too busy looking for you to even think about it."

My stomach bottoms out, and all the hope I felt that this plan was going to save us all disappears.

"Oh. Looking for an answer is so important. I'm sorry I caused such a distraction." I don't even have to pretend. My voice betrays all of my sadness and guilt.

"You aren't a distraction," he says, his smile dazzling as his eyes trace over my face. "But now we can look together."

I nod quickly and then yawn, trying to end this conversation so I can be alone.

We exit the infirmary and Dane leaves me at the ladder to my bunk, promising he will come get me in a few hours when the suns come up. I settle in my same bed and let out a breath, letting some relief wash over me, but also some dread.

I think Dane believes me. I've given him no reason not to. My time here is limited, so I only have to keep the facade up for a little while longer. With Dane's threat to Mara, I don't think she will be as much of an issue as I thought.

But the dust...

Dane still hasn't figured it out. I've been gone for months, and he's made no progress. I have only two days to find anything in camp that might give us a clue or direction, and if I don't, we will only have whatever dust is left.

The rest of us will be stranded.

Weston will try to send me back, and I don't know if I want to go back to Blackwood without him.

I suck in a deep breath, trying to hold on to the hope I know I need to have.

The island wants me to be here, and that has to mean something.

I must be doing something right.

CHAPTER FORTY-NINE

A few hours later, I wake to the suns beating down on me, drenched in sweat, and exhausted from a nightmare filled restless sleep. I wasn't prepared to have the nightmares again, proving there is more than one reason I miss Weston's bed.

Only one more night.

Rolling my shoulders, I try to loosen the tension in my neck brought on by the fitful sleep and the worry over the rest of this plan. My clothes are still the filthy ones I arrived in, too tired to do anything but go straight to sleep after last night. I need to start the day fresh, wash all the grime off and get a new set of clothes, anything that will make me look like I'm back in the fold and a Voyager once again.

A voice greets me as I hop down off the last rung of the ladder.

"I was just coming to get you," Dane says. He sweeps me into a kiss, and I go through the motions, enough not to rouse suspicion, before pushing him away.

"I'm still filthy. I was just about to go clean up."

"I'm sure you'll feel better after you do. How did you sleep?" he asks.

I shrug. "Not great, honestly."

He wraps an arm around my shoulder and pulls me into his side before setting off down the path toward the showers. "You've been through a lot, Lennox. It might take some time to calm down from it all, but I'll be here for you."

"Thanks Dane," I say, keeping my eyes on the floorboards as we traipse through camp.

"I made Mara sleep in the cabin last night. She needs some time to cool down, and I didn't want her making you feel uncomfortable."

"After your threat to bring her home, I don't think she will try anything. She doesn't want to give up on the cure." I make a mental note not to call it the healing waters. No one here does, not unless they've found it. Dane can't know I have, so I can't do or say anything that might catch his attention.

We round the bend to the showers and Dane sends me off, telling me he will meet me in the tavern once I'm finished.

Camp feels quiet and normal, like nothing has changed in the time I've been gone.

Except me.

I've changed.

But I can't let anyone see how much.

I shower quickly, keeping my dagger hidden in my boot and pulling on a clean set of clothes before I start off toward the tavern. Dane is alone, food spread out on a table, as I slide onto the bench next to him, the same way I would have before.

"Hungry?"

"Starving," I say and reach out to pull some food closer. I need energy to stay alert and focused, especially after a rough night of sleep. Hopefully, eating will help fuel me for the day ahead, but also give me something to do while I sit here with Dane.

"I'm just so relieved you're back where you belong," Dane says. He turns to straddle the bench facing me and pulls me toward him, draping my legs over his. I try not to stiffen, instead focus on giving him a soft smile.

"You know I didn't leave on purpose. It wasn't my choice," I say and reach across the table to grab a piece of food, something, anything, to keep my hands and mouth busy. It isn't a lie. I chose to stay after I found out the truth, but I still need to try to say as many truths as possible so I don't get caught up and discovered.

"I know." He strokes the tops of my thighs leisurely. Before I would have leaned into his touch, but now it takes every shred of control I have not to squirm away from it. "But I had to get you back. I don't know what I'd do without you."

Warnings fill my mind, ones I didn't notice when he said things like this before. After I met him, and when I thought there was more between us, I was so caught up in the excitement and newness of meeting someone from outside the castle, making a friend, and seeking this magical place, that I let all of it cloud my judgment. My emotions overcame me, and I allowed them to control my perceptions instead of doing what I have been taught for years: using my mind and analyzing every piece of information.

Both Brynne and Weston are right. I let my emotions overcome me, but I have to heed their lesson in this fight. This is a fight, just one without the cut of a blade.

I shift the subject quickly. "What is the plan for today?"

"I figured you would want to lie low, recover. I don't expect you to be rushing out of camp right away."

"I can't lose any more time, Dane. I have to find the cure."

His face breaks out in a slow grin.

"What?" I ask warily, worried I said something that tipped him off to my deception.

"Nothing." He leans forward, closing the gap between us. "I just love your determination, that's all."

"We have to find it before he does, remember?" I take another bite, chewing slowly, and he sits back in response. Something in my chest squeezes when I bring Weston up to Dane, because I know the last time they saw each other, Dane tried to kill him. I don't want to fuel any more of Dane's hatred, but I can't get through these two days without mentioning him at all, especially since he's allegedly kept me captive.

"We do, but I'm worried about you staying safe. If you're going to go, I should go with you."

"Do you think they'll be out looking for me?"

"Yes." His gaze is intense, searing into my face, like I'm something he needs to keep. For what reason, I don't know. It's the same look I used to see as desire, and maybe even love. Now I see it differently, and it looks too much like he's claiming me.

My fingers fidget in my lap. "Maybe I should stay at camp for a while. Let them forget about me."

"If that will make you feel safe," he says, continuing to stroke my thighs, and slowly moving to my low back.

I shudder, but he mistakes it for excitement and pulls me even closer.

"But you can't be here forever," he continues. "You made me promise not to distract you from finding the cure, and I'm not breaking it."

"Thank you," I say. "Maybe we can still be productive while I'm at camp. You said you hadn't looked for any clues about the dust. Maybe we should start there."

He nods once, firmly. "I agree. We need to."

"Have you told anyone else that it's almost gone?"

So much time has passed, and I don't know if he has trusted anyone else with the secret. There didn't seem to be any worry or haste among the Voyagers, but whoever he told could be keeping it to themselves, just as I did. With the threat Dane had used last night, I know he definitely didn't tell Mara.

"No. I haven't wanted to cause a panic. I'm the Guardian. I'm supposed to protect everyone here. I don't want anyone to think they can't leave. But we need to be able to leave, Lennox. We have to find an answer."

I swipe my hands on my clothes, dusting off any crumbs. "Then what are we waiting for?"

I swing my legs over the bench, putting some distance between us, which he closes again quickly, placing a hand on my hip as I walk in front of him.

It feels possessive and overbearing, completely opposite of the security and warmth when Weston did the same thing. My skin crawls at the touch, especially knowing I once found it comforting and thrilling.

"Do you have any idea where we should start?" I ask once we are out onto the main walkway again.

"I don't think either of the bunks will have anything, and probably not the armory. Maybe the infirmary has some books tucked away. We could start there."

Spinning around, we head toward the infirmary, unused since we were there last night. We turn it over quickly, looking over every item and searching every surface, only to come up empty. Nothing suggests information about the island itself. There are no books or documents, no records of any kind, only the same salves and other treatments, and bandages that are in the infirmary back on the ship.

I try to stay focused on the task, but my mind keeps drifting back to something Sig said back when we were escaping Mara.

I want you to think really hard about needing safety.

Maybe the island is trying to protect the dust just as it protects the healing waters, which is why no one can find it. The Guardian lives at camp, so it would make sense for the answer, or the actual dust, to be here. I think the same thought repeatedly, asking the island for help, letting it know what I need, just as I did with the map.

Please help us replenish the dust. Please help us replenish the dust.

We barely speak. I'm too busy repeating the phrase over and over with every second of searching, but nothing changes. There's no sign or movement, nothing that indicates the island heard me.

Or wants to help me.

Once the infirmary is completely turned over and put back together, we stop and try to figure out where to go next.

"Just like the bunks, I don't think the showers or the tavern will have any sort of clue. Those are too open, too every day." I stop and gaze out over the clearing, thinking about everything at camp.

The cage. The graves. The training area. The cabin. I hadn't gone too far into the trees during my time here to see if anything else is hiding out in the jungle.

But then I get a thought, and turn to face Dane.

"You sleep in the bunks, right? Did the Guardian always stay there? Or is there somewhere else, like the cabin, that was meant for you?"

"I'm not sure," he says. "I didn't get a chance to learn anything from the last Guardian before Weston slaughtered him."

Lie.

He's still lying to me, but he doesn't know I know the truth.

My body starts to physically react, and I tamp it down quickly, hoping my face doesn't betray me.

"He's a monster," I say, looking away as if it pains me to think about Weston. It does, but not in the way Dane thinks.

"I'm sorry I brought him up," he says, reaching out to pull me closer. "But you don't need to worry about him any longer. He won't do anything as long as I'm with you."

I nod quickly. "I know." I clear my throat and try to get us back on track. "Why don't we try the cabin?"

Storm stayed back in camp today, standing in the same spot he was when I first arrived in Dawnlin, watching over the portal entrance to the clearing. We pass by without as much as an acknowledgement, a scowl painted on his face as he stares across camp.

"Storm doesn't seem very friendly this morning," I say, once we are safely in the cabin with no risk of him overhearing. Turning slowly, I survey the room, taking in the empty space where all the beds from the storm were the last time I was here. Only one remains tucked away in the corner, I assume where Mara slept last night.

"He wasn't supposed to stay back at camp today, but with you coming back last night, we needed to make sure someone was on duty that could handle Weston if he came for you."

"Oh."

"He'll be fine," Dane says, waving it off. "He agrees we need the strength here."

I nod and step toward the center of the room. The walls are smooth, with no doors or storage cupboards of any kind. Everything within it is part of the magic and comes and goes as needed. There's nothing to even search, because with no need for it, the room remains empty.

Shit. Another dead end.

"This room is pointless," I say, frustration leaking into my voice. "There's got to be something we are missing."

I close my eyes, and cycle through everything I've learned about Dawnlin. I think back to Edmond's story, the books I found in the library, the fountain. Both sides of stories I was told from Dane and Sig. The mountain. The healing waters, and the poems the mountain spoke to me.

"I don't think there's anything from the past Guardians anywhere," Dane says.

"What if we're looking for the wrong thing?" I say, throwing my eyes open and spinning around to look at him again.

His brow furrows. "What are you thinking?"

"What if we keep looking for something from the other Guardians, but what if it's not them that would tell us? What if it's Dawnlin itself?"

"How would the island tell us?"

"Just like," I start, but slam my mouth shut, stopping 'the healing waters' from tumbling through my lips. I almost told him, and now I need to cover up for my abrupt change of pace.

Dane cannot know I found the healing waters or that the island helped me make a map that led me to the discovery. He can't know that when I asked for help or needed something, the island helped me along, showing me things and pulling me in certain directions, even revealing the location as I gazed upon the replica of the fountain as I approached the mountain.

The fountain.

Maybe it all comes back to that, to the fountain. The biggest depiction of the island of Dawnlin there is. The fountain brought us all here, and held a clue for how to find the location of the waters, but what if we've all missed it before, because we didn't know we needed to look?

"Just like when I found the fountain," I say, covering my stumble. "Dane, how much do you know about the fountain? Can you draw it? Maybe it holds the key. It's what brings each of us here, just like the dust does."

A light sparks in his eyes. "I never thought to look at the fountain before."

Excitement bubbles inside me. This could be it, the answer the Castaways have been searching for.

"What do you remember about it?" I start rattling off any details that I remember, but there was so much going on in that moment that I can't recall too much, only the details that helped me find the waters and know that it was connected to Dawnlin.

"Honestly, I don't really look at the fountain. That's not my purpose when I'm called back, so I don't really know what is carved into it."

I feel myself deflate. This is going to be harder than I thought. If Dane, the person who has the most interaction with the fountain out of all of us, doesn't know any of the details, then it's possible we will miss something. They've all been on the island much longer than me, but maybe one of the other Voyagers will remember. Collectively, we could try to piece things together.

Or the Castaways, but I can't ask them.

"We should ask everyone when they get back to camp tonight, see what they remember. Maybe with everyone's memory, we can get a good picture and figure it out," I say.

"Why don't we just go look at it ourselves?" he says.

I stare at him, confused. "What do you mean? Is there one on the island? I haven't seen it in all the time I've been here."

"No, Lennox. I mean back in the real world."

I suck in a harsh breath, shaking my head rapidly. "Dane, no, we can't. We can't use the dust. There's not enough left."

No. This cannot happen. If we use *any* of the dust now, the amount to get us there and back would be equivalent to four fewer Castaways that can get home. We can't.

"We have enough to get back. I haven't been called away, so I haven't used any. You wouldn't be trapped there. We could come home so you can keep searching."

He pulls the pouch off his belt and opens it up in front of me, the golden glow illuminating the inside.

My heart pounds in my ears and my breaths become shallow as I try to talk my way out of this without seeming suspicious.

"But what if it's a dead end? We'll only have wasted what little we have left—"

"But what if it's not? What if the fountain holds the answer?"

I can't keep the panic from rising in my voice. I'm desperate to find answers, but not at the cost of ruining the life of one more Castaway.

"We can't take that risk, Dane! Every time you use it, we're closer to being trapped here for eternity. No one would even need to find the cure anymore because we could *never leave!*" I yell.

He knows getting back to Blackwood is important to me; it's the entire reason I am here. My time on Dawnlin has been short, so I still have a chance compared to so many of the Voyagers, and even the Castaways. We had this conversation on the cliffs, and again on the beach. I need the ability to leave, even if that means leaving him.

"If the answer is there, on the fountain, it's worth the risk," he says. "We're taking an even bigger risk if we don't follow through with the lead. If we do nothing, we're at the mercy of me getting called and using dust, and I can't control that. Either way, use it or don't. It's still almost gone."

He's right, it is, but I can't allow myself to use any more of it.

"We can talk to everyone. I'm sure between all of us, we can figure it out."

"No. No one else can know."

"Why? Why wouldn't you want them to know that even if they find the cure, they can't do anything with it?"

"Because it will not get to that. I'm not trying to keep anyone here."

A small seed of doubt burrows in me at his statement. Is he telling the truth? Would he have let any of the Castaways leave if they had asked? Is he truly not trying to keep anyone here? Or would he have demanded they tell him the location of the healing waters like Weston and Sig suspected because of how he arrived on the island?

It may not have been worth the risk of finding out, but if Dane is telling the truth, maybe they have all been stuck on the island for so long for no reason.

"Then there must be another way," I say, and swallow down the fear.

This was a mistake. I shouldn't have come back. I'm making it worse.

"We can't risk not checking. It is worth the use of the dust," he says. He reaches into the bag and pulls his hand out, as a glow seeps between the fingers of his clenched fist.

"Dane, no!"

The scream barely leaves my lips before he is stepping toward me, pulling my chest to his and tossing the dust over our heads.

CHAPTER FIFTY

My feet slam into the ground an instant later, my knuckles white as they grip onto Dane's forearms, steadying me after the onslaught of magic that dropped us here. Blinking rapidly, I watch the glow of the dust fade on our clothes, and snap my head up to take in the surroundings. My knees almost buckle as everything catches up to me. We just wasted enough dust for two people, and we aren't in Dawnlin anymore.

We aren't in Blackwood, either.

My eyes flit around the alley, climbing the buildings, the packed dirt ground, the bright skies.

This isn't the same alley we stood in the last time we were in the real world, the last time before I was in Dawnlin.

Dane didn't bring me home.

I step away from him quickly, anger and panic overwhelming me. He wasted it. Not just to get here, but for us to get back, too. He ensured I would go back by bringing me somewhere else, so I wouldn't change my mind and go back to the castle. Now, we have no choice but to use even more dust, and if there isn't an answer on the fountain, we've done nothing but draw closer to sealing our fate. All of this would be in vain.

"I can't believe you did that, Dane! What were you thinking?" I yell, taking another step back and wringing my fingers through my hair.

"Checking the fountain is important, and we needed a fountain." He gestures to the fountain beside us, and I follow his motion.

It is a duplicate of the one in Blackwood, and my face falls as I take it in. No water flows from the openings, the pool below the same stagnant mess as at home.

Is it because of the dust?

Has the magic of the island dried up, just like the fountain? Will the myth of Dawnlin cease to exist as soon as the dust is gone?

"Let's just look for clues," I grind out, and step to the edge of the fountain, turning my back on him.

"You're mad," he says flatly.

"What was your first clue, Dane?" I snap, my anger breaking through the box I'm trying to hold it in.

"There's no reason to be mad," he says, grabbing my arms and pulling me toward him. Wrenching my arms from his grasp, I shrug him off, but he steps between me and the aged white stone. I glare up at him, my jaw aching from clenching it so tightly, trying not to say the venomous thoughts running through my mind.

"It's important we find an answer, and if this is the best idea we have, we need to try. If it doesn't work out, we're stuck either way. Someone had to decide, and the island is my responsibility, so I made it."

I understand his point, but he believes his way is the only answer. He doesn't know about how many Castaways I'm trying to save dust for, in the event we find nothing. He knows every single one of them, and he doesn't care about what happens to them, even though he says he's not trying to trap anyone. He vilifies them, making the Voyagers turn on people they knew and cared about, leaving them stranded and hunted while he continues to search.

Auralie. Stassia. Jorn. Eirlik. Veck. Fern. Everyone.

He knew them all.

And he isn't considering them in any of this. He only is considering what he wants done, in the name of protecting Dawnlin.

But he's not protecting Dawnlin, not after he cheated the magic and wants the cure for himself.

"So let's find the answers," I say and step around him, training my gaze on the fountain.

I scan the surface, the carvings dusted with a thick layer of grime from years without flowing water, making them somewhat difficult to see. Dane hovers behind me, looking at the fountain over my shoulder, and the skin on the back of my neck prickles.

Wasting the opportunity that using the dust gave us would be wrong. Despite how much I hate how Dane went about this, I'm going to use it. Dread pools in my stomach as I stare at the stone, thinking about how I am going to tell the Castaways there is even less dust now.

And why.

If there's a clue here, I need to find it.

Crouching down, I reach into the pool and cup some stagnant water in my hand before dripping it over the surface of the fountain. I run my fingertips over the stone, rubbing the moisture on to try to wash away some of the filth.

Dane picks up on my plan and follows suit, starting in the other direction. It takes a minute of scrubbing before I can see enough of the carvings to analyze, and once I have enough uncovered, I move on to the next section. We work silently, annoyance seething from me, until we meet again on the other side.

The fountain is legible now, at least for our purposes. I rinse my hands in the water and take the moment to run my fingertips along the bottom of the pool. The stone is just as smooth as the fountain in Blackwood, so I mentally check off that area to search.

"Any ideas as to what we should look for?" I ask. I can use him for all his knowledge while I can. He's been the Guardian for twenty years. He knows more about Dawnlin than I do, despite never being able to find the waters.

Please don't let him figure it out now.

"Lennox," Dane says, but I ignore him.

"Any sort of symbol or unexplained shape you've seen on the island that could have something to do with the dust?"

"Lennox," he says again.

"Because I don't recall anything spec—"

"Lennox, will you talk to me, please?"

"What?" I say, irritation slicing through the word as I glare at him.

"I want to find answers, but you're angry because I made a decision that was supposed to help you. I don't know why you're blaming me for doing something because I care about you."

My blood begins to boil. He doesn't understand the gravity of what he did, and he's blaming me for being upset? My mouth falls open, ready to shout my first words, but Edmond's voice pops into my head, reminding me to focus on my goals and find the path that will get me what I want.

Dane may believe he was doing the right thing, and maybe he was. We've still yet to determine if we actually wasted the dust, so we need to get looking. I can't let him believe there is anything wrong, and getting on his bad side or raising suspicion right now won't get me any closer to an answer.

I let out a breath. "You're right," I say. "I'm sorry. I'm just really trying to find anything that can help us."

"I forgive you," he says with a smile, and I do everything I can to keep my fists from clenching.

His face falls slightly, and he takes a half step closer. "You're really that focused on getting home?"

"I told you I can't stay," I say, meeting his gaze.

"I know, I just..." He takes my hands in his and squeezes them. "I guess I just hoped you had considered staying if you don't find it."

I shake my head. "I have to go back, whether or not I find it, but I'm not done looking. I'll be here for a while longer. I just don't want to lose the chance to go home, for me, or for anyone else, if they find it first."

"I understand," he murmurs. He leans forward, closing the gap between us, but I turn toward the fountain, leaning close and examining the carvings.

"Any ideas? Any symbols on the island you noticed?" I say, ignoring the way he shifts uncomfortably after my obvious denial of his kiss.

He clears his throat, his tone dropping lower. "None that I have noticed. Besides the island shifting at any moment, there aren't really any symbols or carvings I've seen. There's definitely nothing that looks like any of this." He gestures to the intricacies of the stone.

Walking around it slowly, my eyes scan every carved detail. I pause when I get to the chalice; the exact replica of the mountain falls.

He can't see it...and this is why he won't find the waters.

Not a single symbol on the fountain points to the dust, not even a suggestion. No pouch, no Guardian figure, no plateau. There's nothing showing how to get on or off the island carved into the gate.

We've spent hours pouring over the details, and my fears have been realized.

We wasted the dust.

The fountain doesn't hold any answers about the Guardian, it is only the way to call him. Tears pool in my eyes as I step away, looking around us, and finally remembering that anyone could have seen us at any time.

We're alone, thank the gods, and the blue sky above is starting to change color, resembling Dawnlin's pinks and oranges.

"Where are we?" I ask.

"Berrendahr," Dane says, stepping up alongside me.

Sig's kingdom.

This is the same fountain Sig used to get to Dawnlin twenty years ago. I wonder if it looked the same when she called the Guardian, the one *before* Dane. I wonder if she knew what she was doing, and didn't stumble upon it like I did, leaving her home behind at the last moment.

"I remember you saying you never left Blackwood, so I thought you might want to see another kingdom," he says.

A few months ago, I would have seen this gesture as heartfelt and caring, but that was before. That was before I knew about all the lies and manipulations. That was before I had tried to figure out his motivations. He doesn't want me to leave, so he ensured I couldn't change my mind.

I still need to act like it is before.

"That was really thoughtful of you," I say, the sweet words feeling like ash in my mouth. "Maybe once we find an answer, we could actually visit it together. Maybe after I find the cure."

His face lights up at my praise. "I would take you anywhere you want," he says as he reaches out to stroke the side of my face.

I smile up at him, then my lips drop again. "I don't think the fountain holds any answers."

"I agree. We would have noticed something."

I let out a harsh sigh. "We just wasted so much time," I say, dropping my gaze to the ground.

"It wasn't a waste, because we aren't left wondering. Now we know for sure that we didn't miss something, and can move on to find what we need on the island."

I nod quietly and take a deep breath.

Wasted. This entire trip was wasted time and wasted dust. The whole point of the plan lasting for two days is to get information on how to replenish it directly from the Guardian, and I'm starting to feel like I'm going to get back to the ship only bearing bittersweet news.

"We should go back," I whisper.

"Do you want to see the city before we do?" he asks, gesturing over his shoulder. "We could find a tavern, get some food. Just like before." Hope gleams in his eyes, but I shake my head.

"No, I want to go back. I'm not done looking."

He nods and glances around the space, just as he did when we left Blackwood a lifetime ago, and it hits me like a blow to the chest.

He's looking to see if anyone is around, making sure no one sneaks in.

Just like he did.

I clench my teeth, trying to keep my face neutral, as he steps in front of me. He wraps his arm around my waist, pulling me into him before reaching into the pouch. My breaths shorten and I try not to flinch as his hand descends toward the glowing gold. How much dust is he going to use? Could he use less and we still make it?

"Use as little as possible," I rush out before he lifts his hand.

"I will. I did before too," he says. I'm sure it was meant to be reassuring, but it only acts as a reminder that I am running out of time.

I need answers.

CHAPTER FIFTY-ONE

Dane drops the dust over our heads and we disappear, magic pulsing around us before we slam back into the ground. Gone is the sea air and cool breeze of Berrendahr, and we are surrounded once again by the stifling humidity of Dawnlin. Darkness has fallen, and the scene from the plateau is much different from the last time I landed here. A sole torch lights the space, and Dane walks over toward it, pulling it from its perch.

"We need to move quickly. It's not safe to be out in the open like this."

Dane's urgency tonight is a stark contrast to his behavior the last time he was here. We watched, hidden in the marshes, as he and Storm walked down the path, casually at ease, anger being the only sign of discomfort. They didn't seem to have any concern about being discovered or confronted by the Castaways. Has this all just been part of the lie Dane has spun? Was he ever truly worried about us running into them?

It's not me you need to protect yourself against.

Weston said it back when I first met him, when he threw my weapons into the lagoon, so I didn't use them against him. I didn't believe him at the time, but now it's just another element of Dane's deception that falls into place.

I nod quickly, agreeing so we can get back to camp faster.

"How is it dark already? Were we gone that long?" I ask.

"Time passes differently here, remember? We don't really know how fast it moves compared to home."

An entire day, wasted. I can feel the pressure settling on my shoulders, knowing that I only have one more day to figure this out before my time is up, and I have no choice but to take the dust and leave. But now, because we went back to the real world, we didn't get the chance to look anywhere else here, or follow any leads. There isn't enough time left.

Dane keeps his hand on the small of my back as we traipse down the path, his head swiveling back and forth, constantly monitoring our surroundings and assessing for danger. It's like he's expecting someone to jump out of the trees and snatch me from his grasp. Now knowing that Weston followed me around the island, and after begging Sig to keep him back on the ship so I could finish this task, I know Dane's worries aren't really that unreasonable. I don't know if any of the Castaways are out on shift tonight, and I can't risk someone seeing me, especially if Sig couldn't convince Weston.

We need to get back into the safety of camp.

The moment we step through the portal, the gravity of the day settles on me like a crushing weight. We found nothing. My time to find answers is running out, and all we accomplished was stealing a future from more people.

I want to curl up into a ball and cry. I want to wallow in the failure I feel, but I can't. I may have lost precious time, but the stakes are too high to give up, and I can't do anything that would make it seem like

I'm in a hurry. I have to act normally, like we have all the time in the world, because Dane thinks we do.

As long as no one calls the Guardian.

The clearing is lively, filled with Voyagers winding down for the evening. Crackling of burning logs echoes through the air, alongside voices and laughter. It's just like before I left. Nothing has changed, except Taril isn't here.

The Voyagers before me have no reason to behave any differently. They don't know what Dane knows, what I know. None of them have any clue their lives are about to be halted in a never-ending cycle.

I spot Roley over at the archery lanes and turn to Dane. "I'm going to go shoot with Roley for a bit. I promised him I would now that I am back."

"Sure," Dane says with a small smile. "I'm going to go check in with Storm and make sure nothing happened today I need to know about. Meet you after?"

He brushes a kiss on my cheek, and I give him a curt smile. After my anger and evasion earlier, I'm glad he didn't push and is letting me have space. He sets off toward the ladder, and I toward the lanes.

Roley is alone. His normal practice partner is off on the ship, probably being told a bedtime story by Weston at this very moment.

My chest aches thinking about it.

I clear my throat as I approach. "Hey Roley." My voice comes out high, filled with emotion. "Hitting that bullseye?" I stop next to him and peer down at the target. Arrows are scattered all over, some sticking out of the ground in the middle of the lane.

"Hi Lennox," Roley says, the usually energetic and chipper child is now sullen and quiet, just like Taril said.

"What's wrong?" I ask, kneeling down in front of him. "Did something happen?"

He shakes his head, but doesn't make eye contact with me.

"You can tell me Roley."

Keeping his eyes on the lane, he nocks an arrow and lifts his arms, pulling back the string until it is taut. I quickly reach out, adjusting his stance and hold, then pull my hands back. He looses the arrow and strikes the target on the outer ring. Surprise lights in his eyes for a split second before the sadness returns and he lowers the bow.

He kicks the grass, eyes trained on the ground, and mumbles, "Mara says we're all supposed to hate you. She says you're not one of us anymore."

My heart sinks. He's only a child, barely older than Fin. I don't expect him to understand the intricacies of the situation. All he can do is pick up on the emotions and words of everyone around him, and it's clearly bothering him.

"Is that what you think?" I ask, keeping my voice calm. I'm not mad at Mara. She's not technically wrong about me anyway. But she doesn't understand the complete picture. She's been lied to as I have, but there's nothing I can do or say to convince her that she wouldn't attribute to the Castaway mind games.

Now I know how Weston felt.

I sit on that realization for a moment, then shake my head. I can't dwell on that. I need to focus on my purpose, and Roley, standing here in front of me.

Roley shakes his head. "No," he murmurs.

"Then that's all that matters. No one should change how you feel about someone else. That is up to you to decide." Another weight settles in my stomach. Dane did exactly this to all of us about Weston and the crew. If only I had someone telling me I didn't have to listen when I first arrived, things may have been very different.

I'm grateful I've at least learned these lessons now.

"I don't want you to be one of them," he says, his voice wobbly. "I want Fin back, too." My heart breaks as I watch tears fall onto his cheeks.

I don't think. I don't even know what prompts me to do this, besides watching this innocent little boy, my friend, suffer under the control of Dane.

Looking around to make sure we are alone, I drop my voice to a whisper.

"Roley, I need you to listen to me, okay? Please raise your bow if you understand." He pauses for a moment, then lifts his bow.

"I'm going to keep talking, but I'm going to move around like I'm showing you something with the bow. Say 'yes' if you understand."

"Yes," he says.

"Do you trust me, Roley? I mean, really trust me?" I reach over and adjust his stance, shifting his hips to align with the target, waiting for his answer.

"Yes."

"Can I trust you? I'm going to tell you something, but I need it to stay between us."

He looks straight at me then, eyes still glassy from the tears only a few moments ago. He nods.

"Look toward the target," I say, and he does. "I promise I am telling you the truth. Fin is fine, he's doing great. He really misses you, too." I lift his elbow so it is parallel to the ground. "The Castaways aren't what everyone thinks. Dane hasn't been honest about them."

Roley's eyes widen slightly as he listens to me. His lips stay pursed, and he doesn't move.

"I'm not staying here, Roley. I'm going back. You can't tell anyone, not a single word, understand?"

His lip starts to quiver as he realizes what I'm telling him. I jump in, trying to explain and give him some hope.

"We're trying to fix things. They're kind of broken, right now, and I'm trying to help fix them. But Dane is lying to you. I can bring you back with me, but it can't be right away." I push his bow closer to his body and reach over to grab an arrow, placing it in the right spot and helping him pull it back.

"If you want to go with me, you need to tell me. I promise it is safe, and Fin is there. I would never hurt you, Roley."

He lets the arrow fly, and it strikes the target on the second ring. His arms fall, lowering the bow, and he turns to face me.

"I know Lennox. I believe you." Childlike innocence fills his face, but more than that, it's trust. "You helped me, before. And so did she. That girl, the one who was with you. They can't be bad if she still let you help me."

Sig. He remembers Sig trying to help him, just before we were attacked from behind.

"That's right. She's not bad. None of them are. They were all once Voyagers too."

"So what do we do?" he whispers, his eyes widening as they dart toward the clearing and then back to me.

My lips turn up slightly and I hand him another arrow. To anyone watching, it hopefully looks like instruction, but to me, it's saving someone I care about.

"In four nights, I want you to meet me somewhere. You'll have to sneak out at night, alright?"

He starts to object, but I cut him off. "I promise you, it is safe. They will not hurt you. Remember? It's not like Dane says."

I try to come up with a place he can meet me, somewhere that isn't too far, so he isn't scared, but also isn't too close to something important. If anyone follows him, I don't want them catching on.

"Do you know the rocks, just on the other side of the rope bridge?"

He nods. Obviously, he does, but what he doesn't know is that the tunnel we used on the night of the marsh incident pops open right there.

"Meet me there, near the edge of the trees. But don't take the rope bridge. It's too dangerous. Take the long way."

"But I've been over that bridge a bunch of times," he says.

"I know. It's different at night. I want you to be safe."

He nods and shoots another arrow.

"Four nights, remember? Tonight is night one. That way, no one will suspect anything. Just be patient, I'll be there, and I'll bring you back with me. I promise you it is safe."

"And Fin will be there?" he asks, his eyes lighting up with hope.

"I'm not going to bring him with me, but he will be there when we get back."

"Alright Lennox," he whispers. "I trust you."

My body warms as I smile at him, and he returns it. Fin will be so happy to see him, and I'll have saved another person I care about from Dane's clutches.

"And remember, Roley. You can't tell anyone. No one at all." My smile drops and I show him how serious this is. His understanding is crucial to his safety, and for the safety of the Castaways.

"I won't," he says. "Promise."

I wrap my arms around him, squeezing him into a big hug. I can't leave him behind, not after everything I know, and how clearly this entire situation is affecting him. Weston is going to be furious with me once he finds out my plan, but I don't care. If the dust runs out, I don't want Roley living for eternity in camp, alone and upset by the influence of everyone older than him. The least I can do is bring him home with me for his own happiness and safety.

I just hope he keeps his word and stays silent. Sending a quick prayer to the gods and the island, I beg everything works out smoothly, and we all get what we need.

CHAPTER FIFTY-TWO

My eyelids are heavy with exhaustion after searching camp late into the night. Once Dane returned to the training area and Roley and I were no longer alone, I told him I wanted to make up for the hours I normally would have searched for the cure. We went to the bunks empty handed once again, after calling it a night once the last sounds of Voyagers had died away hours before.

I'm panicking.

Searching today has been just as fruitless as yesterday, and I leave tonight.

This is the night I've been preparing for, the night to get Dane alone, and get back to the ship with whatever dust I can.

My fingertips start to tingle and my chest heaves with breaths as I tip my head back toward the sky. The suns are already well into their descent, the sky morphing into a flurry of colors, and hits me like a blow to the chest.

I'm out of time.

I found nothing that will help us all get home. Tears prick at my eyes as I think about the handful of Castaways we are going to have to choose. How are we ever going to decide? And how am I going to convince Weston not to choose me just because of my title and responsibility, and to give me the same consideration as everyone else?

How am I going to handle it if he does it anyway, and forces me to leave them all behind?

To leave him behind?

I can't think about that now. The next part of the plan is too important. If I fail, we won't have the opportunity to make any decisions, so my concentration and execution are crucial.

Blinking away the tears, I take a deep breath and let it out slowly. It's time, and I need to be mentally prepared for everything that comes next.

The trees are thick on this side of camp, but that is all they are. Trees. There are no hidden structures or paths, just what seems like fields of trees that might not even be real. The magic hiding camp could make me feel like I'm walking forever, but in reality I'm going in circles, finding nothing.

"Dane!" I yell, stepping past large trunks and over leaves covering the floor. We split up earlier to cover more ground, but now I'm kicking myself, wondering if it was indeed magic that kept us occupied all day.

"Lennox?" he calls from somewhere out of view.

"Where are you?"

"I'm coming!" He appears in the trees ahead a moment later, winding through the trunks and brush directly toward me. "Did you find something?" he asks hopefully.

"No," I say, shaking my head. "I thought we could call it a night. The suns will be down soon and I…" My voice trails off and I drop my gaze to the ground. Heart pounding in my ears, and nervous energy coursing through me, I hope I look more embarrassed than I feel.

"What is it?"

"I just...sort of...wanted to be alone," I say, anxiously meeting his gaze.

Dane's face softens, and he steps up to me, his chest brushing against mine as he weaves his fingers through the hair on the back of my neck.

"I can have Mara move out of the cabin if you'd feel more comfortable there. You were gone a long time. I know it might take a while before you feel comfortable here again."

"No, I, uh," I stammer. "That's not what I meant." I lift my shoulders to my ears, curling in on myself before letting out a sharp breath. "I, um, wanted to be alone. With you." I meet his gaze, and watch as his eyes sparkle, making me shiver, but not in the way I used to.

Not the way that Weston makes me.

This shiver is cold and fearful, because I can't tell what is going on behind those eyes anymore. I can't tell what game he's playing, or my role in it.

"I like that idea," he says, then leans down, pressing a kiss to my lips. I let him, unable to keep hold of the distance I created yesterday for any longer, especially going into tonight.

He breaks away and his thumb reaches back to stroke my cheek. "Do you want to go to our beach?" he murmurs.

"No!" I blurt out before regaining my composure. He rears back slightly, my shout taking him off guard, and I scramble to find an excuse not to return to the beach.

"No, sorry. I just mean, I hoped that maybe it could just be you and me tonight."

A grin widens across his face. "Yeah, we can do that."

I look up through the canopy of trees at the sky again. "I wanted to ask when it was early enough so we didn't leave after dark. I don't want to be out in the dark." I let my voice tremble with fear, and he pulls me closer, lowering his face so our noses almost touch.

"I won't let anything happen to you. You're too important to me." I give him a soft smile, and he brushes another quick kiss over my lips before grasping my hand and pulling me through the trees. "Let's get moving so we can make it before the suns go down."

Back in the clearing, Voyagers are trickling in as everyone heads up to the tavern for dinner. I quickly assess my bunk, trying to remember if I left anything I need there, but I didn't. I don't care about any of it.

Everything I need is back on the ship.

Everyone I need.

Except Roley. There's no choice but to leave him here, if only for another few days. I hope he keeps his promise and meets me so we can keep him safe.

Acting like I won't be back tomorrow would raise suspicion. I can't say goodbye, or do anything unusual. I need to walk through that portal and not look back.

"Lilly," Dane calls as she appears in the clearing, coming in from her day of searching. I haven't really seen her since I've been back, but I can tell being on the island has changed her. I wonder if the change in me was just as noticeable.

She looks up at Dane, waiting for direction.

"Tell Storm I'll be out tonight. He's in charge."

"I will," she says and passes us with a wave, heading toward the ladder.

Once we're on the main path, I take a deep breath, steadying myself and bracing for the next step in the plan.

Here we go. I can't be too obvious.

I start the conversation I've been practicing in my mind every night since Sig and I made this plan, the conversation that would ensure I was safe and on my way home.

"I didn't even think about staying to eat first. Do the safe houses usually have food? I've never stayed at one before."

"They're just like camp. They'll have everything we need. You don't have to worry." He gives me a closed lipped smile, and leads me down the path, heading toward the mountain.

My footsteps stutter as I let him lead me. Sig will be waiting at the safe house on the other side of the island, so I need to get him to turn around.

"Where are we going?" I ask hesitantly. "You said you wanted to go to the beach before. Why don't we go to the house on the other beach? The one right around the bend? Maybe we could walk over and watch the waves."

My heart pounds in my ears, waiting for his answer as I gradually slow my steps and tug on his hand, pulling him in the opposite direction.

"Well, I was going to surprise you. Once you mentioned the safe houses, I got an idea. There's one I want to take you to. It's possible there's a clue about the dust there."

No, no, no, no.

My time to worry about replenishing the dust is gone, no matter what clue Dane thinks there might be.

I can't go to another safe house. I need to get to *that* safe house. Sig will be waiting for me, and if something goes wrong, if he catches me trying to take the dust, I need the backup.

I have to get out of this.

I pull back on his hand a little harder. "But I wanted to take a break from searching for a night."

His hand squeezes mine then quickly releases, but his steps don't falter as he chuckles softly. "We don't have to do anything tonight. We can search in the morning."

Fuck.

This isn't working. My mind races, trying to come up with a new excuse, one that won't seem too obvious.

"I just think it would be nice being near the beach, listening to the waves. You helped me get over my fear there." I hold my breath, hoping the sentimentality will convince him.

Dane didn't help me get over my fear of the water. Weston did. All Dane did that night was shower me with extraordinary experiences, then feed me lies to keep me under his control.

He stops abruptly and I almost run into him, but he doesn't notice. He weaves his fingers through mine and gazes down at me. "I just thought you wanted to be alone, and this one is secluded. No one will bother us."

Panic.

Sheer panic floods my body.

He's not taking any of my bait, only giving me solutions I should have no problem agreeing to. Denying an idea for replenishing the dust after spending the last two days tirelessly searching for answers would not fit the narrative I've woven since I've been back at camp. If I fight him any more, he might think something is wrong, that I'm up to something.

But if I don't, everything will go wrong.

All I can do is smile, which he returns before stepping forward again and tugging me along.

"We need to hurry. We're losing daylight."

"Lead the way," I say, doing everything in my power to keep my voice steady.

Fuck.

Fuck, fuck, FUCK.

Sig does not know where Dane is about to take me, and I have no way of communicating with her. No one should be following me after I told her to trust me, and dread fills my stomach as I curse myself for forcing that.

What is she going to think when I don't show up at the safe house? Is she going to think something happened? Will she think Dane took me somewhere else?

Or is she going to think I double crossed her?

Sweat coats my palms, and my hand slides in Dane's as we walk. He doesn't seem to notice, but I feel as if my body is on fire.

Everything is going wrong.

This entire plan, so meticulously crafted, has been turned upside down.

I didn't find how to replenish the dust, and now I am not at our designated location.

I'm alone.

No one knows where I am.

Using the same calming technique as when I shoot, I inhale deeply through my nose and let it out of my mouth, trying to slow the pounding of my heart.

At least I still have my dagger, even if I don't have Sig there with me.

Edmond's voice pops into my mind, and I realize through all of this planning, my crucial error. I didn't account for any changes in the plan. I only focused on one angle. We had no contingencies, no backups.

I've made a huge mistake.

I'm in this alone, and I have to get out of it alone.

I can handle this.

I just need to get the dust, and get back to the ship, back to the people I love, and hope Weston doesn't hate me because I left.

CHAPTER FIFTY-THREE

*D*ane leads me across the bridge to the other side of the island, the forest that reminds me of Blackwood looming before us. I'd hoped we would take the long way around, not out of nervousness crossing the bridge where I almost fell into the depths with the monsters below, but because I wanted to be seen.

My hope of passing in front of the mountain was dashed as soon as Dane turned off the main path, cutting through the center of the island. I wanted to be seen by whoever was in the lookout on shift today. Walking over that stone bridge was my last hope of Sig finding out that I wasn't where I was supposed to be.

But we didn't, so she will never know.

I'm truly alone.

No one is coming for me.

"This way." Trailing behind him, I follow as Dane cuts off the path, walking straight into the trees. The forest is dark, the trees so dense that all the remaining light from the sunset above us is blocked by the towering trees.

This part of the island is new to me, the forest unfamiliar, even though I've spent my life looking out my windows at a similar one. Once I was searching on my own, I started on the other side of the island, purposely staying close to camp until I was familiar and confident I could make it back before dusk. When I drew my map, I was methodical, and when the time came to cross over and search the other side, I'd already found the waters. The forest is unfamiliar territory, and I don't know where we are going, or even worse, how to get out.

I try to remember the nearest entrance to the tunnels, but we never took one this far into the forest. The closest I know of is at the edge, just beyond the bridge, the same one I told Roley to meet me at in three more nights.

The Oasis is on the other side of the trees.

Depending how far into the forest we end up, if I need to escape I can continue on through the other side, to the dunes. If I could find the magical cut in the ceiling, maybe the island would let me drop through into the pool below.

Maybe I'd have to beg the island for safety, just as Sig and I did before.

I hope it doesn't get to that.

"We're almost there," Dane says over his shoulder, his hand still clutching mine tightly as we tramp through the brush and needles.

I stay silent, lost in my thoughts and observing anything that could help me, or anywhere I could hide if I need it. Nothing stands out or catches my eye that might lead me to safety, and I can't help but notice the scent as we weave through the trees.

With the endless fog and clouds and the moisture in the air, Blackwood smells damp and musty. The wet soil and dewy vegetation give off a scent that means home, but here, even with all the moisture in the air, it is completely different. The forest smells... happy...the trees fragrant. It feels familiar, even though it is the exact opposite of home.

"It's just ahead," Dane says, breaking the silence, as well as my concentration. Leaning to the side, I sneak a glance past him, and my eyes fall on a tiny structure tucked away in a slight break in the trees. Felled logs make up the peaked framework, with only a single door and a small dark window set into it. It barely looks like two people could fit inside, let alone someone as tall as Dane.

"After you," Dane says, and pushes open the door, gesturing for me to enter first. The room lights up before me, and I take in the space, the same magic that creates the cabin back at camp at work here as well.

A wall of windows sits opposite the door, the view of the forest through them peaceful and stunning. Everything else is simple; small wooden table with a few chairs is tucked into the corner near the door. Next to it, a smooth stone hearth that lies across from a single bed.

"Make yourself comfortable," Dane says behind me, and I startle slightly. My eyes are fixed on the single bed, and I gulp down the lump forming in my throat.

It wasn't long ago that the thought of being alone with Dane was thrilling, and something I hoped would happen. I never would have balked at sharing a bed, or whatever followed.

But now my mouth goes dry as I stare at it, anticipating any expectations he might have based on how I was before. *Who* I was before.

Now, there's only one man I want to share a bed with.

Dane steps around me, crossing the room and kneeling before the hearth. He arranges some chopped wood inside and works to strike sparks into the kindling underneath. My gaze drifts down to his bare feet, then to his discarded boots beside me, and my heartbeat hastens. Suspicions might rise if I don't take mine off too, but if I do, I risk him finding my dagger.

And I'm left unprotected.

I'm too close. I can't risk being discovered now.

"Do we really need a fire?" I ask as I crouch down to untie my boots, sliding each of them off, and making sure my dagger slips down inside as far as possible.

"This deep into the forest actually can get pretty cold. You'll be glad later once the suns are all the way down."

The kindling catches and I watch the flames engulf the logs. It almost feels like a sign, as if this is the moment where our entire plan sparks to life and gives us hope of getting home.

"Are all the safe houses like this? I mean—" I gesture to the bed behind him, and he glances over his shoulder, following my point. "Only one bed?"

"The rooms can change depending on how many people need it, but most Voyagers search alone, so they only ever need one." He drops another log inside as crackling and popping fills the air between us.

"There's two of us. Pretty presumptuous of Dawnlin, isn't it?" I say, folding my arms across my chest.

Dane stands and chuckles before crossing the room to stop in front of me. He brushes a piece of hair off my face, his eyes softening as he looks into mine. "We don't have to do anything you aren't comfortable with, one bed or not."

I let out a breath, relief flooding my body, and I think he notices. Before either of us can say anything more, a loud growl from my stomach breaks the tension, and a loud laugh erupts from his mouth. "Let's get you fed."

Before he finishes his statement, a spread of food appears on the table next to us. Pulling out a chair, I sit hastily, digging in to the food and using it as an excuse to figure out how to keep pushing forward despite the location impediment. I need to stick to the plan and get out, but I'm still going to gather any information that might help us later. My time isn't up yet.

"So," I say between bites. "Why did we come here? What was your idea about the dust?"

Dane slides into the chair next to me and drapes his arm across the back of mine. "I want to check all the safe houses. I haven't thought to search them before, but what if, like you said, the previous Guardians used them? What if they stored something that would be a clue, like books or maps?"

"I thought we weren't allowed to have maps," I say automatically. He still has no clue about mine.

"We can't," he answers. "But if there were old ones hidden in our safe houses, they would be protected. We've never had a Castaway inside one before. It's the perfect place to keep important information hidden."

I look around the room, trying to spot anything that could be a secret compartment, or any items that looked like they were left behind, but there is nothing out of the ordinary. The walls are bare, there's no extra furniture. If there is anything hidden in this safe house, the magic decided not to show it to us.

"I wanted to check this one first because it is so secluded. It would make sense if something is hidden here."

It does make sense. The isolation and darkness that surrounds it would make it easily forgotten or never found, as opposed to the houses that are more out in the open, like the one I was supposed to be in tonight. The seclusion makes for a great hiding place, but for my purposes tonight, all it brings is fear.

"But the safe houses are just like the cabin, right?" I ask. "They change depending on who needs it?"

"Right," he says, and reaches out to grab a piece of meat.

My stomach sinks as I formulate my next question. The realization of what Dane's idea could mean hitting me as hard as Sig's fist.

"Are you the only one that can search them then? Will the magic only reveal whatever is hidden to the Guardian?"

His head tilts to the side as he considers it, perking up slightly with his response. "It's possible. I haven't tried, but maybe I should."

If Dane is right, and the Guardians of the past used one of the safe houses to store information on Dawnlin, specifically how to get the dust, he might be the only one that can access it. If the magic protects the island, anything that could risk the dust falling into the wrong hands would stay hidden, only to be revealed to the Guardian.

Which means, if I take the pouch tonight, that's all the dust we will ever have.

But what if the Guardian is the one who is causing the harm? Is the island protecting it from him, too?

I reach out for a cup of water and take a large gulp, trying to hide the worry on my face with this new possibility.

"Should I leave so you can look, then?" I ask.

Dane scoffs, as if what I asked was an absurd request. "Of course not. We're taking a break tonight, remember?"

Of course. A break.

Tension coils in my shoulders, but I smile softly to hide the unease.

Dane was right before. The warmth from the fire that fills the room isn't too much from the coolness of the dark forest around us. The suns fell below the trees long ago, and the windows on the opposite side of the room are black. The only thing visible is our reflections in the dark glass. The island is silent around us, except for the crackling of the fire, and I let out a loud yawn. I am exhausted, but getting to sleep is the next step of my plan. I need Dane to let his guard down enough to take the dust off and fall asleep so I can take it and escape.

Dane stands, his chair scraping against the floor as he leans over and presses a quick kiss to my hair. "I'm going to go get some more firewood. Why don't you lay down? I'll be back in a minute."

"Alright," I say with a nod, as I fight off another yawn.

He walks to the door and slips on his boots while I cross the room to the bed. I need the best advantage possible to escape, so I sink into the bedding and curl up on the side closest to the door, pleading with my body not to fall asleep.

Not in outdoor clothes, you aren't.

I shiver as Weston's words play in my mind, and close my eyes for a moment, pretending I'm back on the ship, getting ready for bed.

But I'm leaving these clothes *on.*

I can do this. I can do this.

Please help me do this.

The island wanted me to be here, wanted me to leave the ship and go through with my plan, so now I plead with it to let me get through this to help my friends. My family. There has to be a reason it let me off the ship, because if there wasn't, if I wasn't meant to be here to steal the dust from Dane's belt, I would have stayed locked in Weston's room, with the entire plan thwarted.

CHAPTER FIFTY-FOUR

Only a few moments later, Dane returns, arms piled high with firewood. He kicks the door closed behind him and steps out of his boots, before crossing the room to the hearth and setting the wood down beside it. The fire pops and flares as he adds more of the dry logs to it, and another wave of heat erupts into the room.

Unstrapping his serrated blade from his belt, he sets it on the hearth next to the wood. I'd never given it a second glance before, but now I can't seem to draw my eyes away from it; the same blade that carved up Weston's abdomen, leaving the mangled, wretched scar from the wound that almost killed him.

I pull my gaze away, and focus back on Dane as he crawls toward me from the foot of the bed, laying on his side and propping his head up on his hand. I try not to sneak another glance at his belt, trying to keep my intentions hidden but also preventing him from thinking that I have others.

He didn't take the dust off.

I don't know why I thought he would; I've never seen him take it off. Now, trying to remove the pouch from his belt without waking him up is going to be a significant challenge, and might get me caught.

"Is something bothering you?" He reaches up and brushes a piece of hair off my face. His touch is gentle, but my body stiffens beneath his fingertips. I don't know what his expectations are for tonight, for this alone time that I requested, but he assured me we wouldn't do anything I was uncomfortable with. Flashes of what we had done before, the few times we'd been alone together, plague my thoughts, and my skin crawls thinking about him touching me that way again.

His hand settles on the curve of my hip, and I cringe inwardly as he pulls me closer. I need to pretend, even if that means getting close to him, not like before, but enough to convince him to let his guard down.

"No. I'm fine," I say. "I'm just really tired. Searching and thinking all day and late last night wore me out."

"It might be helpful if I'm the only one who can search the safe houses," he says. "That way, you can take a break and get some rest back at camp."

"I don't think I'll be able to stay still while you're out searching. I'll have to keep looking too, or I'll keep searching for the cure. Either way, I have to do something."

His thumb slips under the hem of my shirt and strokes the skin just above my pants, and my lips flatten into a tight smile.

Don't think about it, Lennox.

"I think we should give it a few more days before sending you back out. At least let me check all the safe houses first so I can go search with you. That way, no one can touch you."

"Whatever you think is best," I say.

He leans forward, eyes fixed on mine. "I'll do anything to keep you safe." He closes the distance and presses his lips to mine, and I can feel the question in his movements.

I stay focused on my breathing, preventing the short pants from taking hold of me, letting his lips stay pressed to mine before I pull back. I glance down, hoping it seems more nervous and less uninterested.

As I look back up, my eyes catch on his scar, and I reach out, running my fingertips over it, the same way I had all that time ago. His lips part slightly at my touch, but as he leans forward again, I press into them, holding him in place.

"Tell me the story again?"

He's already told me once, but I want to hear it from his lips again and see how easily the lie rolls off his tongue.

"It was nothing special," he says with a shrug, "just kids being kids."

"With your sister, right?"

"Right," he says. "I was too clumsy as a kid and fell when we were playing outside. Had to run all the way home with blood dripping down my face. It was traumatizing for such a young kid, believe me."

Not a change in his voice, not a flutter of a muscle in his face.

How many lies has Dane told us so easily that flowed from his mouth as if they were true?

If I had any doubts Weston and Sig were the ones lying to me, they are gone now. I know they are telling the truth because Dane's story has changed.

He was no longer running through his family home and falling to the doorjamb.

And he no longer has my trust, despite trying to convince me he is worthy of it.

Before I can respond, he leans forward again, his lips cutting me off as they move against mine. The kiss is more insistent as his fingers tighten around my hip. He pushes me gently, rolling me to my back so he is laying on top of me, his weight all but suffocating me as his kiss still draws my breath.

The moment his lips pull away, I suck in a deep breath, trying to steady the trapped feeling that is stirring in my chest. He shifts slightly and begins peppering my jawline with small kisses, making his way up to my ear.

"I can't believe I found you," he murmurs, kissing just under my lobe, then dragging his lips down the column of my neck. He nudges the neck of my shirt to the side, and kisses along the length of my collarbone until it disappears under the fabric, and I keep breathing deeply, trying to come up with an excuse to stop him.

Then his lips are on mine again. I return the kisses, less enthusiastically than him, and I don't care if he notices. If he questions it, I can easily blame being so run down and needing sleep.

He breaks away and leans back slightly, his eyes roaming over my face, my lips, before meeting my gaze again.

"I've been meaning to tell you something for a while now. I don't want it to change anything between us, but I need to say it."

My heart pounds, so hard that I'm sure he can hear it, and bile burns the back of my throat. What could Dane possibly have to tell me? What new lie is he using to reel me in, to manipulate me into believing everything he says?

He reaches up and strokes the side of my face, his eyes scanning between mine for a moment before he speaks.

"I've known it since the moment I saw you, but I've been keeping it to myself. I hope you feel the same, but even if you don't yet, that won't change anything for me. I just can't keep it to myself any longer." He pauses, eyes locking on mine again. "I love you, Lyla."

My mouth falls open as the world around me comes to a crashing halt.

Humming fills my ears, blocking out any other sound as it gets louder and louder, like I've just jumped off the cliff and am still underwater.

My vision blurs and I blink rapidly until my eyes focus on Dane's again, an earnest expression on his face, as he waits for my response.

The moment snaps back into place, and I push at his shoulders, trying to get out from under him. My chest heaves rapidly as he rolls to the side, and I scramble across the bed.

But now, he's between me and the door.

"I'm sorry," he says as he stands, turning to face me. His brow is furrowed and worry paints his features. "I'm sorry, I probably shouldn't have said anything, but I couldn't go another day without you at least knowing how I felt. I don't want it to change our life together."

My mouth is open, my jaw slack as my mind reels, processing what just happened.

"You don't have to say it back," he says, taking a step closer to the bed until his knees bump it.

As if the jolt of the bed wakes me up from a stupor, my eyes snap to his. I gape at him before I finally find the words, my voice coming out in a rasp.

"What did you just call me?"

The worry turns into confusion, as his head tilts to the side. "What do you mean?"

"That name. You called me a different name," I say, pushing up onto my knees and walking back a few paces across the bed.

My hands go numb as I realize I've set myself up in the worst position possible.

There's nowhere to go.

I'm trapped in this room. Dane stands between me and the only exit, and I have no weapon.

"No, I didn't," he says, shaking his head like he's shocked at the accusation.

"How do you know that name, Dane?" My voice rises, panic and fury bubbling under my skin, begging to be unleashed.

"Lennox, I don't know what you think you heard, but I didn't call you another name."

"You did!" I scream. The panic is taking over, along with rising uncertainty. I question myself, doubting my own senses and memory as I play back the last few moments in my head.

But no.

I'm *not* wrong.

I know what I heard.

I know what he said.

And I know he's a liar.

"Don't lie to me again, Dane. Why did you call me Lyla?"

Stepping back from the bed, he crosses his arms over his chest. His jaw hardens and his gaze intensifies as he glares down at me, irritation touching his voice. "Lennox, I don't know what you're accusing me of or why, but you need to get past it. Let's just go to sleep."

He moves toward the bed again, but I stop him.

"No!" I scream, throwing an arm out in front of me. It's enough to startle him, causing him to halt where he stands.

My entire plan unravels before me; everything I worked to fix is disappearing into thin air. My chances of helping even some Castaways get home are dwindling, all because of this man.

This man with the key to our return hanging from his belt.

Who tried to kill the man I love.

Who is trying to convince me I didn't hear what he said correctly.

This man who called me my mother's name.

"Stop lying to me, Dane. I know you're lying." My voice trembles as I stare him down, waiting to see if he'll lie again.

But he says nothing. The corners of his lips turn up into a smug smirk, and my stomach drops.

"How do you know who I am?" I whisper.

I've kept my identity hidden from everyone on this island. Weston knew, and told Sig, but Dane shouldn't have. The only way he would know that name meant something to me, is if he knows who I am, and lied to try to hide his mistake.

"I knew the second I saw you walk into that library who you were. There was no mistaking you were her daughter."

Nausea churns in my stomach, and I feel acid burning in the back of my throat. Dane knew who I was this entire time. But how? Why?

Why did he never say anything?

"You lied to me," I grind out, my panic and fear subsiding, replaced with white hot anger. I'm not afraid anymore, not of hiding anything from him. That part of the plan is long over. "You lied about everything."

"Not everything," he says. "You *are* exactly what I've been waiting for."

"Why?" I snap. "What do you want with me?"

This was my question, back when I found out Dane had been lying. What did he want with *me*? Why was he doing this to *me*?

"I don't want *you*," he says casually, like everything he told me since the moment I met him meant absolutely nothing, and like losing it hasn't affected him at all. "I want what you can give me, and that's the cure."

I shake my head. "Anyone on this island can give you the cure. Why did you do this to *me*?"

"Sure, anyone can, but no one has, despite being here year after year. But then you came along." He takes a slow step forward, like he's stalking me, the ferocity in his eyes making goosebumps erupt on my skin. "I thought who better to get it than you? You're smart, methodical, motivated. Who better to get it for Lyla than her own daughter?"

"You're using me," I say, my chest heaving as I take another small pace backward across the bed, but before I can blink, he's charging at me. His hands slam into the bed on either side of me, his scowling face only a breath from mine.

"I would use anyone to heal her!" he yells, his voice a loud snarl, the volume causing me to stagger back, falling onto my hands behind me. "But when I saw you, searching desperately for an answer, I knew you were the one. I knew you could find it, and the island would help you. It has been years, and it has never helped me, but you? Her daughter? Saving the mother she never knew? That's what Dawnlin is here for."

"You came here for her..." I breathe, the weight of the confession hitting me like a blow to the chest.

Dane knew my mother. He knew her enough to try to save her, when he snuck onto the island expecting the cure and cheating the magic. Now the magic has been kept from him for all these years.

"I would do anything for her! She is everything, and he took her away from me!"

I shake my head. "I don't know what you're taking about."

"Of course you don't. Who would tell you the truth? Surely not him. Not after he stole her. Waltzing into the city and throwing around his royalty, convincing her to leave her life and everything behind. For what? For him?"

My father. He's talking about my father.

My lips seal shut, and I watch as his eyes become frenzied, as flashes of emotions flicker through them.

"She forgot about me. Forgot about everyone who had been there for her, who loved her. All she could see was him."

Oh gods.

Was Dane in love with my mother? That is the only explanation that makes sense, how he's held onto this hope for so long, why he was desperate for the cure when he arrived. Why he would kill for it.

"None of it was real," I say, more to myself than to him.

"Of course it was all real. Everything is real. The island is real, the magic is real. But you and me? I did what I needed to do to get you here, to make sure you gave her another chance."

My voice catches in my throat and I can't say anything, my mind reeling back through everything from before.

Bumping into me at the library.

Telling me about Dawnlin in the tavern.

Assuring me I could trust him.

You're everything I've been waiting for.

He'd been waiting for me the entire time. The Guardian of Dawnlin, trapped in the one place that could heal the woman he loved, the woman that wasn't his.

And he used me.

"It was too easy. Remmington made sure of that, locking you up and starving you of attention. It was nothing for me to whisper what you wanted to hear, watch you fall even harder with every smile and touch. Every single word was nothing except to convince you to do exactly what I needed you to. You soaked up the love like water in a fucking desert."

His words slice through me, the truth cutting through me as if he'd held my dagger to my skin, shredding any remaining thread of doubt deep inside me.

It was all a lie. The entire time. He used me, manipulated me, convinced me he loved me.

He doesn't.

He never wanted me, never cared about me.

But there are people on this island who do.

And despite this entire plan imploding before my eyes, I'm going to fight and get out of it for them.

"And even though you know now," Dane continues, his voice cruel and punishing as he inches closer to me. "You're still going to do what I say, because I'm the only way you can leave. You are still going to find the cure for her."

I almost laugh, but I hold it in. The island has given me the only way I can truly hurt him. Back when it happened, I saw it as a curse, as the lowest point of my time here, being deemed unworthy. Now, I realize what a gift it was.

Dane doesn't care about me, about anyone here. He only cares about one thing, and I'm about to rip the hope right from his chest.

I steel my face, the fury I feel inside flaring in my eyes as I stare him down and grit my teeth.

"I already found it."

The shock on his face is immediate, and a wave of triumph washes over me. Knowing how much he manipulated me, how he thought he had me wrapped around his finger, succumbing to his every whim and push, I can't help but feel satisfaction and pride at having bested him. He thought I would run to him, tell him everything I learned and everything I found, but I didn't. I hid something from him, more than he truly knows, and watching the confidence fall from his face brings me a sick sense of joy.

I watch as the hurt crosses his face. Whether that's for my betrayal or losing hope for helping my mother, I don't know. As much as I can see this hurts him, I'm not through hurting this man that hurt me and people I love. He needs to pay for everything he has done to everyone here, and all the families he's ripped the hope away from.

"It doesn't matter what you want, or what you think I can give to you," I snarl. "The island didn't give it to me. So you can't have anything. You can't save her."

His eyes darken and his lips pull back in a sneer.

"Then you're fucking useless to me."

CHAPTER FIFTY-FIVE

Useless.

The word stings like a slap across my face as years of emotions come cascading over me, pushing me back down into the shell of the person I was before. It's all I've ever felt.

Useless to my father, to my kingdom. Useless to my mother, unworthy of bringing the healing waters home to her.

My entire life has consisted of the driving need to prove myself, to be worth my place and worthy of notice.

Until now.

From the moment I stepped onto that ship, even before I saw it myself, I wasn't useless. I became part of something, part of a crew, who saw me for who I was.

Lennox.

Someone who isn't useless with a blade, who protects and defends those she loves, and who is a new part of this crew, this family, a place no one else can fill.

They never saw me as useless.

Because I'm not.

Dane may know who I am, where I come from, but he doesn't know the real me. Something deep inside urged me to hold that part close, to keep it hidden from him. It urged me to hide things from him, not to tell him about the map, about meeting Weston, all things that completely altered the trajectory of my time on Dawnlin, and brought the truth to light.

Maybe it was the magic, or maybe it was me, but whatever it was, I'm grateful for it, even down to the nightmares that have plagued me, planting a seed of uncertainty about him that ended up being real.

Like Sig said before I left her and the rest of the Castaways behind, I know who I am.

I will not let him control me or influence me any longer.

And I'm going to fight.

There's no one waiting for me outside, no one to count on if something goes wrong, no one to scream for. It's just me and Dane, and I have a family to get home to.

I lunge quickly, rolling off the end of the bed toward the hearth with one sole focus. My fingers wrap around the scabbard as I yank it toward me, trying desperately to pull the blade free, but Dane is too quick. As if he read my intentions, he's on me in a flash. His thick arms wrap around me, pinning mine to my sides, and I thrash wildly against him, trying to get enough space to release the knife.

What justice it would be to use the same knife against Dane that he tried to strike Weston down with.

The thought makes me fight harder, kicking and elbowing, trying to break free. His arms cinch down on me as he reaches for the hilt, prying it from my fingers, before tossing it directly into the roaring flames.

"No!" I scream, reaching toward the fire, but pulling back immediately. The metal is already red hot, and useless to me now.

"Did you really think that would work?" Dane sneers in my ear. "Did you think you could use my knife against me?"

My bare feet glide across the wooden boards as I try to kick out of his grasp, but I can't get any leverage. I need to get away from him. I need a weapon.

My boots. I need to get back to my boots.

"Calm down, Lennox," Dane croons, his cruel voice barely recognizable from the one I've come to know, and it sends shivers of terror up my spine. "You're going to listen, and listen carefully."

My elbow collides with his abdomen, and he lets out a grunt, but his grip doesn't loosen.

"Fuck you!" I scream and he squeezes me tighter, my training no match for his size and brute strength, especially without a weapon.

Dane drags me across the room, away from the hearth and anything that I could have used against him there. I thrash harder. My boots are so close; I just need to get out of his clutches and get to my dagger.

A sickening crunch echoes in my ears when I throw my head back and collide with Dane's face. He cries out, but I ignore it, because it gave me the distraction I needed. Dane's arms release me as he tends to his face, and I crash to the floor, my knees hitting the wood hard under the full weight of my body.

Crawling across the floor as fast as my limbs will carry me, I scramble to my boots and shove my hand inside, feeling for the familiar touch of the metal hilt, but my hand comes up empty.

Fuck! Wrong boot!

The thought barely gets through my mind before Dane's bruising grasp is on my hips. He drags me across the floor and tosses me as if I weigh nothing. Pain erupts as my head cracks on the wooden frame of the bed, and I crumple in front of it with a thud. Dark spots appear over my spinning vision as I try to push away the daze.

They clear as I blink rapidly, only to find Dane stalking toward me, blood streaming down his face into the wicked smile across his lips.

"You're never going to win, Lennox. You can keep fighting, but you're not in charge here. I am." He crouches down in front of me, his icy glare and wicked smirk sending fear coursing through me. "You're going to bring me to the cure. One way or another, I'm going to get it. I don't care if I have to take it from any of the children at camp who worship the ground I walk on. I will get her back!"

"I'll never show you where it is," I force out, my voice echoing around me, feeling like it is separate from my body.

"You will," he says, his eyes narrowing as he reaches toward me. He fists my shirt and yanks me to my feet, dragging my face toward his as he hovers just a breath away.

"I was going to let you get away with it, whatever your little plan was, but you're hiding things from me. No one hides things from me on *my* island."

My breath stutters as I stare into his eyes, the once comforting amber now hard and deadly. The glint of metal catches my eye as his arm lifts, and I see what is sparkling in the firelight.

My dagger.

Dane has my dagger.

I wasn't wrong before; I didn't choose the wrong boot. My dagger wasn't inside because Dane found it.

The gleam in his eye shines as he brings the blade closer to my face, sliding the edge under my chin, far enough away that my skin tingles with the proximity.

"Tell me, Lennox," he says with a tilt of his head. "If your story is true, and you were held captive and *escaped*, why would you have this?"

My instinct takes over, and I grab his wrist, wrenching the muscles in his hand and bending it just like Weston taught me, like Sig and I practiced, but it doesn't move. His hands are too large, his knuckles white as he holds the hilt in a death grip, making the muscles I targeted too taut to move. My efforts only garner a depraved chuckle, just before there's a flash of movement.

His hand wraps around the back of my neck, pulling me toward him as the cold blade settles across my throat. The face presses firmly against my skin, and my entire body stiffens in his tight hold.

My teeth clench as I bite back the panic. He's won. He's bested me. I'm at his mercy, and my only consolation is that he won't kill me, because he still needs me.

But I failed, again. I failed the Castaways, I failed Weston, I failed myself. The sinking feeling in my stomach that threatens to swallow me whole, the one I've been so familiar with in the last twenty-one years, makes me question why I continue to try.

It's for them. I'm trying for them.

I blink away the tears welling in my eyes and see something flicker in Dane's. He thinks I'm afraid of him, that I've surrendered to him, but I won't. I won't stop trying to get out, no matter how long it takes.

All the love in Dane's eyes has vanished, and I stare at him, raising my chin to avoid the cut of the edge, waiting for his next move. I'm nothing to him. I never was anything more than the means to get what he wants.

"I won't help you. You'll have to kill me," I spit at him, and he pushes the blade deeper into my throat.

"You will," he spits back. "Because if you don't, I will spend the rest of eternity hunting down every single fucking Castaway, and making sure they know exactly who is responsible for their fate."

My throat bobs at his threat. He chose the one thing he knows would make me suffer.

"You know," he continues, "I thought maybe you would be enough and I could just have you instead. You were so willing and desperate. Since I couldn't have her, I'd just take you. You look enough like her that it was easy at first." A look of disgust passes over his face and his lip curls up before he spits out the next words. "But you're too much like him."

My heart pounds in my ears and my body shakes as Dane's fingertips dig deeper into the sides of my neck.

I'm too much like my father. Something that weeks ago I told Weston I never wanted, but maybe here, with Dane, that piece of me I tried to fight may have helped save me from being completely under his spell.

I open my mouth to respond, trying to find the right words to sling back at the obvious disgust he has for me. My thoughts are muddled with everything that has happened and the throbbing pain in my skull, and I can't find the right ones. My throat works in silence, for barely a moment, before something happens.

Dane's face changes before my eyes. His mouth falls slack and his shoulders stiffen, but he doesn't move, not even a hairsbreadth as a voice breaks the silence between us.

"I will plunge this sword straight through your gods damn throat if you don't get your fucking hands off her."

CHAPTER FIFTY-SIX

Weston.

I can barely contain a sob when I hear the growl of his voice. He found me. I don't know how, but he did. A slow, wicked smile spreads over Dane's bloodied face.

"So, after all this time, Weston finally decides to come out of hiding."

"No one is hiding. I just had no reason to speak to you ever again," he grumbles.

I can't see him. Dane is holding me too close that I can't see past him, but the relief that washes over me knowing he's there, that I'm not alone, is immediate.

"Until now, it seems." Dane's eyes are wild, but he stays unmoving, and I have no doubt that Weston has his sword trained on Dane's neck, just like he promised.

"Drop the dagger. Now," Weston barks, but Dane doesn't lower it.

"Or what? You're going to kill me?" he sneers. "I don't think you will."

"For her I will," Weston snarls. "Put. Her. Down."

Bile rises in my throat at the thought of Weston following through with his threat. He can't kill Dane, no matter what he does to me. My eyes scan Dane's face, his gaze boring into me as he addresses Weston behind him.

"You're really going to splatter my blood all over her pretty face?" he taunts.

"If it means keeping you away from every person in that family, I'll do it right now."

I can't stay quiet any longer, and I push back against Dane's hand, trying to wrench myself from his grip.

"Weston!" I scream. "Don't! Don't kill him!" Panic laces my voice as I plead with him.

I can't think about what would happen if Weston became the Guardian. He would be trapped here for eternity or until death, after so many years of trying to return home. I'd have to live without him, or stay here with him, but he would never let me.

"Interesting," Dane says quietly, scanning my face. He makes a clucking noise with his tongue, and his eyes turn devious. "Seems like you have been unfaithful, Lennox. Not a noble quality in a future queen, if you ask me."

"You can't be faithful to something that was all lies," I grind out.

"Last chance Dane!" Weston roars.

Dane jolts slightly, as if Weston pushed the sword deeper into his skin, warning him he is serious, and I start begging. I beg the gods, beg the island, beg whoever is listening to keep Weston from killing Dane.

Suddenly, the pressure around my neck falls away, and the bite of my dagger is gone. It hits the floor with a loud thump, and I follow it, my knees crumbling underneath me. I scramble around, searching for my weapon until my hand wraps around the hilt and I instantly feel secure.

I stand just as Dane whips around to face Weston, and my eyes finally lock on him. The point of his sword is aimed at the base of Dane's throat, and the ferocity in his eyes makes my stomach tumble. They glare at each other face to face, neither willing to make the first move.

"Willing to stab a man in the back, Weston? I didn't realize the First Guard was such a fucking coward." Dane's grimace is met by Weston's unmoving stare, as if his words have no effect on him.

But they have an effect on me.

Do they *know* each other? More than just from being on the island? Why else would Dane know Weston is the First Guard?

I replay everything from the story Sig told me. The fight between them, giving Dane his scar, the slash of Dane's knife through Weston's abdomen.

Now that I hear the words from Dane's mouth, the fight feels like more than just retaliation for killing the Guardian. But I was so focused on the fight and learning that Dane lied about his scar that I completely forgot the first part of the story.

Dane jumped through the remnants of the dust as Weston traveled through the magic with the Guardian. Dane is from Blackwood. Dane knows my mother, so Dane must know Weston.

And Weston didn't tell me about any of it.

I can't be angry about it. Not now. Not when we need to get away from this manipulative monster. Both of us.

"Get behind me," Weston grumbles, and I know the command is directed at me. His eyes don't leave Dane's, his training keeping him poised to respond to any attack.

I scamper past Dane, my bare feet slapping on the wooden floor as I slide behind him. His free arm extends backward, herding me farther back and making sure I'm safe. I reach out, wrapping my hand around his belt, the feel of the leather grounding me as I hold my resolve and keep my dagger trained toward Dane.

"This isn't over, Weston," Dane says. He doesn't advance toward us, doesn't attack. He didn't even spare me a glance as I moved away from him. Dane just stares Weston down, with obvious hatred written all over his face.

"Here's what's going to happen," Weston says, his voice full of the commanding authority that I recognize only appears when he is deathly serious. "We are going to walk out that door. I have archers trained on it, waiting to put an arrow through you. If you so much as step foot out of this cabin to follow us, they will take you down."

Dane scoffs. "You're going to take the coward's way out and let someone else have the fate that should be meant for you?"

"I said put an arrow through you," he snaps. "Their orders are to maim, not kill."

An eerie smile pulls at the corners of Dane's lips. "Just remember, you can't leave without me." He pats the pouch at his side and my eyes flicker to it.

I didn't even think to take it while I was still near him, while Weston had him held down with the threat of the sword. I was too focused on getting as far away from him as I could, and I don't know what would have happened if I tried. He probably wouldn't have let it go without a fight, and Weston wouldn't let me fight it. I can't put him at risk.

Dane's eyes shift to me. "That was your plan, wasn't it? You were trying to get the dust." I glare back at him, not giving him the satisfaction of confirmation. He doesn't need it though. He knows that's what I wanted.

He huffs a laugh, a small smile playing at his lips as he shakes his head at me.

"Like I said. Useless."

"Remember what I said, Dane," Weston growls, and takes a step backward into me, urging me toward the open door. His sword stays leveled at Dane, his focus still on him until we are outside and Dane still hasn't moved.

Weston grabs the door and slams it shut before he's moving frantically, sheathing his sword and wrapping his hand around mine, squeezing tighter than he ever has before.

"Run."

He takes off, yanking me behind him as we tear through the trees, darting to the side of the safe house, in a completely different direction than when Dane and I arrived. The soles of my feet scream as every rock and branch they hit pierce through them. My boots are still sitting just inside the house; I didn't have time to put them back on before our escape, and I'm feeling it now as I try to keep up with Weston's long strides.

I'm so focused on getting as far away from the cabin as we can that I didn't even think about the Castaways we left behind, the ones who were waiting to protect us against Dane.

"The archers! We can't leave them behind!" I cry. "What if Dane finds one of them?" Whoever Weston has hidden in the forest needs to get back to the ship immediately. I don't want Dane or any of the Voyagers to catch them and harm them in retaliation.

"There are no archers. Just fucking run."

My chest fills with relief. Weston would never leave his people behind or leave them in danger. He would shoulder it all himself before putting any of the crew in harm's way. My legs pump harder, as we fly through the trees, and I gasp every time something pierces through the flesh of my feet, but I can't slow down. A shriek gathers in my throat when I hear footsteps pounding behind us.

"It's Sig!" Weston yells. "Keep moving!"

Sig's steps get closer and stay steady, matching our pace until we burst through the edge of the forest. I can see the mountain and the cliffs just ahead, and I know exactly where we are headed.

We fly down the stone steps, and stumble through the sand of the collection beach, straight to the stone wall. The door swings open before us, the darkness of the tunnel welcoming as we throw ourselves into it and slam the stone behind us.

Safe.

We're safe.

Dane didn't follow. There were no sounds of pursuit, except from Sig, and no sign of anyone else on the island that may have spotted us.

I crash to the floor, my hands and knees hitting the rough surface as I gasp for air. My chest is on fire from the sprint, and the pain masked by the rush of escape is returning. Weston leans forward, his hands on his knees, heaving breaths, while Sig sinks her back against the wall.

"Lennox," she pants, "are you alright?"

I can barely breathe and can't even get a word out to reassure her before Weston speaks.

"We don't have time to fucking talk," he snaps. "We need to get back to the ship."

"Aye, Cap," Sig says, pushing off from the wall.

Weston straightens and extends his hand toward me. I grab hold and he pulls me to stand, noticing my wince as soon as my weight is on my feet again. I don't need to look down at them to know they are shredded and bleeding from the run. I try to take a step and suck in a breath as pain shoots up my legs.

Weston glances down at them, his jaw clenching as he takes in their state. I don't make it another step before he is crouching down and scooping me into his arms and striding swiftly through the tunnel.

I wrap my arms around his neck and let my head fall to his shoulder. My entire body relaxes, sinking into his, and his arms tense underneath me.

"Thank you," I mutter, glancing up at him shyly. A muscle in his jaw ticks, the only sign he heard me. He doesn't look at me or utter a sound, he just continues barreling through the tunnels as Sig follows quietly behind. We aren't safe yet. We still have to get to the ship and hope that Dane or anyone else isn't near the beach to discover us.

The fury seeping off him is palpable, and I can only imagine what Sig has been through since I've been gone. I breathe in his scent, the smell immediately settling my rattled nerves, and making me feel safe again.

It's only been two days, and I've missed him.

Weston steps through the portal, looking quickly at the surroundings to ensure we aren't stepping into an ambush before striding directly to the jagged rock toward the ship. The gangway rolls out as we approach, and Weston and Sig bound up it, the sound of it retracting almost immediately after their boots hit the deck. I let out a breath, thankful that we made it back almost unscathed.

"Lock it down," Weston growls, and Sig steps into action.

"Below deck, now!" Sig orders the few Castaways who are still on deck, watching us cross the space with shock painted on their faces.

Stassia sits on a crate next to Taril, her eyes wide as she lowers the wine bottle she was about to drink.

"Lennox?" she calls out, hopping off the crate and taking a step toward me.

"I'm alright, Stass," I get out, before Weston takes the steps rapidly, descending below deck.

I expect him to turn immediately and take me to our room, but he doesn't. Instead, he flies down the second set of stairs as commotion sounds behind us. Sig rallies everyone, barking orders to stay off deck and not to leave the ship. I hear the slam of a wooden door followed by a bolt snapping into place right as we hit the base of the stairs, putting Sig out of sight.

Weston turns sharply, then pushes the door to the infirmary open with his back, kicking it closed behind us once we are inside. A flame flickers to life in the lamp on the shelf, casting the room in a dim glow.

It barely takes two strides for him to cross the room to the table, where he sets me down gently, turning me so my knees hang over the side as he towers over me.

"Weston, I—"

"Don't talk to me right now."

I snap my mouth shut. I shouldn't be surprised he's angry. I expected it, but what I didn't expect was the concern and worry lacing his voice, mixing with the grumbly fury.

Weston drops his head between his shoulders, leaning forward until his hands rest on the table on either side of my thighs. His fists clench tightly, his knuckles white as his chest releases harsh breaths, rising and falling raggedly.

It's taking everything not to reach out and touch him, to run my fingers through his hair and wrap my arms around him. I want to reassure him I'm safe, and I'm here.

But I don't. I let him have the moments he asked for. He didn't want to talk, and if he wanted to touch me, he would have. Instead, I swallow the feelings down and hope I haven't done irreparable damage to whatever was between us before I left.

His breaths eventually slow and his fists relax, his palms flattening on the table before he rises back to his full height. Teal eyes bore into mine, and my breath catches in my throat.

"Where did he hurt you?"

Gravel coats his voice as his throat works, and my muscles turn fluid. Any worry that I'd broken the invisible thread that was holding us together disappears as I scan his face. The serious mask he wears so well has fallen, just for a second, and I see how much he still cares before he pulls himself back together, hiding it once again behind the semblance of anger.

"It's mainly my feet from the run. And, uh, I hit my head when I fell."

His hands are on me in the next instant. All hesitation about touching me that he had from my command months ago is gone. I let him, trying hard not to lean into his touch as his fingers work through my hair.

His fingers brush the tenderness at the back of my head, and I wince, drawing his attention back to my face. A muscle ticks in his jaw, and his stare is hard as his hands continue roaming, working a path down my body to make sure he isn't missing any injuries.

Once he's satisfied, he turns toward the cabinet and rifles through it, pulling out a small vial. Uncorking it and tossing the stopper on the table beside me, he reaches out and hands it to me.

"Drink this."

"What is—"

"For once, just don't argue with me," he growls.

I don't argue. This isn't the time to push back at him, not after he risked everything to come after me, and is taking care of me even though he could have delegated it to Sig. I lift the vial to my lips and tilt it back, and watch his back from the corner of my eye as he pulls more supplies out of the cupboards and drawers, slamming them closed as he goes.

He's still pissed.

The throbbing pain in my head subsides almost instantly, and I feel the pulse of magic thrum through to my fingertips. I reach back and run my fingers over the knot to find the tenderness is already almost gone.

Weston drags a stool across the floor, stopping in front of me, and sits down, pulling the supplies closer on the table. He reaches down into a bucket that instantly fills with water, dipping a rag and wringing out the extra liquid.

A small shiver runs up my spine as his fingers wrap around my ankle and lift my foot slightly, his gentle touch not at all reflecting the mood he's in. His gaze never lifts from his task, and we sit in silence while he tends to every injury, cleaning the cuts and applying the salve. None of the wounds seem to be deep, and start healing quickly once the salve soaks into my skin.

I don't know how long to stay quiet. He didn't want to talk to me, and I think it is helping him focus on a task that will relieve whatever turmoil is going on in his head. So I just watch, grateful that I am back on this ship, despite having to come to terms with my failure.

Once he's finished, he tosses the rag in the bucket and slides it across the floor. I start to slide forward off the table, but his hands clamp down on my thighs, pushing me back to where I was seated. Heat pools low in my stomach, but he doesn't look up. He just holds me in place until I readjust, scooting back into place.

I guess he's not done then.

He stands and reaches for another rag, wetting it in a small bowl on the table beside me. My knees part as he steps in front of me, and my mind flashes to a few nights ago, on the deck of the ship when we stood just like this, only reversed.

His eyes grow dark as they travel up my body, falling on my neck. Goosebumps erupt on my skin as he wraps a hand around my neck, his thumb brushing back and forth softly as his other hand wipes the wet rag across it. I flinch as stinging prickles under the warm cloth, and I try not to draw back, but he notices and huffs a quick breath from his nose.

"I'm going to fucking kill him," he growls, eyes fixed on the spot he is cleaning.

Dane must have broken the skin when he held the dagger to my throat, but in the moment, I was so focused on getting out that I didn't feel a thing.

"No," I say, staring him down, but his eyes stay fixed on my neck and the wound he's cleaning. "Weston, look at me."

The stubborn asshole still refuses, but I won't let him think it's even an option. I reach out and clutch his face between my hands, the stubble on his jaw tickling my palms as I force him to look me in the eye. His gaze meets mine reluctantly.

"No. You're not," I say. Our gazes stay locked, and I hope he knows how serious I am. He cannot kill Dane, especially not for a flesh wound that will be healed as soon as I get some salve on it.

He tears his eyes away and drops the soiled rag on the table next to me before swiping a finger through the pot of salve. The magic tingles as he slowly rubs it into my skin, and my entire body heats despite the chaos of the night and his surly mood.

We've argued before about how I always seem to come back to the ship injured, but how different it is now compared to the first time it happened. I welcome the touch of his hands on my body now, especially after his indifferent response to the terms of the bet a few nights ago. Where before I wanted him nowhere near me, finding his assessing overbearing and unnecessary, now I see it for what it is. Caring. Loving. His way of showing affection.

He wipes his hand on the rag, then loops one arm under my knees, and the other around my back. Before I can protest, he's lifting me off the table and crossing the room.

"I can walk, Weston," I say, trying to wiggle out of his arms, but he only holds me tighter, his chest vibrating against my shoulder with a low grumble.

How long is he going to stay mad before he talks to me again?

He yanks the door open and steps out into the hallway, only to be met by Sig leaning against the opposite wall. She straightens when we emerge, eyes flying over me, and her shoulders sag in relief when she realizes I'm not seriously hurt.

"Cap—"

"Go to bed Signee."

"Stop being an asshole," I mutter so only he can hear me.

A harsh huff of a laugh escapes him as he bounds up the stairs, his angry footsteps echoing through the decks all the way to our room. The door slams behind him, making me jump when he kicks it closed. I should have expected it. He hasn't closed anything quietly since we've been back on this ship, but it feels different now that we're alone.

It's not the same alone as in the infirmary when he was focused on a task. Something tells me the time of no talking is coming to an end, and I'm going to have to face his anger now that I'm no longer hurt.

Crossing the room, he strides straight to the tub, pulling me in tighter to his chest as he leans forward and turns the knob. Water splashes into the porcelain, the sound breaking the tense silence, and steam rises into the air. I always bathe before bed, at least I have after every shift out on the island, and it's apparent how much he pays attention to my moves and patterns. I almost protest, saying I'll use the crew showers because using this tub feels like too much, but I keep my mouth shut. He doesn't want to let me out of his sight, and after disappearing before, I can't say I blame him.

Stepping away from the edge, he finally lowers me down, releasing my legs first and supporting my back so my injured feet meet the ground gently. The shallow cuts are mostly healed by now, the salve working so quickly paired with whatever potion I drank for my head. I flatten my feet on the floor, flexing my toes and feeling no pain.

Weston disappears behind the screen, and the thud of the trunk sounds loudly through the room. He's back in the next moment, holding his shirt, *my* shirt, and drapes it over a wooden bench next to the screen.

"I'm not leaving," he says gruffly, his hands on his hips and his eyes still looking anywhere but at me. He gestures to the room on the other side of the screen. "I'll be over here when you're done. And then you've got some explaining to do, princess."

CHAPTER FIFTY-SEVEN

Knowing that Weston is just on the other side of that screen makes my skin tingle as I peel myself out of my Voyager clothes and step into the tub. The sharp burn of the water is welcoming as I sink my shoulders below the surface. I wasn't planning on having time to collect my thoughts before Weston forced the inevitable conversation on me, but I'm thankful for it.

So I take my time, soaking in the tub, letting the heat break down every single tremor in my muscles from the fight earlier this evening as I go through everything I learned, and find the right words to explain what happened.

Dane convinced me that Weston was a monster, and the Castaways were complicit in his schemes, when, in fact, it has been him all along. He's the one who had been biding his time, waiting for someone to find the healing waters so he could take them for himself.

To heal my mother, the woman he loves.

A hole opens in my chest as I remember what Dane said. It was too easy for him to trick and manipulate me, all because I wanted to be loved. I fell right into his hands, a willing pawn that fell prey to all his words and touches.

Did I do the same thing with Weston? Have I misinterpreted every look, every touch, every conversation? Are my feelings for him real, or is he just another man who has tricked me into loving him because he gave me a scrap of attention?

I hate that Dane's words have affected me this way, casting doubt over everything I felt for someone else and making me question myself. He's cruel, his intentions made that clear, and he should not have any effect on me from this point forward, but I can't stop the echo of them in the back of my mind.

Footsteps reverberate off the walls, drawing my attention.

He's pacing.

I've been sitting here immersed in my thoughts long enough for the water to cool, and Weston must be getting impatient. I can't avoid the conversation any longer, and I won't run away. Going back to camp may not have been easy on everyone I left behind, but my intentions were real, and I was coming home. I couldn't let the opportunity to help everyone here pass by. He needs to understand that.

I grab a sponge off the small table next to the tub and douse it with soap. The water sloshes slightly as I sit up and scrub my skin raw, washing away any reminder of everywhere Dane touched me. I dunk my head under the surface and wash my hair, rinsing the suds from my waves and running some oil through them before I step out of the tub. Weston is still pacing, and thank the gods no one lives under his room because the angry pounding of his feet would wake even the heaviest sleepers.

I towel off quickly, squeezing all the extra water from my hair, and grab hold of my sleep shirt, slipping it over my head. The fabric feels soft and fresh against my clean and sensitive skin, and my shoulders relax with the comfort.

I made it home. No matter how badly this conversation goes and how angry he is with me, I'm where I belong. I need sleep after the whirlwind that has been these past few days. If it wasn't for the anticipation of this fight with Weston, I'd walk straight over to the bed and collapse into it, letting the exhaustion overtake me.

Please don't let me have any nightmares tonight.

I barely make it past the screen before Weston turns on me, his pacing immediately halted and his eyes wild.

"What were you thinking?" he says brusquely.

After all the grumbles and stares, he's finally ready to talk.

"Someone had to do something," I say firmly, squaring myself to him and crossing my arms over my chest. His eyes flick down to my thighs, where my movement pulled the hem higher, so it brushes the top of my exposed skin. They slowly trail back up to my face and my body feels like it is on fire.

"We were doing something. We have been for years," he grinds out.

"We are out of time! I at least needed to try. I couldn't have lived here for eternity if it ran out, knowing I might have been able to do something and didn't. I tried to ask you, but when I brought it up, you shut me down, so I did it on my own."

"I told you to trust me!"

My own anger grows, matching his, as I remember an important detail I need explained. In the cave, Weston told me to trust him, but I knew he was still hiding something. Now I know, but I want to hear it from him. Weston knew Dane had come here for my mother, but he said nothing.

"Trust you?" I snap. "Let's talk about trust, Weston. I knew there was something more you weren't telling me. How can I trust you after you kept something like that from me? How could you? You knew Dane was here to save my mother, and you knew he was using me!" Now I'm yelling, my volume rivaling his.

"I was trying to protect you! I didn't want you to ever find out, because I knew it would crush you. I begged you to trust me, but you didn't." A flash of hurt flickers over his eyes, but it's gone almost instantly.

"I would have trusted you if you'd just told me!"

"You know you wouldn't have. You wouldn't have believed me without questioning everything all over again."

My head shakes harshly, like I'm trying to force his explanation out of it. "That was the excuse you used last time. You can't use it again."

"What do you want me to say, princess? You don't trust anyone unless you figure it out on your own. I can't help that my dumbass friend fucked up and hurt you. All I can do is try to prove to you again and again that you can trust me, that I will always be there for you."

"But you didn't tell me, Weston! You didn't give me a chance to trust you!"

"I didn't tell you because I didn't expect you to go running back to him after I fucking ordered you not to!" He flings his hand toward the island, then scrubs it through his hair. His frustration with my decision is palpable, but I can't contain mine any longer.

"You can't order me to do anything."

"On this ship I can."

"Fuck that, Weston. No. You can't. If you're going to treat me like a princess here, then I'll be the fucking princess. If you're going to push me away and leave me to figure things out on my own, fine. But you can't just change your gods damn mind whenever you want to be the captain instead of the First Guard. It doesn't work like that!"

I'm grateful his desk is between us, preventing me from getting too close to him, because at this point I don't know if I'd pull my dagger on him or drag my body against his.

"I took an oath, princess. I can't just break it." His voice drops low, and my stomach goes with it.

Everything changed the other night the moment I uttered his title, reminding him of the oath he took as the First Guard. He shut down, pushing me away, and I couldn't help but feel his title and his relationship with my father was more important to him than whatever shreds of feelings he had for me.

"So, this has all been about your duty? About my father? You're just following orders?" My jaw clenches as I bite out the words and try to choke down the knot in my throat.

He storms around the desk until he's toe to toe with me, and I have to crane my neck back to keep his gaze and hold my ground.

"It may have started that way, but it's not now, and you know it. Since the second I pulled you out of that water, this has been about you and only you. I watched you die, and fought to bring you back, for your father, for my kingdom, for my oath. But the moment you took a breath, and I looked into your eyes, it was over. Everything changed. It was all about keeping you safe, and keeping you away from him."

His hands are clenched at his sides, like it's taking all of his strength to keep from reaching out and touching me.

Angry tears prick at my eyes. My teeth are clenched so hard that my jaw pops.

"I don't believe you," I grind out. "If it was, you wouldn't have pushed me away. You wouldn't keep talking about your duty and my title. You would have told me how you felt!"

"What do you want me to say?" he yells as he throws his arms out to the sides, the motion an act of vulnerability, like he's trying to finally open himself up to me. "What do you want to hear, princess? That every time you challenged me, or fought me, or yelled at me, I fell fucking harder?"

He steps forward and I step back, our gazes locked, the minuscule space between us crackling with energy like a thunderstorm ready to erupt.

"That every time I watched him manipulate you and take advantage of your mind and your body, I wanted to tell you everything? Do you know how hard it was to stop myself from giving him another scar to remember me by?"

I swallow hard, and he takes another step, which I match.

"Would you believe me if I said I couldn't stay away from you, even before I brought you back to this ship? I finally felt like I could protect you here, but you pushed and pushed, defying me at every moment and trying to get away. I felt like a complete asshole trying to pull you back in, but I did it anyway, because I knew that was the only way I could control how out of my mind I was with worry every time you left."

My mouth goes dry and my jaw falls open as I watch him lay everything out between us.

"I would have fallen in love with you, in whatever place or time the gods granted me, but it wouldn't have changed the fact that I could do nothing about it. Either way, I would have to watch as someone else captured your attention, or was promised your hand."

My chest heaves as I gasp for breath.

Love. Weston loves me.

Before I can say anything, he keeps speaking, his gaze falling to the floor as a sullen expression overtakes him. His voice drops just above a whisper, and I feel it echoing in my chest.

"I used to think being trapped here was a curse, that I was stuck in the same body with the same mind as the moment I left. I used to sit around thinking about everyone I left behind, and how they would have lived an entire life by the time I returned, if I ever did. All I would be is the young First Guard left to protect an aging king, and I'd be alone.

"But then you showed up, and everything I thought was a curse wasn't anymore. I stopped begging the gods to take back the years I spent in this purgatory. I saw you, and I had hope that maybe I could have a life, and that my time wasn't wasted. But as quickly as the hope filled me, it disappeared just as fast. I remembered it didn't matter, and that I still couldn't do anything about it."

"What do you mean?" I finally manage to say, my chin quivering and making my voice shake.

His groan comes out more like a roar as he throws his hands up, clutching his hair at the back of his head. He takes a few quick steps away, breaking the trance between us.

"I can't have you, Lennox! Not the way I want you. The rules don't disappear just because we're here! It doesn't matter what I feel or what I want. I could love you with every fiber of my being, and it wouldn't be enough."

My spine stiffens and my body freezes as my name rolls so easily off his tongue.

Not princess.

Lennox.

Then the rest of what he said registers in my mind.

I can't have you.

Love you with every fiber of my being.

"I'm the only one who can say who can have me and who can't," I say, my voice oddly calm in the wake of his confession.

He shakes his head and pain fills his eyes as his hands drop back down to his sides.

"When we get home, our titles won't disappear. You're going to be the princess again, whether you want to be here or not. And since I was never replaced, I'm going to be First Guard."

He lifts his hand and the ring that symbolizes his commitment to the crown glints in the room's dim light.

"I can never be with you, never provide you with alliances or wealth." He closes the space between us and cups my face in his hands, eyes imploring, forgetting his previous commitment not to touch me. "But I will be yours. I will do anything to remain at your back and keep you safe. I don't care how much I have to suffer watching you choose someone else and build a life with him. It doesn't matter, as long as I can be close to you."

The tears that had been filling my eyes over the last few minutes finally fall in steady streams, and his face blurs in the onslaught.

His voice drops low, still full of intensity as his thumbs swipe across my cheeks.

"I was furious when I woke up and you were gone, but I was also terrified." His throat bobs as he swallows hard. "I could have lost you. Once Dane found out he couldn't get what he wanted anymore, he didn't need you, and I wasn't there to protect you."

"But you were," I choke out. "You found me."

"He still hurt you," he mumbles, one hand shifting to the back of my head where the tenderness has disappeared. His eyes fall to my neck, down to where the cut from my dagger has already healed. "I won't let him hurt you again."

Of all the ways I'd expected this conversation to go, I did not expect this. I'm stunned. I don't know what to say. I expected Weston to yell at me tonight, to be furious for going behind his back, but to confess all of this, and tell me nothing could come of it? All I want to do is shout back at him and convince him he is wrong. I want to tell him how I feel and order him to break his oath.

I can't find the words. Instead, I just stare at him, taking in every detail of his sparkling teal eyes as they roam my face, settling on my lips.

"Why did you beg me not to kill him?" Weston murmurs, and I don't even think before my response comes spilling from my mouth.

"Because I wouldn't be able to live with you trapped here forever." The words are a rushed whisper, and his eyes meet mine.

I don't know what I see there. Acceptance? Excitement? Gratitude?

Did he think I was begging for Dane's life instead of begging for his? Was he expecting me to say because I still had feelings for Dane?

My palms come to rest on his chest, and I push him away. His hands drop from my face and he steps back immediately, a look of confusion coming over him as he watches me cross the room. I walk to the chair with his belt hanging off the side, his scabbard and sword still present since we didn't go to the armory once we returned. The metal zings as I unsheathe it, moving quickly until I'm standing in front of him again. I extend the hilt toward him, and his head quirks to the side as he wraps his fingers around it.

"You said you swore an oath that you can't break," I say. My shoulders settle and I don't look away as I conjure all the confidence and regality I never once felt worthy of.

"Swear a new one," I command.

Weston drops to one knee, so fast I barely register it. The point of the sword stabs into the wooden floor as he holds it out in front of him, both hands wrapped around the hilt firmly, his head bowed the same way I had seen every guard recite their pledge in the past.

"I pledge my service to the kingdom of Blackwood," he starts, the traditional pledge that I have heard so many times in my life, but instead of keeping his head bowed, he lifts his chin, his gaze piercing mine as he pins me to the spot.

"I give my sword."

I swallow hard, the tension and desire in his face too much.

"My body."

My heart pounds, the pace rising in my chest as I register that he's changed the pledge. This isn't the pledge of loyalty to Blackwood. This is *Weston's* pledge, his oath to *me*.

"My life and my heart to my queen."

My chest heaves and I can't catch a breath. I just stare into his eyes, using every ounce of strength I have not to throw myself at him before he finishes.

"I swear my loyalty to her, Lennox Holt, and vow to stay by her side in whatever way she will have me, until the breath stills in my lungs."

His eyes smolder, and the ember within them lights a deep flame, burning me from the inside out.

He clears his throat, his voice dropping to a gravelly whisper.

"Long live the queen."

CHAPTER FIFTY-EIGHT

The proper response is on the tip of my tongue. I know it. I've said it countless times.

Blackwood honors your service and loyalty. You may rise.

But I can't say it, because this isn't the proper oath.

This is Weston's oath, his oath to me and only me. Not to our kingdom, not to the throne. This is his promise, his confession.

No words will convey how I feel.

No one in my life has ever cared for and protected me like Weston, who has done anything and everything to make me feel safe, even if I hated him for it.

I eventually grew to love him.

The thought of returning home, of him being my father's guard, being so close but unable to act on his feelings because of his position, is unthinkable.

So I don't think about it.

I've begged him to stop treating Dawnlin as if we are back in Blackwood, to forget about our titles and duties, and to just be us, so now I'm following my own command.

The sword clatters to the ground as he releases it, catching me as I leap at him and wrap my arms around his neck. His hands fist in the fabric at my hips, holding me steady, but not letting me get too close.

I lean in until there's barely a breath between us, and gaze into his teal eyes, the eyes that brought me back to life in more ways than one.

"You can have me," I say against his lips, and it's like a barrier breaks between us. His mouth crashes against mine, his lips bruising as the kiss becomes more demanding. My body hums with desire, and I need to be closer, my hands moving as if they have a mind of their own, clawing at his back and fisting the hair at the nape of his neck.

His lips are relentless as his hands release my shirt and slide down the curves of my body. Fingertips press deep into the muscle as he lifts me off the floor and wraps my legs around his waist. Standing swiftly, his arms tighten and crush my body against his. My core presses into him, and a gasp rips from my chest.

He takes advantage of it, sweeping his tongue in and brushing it against mine. I moan into his mouth, the sound only urging him on, his tongue working mine deeper than before. Weston lets go of me with one arm and swipes it across the desk, all the maps and weapons and trinkets clattering loudly to the floor. My back meets the smooth wood next as he leans over me, pressing me into the hard surface.

A shiver courses through me when his hands find my thighs, squeezing firmly before they move, torturously slow, fingers caressing my soft skin as they slide under the hem of the shirt. They brush over my hips only to find bare skin, and his lips break away, a loud groan rumbling against my neck as his head falls into the space next to my shoulder.

"Was it your plan to drive me wild, my queen?"

His hand wraps around my hip, the brush of his thumb teasing, and I let out a loud sigh. A low chuckle tickles my ear from where he licks and sucks his way down the side of my neck, into the plunging neckline of the shirt.

I didn't expect this turn of events when I left off my undergarments. All I really wanted was to feel as if Weston was wrapped around me, touching me everywhere, his scent overwhelming me, even if it was only the fabric of his shirt.

Now I'm glad I did.

My eyes flutter shut as I focus on the feel of his lips on my skin and the press of his hands holding me underneath the weight of his body.

But the weight lifts, gone in an instant, and my eyes fly open in shock.

"Weston?" I say, breathless. Pushing up onto my elbows, I try to see where he went.

Did I do something wrong?

Sig told me Weston hadn't been with anyone on the ship since they arrived, but I don't know what his life was like back in Blackwood. It wasn't something I ever wanted to have come up in conversation, but now I'm worried about being inadequate.

My thoughts are interrupted when his hands find my hips, gripping them and sliding me to the edge of the desk. There's a glimmer in his eye as he takes me in, and my worries from moments ago vanish.

His hands slide up the insides of my thighs, fingertips leaving a tingling trail of desire in their wake. His eyes darken when he reaches the hem of my shirt, pushing it up over my hips and exposing me to him. My mouth dries as I watch him, looking at me like I'm a piece of treasure that he's been searching for.

"I have wanted to do this ever since I watched you moan another man's name in my bed," he growls, and liquid pools between my thighs. Dropping to his knees, he spreads my legs wider, draping them over his shoulders.

"What are you doing?" I ask, my breaths coming out in heavy pants as I watch his eyes consume every inch of me. I'm not completely ignorant of what goes on behind closed doors, especially with as descriptive as Tila's books can be, but a man kneeling before a woman is unknown to me. The look in Weston's eyes leaves me wanting, and completely at the mercy of whatever he has in mind.

"Making you forget any other man exists," he says, then lowers his lips to the inside of my thigh, trailing kisses higher, closer to where I'm aching for him to touch. "Do you trust me, Lennox?"

"Yes," I pant, trying hard not to squirm.

A wicked grin pulls at his lips as his gaze locks on mine.

"Good girl."

He lowers his face to my core, his tongue flicking out over me, and my body explodes. Back arching, and eyes rolling back, I moan loudly as the throbbing heat intensifies. His hands grip my hips harder, pressing me into the desk so I can't move. His strokes continue, lapping me up while I try to writhe under him, but he doesn't let me budge.

"You taste even better than I imagined, and trust me, my queen, I have been dreaming about this for months."

I cry out, his words driving me even more wild before his tongue starts again, swirling and flicking around my most sensitive spot. My hands fly across the desk trying to grasp something, anything, but the smooth wood leaves nothing to ground me. I reach down, threading my fingers through Weston's hair, fisting it tightly, and he growls against me.

"Oh gods," I pant, throwing my head back as his movements become more rapid, before he sucks on my sensitive bundle of nerves, the place only I've ever touched, flicking his tongue over it and driving me wild.

"Fuck," I hiss, and he chuckles, the vibration sending my hips jolting, only to be held still by his powerful grip. My heels dig into his back as the pressure builds, the fire licking at my spine, raging harder with every stroke.

"Come for me, Lennox," he orders, just before his tongue pushes inside me.

A scream erupts from my throat, and the pressure climaxes, bursting into flames that engulf me completely until I'm falling back down into the moment as his tongue strokes slowly, coaxing the rest of the pleasure out of me.

My muscles are liquid and my hands fall from his hair as he stands, a satisfied smirk on his face. Lifting my weak arms, I reach out for him, and he laces his fingers with mine, pulling me up until I'm sitting on the edge of the desk.

He plants a heated kiss on my lips, and my body ignites again.

I want him. I want to feel his skin on mine, and I want it now.

My fingers find the laces on his vest, tugging at the knots. I pull my lips away from his so I can see what my hands are doing and rid him of these clothes faster. He watches me yank at the strings until they fall away and holds his arms out so I can push the vest over his shoulders. It falls to the ground with a soft thud, but before it even hits, I'm grabbing at his shirt, yanking it from the front of his pants.

"Take this off," I say, and his arm is already moving, reaching over his head and pulling it forward before tossing it off to the side.

My mouth dries as my eyes drag over his broad shoulders, the taut round muscles of his chest and abdomen. I've been sleeping next to him shirtless for months, but never truly appreciated the beauty that is Weston. I was too busy trying to fight the attraction, and trying to keep my eyes and my imagination away from him. But I don't have to any longer.

"Can I touch you?" The words barely leave my mouth before he's grabbing my wrists, flattening my palms against his chest.

"You don't have to ask," he grumbles in my ear, his forehead pressed into my hair. My hands move on their own, trailing over every surface, reveling in the feel of his strength, the strength he uses for me. I lean forward, brushing my lips across his collarbone, kissing him softly as my hands roam over his smooth skin.

My attention snags when they brush over the rough raised scar splitting across his abdomen. Pulling my lips away from his skin, I stare down at it and watch my fingers trail over the evidence of Dane's violence. Tears prick at my eyes and my breath hitches at the fear that works its way into my thoughts.

What would have happened if Weston hadn't survived? Would I ever have gotten to experience these feelings and emotions that only he has pulled from me? Would I have known any different?

"Hey," he says, hooking his finger under my chin and pulling my gaze away from the scar. "Eyes up here."

There's only tenderness as his gaze bores into mine, as if he can read my thoughts. I don't want to think about them, or about Dane, or the dust. I don't want to have any worries beyond this moment. I just want to get lost in the sea of his teal eyes and succumb to the pleasure that I know he wants to give me.

Raising my hands to his shoulders, I slide them over the solid muscles to his neck before I pull his lips back to mine. Urging my lips open, his tongue dives in, stroking languidly until the throbbing in my core intensifies.

I scoot forward toward the edge of the desk, nudging him backward so I can slide off. He guides me down gently, never breaking the steady rhythm of the kiss as he walks me backwards toward the bed. His hands run up my thighs, gathering the hem of my shirt, and I break away, lifting my arms so he can slide the smooth fabric over my head.

His throat bobs as his eyes devour me, and my nipples peak and skin tingles under the adoration.

"You're so fucking beautiful," he breathes, diving in for a deep kiss again. His fingertips press into my waist before I'm flying through the air, landing in the middle of the bed.

A fit of giggles overtakes me, and I look over to find him crawling across the bed toward me, a wide grin splitting his face.

"Do that again," he says, his voice laced with longing as he kneels between my legs. His knees nudge my thighs wider, and I suck in a breath as his hands capture my wrists, pinning them on either side of my head. My eyes roll back as his hips press into mine, his hard length hitting me just right, and I have to bite my lip to hide a gasp.

"Do what?" I manage to get out, trying to control myself enough to look back at his smile, the wide radiant smile that doesn't appear often.

His eyes sparkle as he leans closer, his breath mingling with mine. "Laugh."

I giggle again at such a simple request, but realize I couldn't even say how many times I've laughed on this ship. It feels good to be happy about something, especially if he is part of it. Weston's face lights up only for a moment, then darkens again as his eyes trail down my naked body.

"Don't tell me what to do," I say with a fake scowl. "I'm the one that gives orders, remember?"

Lifting my arms over my head, he shifts so both my wrists are in one of his hands, still pinning me down to the soft mattress. The now free hand moves lower, beginning a slow, torturous journey down my flesh.

"Now that is where you're mistaken. You may be my queen…" He places a firm kiss on the side of my neck, just as his fingertips trail over one nipple, circling it before squeezing firmly. My hips wiggle at the sensation, but his thighs hold me in place. "But when you're in my bed, Lennox, I'm in charge."

Heat floods my body at his words, and I arch my back when he takes the other nipple into his mouth, sucking and pulling before moving to nip at my breast.

"Weston, I—" I'm cut off with a quick breath as he moves to the other nipple, rolling his tongue around it and sucking into his mouth firmly. When he releases it, he moves on, peppering my chest with kisses as he slowly moves back up to my neck.

"What were you going to say?" he whispers into my skin as his fingers start their torturous trail again, inching lower toward the point where I want to feel him most.

"Dane and I, we never…we didn't…" I try to find the right words, but I'm too distracted by what he is doing to my body, and slightly embarrassed about my clear lack of experience compared to his. His fingers still, moving up to stroke the underside of my jaw as he looks down at me. I try to hide my nervousness, but his face softens, a small, understanding smile on his lips. I can tell he knows what I'm trying to say, even though I haven't spoken the words.

He strokes my face, his fingertips pushing into my hair. "Hey, it's alright." He brushes a soft kiss to my lips that makes me melt further into the bed. "We can stop."

My eyes widen as my jaw falls open with shock.

"No!" I yell at him, and a burst of laughter erupts from deep in his chest and echoes through the room. I push against his hand, trying to adjust so I can look him better in the face. "I swear to the gods Weston, if you stop, I will go sleep in the brig!"

His lips lower to mine and the laughter is gone instantly.

"That's not happening," he murmurs. He presses down with a demanding kiss and pries my mouth open with his lips, breathing in my breath as a sultry smile tips the corners of his lips. "You belong in my bed," he grumbles, and the muscles in my core flutter, my hips shifting against his.

"Do you know how hard it has been to keep my hands off of you?" His free hand moves again, his palm flat against my skin, and I gulp in anticipation of his touch. "Do you know it's been driving me insane laying next to you every night knowing I couldn't come near you?" He shifts his body, his hips falling to the side as his hand travels lower, the calluses from years of handling a sword rough on my skin as he continues to tease me.

"I seem to remember you inflicting that torture on yourself," I rasp.

"And I'd do it again and again if it means you're the last thing I see before I fall asleep, and the first thing I see when I wake. I'd gladly endure that pain just so I get to breathe in your scent on my sheets and lie in jealousy that my shirt gets to touch every inch of you when it should be me caressing your skin. I'd do it all again knowing you are safe, and nothing can harm you even though the guilt I live with every day, feeling like I hurt you by trapping you here, feels like a thousand blades stabbing through my chest."

A lump forms in my throat and I try to swallow it down. This whole time I thought Weston was annoyed by me, that he was using me as a pawn in his fight against Dane, but really I was torturing him, making him feel things he hasn't for years, if ever. Even when we were becoming friends, when I started developing true feelings for him that would one day turn into more, he kept enduring the pain just so he could be around me.

I thought this was all because of his duty and oath, that he was just like everyone else back in the castle, their relationships with me based on requirement first, and friendship next, but it wasn't. It was for me, all of it.

How wrong I have been.

I tug my wrists down, fighting against his firm grip. I need to touch him, to feel the warmth of his skin and ground myself to this man who has held himself back from me for so long. He releases them, and my hands find his face, pulling him back down to me and pouring everything I feel into this kiss. My blood heats even more as his body presses into mine, his skin soft and flush against me, and I want more.

"Weston," I moan, reaching down toward his pants.

He plants another firm kiss before leaning back, a small crease between his brows.

"There's been no one else?" he asks, his chest grumbling against mine.

"No," I say, and pull my lower lip between my teeth. "Only you."

"Do you know——" he starts, but I cut him off, nodding rapidly.

"Yes. I know. I've read enough of Tila's books."

A slow smile brightens his face. "We're going to talk about how Tila hid those books from two young boys another time," he says, and I can't contain my laughter. His eyes sparkle as he watches me laugh, but it stops quickly, replaced with heaving breaths as I watch him move to kneel between my legs.

"I'll go slow," he says softly, running his fingers up the inside of my thighs, then circling around and down, just to repeat it all again. My eyes fall down, his obvious excitement bulging in his pants, and my hips wiggle with anticipation. "Tell me if you want to stop, and I will. There's nothing to be ashamed of."

I nod quickly, and watch as he reaches for the top of his pants, undoing the button and laces, his focus not straying from me the entire time.

My face tingles under his gaze as I watch him slowly lower his pants, freeing himself from the confines. The only male form I've ever seen is a figment of my imagination, but even Weston outshines anything I'd conjured in my mind. My mouth dries at the sight of him; his impressive length hard and smooth, with a bead of liquid at the tip.

I can't look away. Excitement and nerves course through me as he slowly removes the rest of his pants, tossing them off the side of the bed and kneeling back between my thighs. Wrapping his hand around his cock, he slowly strokes himself, and my core throbs, anticipating the feel of him inside me.

"It will be better if you're ready for it," he says quietly. "Do you want my tongue again?" he asks, and I nod vigorously, my legs falling wider as I open myself up to him. He smirks and leans forward, adjusting himself so he can run the tip of his tongue up my core, keeping his eyes on me the entire time. I buck my hips and cry out, my hands fisting the sheets, this time having something to grab on to. He licks again, flattening his tongue before swirling it repeatedly, and I see stars.

"Fuck, Weston!" I scream and look down to find him grinning at me.

"You can scream my name as much as you want, my queen." He swirls his tongue again, and I clamp my eyes shut, reveling in the feel of him. The wet heat turns to pressure as he slides a finger inside of me, a low moan sounding in the room as my hips writhe against his hand.

"Fuck," he hisses, his hand moving to slowly pump it in and out. My body adjusts, taking his finger slowly, until there's a slight twinge of pain, the pressure growing as he adds another.

My mouth falls open when he twirls them, his tongue flicking out at the same time and hitting the spot that makes me shake.

"Gods!" I scream, tilting my hips to try to feel more of him. He pumps his fingers again, pulling them in and out slowly before they're gone completely. The bed shifts under me as he moves, his thighs urging my knees farther up.

"Open your eyes, sweetheart," Weston says, and they flutter open to find him hovering over me, his body completely overwhelming mine as he waits for me to be ready.

I pull his face to mine, urging him on. He strokes the tip of himself over my core, the bead of liquid mixing with the slick between my thighs, and I gasp into his mouth. His teal eyes lock on mine as he lines himself up and slowly pushes inside, just the tip, before he stops and waits for me to adjust. My fingers dig into his shoulders, and I pull him closer, silently telling him to keep moving.

He pushes in farther and the pressure overwhelms me, pulling and stretching me to take him. My back arches, a cry catching in my throat, as he continues the slow torture, never rushing, and his eyes never leaving me.

I feel like I'm being split in half, the size of him impossible to fully allow, but I know when he is fully seated. His forehead drops to my shoulder, and he holds himself over me, groaning into my skin.

"You feel so fucking perfect."

He captures my lips with his, and an involuntary tear slides out of the corner of my eye. Concern etches across his face, his brow furrowing the moment he sees it, but I shake my head.

"Don't stop," I whisper, and he listens. The strokes are slow and deep as he rocks into me, his lips and tongue caressing mine in the same rhythm. I close my eyes again and soak up the feel of him, wrapping my arms around his back, and pulling him to me. It isn't enough. I want to be closer, to be crushed and overwhelmed by him. After fighting it for so long, I want to give in, to be consumed by Weston and memorize every inch of him.

My fingers dig into the taut muscles in his back and shoulders, my nails scraping across his skin as I pull him closer, our bodies communicating silently against each other. His thick arm wraps underneath me, clutching my body to his tightly in answer to my wordless plea. The sensation between my thighs quickly changes and the pain disappears, just before heat and pressure heighten. He reaches down with his other arm and hooks it under my knee, wrapping it around his waist, his hips shifting to change the angle. With the next thrust, I break away from his kiss, crying out as the unbelievable pressure intensifies.

Fire licks over my skin, the heat burning from the inside out. My limbs are tight around him as he crushes my body to his. The feel of his hard cock sliding in and out of me pushes me impossibly higher, until I feel like I can't take any more. His lips press into the base of my neck, where my pulse pounds beneath the skin, and he grunts softly with each long thrust, growing deeper and harder as I gasp for breath. Then my body shatters, the muscles in my core clenching around him, eliciting a gruff moan in my ear. Heat fills me as his hips pulse a few more times before stilling.

My limbs are liquid and my eyes flutter shut, as he gently covers my face with kisses until he finds my lips again, his tongue delving deep into my mouth. The gentle caress of fingertips across my forehead brings out a soft sigh, and he brushes my hair back, his fingers twining in the curls.

"Are you alright?" he asks, his thumb stroking my cheekbone.

I make a low humming sound, keeping my eyes closed and soaking up every remaining sensation I can. He chuckles softly, and the scruff on his chin nuzzles against my jaw.

"Why haven't we been doing that forever?" I mutter, reveling in the hard planes of his body pressing in to mine.

He laughs, and my eyes fly open to catch his rare smile again. He closes the space between our faces, his movement shifting him still inside me, and I suck in a breath as he mumbles against my lips. "Because I'm an asshole, remember?"

"You can keep being an asshole as long as we get to do that again."

"Whatever you say, my queen." He peppers kisses along my jaw until his lips brush my ear, the grumble of his voice making my muscles clench around him again. "Now that I've had a taste of you, nothing could keep me from being buried inside you again."

Pressure mounts as I feel his cock swell inside me again the moment I catch his lips with mine and breathe into another deep kiss.

He breaks away, propping himself up on his forearms. "You can't kiss me like that or we'll never sleep."

A yawn breaks free at the mention of sleep, and I slap a hand over my face. He chuckles and wraps a hand around my hip as he slowly slides out of me, and I wince at the twinge of pain once he's gone. His feet hit the floor as he gets out of bed, and my stomach sinks.

"Don't leave," I murmur, my cheeks heating from embarrassment at how the plea sounds.

"I'm not going anywhere," he says, leaning over the edge and brushing his lips over mine. Before I know it, Weston scoops me up in his arms and walks me over to the tub again. I nestle my head into the crook of his shoulder and lean into his chest. Exhaustion comes over me in a wave, and I barely move when he turns the water on again, letting the tub fill before setting me inside.

"Slide forward," he says, and I follow his order, giving him enough room to lower himself behind me. Once he's seated, he reaches out and pulls my back to his front, laying my head on his shoulder and wrapping his arms around me.

I don't know how long we sit like that, folded together in the warm water. My mind goes in and out of sleep, the heat of the tub relaxing me until I feel the firm press of his lips against my hair.

"How did you find me?" I ask, my question barely a murmur as I try to fight the fatigue. Strong hands move beneath the water, kneading the muscles of my thighs and hips, and I sink deeper into the water, pushing against him and waiting for him to answer.

"I wouldn't let Sig go alone. She told me what your plan was and where you were supposed to meet, so we went together. When you didn't show up—" He pauses and I feel the tension stiffen his body behind me. Did Weston think I wasn't going to come back? Was he really worried I would leave them, even after everything I discovered about Dane? He lets out a sigh. "I knew something was wrong. I begged the island to bring me to you."

"And it did?"

I can feel the bob of his throat from where I'm nestled under his chin. "It did."

I lace my fingers through his where his hands stopped on the tops of my thighs and squeeze gently. He moves us then, wrapping our arms around my middle and pulling me in tighter.

"I told you I'd always rescue you," he murmurs in my ear. "I wasn't lying."

My chest swells as I remember the relief of hearing his voice in that safe house, knowing he had come for me. The island let him. Dawnlin brought him to me, and if there was any doubt before that this wasn't where I was supposed to be, it was answered.

I tilt my head back and weave my fingers through the hair on the back of his head, lowering his face to mine for one kiss, thanking him with the press of my lips for not doubting me.

"But now I'm begging you," he says. "Please don't fucking do that again."

Repeating his words back to him, I smile softly. "I'm not going anywhere."

Weston grabs the sponge and soap from beside the tub and starts lathering it up in front of me.

"Let me take care of you," he says, and I nod lazily, my eyelids heavy and drooping after everything that happened tonight. He washes me gently, and I'm surprised to find that I'm not even a little uncomfortable having his hands roam caressingly over every inch of my body. It's gentle and relaxing, the complete opposite of the way he can be out on deck when he has to be the captain.

When he's finished with me, he moves me to the other side of the tub, giving me the perfect view of him as he washes himself. Rivulets of water stream down his body as he stands and rubs suds over his skin, and I get to gape at the perfection that is Weston. He steps out of the tub, and holds his hands out to me, pulling me to stand and lifting me out gently, setting me on my feet beside him. He has a towel a moment later, and dries me off quickly, doing the same with himself before he scoops me up again and carries me back to bed.

He doesn't bother with the sleep shirt or his pants, he just sets me in the middle of the bed and climbs in behind me. I roll on my side, pressing my back to his front as he wraps his arms around me, pulling me close and pressing a long kiss to the tip of my shoulder.

"Are you going to run away in the morning if we wake up like this again?" I say sleepily, not realizing what I said until the words leave my mouth.

"You remember that?" he asks, shock clear in his voice.

I nod and yawn. "I woke up before you did. Are you going to regret it like before?"

"No, Lennox. I don't regret it." He pulls me closer, his hand splayed firmly across my stomach, and his arm sliding beneath my neck.

I don't know how long we lay silently listening to each other breathe before I can't keep my eyes open any longer, and drift off to sleep with the faint memory of a brush of his lips against my temple, and a mumbled, "Goodnight, Lennox," against my skin.

CHAPTER FIFTY-NINE

Sunlight brightens the room and dances across my closed eyes. I let out a groan and turn my face away, sinking into the warmth wrapped around me. The events of last night come rushing back to me as the sleep slowly drifts away. Weston's bare chest is under my cheek, and I'm tucked tightly into his side, while his fingers trace lazy circles over my back.

Waking up this morning, everything feels different. Dawnlin isn't the same world, and I'm not the same person. But now, I know for certain I don't want to stay here forever. Now more than ever, we need to find a way home. Spending eternity waking up like this would be amazing, but I don't want to be robbed of the life we could have together back home. It doesn't have to be how Weston thinks. I could change anything once I'm queen. We'd just have to contend with the kingdom and my father until then.

But right now, I don't want to think about any of it. If there is anything I have learned on this island, it is to appreciate every moment because you don't know when everything can change.

"You're thinking too loud," Weston says, the rumble in his chest loud against my ear. Fingertips skate up my bare back, my skin tingling in their wake, until they reach my head, and twirl through my hair and grazing my scalp.

"No, I'm not," I grumble and turn my face farther into his skin, breathing deep and soaking up his scent. I'll never understand how he always seems to know what's going on in my mind, and my chest tightens, knowing it only means he understands me like no one else ever has.

"We still have a lot to talk about," he mumbles.

"I don't want to think about it yet," I say, my voice muffled against his skin. The muscles of his abdomen tighten as I skate my hands over them, trailing my fingers down his stomach. My stomach flutters and I press my lips to his skin. I want him to distract me for a little longer before we have to leave the safety of this room and face the reality of everything that happened with Dane.

Weston's fingers wrap around my wrist, stopping my hand from drifting any lower before he lifts, flattening my palm to his chest.

"You're probably going to be sore. I don't want to hurt you."

I tilt my chin up to look at him, only to find him watching me intently.

"I think there's only one way for you to help me with that," I mutter. His eyes darken, his pupils widening as a low rumble vibrates in this chest.

The next second, I'm on my back and he's rolling on top of me, his fingers sliding up my sides and pushing my arms up around my head.

"We can ignore everything for a little longer," he says between kisses across my chest. "But we need to talk about it, Lennox. We need to figure out what to do now that Dane knows what we're after."

The sound of my name on his lips makes my chest squeeze and fire burn through me. He's finally seeing me for me, not focusing on the title that will keep us apart.

"I don't want to talk about him. Not right now," I say. I try to pull my arms out of his grasp, wanting to run my fingers over his skin, but he tightens his grip, the thrill causing me to wiggle underneath him. The muscles in his arms ripple as he pushes his chest off mine, his hips lining up with mine as he towers over me. The sheets pool around his hips, and I gaze up at him, his broad shoulders blocking out everything beyond so all I can see is him.

All I want to see is him.

"Spread those pretty thighs for me," he says, desire lacing his words. I respond, my eyes not leaving his as I wrap my legs around his hips, a jolt singing through me as his hard length presses against my core. He leans forward, tantalizingly slow, and brushes his lips over mine, and I part them, begging for more.

Weston's lips part in a teasing smile, but his eyes don't stray from my lips as he leans in again, but just as he's about to seal the kiss, he stops abruptly as the door to the room flies open, slamming into the wall with a thud.

"Hey, Cap, when are we going to lift lockdown ohhh shit." Jorn's curse echoes through the room, and Weston's face turns murderous.

"Get out!" he bellows over his shoulder.

"Shit. Fuck. Sorry. Shit. Sorry Cap," Jorn stammers, then the door slams again, the room falling back into silence.

Weston's head droops between his shoulders, and he heaves a sigh. I can't contain my giggles any longer, and my entire body shakes as I try to stifle them. The corners of his lips tip up at the sound of my laughter, and his hips press tantalizingly deeper into mine.

"I hope you didn't plan on keeping this a secret because the entire crew probably already knows," I say through the giggles.

He looses another harsh sigh. "One day. I couldn't have you to myself for one gods damned day."

"It doesn't change anything for me if they know," I say. He looks up then, a crease between his brows. "You're the one worried about titles and duty, Weston. I told you, I'm not."

He leans forward and presses a searing kiss to my lips before wrapping his hand around my head, tilting it to deepen the kiss. I turn my head, breaking away from him before I can't stop myself.

"Don't you need to go open up the ship? Go be the captain," I say, slightly breathless and trying to ignore the slow rocking of his hips into mine that's driving me wild.

"Do you really think I'm going to let Jorn stop me from starting my day buried inside you?"

My face is on fire, and I know there's no hiding how his words affect me. I don't know why this side of Weston seems…unexpected, but I want more of it.

He frees my hands, and they instantly find his face, wrapping around his strong jaw. I've spent months defying his touch, and now I'm craving everything I've been missing. My fingers brush over the stubble as he dives in for another kiss. His tongue is smooth and challenging, almost distracting me from the drift of his hand between my breasts and down my stomach. He cups between my thighs, the heel of his hand pressing down and slowly circling, and sending fire licking up my spine. I gasp into his mouth; the noise turning into a low groan as his fingers move, sliding through my wetness before pushing inside.

The stretch is intoxicating, the dull ache driving me wild and making me crave all of him even more.

"I love feeling how much you want me," he growls, swirling his fingers inside, before slowly pumping them in and out, pressing deeper with each stroke.

"I've wanted you for longer than I am willing to admit," I pant. My eyes are screwed shut as I try to keep the release at bay. I don't want this to be over too soon, lockdown be damned. Weston was right. I just got him to myself, and I am not ready to share.

His eyes flare. "I kept trying to talk myself out of it, but I couldn't," he says, his fingers still working inside me, drawing heavy breaths from my chest. "I'm glad because I don't know how I've lived my life without this. Without you."

My heart feels like it is going to burst. I thought he would never let go of whatever was holding him back, and I didn't know how I would return to the ship only to be met with another rejection. If almost losing me helped push him over the edge and stop denying what has been building between us for months, then I am glad I did it. Even though I didn't get the dust, it was worth it, because I got him.

The building pressure subsides as he slowly slips his fingers out of me, rubbing my wet excitement over me and sending shockwaves through my body. Then he's kneeling between my legs, his hands wrapping firmly around my forearms and lifting me to his chest, wrapping my legs around his waist. Circling his neck with my arms, I press my breasts into him, reveling in the heat of his skin as our bodies mold together.

Fingertips sink into my flesh as he holds me above him, the tip of his length teasing my entrance. His eyes find mine, the teal darkened with desire, and his voice drops almost to a whisper. "I don't care what happens, here, or if we ever get back home. None of it matters, so long as you always remember, you're mine."

"I'm yours," I say, as I blink away the prick of tears beginning to form. He doesn't look away. His gaze stays locked on mine as he thrusts inside me, impossibly deep, and my head falls back as an involuntary moan rips from my chest. Muscles ripple in his thighs and hips as he drives into me, the delicious friction causing the base of my spine to tingle.

Chest taut and arms bulging as he holds me above him, I press harder, molding my lips over his, sucking his tongue into my mouth, trying to get impossibly closer. A hand moves from my ass and dives between us, his thumb hitting me at the right spot, and rubbing quick circles as he pulses in and out. I cry out, squeezing my eyes shut, as my core contracts around him again and again. His speed increases, chest heaving with quick breaths and grunts, and sweat glistening across his shoulders. My jaw falls open in a silent cry, my pleasure exploding, tearing me apart from the inside out, and he follows, groaning into my neck with one final buck of his hips.

I collapse onto him as his lips trail from my neck to my shoulder, nipping at my skin as I come down from the high.

"Jorn can go fuck himself," Weston pants, his shoulders still heaving with exertion.

I laugh into his chest and feel his smile against my skin.

"He's done enough already," he grumbles. "I was not missing that, too."

I straighten abruptly, the shift of my hips on his cock making him suck in a breath.

"You *were* jealous," I say with a laugh as he sits back on his heels, settling me into his lap with a smug look on his face.

"I had to stop myself from ripping his arm off every time he touched you."

I snicker, and lean in to him, running my fingernails through his hair at the base of his head. He lets out a low grumble and his eyes flutter closed as I brush my lips over his.

"You have nothing to be jealous of. But you can't hurt everyone who touches me, Weston."

His eyes fly open, finding mine, and I melt with the glimmer of challenge I see there.

"Watch me."

I shove his shoulder and he chuckles, before untangling my limbs from around his body and slowly lifting me off him. He grabs a towel and cleans us both up before striding over to the armoire and opening the doors, his naked body on full display bringing heat to my cheeks.

I could get used to unashamed Weston.

Two sets of clothes appear in the armoire, one for each of us, and he pulls them out, tossing mine to me before pulling on his own. We dress quickly, and I run my fingers through my hair, trying to tame the wild waves, getting rid of any knots to not give away exactly what has been going on in here. Not that they don't probably already know because of Jorn's inability to stop talking.

Weston straps his belt around his waist, picking his sword up off the floor amid all the discarded desk trinkets, and slides it into the scabbard while I retrieve my dagger and settle it in the back of my waistband.

We do not know what the day will bring now that Dane is aware I double crossed him. We know the island will continue to protect us on the ship, but the danger for everyone off deck is heightened.

We can't stop searching.

Weston sets his hand on the doorknob, ready to pull it open and face the rest of the crew, but before he does, he turns back to me, pinching my chin between two fingers and lifting my face, giving me a soft, warm kiss that makes my stomach tumble.

"Let me handle them," he says as he backs away, then pulls open the door.

CHAPTER SIXTY

Chatter carries down the hallway as soon as the door opens, almost as if we were cocooned in our own world moments ago. With the deck locked down, the entire crew is below, and by the sounds of it, it's late morning and they are getting antsy.

Weston bounds down the hallway ahead of me, his footsteps loud on the floor, the full captain authority back in place. Stopping just before the wooden steps, he crosses his arms and looks out over everyone filling the space. Bodies line the hallway, people sit on the steps, everyone waiting to hear what caused the sudden change in protocol.

"It's about time," Jorn calls out from somewhere down the hallway. My cheeks heat as I hover in the shadows behind Weston. I don't know if Jorn is talking about what he walked in on, or how long it took us to leave Weston's quarters, but either way, I have no doubt most, if not all the crew already know what we were up to.

"What took you so long, mister Weston?" Fin cries from somewhere in the group.

"Yeah, what took you so long?" Jorn echoes. The mischief ringing in his voice is met with a few low snickers, and I drop my chin to my chest, trying to hide my smile.

"Alright, alright, enough," Weston huffs.

"Why are we locked down, Captain?" someone calls out from the second set of steps.

"There was an incident with the Voyagers last night, and I needed to make sure no one left the ship last night or this morning," he calls out. "No one is to step foot on the island until I give the go ahead. Collection crew, meet me on the quarterdeck in fifteen minutes."

A chorus of ayes sound from all over as Weston weaves through the crew to unlock the hatch. Light pours in from above as he flips the wooden doors out, and they land with a thud on the deck. The shadows disappear around me, and murmurs creep through the crew as they see me standing there. I guess my disappearance was noticed, and I'm worried what they will all think of me now that I've returned.

"Lennox! You're back!" Fin yells, running toward me and flinging his body into my legs like he normally does.

"I'm back." I bend and wrap my arms around him, squeezing him in a tight hug. I knew he was safe back on the ship, that Weston would never let anything happen to him, but after being with Roley for such a short time, I missed this chosen little brother.

"No one would tell me where you went, but I knew you'd be back!"

"You were right." I laugh as Weston's footsteps thud toward us. He steps up beside me, wrapping his arm around the small of my back, his hand settling possessively on my hip.

"Are you hungry?" he asks, and the mention of food makes my stomach rumble.

"I will feed her, Captain!" Stassia cuts through the group, stopping just in front of me and shooting Weston a dazzling smile. "We'll meet you on deck."

Weston's fingers flex slightly against my hip before he reluctantly releases me. His hand brushes over the curve of my ass before dropping away, and I swallow hard. I hadn't really thought about how things would change after last night, but one thing is clear. Weston wasn't lying about fighting his desire to touch me, and I doubt he is going to hide it from the rest of the crew.

A shiver of anticipation runs through me.

"Race you to the deck, Fin," Weston says, and Fin is gone before Weston can even take a step, his little feet pounding up the stairs and disappearing through the opening.

Stassia grabs my hand and drags me toward the second steps, ignoring everyone and dodging bodies as we walk against the current.

"Slow down, Stass, I'm not that hungry." That is a lie. I am starving. The last thing I ate was dinner with Dane, and I don't know how long ago that was.

She cuts through the remaining crew gathered near the lounge, and I try not to stumble as she drags me down the hallway toward the empty galley. Thankfully, everyone had enough time to get a meal in while they were waiting for lockdown to be lifted. Stass turns on her heel, completely forgetting that we are actually here to get food.

"First of all, are you alright? I wanted to check on you last night, but you disappeared once you were below deck."

"Yes, I'm alright," I say. "I lost my boots so my feet were torn up, and I knocked my head pretty hard. Weston brought me straight to the infirmary to take care of everything."

It seems like so long ago now that he was barreling down the steps and locking us in the infirmary. He wouldn't speak to me, let alone look at me, but since then he's had quite the loose tongue.

"From what I hear, that isn't the only thing he wanted to take care of." A single eyebrow raises and her head quirks to the side as she waits for me to answer.

"Wow, Jorn really can't keep his mouth shut, can he?"

"So it's true?!" She all but squeals the last words.

Blood rushes to my face and suddenly my clothes are too warm. It's not that I want to keep things from her, I've just never talked to anyone about anything so personal like this before. Even though she knows because of Jorn's inability to keep a secret, the words still catch in my throat.

"Finally!" she cries, completely ignoring my hesitancy, and my shoulders slump in relief that I didn't upset her. "That man fell hard. We all saw it. Maybe now he'll loosen up again. He's been in a grumpy mood for too long."

My chest squeezes. Stassia obviously cares about him. The entire crew does, but I feel lucky to have made such a loyal friend like her. Despite all her jokes, Stassia truly wants everyone on this ship to have the best life here that we can. I hope for her sake that if we end up here for eternity that she can find the same happiness.

"How was it? Was it amazing? You don't have to tell me Just stay quiet if it was absolutely phenomenal."

And there is the real Stass.

Clamping my lips closed, I stifle a giggle, and there's only a brief pause before she can't control herself any longer.

"I knew it! I am so happy for you. Jealous of course, because who wouldn't want the captain in their bed?" I laugh fully, no longer afraid of hiding things from her.

"Technically, I'm in his bed," I say, and she waves me off.

"Who it belongs to doesn't matter as long as everyone is naked."

I slap a hand over my mouth as an obnoxious snort erupts from my nose. Stassia grins, and my shoulders shake with laughter, but there's a twinge of sadness in my chest. If we make it back home, who knows if I will ever see Stassia or anyone else in the crew ever again. The thought makes my stomach sink, and I know I need to focus on just enjoying whatever time I do have with them, because the future is so uncertain.

"I'm really happy you don't hate each other anymore," she says, her eyes softening as she reaches out and squeezes my hand. "Although hate sex could be a lot of fun."

"Stass!" I cry, my mouth falling open as even more laughter billows from my chest. She's laughing now too, and she weaves her arm through mine as we cross the mess to the galley line.

I realize quickly that I don't know what Weston likes to eat, having avoided him at every meal since being here. I fill a small plate for me, enough to tide over my growling stomach and shovel it in quickly while Stassia fills me in on anything I missed in the last few days. Not much has happened. It's mainly fun stories, but she keeps mentioning Taril, and I can't help but wonder if something is going on between them.

On our way out, I grab a piece of fruit and a pastry before we make our way back to the main deck.

"Are you going to tell me what was going on? Why'd you leave?" she asks as we climb the stairs.

"I have a feeling that is what we're about to talk about, but I, uh," I trail off, wondering how much I should share right now versus letting Weston tell the crew. I decide it doesn't really matter, because whether I tell her or he does, it won't change what happened and how it all turned out.

"I went back to the Voyagers to steal the dust from Dane."

Stassia gasps, her hand reaching out to grasp my forearm. "What happened? Did you get it?"

I shake my head. "No. I tried, but things didn't go how I planned, and I uncovered how much Dane had been lying to me. I was trying to get away when he attacked me. He was going to force me to tell him where the waters are, but Weston found me."

I was lucky he found me when he did, especially if Weston was worried that Dane no longer cared about my well being after he found out I couldn't help him.

"Oh gods, Lennox," she says, her eyes glistening with unshed tears. "I'm sad it didn't work, but I'm so grateful you made it back to us." She wraps me in a hug and squeezes tight.

Tears mist my own eyes as I squeeze her back. I was so close to never seeing any of them again. When Sig and I made the plan, I was so focused on helping everyone, I never considered that it could hurt any of them instead. I've never had my presence affect other people like this, different from that of my kingdom, and I am still learning how to navigate the relationships.

"Me too," is all I say in return.

Once we're on the quarterdeck, Stassia snags a crate in the shade and shoos me away from her. Not everyone in the collection crew has gathered yet, and I look around for Weston to find him standing alone at the helm.

"I thought you might be hungry too," I say, holding the fruit and pastry out to him. His fingers brush mine as he takes them from me, before lifting the fruit to his mouth and taking a large bite. Juice dribbles over his lips and his tongue flicks out to catch it, and I can't look away. My thighs squeeze together involuntarily, now knowing what kinds of things he does with that tongue.

He chuckles softly, breaking my trance, a fire lit in his eyes. "Thank you."

"Um," I stammer, trying to regain my composure under his playful stare. "Should we talk now? Before everyone else gets here?"

He nods once, setting the food down on the railing. "It would be best if I know everything before I talk to them, so yes. We should." His hips settle on the rail behind the helm, and he crosses his feet out in front of him, the same way he stood the other night when my courage took over me and I worked my way close to him. With everything I need to tell him, I'm nervous to be that close now. My feet stay planted on the deck, and I bite my lip nervously, trying to figure out where to start.

His eyes track the movement before flicking back up again. "Just tell me, Lennox. You don't have to be nervous about it."

"I'm just trying to figure out how not to make you turn back into the furious captain I know so well. I know you're mad at me."

"I'm not angry with you, but I can be mad at what you did. I'm upset you didn't tell me, and that you just disappeared. I'd be lying if I said it didn't hurt that you didn't trust me. But you're here, and you're safe. We'll figure the rest out."

I let out a long breath. I stand by what I did, especially after his refusal to let me leave so many times, but I knew it might cause problems between us. I didn't want him to hate me when I got back, and the relief that floods me knowing he doesn't is consuming.

"Alright. Well, the night I asked you to send me back to the Voyagers, and you refused, I…went to Sig. We had talked about it before. That's why I was the one who asked you this time. We thought I'd have a better chance than she did, but we were wrong."

His jaw tenses, and he motions with his finger for me to keep going.

"I told her I had already decided that I was going back, so she could help me or not. Don't blame her for any of it. She was only helping me to give us the best chance. I begged her not to tell you for as long as possible after you figured out I was gone. I needed time to get back, and convince them I had been faking everything Mara saw in order to stay alive and wait for my opportunity to get back to them."

"Like your original plan," he says.

"Yes. But obviously, I was coming back."

"That's good to hear," he says. I level him with a look, and he smirks again. "Go on."

"The plan was to figure out how to replenish the dust during the days I was there. Dane and I were going to look for clues before you took me, so I had hoped he found something. I was going to get him to tell me, but when I got there, he had found nothing. He hadn't even looked because he was too busy searching for me." He huffs a laugh, because he knows there's no way Dane could find me under the island's protection, especially since he hadn't found the Castaways for so many years.

"I spent the two days trying to find answers. We didn't stop searching, but there was nothing. I, uh…"

My voice trails away as I try to find the courage to admit the next part. Tingling fingertips distract me and I clench my hands together and release repeatedly, working the nerves from my body.

I wince slightly and force myself to continue. "I even looked on the fountain."

His spine straightens and his brows furrow. "You went back?" There's something in his voice that I can't place. Worry? Fear? Longing?

"It wasn't my choice. I remembered the imagery on the fountain that helped me find the healing waters, and thought, maybe there was something for the dust, too. I racked my mind trying to remember the other images, but Dane thought it would be worth the risk of using the dust to go back and look. I tried to talk him out of it so we didn't waste the it, but he didn't listen. I was furious, and I panicked as soon as I got there. All I could think about was how many of us could have gotten back with it, and it was wasted."

"You didn't stay?"

"What?" My focus on the story is broken as I try to figure out what he is asking. He pushes off the rail and steps closer to me, coming toe to toe with the new boots the island gifted me this morning. I crane my neck up, flinching as the light of the suns flares in my vision, and he shifts, casting his shadow over me so I can look into his face.

"You didn't stay in Blackwood?" he repeats, as he scans my face.

Throughout the entire story, this is the piece he holds onto? He isn't concerned about using more of the dust, about not finding answers? He only wants to know why I didn't stay without uttering those specific words.

I shake my head. "Dane didn't bring me to Blackwood. But Weston," I reach out and lace my fingers through his, nervous that he's going to pull away, afraid of showing any sort of affection in front of the crew. His hand squeezes mine, his thumb brushing over the back of my palm, and my shoulders sag with relief. "I wouldn't have stayed. I wasn't going to leave you here."

His throat bobs and he plants a kiss on the top of my head. "Then what?" he asks.

I go through the entire story, telling him about how Sig and I planned to meet at one house, and he brought me to another, not listening to any of my attempts to make the night go according to plan. I recite everything, and he listens intently, his normal potent silence no longer intimidating.

"Just before everything went wrong, we talked about searching the safe houses because of the magic that protects them, and how they morph and change. The problem is, if the answer to replenishing the dust is in one of the houses, we don't know if it will only be revealed to the Guardian, and no one else."

"So if that is the case, there's no way we could find it, anyway. We'd also never know."

"Exactly," I murmur.

He rubs his chin and his lips, processing what I'm saying. I'm sure he's trying to think of another plan or loophole that would help, but there's nothing. If the Guardian is the only one who can find it, then Dane truly is in control of everything. The only other way would be if Dane was no longer the Guardian, but I will not let that happen.

"Don't even think about it," I snap at him, and he looks back at me, guilt settling over his features that tells me I was exactly right at where his mind was headed.

"We don't even know if that would work. You will not sacrifice yourself on that uncertainty. If I won't leave you, then you won't leave me, understood?" I say, the royal authority seeping into my voice, sounding so much like my father, and I watch him recognize it immediately.

"Understood, my queen," he rumbles.

"Then he called me Lyla, and you basically know the rest," I finish.

He stays silent, staring at the floor, still lost in thought.

"Are you going to say something?" I ask, but he doesn't move. "You know I was going to come back, right?"

A beat passes before he answers. "I hoped."

My chest clenches as I think about how he must have felt when he woke up to an empty room, and the chaos Sig had to endure trying to explain.

"What you found out is important for all of us. We wouldn't have known it if you didn't go back, so thank you for that."

As worried as I was to have this conversation, pride is now all I feel, proud that I could help my family here, even if it wasn't the result we'd hoped for.

"Let's go tell the crew," he says, and pulls me along behind him toward the group of Castaways that have formed on the quarterdeck. Releasing his hand, I cross the rest of the deck and sit on the floor in front of Stassia's crate, and watch as Weston looks over everyone.

"You all know the announcement I made the other day about the dust running out." There's a collective mumble from the group before he starts again.

"*Someone*," he says, refusing to look at me, "decided to sneak back to the Voyagers and try to steal the dust from Dane so we could have a chance at getting home."

"*That's* where you were?" Jorn calls out, hopping down from his perch on a beam above. He slides across the ground until he's sidled up next to me, and throws an arm over my shoulders, squeezing me in a side hug. "Little Lennox! You did that for us?"

Weston glares at him, his eyes falling on where Jorn holds me close. I bite my tongue, trying to hide a smile as I drop my head to Jorn's shoulder, and watch as Weston's arms cross slowly across his chest, the muscles in his forearms rippling with tension. Jorn laughs, his face beaming with a smile, and I catch Sig smirking to herself as she watches.

Sig knows then, too.

"Things didn't go as planned," Weston says, his voice a little more gruff than before. His eyes stay pinned on Jorn's arm for a second longer, before he turns away to keep addressing the group. "Unfortunately, we didn't get the dust. The situation became too dangerous, and it wasn't possible. But we got some new leads. I don't know where they will take us yet, but we'll keep trying. That's where all of you come in. We're going to have to pick up all the shifts between us. Dane knows what we're after now, and it just made leaving the ship more dangerous for everyone."

"Should we let things simmer for a bit? Let him cool down?" Eirlik asks.

"I think that would be best. I don't know if he will, not this time, but it's safer for everyone if we do."

"What new lead did we get?" Sig asks. Hope fills her face, and I remember I haven't even had time to talk to her since I've been back.

Weston explains what I told him about the safe houses, and the silence of the group is somber.

"We knew the situation was getting serious. We talked about it the other night. But I won't give up," Weston says, followed by a melancholy chorus of aye's.

"That's all," he says. "Stay on the ship, and I'll let you know when we are going to start back up again."

The group disperses, and Jorn stays put, his arm still slung around me.

"You're a Castaway through and through, you know that?" He nudges me with his side and my chest squeezes. I didn't need Jorn to say it, but it doesn't hurt hearing it. I know I belong here. These are my people, and if I have to spend eternity with anyone, I'm grateful it's them.

Sig crosses the quarterdeck and pulls me to stand before throwing her arms around me, hugging me fiercely.

"You fucking scared me," she hisses in my ear.

"I'm sorry, I tried."

She releases me and steps back. "I knew something was wrong. I knew you wouldn't go back to him."

"I was so worried you would think I lied to you," I say, tears welling in my eyes. Then I chuckle and nod my head toward Weston. "Hopefully he wasn't too hard on you."

"Oh, he was. I don't think I've ever seen him that out of his mind. It was hell on this ship for two days, but it was worth the risk. And something tells me he is happy to have you back." She quirks a brow and her lips tip up into a smug smile.

"Yeah," Jorn yells as he jumps up and drapes himself over Sig's back. "No more barging into Captain's room."

My cheeks burn as Sig laughs loudly. I was prepared for Jorn to have talked, obviously Stassia knew, but openly talking about it on deck with everyone around was unexpected.

"Next time, fucking knock," Weston orders as he walks up behind Jorn, clearly having heard our conversation. "And keep your hands to yourself," he growls as his hand finds my low back.

"Aye, Captain." Jorn offers him an exaggerated salute and Sig rolls her eyes.

"I actually have something else to tell you," I say, tipping my head up toward Weston. Curiosity flashes over his face before Sig says, "And that's our cue to leave." She grabs Jorn's hand on her shoulder and turns them toward the deck, quickly descending the stairs and leaving us alone on the quarterdeck.

"Don't be mad, alright?"

His head falls back with a groan. "Please don't let every conversation we have start with something that will make me mad."

"Actually, I don't really care if you're mad about this one, because it needed to be done." He can be upset with me all he wants. I do not regret my decision to tell Roley. After seeing the malice in Dane's eyes and hearing that he would force all the Voyagers to get the cure for him, I knew I needed to get Roley out.

"What is it?"

"Do you remember Roley? The boy Sig and I saved? Fin's friend?"

"Yes." He nods.

"I told him the truth and told him to keep quiet. I'm supposed to meet him tomorrow night on the island to bring him here."

Weston stays quiet, his expression unreadable.

"He's a child," I say, trying to explain. "I couldn't leave him there for eternity if none of this works out, not with everything you and Sig told me about Dane's lies. And now, with how everything ended up, I'm glad I told him. He needs to get out of there, Weston."

"I agree with you."

I lean back, shocked. "You do?"

"Of course. I would have done the same thing."

Just like he would have saved Roley and risked himself getting discovered. Just like he saved me. I don't know why I thought he would be mad, but again, he continues to surprise me.

"I need to leave the ship tomorrow to meet him. I don't want to put anyone else in danger for something I decided. Dane might have hurt me, but he still needs me. He wouldn't do anything too bad."

Suddenly, his hands are on my waist and I'm stumbling backward until my back meets the smooth panel of the wooden wall behind us. Weston leans over me, his body caging me in, his hips pinning me so I can't move. He tilts my head back with a nudge of his fingers until I can look nowhere else but at him.

"If you think I'm letting you go alone, you're out of your mind," he grumbles.

"I can handle myself." The words come out breathy, his proximity and the delicious press of his hips completely distracting.

"I know you can," he says, "but that doesn't mean I won't be alongside you." His fingers wrap around the side of my neck, his thumb stroking the long column and sending flutters of heat down to my core. His voice drops impossibly lower, and I'm lost in him, the ship around us completely falling away. "You ordered me, so now I'm ordering you. I don't care where we are, Lennox. I will keep you safe. I won't let him hurt you or take you again. It was hard enough to get you here before. Please don't make me go through it again."

My heart pounds out of my chest, and my response comes out in a hushed breath. "Understood, Captain."

"Then we'll go get Roley. Together."

His lips crash to mine, heated and wanting, and my mouth opens instantly, welcoming the steady push of his needy tongue. I'm breathless in moments, the ferocity in his kiss only adding to the intensity of his order. Sliding my hands under the edge of his vest, I ache to pull him closer and show him how much I now understand that this protectiveness is his way of caring. My stomach flips as his hand slides up my body, his thumb brushing the underside of my breast as his fingers dig into my ribs.

A taunting whistle sounds from somewhere near the mainmast, and Weston breaks away, the sudden withdrawal leaving me spinning. He rests his forehead on mine, as Jorn crows behind him, laughter ringing out right after. Weston sighs and shakes his head, and I can't help but giggle along.

"If he keeps this up," Weston grumbles against my lips, "he's going to find himself scrubbing the deck. Without the fucking mop."

CHAPTER SIXTY-ONE

Nerves course through my body as I wait on deck with Sig. The night is dark, the thinnest sliver of the moon high in the sky is almost invisible in the vast expanse. Tonight needs to go to plan. After my last failed attempt, I don't want to deal with the repercussions if the worst happens. Hopefully, Roley trusted me and is waiting alone for us to arrive.

The danger we face is more real than any other shift or interaction with the Voyagers. My stomach is in knots as my mind conjures all the things that could happen to Weston if Dane had somehow found out. Weston would put himself between us, and it isn't below Dane to use him against me to get what he wants.

The healing waters. My mother.

My body shudders and I push the thought out of my mind.

That will not happen.

Sig is quiet. She stands beside me, hands on her hips, as she watches the steps, waiting for Weston to emerge. My mouth dries the moment he does, and my eyes trail over his body. More weapons than usual are strapped to almost every surface, looking like he's going into battle. A second sword hilt peeks over his shoulder, and every slot in his vest is filled with a variety of sized blades. His sleeves are rolled to his elbows, the fabric tucked away so it won't interfere in a fight, and his hands are filled with even more as he strides toward us.

He hands the weapons off to Sig, then holds a dark brown leather vest behind my shoulders. I slide my arms through the holes, and he pulls the laces taut, the backs of his fingers brushing against me as he secures the knots. It's just like his, and I'm not surprised at all when he turns back to Sig, taking the weapons from her and fitting them in my vest.

A sword is all that's left, and he reaches down, hooking the scabbard to my belt, the one I stole from him. He doesn't have to say a word, because I know what he is doing. He needs to make sure I can defend myself in the event he cannot. Knowing I am protected gives him peace of mind going into tonight.

Weston turns to Sig then. "You know what to do if I don't come back. You take care of everyone, and never stop trying to get them home."

"You're going to come back, Cap. Both of you," she says, looking between us.

Weston reaches out, wrapping his arms around her shoulders, and pulls her into his chest. It's the first time I've ever seen him affectionate with anyone else in the crew, and a pang fills my chest. They've been through everything together. Weston wouldn't have lived if it hadn't been for Sig, and I finally understand what Sig meant all those months ago, when she said Weston was like a brother.

She pushes him off with tears in her eyes.

"Stop. Just go get the kid," she demands, looking at me next. "You make sure he comes back. Both of you better come back." She turns on her heel, and descends the steps quickly, disappearing into the deck below.

Once we're alone, Weston steps back to me, our bodies barely brushing. I crane my neck to look into his face just as he wraps his hand around the back of my neck in a soft caress, his thumb softly stroking my jaw.

"If we run into Dane," he says, "you let me deal with him. If something happens to me, you don't hesitate. You get back to this ship."

My throat feels like it's closing and my voice catches on it. "I'm not going to leave you, Weston," I croak.

He reaches up and brushes a piece of hair off my forehead, and my chest warms. "You know what you should do. You've had all the training and the lessons. I know you have. You know it's more important for you to get out than me."

"Stop talking like that," I say. My nose burns as I try to will away tears. "We're going to get Roley, and we're coming back."

"Promise me, Lennox."

His eyes trail over my face, as if he's memorizing every piece of it. Tenderness fills his expression, and it feels like my chest is cracking in half when I realize what he's doing.

"I promise," I whisper.

He leans down slowly and presses his lips gently to mine. This kiss is so much different from the others we've shared. Before, they were filled with passion and desire, impatience and hunger. This one says more than his words do. The gentle caress of his lush lips tells me everything I need, and more than I want him to say.

A single tear falls onto my cheek and I swipe it away, pulling my face from his. "Don't you dare say goodbye to me, Weston. This isn't over." I sniff, and he smiles down at me softly.

"No, sweetheart, it isn't over." He presses a kiss to my forehead, then laces his fingers through mine.

"Let's go."

I pick my bow and quiver up off the deck and drape them over my shoulder. Weston leads me down the gangway, the mask of the abrasive and intense First Guard and Captain firmly back in place, as if that moment between us hadn't just happened.

Weston is always on high alert whenever we leave the ship, the result of being responsible for everyone else's well being, but he has never been as attentive to our surroundings as tonight. He watches everything, keeping me hauled in close to him as he constantly scans the terrain while we move swiftly to the portal.

Once we're safely inside, his shoulders relax slightly, but his pace doesn't slow. I'm almost running to keep up with his long strides as we weave through the tunnels.

"Near the edge of the forest, right?"

"Yes," I say. "I told him to wait there for me and I would be there after dark."

We reach the steps quickly, and Weston takes them first, his head poking through the portal in the ground just enough to make sure we aren't about to be ambushed. I hold my breath until he sinks back down into safety.

"There's no one waiting, but that doesn't mean they aren't hiding. Be prepared for an ambush and drop back into the portal. We're going to do this fast."

I nod, and he draws his sword, the sing of the blade echoing in the tunnel. I lift my bow off my chest and pull an arrow from the quiver, nocking it and raising it to the ready. Hopefully, I can get to anyone before they make it to him. I'm not taking any chances.

He peeks out of the portal again, looking around before climbing the last steps and disappearing. Running up the stairs behind him, I burst through the portal, not wanting to leave him uncovered for long. The darkness of the forest makes it even more difficult to see in the already pitch black night. It takes a moment for my eyes to adjust so I can see things clearly, still holding my bow up and ready to fire.

The area before us is empty; not a hint of Roley in sight.

"I told him to wait near the bridge. Maybe he is closer to it."

"Quickly," Weston says, peering into the trees as we take the path toward the bridge. The island is silent, the only sound the rush of water in the canyon alongside us, and it feels eerie, like at any moment the world will explode with danger.

No. We're just here to get Roley. Then we're going home.

The entrance to the bridge appears just ahead and Weston slows his steps. I match his pace so I don't walk past him, keeping my bow out in front, ready to pull back. Looking around, everything looks undisturbed. There's nothing, no sign of Roley at all.

"Lennox," Weston says warily. "I don't think he's coming."

"No, he has to. He told me he would." Worry fills me as I look around for him, hoping he didn't choose to stay, or worse, let someone know about the plan.

"Roley!" I call out, my voice a coarse whisper, hoping he is just hiding.

Footsteps shuffle in the dirt as a small shadow appears ahead, emerging from the edge of the trees.

"Lennox?" Roley says weakly and steps out onto the path in front of us.

Relief floods through me as I take him in.

He came.

I lower my bow, pointing the arrow to the ground when movement catches in the corner of my eye. Weston stiffens and takes a step forward, using his body to shield me as someone larger emerges from the trees, just in front of Roley.

"So, you must be Weston."

Mara.

Weston pulls the other sword from his back, knees bending, ready for an attack. I level my bow at her, pulling the string taught and taking aim.

Fuck.

He told them, or he was followed. I risk a glance at the trees, as my breaths heave. Where is Dane? Are there others here? It is too dark. I can't see if we are surrounded, trapped against the monster filled river and not close enough to a portal.

My shoulders tighten as my training kicks in. Situations with multiple attackers start cycling through my mind. I know Weston feels it, too. I can tell by the way his body leans slightly toward me.

"Lower your bow, Lennox!" Mara calls out.

"Not a chance!" I yell back.

"I'm serious Lennox, lower it!"

"I don't feel like a knife to the back again, Mara."

She knows I can make the shot. I've proven it to her already, but I will not do anything to put him or me at risk. I won't let my guard down again.

My ears strain, trying to pick up any sound of Voyagers approaching from behind, all while keeping my eyes locked on Mara. Her sword hangs at her side, not drawn like she normally travels, and a feeling of unease runs through me.

She takes a step forward and Weston does too, angling himself further in front of me with her advance.

"Stay where you are," he growls. "We just came for him."

"And I just came to talk," she says, raising her hands, palms facing us. She doesn't move. Standing in silence, she waits for us to decide.

"It's true, Lennox. She just wants to talk," Roley yells from behind.

"Weston," I mumble. "What do we do?"

I can feel him thinking as he stands in front of me like a statue, muscles taut and ready to spring into action at any sign of deception.

"Throw your sword," he orders, and she quickly complies, pulling it from the scabbard and tossing it out in front of her. She raises her hand up again, waiting to see if that will suffice. A Mara that is quick to agree to leaving herself unprotected doesn't sit right with me.

Something is wrong.

"Is this a trap?" I whisper to him.

"I don't know yet," he murmurs back. He glances around again, looking for any threat that might come as soon as we relax.

"There's no one else here," Mara says. "It's just us. Please, I just want to talk."

"You didn't seem like you wanted to talk to me at all a few days ago," I yell. "Not when you were trying to attack me in the clearing."

Weston grunts in front of me. "You left out that detail," he grumbles.

"It's fine. I had it handled. You taught me how to disarm her, remember?" I murmur back.

"Things have changed," Mara yells. Her voice wavers slightly, and my curiosity piques. Weston's does too, and his head tilts just the slightest bit to the side.

"What's changed?" Weston yells.

"Can you just lower your weapons, please?" She's getting impatient now, and I will admit, the malice and hatred in her voice and eyes from before doesn't seem to be there now.

"I think she's telling the truth," I say to Weston.

"But can you trust her?"

Can I? Could things change so quickly that she is back to the Mara I knew before? My friend? What could make that change happen? Or am I about to learn another serious lesson in warfare and deception, one that Edmond couldn't prepare me for without being thrown directly into it?

"She saved my life before. She didn't even know me then. I trust her."

He pauses for a beat before lowering his swords to his sides. At his cue, I drop my bow, pointing the arrow into the ground and still keeping it nocked so I can react to any trickery.

"Don't move. We'll come to you," Weston orders, and walks toward her. I follow closely. He kicks her sword behind us, stopping just out of her reach.

"Talk," he says gruffly, the all serious Weston back in full force.

Mara eyes him for a moment, before directing her attention to me, her eyes full of emotion, and her eyebrows drawn in.

Has she been crying?

"First, I need to say I'm sorry." She gulps after the statement, eyes pleading with me to believe her. I stare back at her in shock, the apology the last thing I was expecting to hear when I thought she was going to ambush us.

She continues, "I'm sorry I hurt you before. I was too furious that you left us to see that you actually saved Roley." She eyes Weston before turning back to me. "But it seems like you made the right decision."

"What do you mean, Mara?" I ask warily.

She lowers one hand, reaching behind her, and Weston automatically levels a sword at her. She pulls her arm forward and holds her hand out toward us.

My gaze falls to what she holds, and I choke on the air.

The bow drops to the ground at my feet and I stumble into Weston, my fingers digging into his side as I struggle to breathe.

No. This isn't happening. This can't be happening.

Of all the ways my mind conjured tonight could go, the worry that Weston would be hurt, or worse, taken, the nerves about Roley being discovered, the anticipation of an ambush, nothing prepared me for what Mara holds in her hand.

A limp piece of fabric I'd recognize anywhere dangles from her fingers, the circular opening hovering above the ground.

But there's no golden glow.

My eyes fly to hers, streams of tears already falling down her cheeks as she chokes out the next words.

"He's gone, Lennox. Storm left too. You tried to talk to me. You said you weren't a traitor, and you didn't abandon us, but I wouldn't listen. I was wrong."

Weston's sword lowers slowly as he pieces it all together.

Ringing fills my ears and nausea churns in my stomach as I stare at the pouch.

The *empty* pouch.

All these years, Edmond taught me to believe in hope, but he was wrong. Light doesn't always find a way. We have no hope anymore. It was ripped away from us the moment the Guardian chose himself over the island.

Dane left us all here. He's gone, and so is the dust.

We're all trapped on Dawnlin.

BONUS CHAPTER
WESTON

Kissed her.

I fucking kissed her.

My duty, my oath, all my training in self-control, gone in an instant when she showed up on my ship covered in blood.

"Fuck," I mutter again. I can't turn back and look at her. If I do, I don't know if I'll be able to control myself, and I will absolutely fuck everything up. So I leave. Stomp away like a damn coward, but call it self-preservation instead.

I shuffle down the steps and do the first thing that comes to mind.

"Jorn!"

Jorn has always been there. From the moment he walked out of the mountain, he became one of us, but most of all turned into a brother I never had.

The door to Sig's room opens, and he sticks his head out of the crack a moment later. "What's up, Captain?" I must look as unhinged as I feel because his eyes widen when he sees me. "Uh oh. Trouble in paradise?"

I pin my hands to my hips and pace the hallway, trying to calm down, but my breathing is still ragged just thinking about the way it felt.

Her body wrapped around mine, her face in my hands. Her lips and tongue in my mouth. The moan she couldn't control when I tightened my fist in her hair.

My cock hardens just thinking about it.

"I kissed her," I grind out.

"And then walked away?"

I nod, trying to hide my grimace.

"Captain, I'm gonna be honest with you," he says, "not the smoothest of moves."

Then I say something I don't say very often, but apparently I have no self control anymore. I'm already fucked. What's destroying everything a little more?

"I need a drink," I growl. I need to distract myself, forget how she kissed me back, how she rubbed herself against me like she wanted more.

I have to forget, because nothing can ever happen.

"Wait, really?" Jorn says, excitement lighting up his face as he steps out of Sig's room into the hallway. He lets out a crow and starts hopping on his toes.

I release a deep sigh and lace my fingers behind my head. My scalp still tingles from where she scraped her nails across it.

"Why do you look like this is the end of the world?" Jorn asks. "You've been pining over her since you pulled her from the lagoon."

I shoot him a glare and he throws his hands up innocently.

"Everyone can see it, Captain. You aren't hiding anything."

My chest grumbles in response as I turn on my heel and head down the second set of stairs. Jorn's footsteps trail behind closely as I storm into the mess, and thankfully find it empty.

I fall down into a chair, slamming my elbows into the wooden tabletop, and drop my head into my hands. A frustrated groan rips from my chest, just as Jorn falls into the chair across from mine, leaning forward on his forearms.

"I'm confused, Captain. I think you need to dumb this down for me."

I lean back, draping my arms over the chairs beside me, and try to decide if telling him the truth is the best thing. I trust Jorn with my life, but Sig is the only one who knows everything.

Fuck it. He already knows everything else.

"Remember when I told you where I'm from? That I'm the First Guard to the king?"

He makes a sound of acknowledgement, waiting for me to continue.

"The king is my friend. We grew up together, and it was always me and him, until he found Lyla."

"I'm not seeing where you're going with this Cap, but continue," Jorn says.

My fingers raise, pointing up toward the deck while holding Jorn's gaze.

"She is their daughter."

Jorn stays silent, which is not a typical behavior for him, and I know the significance isn't lost anymore. He pushes back in the chair, the legs scraping across the wooden floor before striding to the galley. He pulls out a large bottle of liquor and two smaller cups, then plops back down into his seat. A cup slams down in front of me, and he fills it to the brim before filling his own.

"And now I get it. You're fucked, man."

"I know." I groan, snatching the cup off the table and bringing it to my lips.

I tip it back, reveling in the burn as it goes down, trying to focus on that feeling instead of the burning desire to march back up to the deck and continue what I started.

"Figures, the one woman you've ever shown any interest in is the one you can't have," Jorn says as he takes a sip.

"Thanks for the reminder," I snap and slam my empty cup back down in front of him. He takes the hint and tips the bottle, filling it again.

"Not to mention she's with Dane." I look up and pin him with a death glare. A wicked smirk sits on his lips, like he's goading me on purpose. He probably is.

"Nah," he continues, taking another sip. "That's basically over already. She might not realize it yet, but she's fighting feelings, too."

My head drops back, and I close my eyes with a groan. "I don't need to fucking hear that."

I tip back the second cup, and know I'm going to pay for it later. Sig will handle anything that comes up, because I know she knows exactly where we are. By the look on her face when they stepped on deck, she could tell exactly what was going through my mind.

"What's so bad about it, though? You've been here for how long?"

"Almost twenty-one years," I say, staring at the pattern in the wood. "I left after she was born."

"Right, but you're here. All that time has passed, but we're still us. Nothing has changed, no matter how long it has been. When we get back, I'll still be twenty-five, and you'll still be…" He trails off, waiting for me to fill it in.

"Twenty-seven," I mumble.

"Exactly. Dawnlin may have stolen our time, but it didn't really steal our time, you know?" He takes another drink and I reach over and snatch the bottle off the table.

"She's the princess, Jorn. I'm the First Guard. It's my job to protect her."

"Yeah, and you're doing that. I know you, and I can guarantee that isn't going to stop, whether we're here or home."

My jaw tightens and I stay quiet. It won't stop. I've been there every moment since the crew first came back and told me there was a new girl on the island, since the moment I saw Dane showing her around.

Since the moment I figured out his plan.

"Think about it this way." He leans forward again, like he's trying to tell me a secret. "The king is your best friend, right? Wouldn't he rather she be with you over any random last-born son trying to hitch himself to her for a little bit of power?"

I actually do growl at him now. The thought of some prick buying her with the promise of an alliance sets me on edge. I know that's the way things are done, but I can still fucking hate it. I already got her away from Dane; the thought of her being handed off to someone else makes a fire light inside me.

Honestly, I don't know how Remington would react, but part of me really does not want to find out. I'd like to keep my balls attached to my body.

"I have a feeling Rem wouldn't be happy with me touching his daughter." Another swallow, followed by more burn, as I block out all the ways I've thought about touching her.

"Well, the thing is, you already have. That's first off," Jorn says, ticking off his fingers. "Second, Sig and I have been saying for years you need to get laid."

I glare at him, which only makes him smile more as he continues.

"Your mood has significantly worsened since she's been here, and it was already pretty bad. And she's kind of the only one who can put up with your shit. Third, she's already here. She's with us, and we don't know how long that will be. Could be another twenty years for all we know."

I take another sip and stare out into the empty room.

"We aren't back in our world, Weston. It doesn't matter who we are there, because we're here. Just fucking live a little." He tips the drink to the back of his throat and slams his cup down on the table.

Jorn is the only one that calls me Weston on this ship, well, besides the kid, and it's only ever when we're alone. No matter how many times I have told Sig to, she won't. It's always Cap. Probably stems from her upbringing and time spent on the sea.

"I guess if you want to keep pining, then she's free for anyone else. She's cute. Veck or Eirlik might be interested. Not sure if she'd want either of them over you or Dane, but they can always try," Jorn says.

"Shut your fucking mouth," I snap, my head whirring toward him to find a sly smile there. "Don't even think about it, Jorn." My tone should be enough of a warning, but I can see the mischief in his eye.

He knows how to push my buttons, and I know exactly what he is doing. He's trying to goad me into making a move by threatening the interest of other men. He doesn't understand the severity of the situation. He wasn't raised in a castle, and he doesn't have an oath he swore to the royal family.

"Enough stalling," Jorn says as he stands quickly, knocking the chair to the ground behind him. "You came down here for a reason, and it's time to play."

He strides over to the doorway and calls out, "Hangman is on in the mess! Better get down here now!"

There are some noises and footsteps in response, which Jorn clearly isn't happy about, because he calls out even louder. "Captain is playing!"

Footsteps pound then, followed by cheers and calls out to others, and I roll my eyes. Jorn turns with a smug look on his face and walks back to the table, righting his chair before plopping into it.

"Get ready to be wrecked," he says as more of the crew file in loudly, pulling out chairs and shifting tables around. "As if you weren't already."

"Fuck you," I say and drain the last of my drink.

Jorn chuckles and organizes the game, urging everyone to get their drinks and get in place. A few rounds pass without anyone choosing me for the bluff, which is typical. They all want me to play, but everyone is afraid to make the first move. Jorn's hand carved dice rattle constantly on the table and I take small sips from my cup as everyone cheers and yells with each round.

When she walks into the room, my senses heighten, my gaze snapping to her as she follows Sig over to the galley. I follow her the entire walk, the game around me completely falling away into a dull noise. She cleaned up after today's watch, and her arm is wrapped and treated thanks to Sig.

It should have been me taking care of her, especially with that wound, but I couldn't. I couldn't touch her for another second. That doesn't stop the aching guilt from settling in my chest, knowing that it wasn't me that helped her.

My eyes trail over her face, picking up on subtle tells she thinks aren't there, things that make her emotions stand out like a sail flapping in the breeze. The clench of her jaw, the aversion of her eyes, the set of her shoulders.

She's trying not to look over here.

She doesn't realize how much like her father she is. I'd know that body language anywhere. With Rem, I'd normally train it out of him, and I tried to do the same with her. But with every single spar, every time I saw that glint of defiance in her eye, watching her charge at me, determination in every muscle of her body, it was a miracle I wasn't hard on deck in front of the whole damn crew. I already took enough liberties in that session, pulling her as close to me with any chance I was given. My hands had a mind of their own, and they were begging her to be close.

It took every shred of control I had not to throw her over my shoulder and toss her in my bed to work the stubbornness out of her in a different way. What I wouldn't give to have her stubborn defiance in bed as I was buried inside her.

"Sig! Lennox! Come play!" Jorn yells, breaking through my indecent thoughts.

"Go back to your game, Jorn!" Sig yells, which is met with a chorus of boos from the table.

I take another sip, watching her avoid looking over toward the table. I know I should look away, should focus back on the game and the crew. I should pretend like the kiss didn't happen, because it can't happen again.

No matter how bad I want it to.

Stassia walks in a moment later, blocking my view of her as she disappears through the doorway. The table rings out in cheers for Stass as she pushes her way into a spot to join the game, snagging an extra cup and filling it to the rim.

I reach over to grab the bottle from her, which she hands over happily, and fill mine again, almost knocking the dice out of the way when I set the bottle down in the middle of the table.

"Ha!" Jorn calls out, having rolled a number that lets him choose the next victim. I watch as his eyes slide to me, a glimmer in them as he stares me down, waiting for his question.

I don't move a muscle, my face staying as stoic as possible. I know what is coming, and I know what I have to do to win the round.

"Captain," he says, and everyone around makes some sort of noise of anticipation. He leans forward across the table toward me, looking me dead in the face. "Do you regret it?" he asks, his voice clear and direct despite how much drink he's already had.

I don't move a muscle. I focus on my breathing as I stare him down.

"Ooh, what are we regretting?" Stassia says happily as she scoots closer to the table.

"Yes," I grumble, my glare pinning him down, but it barely affects him. My answer is the truth, or at least what I need to be the truth. If I say it out loud, maybe I can convince not only him, but myself.

He quirks his head to the side, still assessing me, before he says calmly, "You're a fucking liar, Captain."

I pause for a moment before giving in to the actual truth. The truth that I don't regret a fucking second of her lips on mine, that I wish I could do it again, right now, and not care at all about who we are or how we're connected. I let myself admit the truth, if only to Jorn, knowing he will keep it right here, at this table, with this game.

I lift my cup slowly, and his face glows with victory and understanding as the rim meets my lips. I never take my eyes off him as I tip the whole thing back, and crows and calls and laughter erupt around me, the floorboards shaking under the stomps of boots as everyone congratulates Jorn on his win.

My chest burns and I feel the fire breath as I finish every drop, then reach out, slamming my hand onto the table.

"Give me these fucking dice," I say, and cheers and whoops rise again.

I came down here to do one thing, and that was to dull my feelings and forget what happened, even if it is only for a little while, so that is what I'm going to do.

I'm going to play with my crew until I forget I don't regret a damn thing about it.

But the moment I walk out of this room, it's all over, and it will never happen again.

ACKNOWLEDGEMENTS

Even though this isn't the first acknowledgements page I've written, it still feels very surreal writing it. Of course my first thanks is to my husband who has been on this journey every step of the way, even though he seriously procrastinated this book so hard, because he always forgets how much fun he has being creative too, until he sits down to do it.

Thank you to my children (who will probably read this acknowledgements some day *way* in the future) for sleeping at night so I had time to write…at least most nights.

Thank you to my peasant, I mean, sister, for "alpha reading" book two. Even though some of your comments did send me into a full blown crisis tailspin, I still seriously appreciate all of your thoughts and support with this crazy life.

Of course thank you so much to my beta readers, Michelle, JJ, and Alex. Your feedback and support is always so important for this whole process, and I really appreciate you taking time out of your life to help me with mine.

Thank you to my IRL friends who have read and supported me. You all know how big of a change this was in my life, and the fact that you didn't flinch or try to talk me out of it when I told you shows how much you are my people. Found family forever.

Thanks to my editor Kay who didn't flinch when I said this book was significantly longer than the last one.

Thank you so much to my sister, Michelle (thats_what_michelle_read) and Abby (abigailsbooknook) for helping me finalize the synopsis. This is one of the hardest parts for me, and your input was so helpful.

A huge thank you to the artists who have helped bring these characters to life with your art, especially Morgan (illustratedbymorgan). I'm so excited for all of our projects together.

A giant shout out to my ARC Team! Thank you so much for your excitement, both for Dawn of Hope and Blade of Truth. Your enthusiasm and support has kept me going, and I loved seeing all of your posts, videos, comments and love for this story. Thank you all.

And of course, thank you to all of the readers who wanted to continue with Lennox's story after reading Dawn of Hope. Blade of Truth is very near to my heart as the set of scenes that inspired the entire series, and it means so much to me that you wanted to read it. I hope you loved it as much as I do.

Finally, thank you to my characters for letting me go through my own shit through you. Sorry about the anger, hurt, confusion, lack of confidence, and everything else I put you through. Wish I could say it was over.

ABOUT THE AUTHOR

Amanda Briar has been an avid reader of romance, both fantasy and contemporary, since middle school, and loves to watch a good rom-com or fantasy series. After starting a family and deciding her career wasn't for her anymore, she took a chance to fulfill a lifelong dream to write books. As a self-proclaimed Disney Adult who grew up craving a happy ending, she now writes them herself. She currently lives in California with her family, and still loves reading, baking, movies, and going to Disneyland.

@authoramandabriar

@authoramandabriar

www.amandabriar.com

www.ingramcontent.com/pod-product-compliance
Lightning Source LLC
Chambersburg PA
CBHW031149310726
48969CB00001B/23